EMMANUEL: BOOK TWO

CALM THE STORM

JEFF HUTCHISON

WESTBOW
PRESS
A DIVISION OF THOMAS NELSON

ISBN: 978-1-4497-3276-9 (sc)
ISBN: 978-1-4497-3277-6 (e)
ISBN: 978-1-4497-3278-3 (hc)

WestBow Press books may be ordered through booksellers or by contacting:

WestBow Press
A Division of Thomas Nelson
1663 Liberty Drive
Bloomington, IN 47403
www.westbowpress.com
1-(866) 928-1240

Library of Congress Control Number: 2011962309

Printed in the United States of America

WestBow Press rev. date:11/22/2011

CHAPTER 1

Luke James wasn't sure how he got here. He was standing on top of a large wooden platform, rectangular in shape, about thirty feet above the ground. A leather cord bound his wrists together, behind his back. In the same predicament were two of his best friends, John Thomas and Mark Andrews. Standing diagonally behind each of them were huge men with hoods pulled up over their heads, hiding their faces from view. They were prisoners, but he had no idea why.

Luke looked around at his unfamiliar surroundings, trying to figure out where he was. Unable to see anything that he might recognize, he quickly came to the conclusion that he'd never been here before.

They were in a town square, of sorts. A sizable crowd surrounded the platform in which they stood atop. The buildings in the area looked old and primitive.

Although he had never been to a desert environment, Luke acknowledged this as so. The ground below him was a mixture of dirt and sand, and there wasn't a tree anywhere in sight. All of the people watching from the crowd were dressed in robes and sandals. They reminded Luke of the way people dress in biblical based movies. Sporting a t-shirt and jeans, along with John and Mark, he felt very out of place in this strange location. This looked nothing like his hometown of Benworth, Pennsylvania.

Another identical platform stood about fifty feet away. Six men in purple robes stood on the edges of it, three on each side. A tall, thin man, dressed in a scarlet robe, and a golden crown with many jewels on top of his head, stood in the center. He was clearly the leader of this group. Standing next to him was another of Luke's good friends, Matthew Peters. He, like his friends, was wearing a white t-shirt and jeans. A black baseball cap turned backwards adorned his head.

Matthew stood there with his arms folded across his chest, looking very relaxed. Luke wondered why they were being held captive, but Matthew wasn't. For some reason, Luke seemed to believe that Matthew could do something to help them, but was choosing not to.

The leader, on the other platform, raised his hands to the sky, creating a hush over the crowd. When he was sure that he had everyone's attention, he began speaking in a loud, booming voice. "This is what you are commanded to do. When the music begins, you must fall down and worship the image of gold."

With his left hand, he motioned toward a gold statue, in the likeness of the leader, off to the side of the town square. Luke felt a sick feeling in the pit of his stomach.

The leader continued, "Whoever does not fall down and worship will immediately be thrown into the blazing furnace."

With his other hand, he pointed to the side of the platform that Luke and his buddies were being held. Luke looked over and saw a colossal metal structure, cylindrical in shape. The top came to rest at the end of the platform. Flames were shooting out the top. Suddenly, he felt the heat wash across his face, and he thought that he might vomit.

Rage filled the leader's eyes as he looked across at Luke and his friends. "It has been brought to my attention that the three of you refuse to serve my gods or worship the image of gold that I have set up. Now when you hear the music, if you are ready to fall down and worship the image I made, very good. But if you do not worship it, you will be thrown immediately into the blazing furnace. Then what god will be able to rescue you from my hand?" Fear flooded Luke as the thought of being burned alive rushed through his mind. He looked at Matthew standing next to the leader. Why wasn't he doing anything to help them? He actually had a smug look on his face as he looked across at his doomed friends.

Why did the leader want them to worship a false god? So much of this didn't make sense to Luke. He knew that he and his friends would only worship the one, true God. After several visits from Emmanuel, whom they knew to be Jesus Christ himself, had increased the faith of these kids to unbelievable heights. There was no way that they would ever bow down to anyone else.

John, in a loud voice, boldly spoke up, "We do not need to defend ourselves before you in this matter. If we are thrown into the blazing furnace, the God we serve is able to save us from it, and he will rescue us from your hand. But even if he does not, we want you to know that we will not serve your gods or worship the image of gold you have set up."

The leader was furious at John's outburst. His face turned crimson with anger. "Guards! Throw them into the furnace!"

Cheers erupted from the crowd. Luke frantically looked around for some means of escape, but he was quickly grabbed by the guard behind him. He felt weak in the knees as he was forcefully pushed to the edge of the platform. John and Mark were on either side of him.

Luke looked over to the other platform and screamed, "Matthew! Do something!"

Rather than do anything to assist them, Matthew slowly turned around and looked in the opposite direction. Luke felt crushed as he saw his friend, whom he'd known for as long as he could remember, turn his back on him at his biggest time of need. Why wouldn't Matthew help them? And why wasn't he in danger of being thrown into the furnace as well? Surely he hadn't bowed down and worshipped the image of gold, had he?

All three of them were struggling to break free, but with their wrists bound together, it was futile. The heat coming from the furnace was scorching. Luke felt his mouth go dry. He tried to swallow, but couldn't. He was short of breath as he realized that his fate was set.

With one last look over his shoulder, his fear turned to hate as he saw his captor pull his hood down, revealing his identity.

It was Jude Iscoe!

Jude, along with his friends, Ethan Saul and Scott Herod, were three years older and had been terrorizing Luke and his friends for years. They'd been picked on and abused by them for a long time. Mark had even been on the receiving end of a brutal attack from them recently.

The other two guards pulled their hoods down as well, exposing them to be Ethan and Scott. Jude laughed mockingly while his cronies showed sinister smiles.

Not wanting to give them the satisfaction, Luke stood tall and straight. He glanced back down into the furnace and something caught his eye. There was something at the bottom of the furnace. He squinted his eyes, trying to see through the flames. There appeared to be someone standing at the bottom.

It was Emmanuel!

He was looking up at them, smiling. Luke looked to each side of him and saw that both John and Mark could see him as well. All three smiled back. A calmness engulfed Luke, as he suddenly knew that everything was going to be alright.

Luke felt a hard shove from behind, and he fell headlong into the fiery furnace. He braced himself for impact, but it never happened. He felt himself *freefalling through the flames, but felt no heat.   Wondering why he wasn't hitting the bottom, he felt peaceful and relaxed. He knew that Emmanuel wouldn't allow him to be harmed in this way. Laughter escaped from his lungs a he heard his grandfather's voice.*

"Luke, wake up!"

Luke opened his eyes and saw the familiar confines of his bedroom. He breathed a sigh of relief as he became aware of the fact that it was all a dream. He was drenched in sweat from head to toe.

His maternal grandfather, whom everyone referred to as Pops, entered the room and asked, "Are you okay? You were making a lot of noises."

"I'm okay. Just a bad dream."

Pops sat on the edge of the bed. "Must have been real bad. I could hear you all the way from the kitchen. Do you want to talk about it?" Luke felt a little embarrassed. At fourteen years of age, Pops still treated him like a little kid sometimes. He didn't want to tell him, for fear of appearing weak in his grandfather's eyes, but knew that Pops wouldn't let it go, so he reluctantly told him all of the details of his dream, minus seeing Emmanuel in the flames.

Pops didn't approve of Emmanuel, nor did any of the parents of Luke's friends. They didn't believe the kids' claim that he is Jesus, so they were forbidden from having any contact with him. The kids no longer mentioned Emmanuel in front of the adults.

Luke concluded his story by telling Pops about being pushed into the furnace and waking up.

Pops nodded slowly and said, "That sounds an awful lot like the story of Daniel, from the Bible. Matthew was asking me about that the other day. You probably overheard us talking about it and it influenced your dream."

"I don't remember hearing you two talk about that, and I've never read that part of the Bible."

"Well, in any event, it was just a dream. It's getting late. Just because it's Saturday doesn't mean you can sleep the day away. Get up and I'll make us some breakfast."

"Sounds good."

Pops got up and headed toward the kitchen.

After a quick shower, Luke joined Pops at the kitchen table, where a breakfast of scrambled eggs and bacon awaited him. Pops said a quick prayer and they dug into the food.

As they ate, Luke noticed that Pops was eating a lot more bacon than usual. He suddenly remembered something that Emmanuel had told him a few days earlier, warning Luke that Pops needs to watch his eating habits, or it'll lead to health problems.

Luke asked, "How much bacon did you make?"

"I saw that the expiration date was getting close, so I made all of it so it wouldn't go to waste."

Trying to make light of it, Luke said, "Don't eat too much or you'll explode."

Pops ignored the joke and went on eating.

Concern filled Luke as he looked across the table at his grandfather. For as long as he'd known him, Pops had always had a paunch, but over the last year or so, he had gained a considerable amount of weight.

Remembering Emmanuel's advice about encouraging Pops to eat healthier, he suggested, "Why don't we make a big salad later, and have that for dinner?"

Pops looked puzzled as he answered, "Salad is a side, not a meal. I was thinking about ordering a pizza with the works."

"Wouldn't you rather eat something better for you? Wrestling season will be starting in a few months, so I'll have to watch what I eat in order to make weight. I may as well get used to it now."

"It's still football season, so you should be more focused on keeping the weight on for now. You're kind of puny for a tight end."

Seeing that he was getting nowhere, he chose to change the subject. "What did you think about the game last night?"

"Matthew looked great. It looks like football talent runs in that family."

The previous night, Matthew led the Benworth Eagles to an incredible come from behind win. Although only a freshman, he was given the chance to quarterback the varsity team after his older brother, David, was injured with an ACL tear, and Cody Williams, David's initial replacement, was benched after some very poor play. Matthew stepped up, and he performed remarkably, earning him the starting position.

Luke smiled as he thought about the game. He was happy for his friend and was excited for what the future held for him.

As he finished eating, his cell phone rang. He checked the caller ID and saw that it was his friend, Mark.

"Hey, Mark. What's up?"

"My parents are gone for the day, and I'm stuck here, watching my little brother. Why don't you come over and we'll watch college football. I'll call John and Matthew and invite them too."

"I'm on my way."

He hung up and told Pops where he was going. Mark lived on the same street, about a quarter mile down the road.

After retrieving his bike from the garage, he rode it out of his driveway, making a left onto Forest Street. About a hundred yards down the road, a jolt of fear ran through him as he saw Jude, Scott and Ethan walking on the sidewalk to his left, in his direction.

As soon as Jude saw Luke, he shouted, "Stop!"

Luke began pedaling faster, hoping to get past them as fast as he could, and into the safety of Mark's house.

Figuring out that Luke had no intention of obeying his command, Jude ran into the street to cut him off. Luke veered to the right to try to get around him, but quickly saw that he wasn't going to make it.

Panic engulfed him. On the fly, he decided to try to jump the curb in an attempt to get by, but he misjudged the timing. His front tire slammed into the curb, bringing the bike to an abrupt halt. Luke sailed over the handlebars and landed hard on his right shoulder, skidding across the sidewalk and into a grassy field between houses.

Luke laid there, stunned. The pain in his shoulder was excruciating. Before he had a chance to react, Jude came down on top of him, dropping his knee into Luke's groin, driving all of the air out of his lungs. Nausea set in and he thought that he might throw up.

Jude held him down by forcing his left hand against his throat. "You should've stopped when I told you to."

Luke didn't say anything, too dazed to respond.

"You and your friends need to be taught a lesson." Jude proceeded to punch him in the face, repeatedly.

Luke was only partly aware of what was happening, and with each blow, his mind got foggier. On the brink of falling unconscious, he saw Jude rise above him, then come back down full speed, driving his elbow into his jaw, and everything went black.

—

Luke opened his eyes and squinted against the bright sun. Sharp pain filled his right shoulder and jaw. Laying on his back, he moaned softly. He tried to rise to a sitting position, but the throbbing of his body prevented him from doing so.

Two hands touched his shoulders and alarm seized him. He began squirming to get away. A calm voice spoke, "Relax. Jude and his friends aren't here anymore."

He stopped moving. The voice was vaguely familiar, but in his disoriented state, he couldn't quite place it. There was a figure kneeling next to him. He raised his hand to shield his eyes from the glaring sun. Slowly, the recognition came to him.

It was Emmanuel!

Luke tried to say something, but his mouth couldn't form the words.

"Shhhh! Don't try to talk. Your jaw is broken."

Emmanuel put his hands on each side of Luke's face. He looked to the sky, then closed his eyes.

Immediately, Luke felt heat rush through his cheeks and the pain disappeared. The same happened when Emmanuel touched his shoulder.

Once again, Luke tried to sit up, this time succeeding. He looked to his feet and saw that his shoes were missing. Looking at Emmanuel, he asked, "What happened to my shoes?"

"Jude took them."

"Pops just bought those for me last week. They're brand new."

"Don't worry about your shoes for now. Matthew will be coming by any minute now. He'll be able to help you."

Emmanuel guided him back down to the ground, flat on his back. Fatigue washed over him and he couldn't hold his eyes open. He surrendered to the feeling and allowed sleep to come.

—

"Luke! What happened?"

Pops voice jolted him awake. He looked up and saw Pops and Matthew standing over him. The memory of what happened flooded his mind and he broke into tears.

Between sobs, Luke asked, "How long have I been here?"

Pops answered, "You left the house about ten minutes ago."

Matthew added, "I was on my way to Mark's when I saw you laying here, not moving. I called Pops on my cell phone and he came right over. Did you take a spill on your bike?"

"Jude and his friends jumped me. They stole my shoes."

Matthew looked at him sideways. "You couldn't outrun them on your bike?"

"I tried, but they cut me off. I hit the curb and went down. Jude was on top of me before I could react."

Matthew shook his head and said, "You should've been able to get away."

Getting angry, Luke shot back, "You weren't even here. How would you know?"

Pops interjected, "That's enough! Matthew, do you know where we keep our spare key?"

He nodded.

"Good. Ride your bike back to the house and get his old shoes out of his bedroom closet."

Matthew hopped on his bike and took off down the street.

While wiping the tears off of his face, Luke slowly rose to his feet. "I'm sorry, Pops."

"Don't be sorry. This wasn't your fault. Are you hurt?"

"No."

"Are you sure? You were out like a light when I got here. What did they do to you?" Luke shook his head.

He knew that he couldn't tell Pops that Emmanuel healed him, so he needed to think of a quick lie. "I really don't remember anything after crashing my bike. I'm not in any pain."

"You should come home and I'll check you out."

"No. I'm fine. I want to go to Mark's."

"You were just knocked out. We should probably get you to a doctor."

"No way. I'm telling you that I'm fine. I'll be with my friends. I promise to call you if I start to feel bad."

"Alright. I'm going to pay Jude's mother a visit and get your shoes back."

"I doubt if it'll do any good. His mother doesn't care what he does. He'll probably deny doing it, and she'll believe him."

Pops ran his fingers through his thick gray hair. "Well, I have to try."

A couple minutes went by and then Matthew returned with Luke's old pair of shoes. While Luke put them on, Pops said to Matthew, "Keep your eye on him. Call me right away if you need me."

"Will do."

Pops walked off, back toward his house, leaving Luke and Matthew alone. When Pops was out of hearing range, Luke quietly said, "Emmanuel was here. Those guys hurt me pretty bad, but he came along and healed my injuries."

"He was just at my house. We talked in my backyard for a while. Come on. Let's get to Mark's before the game starts."

They got back on their bikes and rode the rest of the way. They saw John's bike in the driveway when they arrived. They parked their bikes next to John's, then walked to the front door. Matthew gave two quick knocks, then opened the door himself without waiting for an answer.

Luke followed Matthew in. Mark and John were sitting in easy chairs in front of the TV, while Jacob, Mark's six year old brother, sat on the floor, putting a jigsaw puzzle together. Matthew and Luke took seats on the sofa, where Luke filled them in on what just happened to him.

John said, "I'm sick of those guys."

Matthew added, "Me too. We need to find a way to get even with them."

Luke nodded. "I wish we could give them a taste of their own medicine."

Matthew said, "I still think that you could've gotten away."

Luke gave him a nasty look, but kept quiet.

The game started, and as it went on, Luke started to get annoyed with Matthew. No matter what happened in the game, Matthew talked about how it could have been done better. It appeared to Luke that Mark and John were irritated with him, too.

At halftime, they passed the time with small talk. John's face lit up as Madison, Mark's sixteen year old sister, came down the stairs. "Hey guys," she announced. With a smile, she added, "How's it going, John?"

Returning the smile, he answered, "I'm good."

She walked through the living room and into the kitchen. John watched her, then got up and followed her in.

Mark got up to get a better look into the kitchen. He gazed at them for a few seconds before returning to his seat.

When the second half started, Mark shouted out, "John, the game's back on."

When a couple minutes went by and John still hadn't returned, Mark repeated the call. Laughter from both John and Madison could be heard, and Mark didn't look happy about it.

When the game cut away to commercial at the end of the third quarter, Mark stormed into the kitchen and asked, "What's so important in here that you're willing to miss the game?"

John and Madison sat facing each other on bar stools lined up along the counter. John laughed and said, "Nothing. I'm just talking to Madison."

Looking at his sister, Mark asked, "Don't you have something better to do? Why do you have to bother my friends?"

She looked offended and said, "Mind your own business."

John added, "She's not bothering me. I came in here on my own because I wanted to talk to her. Do you have a problem with that?"

With a wave of his hand, he said, "Whatever." He turned around and went back to the living room.

He returned to his chair and sat with a scowl on his face. Jacob, leaving his puzzle unfinished on the floor, came over and crawled into Mark's lap.

"What's wrong, buddy? You didn't finish your puzzle."

"I don't feel good."

"Are you sick?"

"I don't know. I'm tired and my tummy hurts."

"Do you want to go upstairs to your room?"

"No. I want to stay here with you."

Luke felt a little envious as he watched. Being an only child, he never got to experience what it was like to have a sibling. The love little Jacob had for his older brother was obvious to anyone watching, and even though Mark wouldn't show it outwardly, it was clear that he felt the same for Jacob.

Mark remained silent for the remainder of the game, remaining motionless with Jacob sleeping in his lap. When it ended, he gently set Jacob on the sofa between John and Luke. He looked back into the kitchen, and saw that John and Madison were still having a good time, laughing and joking together. He shook his head, went back to the sofa and picked Jacob back up, then carefully carried him up the stairs.

Luke watched all this and wondered why Mark was upset. If he had a sister, Luke would be happy if John were interested in her. There were far worse guys out there.

When it appeared that Mark wasn't coming back down, Luke said to Matthew, "Maybe we should go."

Matthew nodded and they went to the kitchen to say goodbye to John. They shouted up the stairs to tell Mark that they were leaving, but got no response.

When they went outside, Luke had a sick feeling in his stomach. He looked around, wondering where Jude was. The thought of seeing him again terrified him. They got on their bikes and headed home. Luke pedaled as hard as he could to keep pace with Matthew, not wanting to be left behind. He did not want to be alone on the street.

Once home, Luke put his bike away and went inside. The pizza that Pops had promised sat on the dining room table, half gone.

Pops said, "Help yourself."

On the floor next to the table, Luke saw a new pair of shoes. He asked, "What's this?"

"You were right about Jude's mother. What a piece of work she is. She thinks her son is an angel. She refused to believe that Jude had anything to do with it. I resigned myself to the fact that your shoes are probably gone for good, so I went to the mall and bought you a new pair."

Luke felt disgusted. He ate a few bites of the pizza, but didn't feel hungry. He felt despair and embarrassment overcome him as he thought about the beating he received. He pushed his plate away and excused himself to his room.

He spent the rest of the night alone in his room. The tears started flowing and he couldn't control them. He didn't understand why, but he was afraid to leave his room. He suddenly feared what was outside the door.

Before the sun went down, he turned off his light and got into bed. He silently wept until sleep overcame him.

CHAPTER 2

From the stillness of his bedroom, Luke could hear Pops moving about the house. A look at the digital clock on his dresser told him that Pops would be coming soon to wake him up for Sunday service, but Luke had no desire to get up. Humiliation surged through him when he thought about what Jude did to him. Even though Emmanuel healed his physical pain, there was a much deeper hurt inside of him.

The knock that he was dreading came, and the door opened a crack. Pops peered in and said, "It's time to get up."

Still laying under the covers, Luke asked, "Can I stay home today?"

Pops opened the door the rest of the way and stepped inside. "Are you sick?"

"No. I just don't want to go anywhere."

A look of worry came across Pops' face. "Are you upset about what happened yesterday?"

Luke answered with a shrug.

"You can't let that bother you."

Luke remained silent.

Pops dismissed his quietness with a wave of his hand. As he left the room, he said, "In any event, you're not missing Sunday school, so get up and get ready."

Alone in his room, Luke reluctantly sat up. He didn't want to face the day. The only thought that appealed to him was to stay in bed all day. He sat on the edge of the bed for a few minutes until he heard Pops call out for him to get moving.

He sighed as he stood up. After a quick shower, he dressed and joined Pops at the kitchen table. Just like the previous night, Luke didn't have much of an appetite. Pops made up for it by eating more than usual.

Just before leaving for church, Luke made one last plea to stay home, but Pops wouldn't give in. Brisk air hit Luke's face as he walked out the front door. The temperature had dropped overnight, causing Luke and Pops both to shiver as they made their way to the minivan parked in the driveway.

Pops stopped and said, "I'm going back inside to get a jacket. Do you want one?"

"I don't care."

While he waited for Pops to return, Luke stood by the passenger side door. Being alone outside made Luke uncomfortable, if not down right scared. He looked around expecting to see Jude in every direction. Pacing around the driveway, jitters ran through his body. He wondered what was taking Pops so long. How long does it take to put a jacket on?

Despite the morning chill, beads of sweat formed on his forehead and the back of his neck. The anxiety of waiting for Pops to come back outside felt like it was going to crush him. He had thoughts of running back inside but was suddenly paralyzed by fear. He stopped pacing and his feet seemed to be rooted to the ground. What was taking Pops so long?

After what seemed like forever and a day, Pops leisurely strolled out the front door, sporting a black and gold windbreaker with a Pittsburgh Pirates logo across the back. He carried a bright blue fleece jacket, which he casually tossed to Luke, saying, "Put this on before you catch pneumonia."

Relief flooded Luke as he put the jacket on. When Pops unlocked the doors with his keyless remote, Luke slipped inside and quickly locked it.

As they drove to church, the scenery showed signs of autumn. The leaves on the trees were turning to shades of red, orange and yellow.

Pops commented, "I love Pennsylvania this time of year. Look at how beautiful the trees are."

Luke didn't even bother to look. He stared out the side window, not really looking at anything. He wasn't in the mood for conversation.

Seeing that Luke didn't seem to care about the trees, Pops went for a different approach. "The Steelers have a tough game today. Are you going to invite your friends over to watch it with us?"

Barely above a whisper, Luke answered, "I guess."

Pops let out a long, deep breath. "I know that you're bothered about getting roughed up yesterday, but you need to snap out of it. You're not the first kid to get victimized by a bully."

Luke turned his head toward Pops and gave him a cold stare. He thought about responding with a wise crack, but decided against it and went back to sulking.

When they arrived at the church, Luke didn't want to get out of the minivan. Knowing that he would be on the receiving end of a tongue lashing from Pops if he didn't get moving, he got out slowly and made his way to his classroom, dragging his feet as he went.

As he got near, he heard a lot of voices coming from the alley between the sanctuary and the youth center. A closer look revealed that the commotion was centered around Matthew, who was surrounded by teenagers and adults, congratulating him and asking questions about the past Friday night's game. Matthew smiled deeply, clearly enjoying the attention.

Luke paused to watch for a minute. Notwithstanding his foul mood, the corners of his mouth went up slightly. He was pleased to see his friend in the spotlight, especially after living in his brother's shadow for so long.

Luke shuffled along and went into the classroom. He took his usual seat and sat quietly, waiting for the rest of the students to show up. His teacher, Zeke, was sitting on a stool at the front of the class, fiddling with his cell phone. Most weeks, Zeke would be telling a story or asking questions while they waited for class to begin, but Luke was thankful for the silence this morning.

Little by little, the room began filling up as the kids filed in. Mark came in and sat next to Luke while John took a seat on the opposite end of the room. Luke sensed that there was still tension between Mark and John.

At the top of the hour, Zeke closed the door and started the class. Luke noticed that Matthew was absent. He had just seen him outside a few minutes earlier. Where was he?

Zeke began teaching about the book of Daniel, which made Luke's ears perk up. Could it be just a coincidence that he was learning about Daniel after dreaming about it two nights ago? He quickly forgot about his bad mood and listened intently. He got lost inside the story as Zeke described it.

About ten minutes into the class, they were interrupted by the door opening. Matthew walked in, followed by Kylie, a pretty blond who was the object of his affection.

Zeke sarcastically said, "I'm glad the two of you could make it on time."

A little embarrassed, Kylie softly said, "Sorry."

Matthew said nothing as he glided across the room and sat next to John. Luke was a little appalled as he watched. Was Matthew strutting?

He definitely wasn't bothered by Zeke's comment. He casually gave John a fist bump and leaned back in his chair. Motioning to an empty seat on his other side, he invited Kylie to sit beside him, which she was eager to do. Zeke shook his head and went back to the lesson.

As the class went on, Luke's attention kept getting diverted by Matthew, who repeatedly whispered in Kylie's ear. She giggled the first few times but then looked to be getting bothered by it. She eventually gave him a soft elbow to his ribs and scooted her chair a few feet away so she could hear what Zeke was saying. Matthew continued smiling as he sat there with his arms folded.

When the class ended, Luke slid out of the classroom unnoticed. He darted into the sanctuary, looking for Pops, and found him talking to Pastor Alex. He tried to be patient while he waited for their conversation to end, but he was getting stirred up on the inside. He wanted nothing more than to get home as fast as possible.

Pops, seeing Luke out of the corner of his eye, politely ended his talk with the pastor. As they walked through the parking lot, he asked, "Did you invite your friends over to watch the game?"

"I didn't say anything, but they know they're always welcome."

Pops stopped in his tracks. "Go back and invite them."

Luke stood still without responding.

Anger began to show in Pops' voice. "We're not leaving until you talk to your friends and invite them over to watch the game."

"Why can't we watch the game by ourselves?"

"We always have your friends over to watch the Steelers, and we always have a great time. Why are you acting like this?"

Luke shook his head in frustration. Disinclined, he headed toward the youth center in an attempt to find his friends. Before he got a few steps, he saw Matthew and Kylie walking toward him. He meekly asked, "Are you coming over to watch the game?"

Matthew replied, "Of course."

Pops added, "You're invited too, Kylie."

With a look of surprise, she said, "Thanks, but I'm going home with my dad to watch the Patriots."

Disguised as a cough, Matthew blurted, "Cheaters."

She gave him a playful shove and said, "Don't be a hater." Pops laughed heartily while Luke stood there, stone faced. Seeing this, Pops said, "Hey grumpy, go find your other friends and let them know that they can come over."

Matthew interjected, "I'll tell them. I'm heading that way." Turning to Kylie, he added, "I'll call you tonight." They hugged quickly and Matthew ran back to the youth center, while Kylie joined her mom and dad by their car.

Pops and Luke silently went to the minivan and started their jaunt home. They made a stop on the way at the local grocery store to pick up some snacks and drinks to enjoy during the game. Luke was aggravated because he didn't want to go into the store, but the thought of staying in the parking lot alone sent shivers up and down his spine. He stayed close to Pops as they filled their cart with chips, pretzel and soda. He was constantly looking over his shoulder, expecting to see Jude around every corner. He anxiously wanted to get back to the safety of their home.

They got into the checkout line, paid for their items, and went the rest of the way home. Luke's stress was eased when they pulled into the driveway. He quickly ran inside and changed into his favorite Steelers jersey, then took his usual spot on the sofa and watched the pre-game show.

One at a time, his friends showed up. Mark, Matthew and Pops discussed their opinions of what they expected in the upcoming game, while Luke sat silently, staring at the TV, not really listening.

John was in the kitchen, talking on his cell phone. Just before kickoff, Pops called out to him, "The game is about to start."

A few seconds later, John reappeared in the living room, putting his phone into his front pocket. Matthew asked him, "Who were you talking to?"

"Madison."

Mark glared at him for a short time, then turned his attention back to the TV as the game got under way.

As the game went on, Luke watched stoically, while the others had a great time cheering for the Steelers big plays, and groaning when their opponents did well.

Just like the previous day, Matthew was very critical of what he saw. He was quick to question every call the coaches made, and even quicker to find fault with decisions made by the quarterback. Luke wondered if everyone else was as bothered by it as he was.

Toward the end of the game, Luke soundlessly excused himself and went to his bedroom, laying down on his bed, staring at the ceiling. He wanted to be left alone.

About five minutes went by before Pops appeared at his doorway. "What are you doing in here by yourself?"

Luke lied, "I don't feel well. I just want to lay here for a while."

"You have guests. Get back into the living room and be a gracious host."

Luke sighed and got back up. He walked back into the living room just as the Steelers scored a touchdown. His friends all stood up and cheered loudly. Luke's bad mood got worse with the noise. He stopped caring about the game early on. Sitting back down, he waited patiently for the game to end so his friends would go back home and he could get his wish of being left alone.

When the game ended, the Steelers had won a thriller, but Luke didn't care. He felt annoyed, especially with Matthew, who continued with his criticism of the game. He was down right cocky in his attitude, and Luke didn't like what he was seeing.

Luke felt a rush of relief when his friends started putting their jackets on, getting ready to go home, but that relief quickly ended when the doorbell rang.

Pops opened the door and his face went white. He angrily asked, "What are you doing here?"

Luke walked over to the door to get a better look. He didn't recognize the man standing there. He appeared to be in his early forties, standing about six feet tall with an athletic build. His reddish brown hair was the same color as Luke's.

The man asked, "Can I come in?"

Pops hesitated a second before taking a step back and motioning with his arm for the man to enter. He boldly stepped inside and looked Luke in the eye, smiling broadly.

Luke immediately felt uncomfortable and asked, "Pops, who is this guy?"

Pops took a deep breath, then calmly said, "Luke, this is your father."

CHAPTER 3

Luke stood there stunned. He had gone the first fourteen years of his life not knowing who his father was. He only knew what Pops had told him.

Luke's mother died from complications while giving birth to him. His father took off when Luke was still a baby and hadn't been heard from since. Pops and his wife had raised him together until her untimely death when Luke was ten years old.

Seeing how disturbed Luke was, John said to the rest, "Let's give them some privacy."

Pops nodded his approval as John, Matthew and Mark quietly walked outside. After closing the door, Pops asked, "Why are you here?"

"I want to see my son."

With irritation in his voice, Pops asked, "Where have you been the last fourteen years?"

Luke's father sighed. "I had a feeling that you would react this way."

"How do you expect me to react? Should I welcome you with open arms and pretend that you never abandoned your son?"

Luke jumped in, "Stop arguing!"

His father looked at him and asked, "Can I buy you dinner? It will be a good way to talk and catch up."

Pops interjected, "You're not going anywhere with him unless I go too. I don't trust you alone with him."

With a shrug he said, "That's fine."

Luke grabbed his jacket from the closet and said, "Let's go to Mario's."

His father chuckled lightly as he asked, "Is that place is still open? I used to go there when I was your age."

Luke shook his head as he went out the door. Pops and his dad followed him out and into the driveway. A white, four door sedan was parked behind Pops' minivan.

Pops asked, "Is that your car?"

"It's a rental. You guys can come with me. I'll drive."

"I think we should drive separately. Luke will come with me."

With slumped shoulders, he said, "You don't have to be this way. I'm trying to make peace here."

Pops glared at him until he turned away. They got into their respective vehicles and drove out of the neighborhood toward Mario's. Luke sat in the passenger seat, staring straight ahead. Pops didn't bother trying to make conversation this time.

Everything seemed surreal. For years, Luke had wondered where his father was and why he had left. Although he felt resentment toward him for leaving, he still longed to have him in his life. Now, his father was here and he wasn't sure how he felt about it. More than anything, he wanted answers.

When they got to Mario's, they parked next to each other in front of the restaurant. Luke got out and jammed his fists into his jacket pockets. He slowly walked to the entrance hunched over and looking at the ground.

The atmosphere inside was completely different from what Luke was used to. It was noisy and energetic on Friday nights after the football games, but now it was quiet and serene. Nobody was playing the video games and only two tables had customers. He walked straight to the back and sat at the table farthest away from the other patrons. Pops and his father sat across from each other with Luke in between them.

After a period of uncomfortable silence, Luke said, "I'm not sure how I should address you?"

His father smiled and said, "Dad would be fine, but if you're not ready for that, you can call me Brad."

He nodded without saying anything. He stole a glance at Pops and saw him looking to the side with a scowl on his face. He gave the impression that he wanted to be anywhere but there.

The waitress came over and took their order. Pops and Luke each ordered a calzone and a soda, while Brad got a Stromboli and a beer.

Pops asked, "Is it necessary to drink?"

Brad looked surprised as he responded, "I'm nervous. I thought it would take the edge off."

Pops shook his head with disgust. "You haven't changed a bit."

"You never approved of me when I dated Stephanie, why would you approve of me now?"

Luke felt awkward hearing his mother being referred to by her first name. He was also annoyed by the bickering back and forth between Pops and Brad. He looked to Pops and asked, "Why didn't you approve of him?"

"Lots of reasons. He couldn't hold a job. He drank too much. He owed half the town money. He was too old for your mother. I could go on, but you get the point. I thought he was a bum and my daughter deserved better."

Surprised, Luke asked, "Too old for my mom? How much older are you?"

Brad leaned backed in his chair. "I was twenty-eight and your mother was seventeen when we met."

Pops looked at him angrily as he said, "If I'd known about you and her at the time, I would've had you arrested."

"We weren't dating at that time. We kept it as friends until she turned eighteen."

Pops dismissed the comment with a wave of his hand.

Luke said, "I'm confused. I know that my mom died just after she turned nineteen. How soon after you started dating did you get married?"

Brad shot a look to Pops and asked, "You never told him?"

Luke asked, "Told me what?"

Brad looked back to Luke and said, "Your mother and I never got married."

A shocked Luke exclaimed, "What?"

"I'm sorry. I thought that your grandfather would have told you."

Anger coursed through Luke's body. He turned to Pops and asked, "Why didn't you ever tell me that?"

Pops ran his fingers through his thick gray hair and sighed. "Because your mother was a wonderful person and I didn't want you to think less of her."

Trying to ignore his irritation with Pops, Luke shifted his attention back to Brad. "I want to know everything. Start from the beginning."

The waitress brought their drinks to the table. Brad took a long swallow from his bottle of beer, then scooted forward in his seat. "I saw your mother for the first time at a fast food restaurant. She was with two of her friends. At the table next to them were three guys who looked to be about college age. They were making some crude comments about the girls and it was obvious to me that they were trying to make unwanted advances.

"I went over to the guys and told them to leave the girls alone. At first they acted tough. They had me outnumbered three to one, so they mouthed off a bit. Instead of starting a fight, I chose to sit with the girls. It didn't take long for the guys to give up. It was only a couple minutes later that they got up and left. As they went outside, I went over to the window and watched them get into their car and drive out of the parking lot.

"I returned to the girls table and asked them if they knew those guys, but they didn't. Your mom thanked me and we said goodbye."

Pops sarcastically said, "I wish you'd said goodbye forever."

"Hey! I was coming to the aid of your daughter!"

Pops mocked, "How noble of you."

Paying no heed to Pops comment, Brad resumed his story. "It very well could have been forever, but the next night, I went to the Benworth basketball game. My friend's younger brother was on the team, so he and I went to watch him play. As fate would have it, your mother was sitting in the row in front of us. She recognized me and we struck up a conversation. After the game ended, she gave me her phone number and asked me to call her.

"I wasn't sure what to do at first. I knew that she was still in high school and too young for me. It would be totally inappropriate to call her. About a week later, I ran into her again at a convenience store. She seemed a little hurt that I hadn't called. I told her that I wanted to but was bothered by the age difference."

Pops cut in, "You're making it sound like Stephanie pursued you."

"In a way, she did. I never asked for her number, she offered it. I never intended to call her, but we kept bumping into each other at unexpected times."

Luke asked, "If you were really troubled by the age difference, then how did you end up together?"

"I'm getting to that. When we left the store, we talked for quite a while in the parking lot. Her friend that was with her was losing patience and wanted to leave. Your mom told her to go ahead and leave and she would catch a ride home with me. I was a little uncomfortable with that, but reluctantly agreed. We drove around for at least an hour or two, talking and enjoying each others company. Eventually we came to the agreement that we would be friends, but try to avoid spending time alone. We would try to plan outings in public places, not allowing ourselves to be alone.

"That worked fine for about a month, but ultimately we admitted that we had developed romantic feelings for each other. She was still about four months away from turning eighteen, so we promised each other that we would behave until her birthday. We continued talking on the phone but avoided seeing each other.

"When her birthday finally came, we went out to celebrate and had our first date. She graduated high school a few weeks later and we started discussing our future together."

Pops said, "I still can't believe that you talked her out of going to college."

"That wasn't my idea. In fact, I encouraged her to go. She wanted to take some time off before making a decision."

"She was all set to go to college before she met you. Don't tell me that you had nothing to do with her changing her mind."

"Inadvertently, I may have, but it wasn't anything that I did consciously or purposely. I loved your daughter and wanted nothing but the best for her."

An awkward silence followed as Pops and Brad stared at each other from across the table. Luke wanted to hear the rest of the story but didn't like the tension he was feeling. Thoughts of going back home appealed to him.

Brad continued his story. "Things went well between us despite the fact that your grandfather was very vocal that he disapproved of our relationship."

"Darn right I disapproved."

Ignoring Pops, Brad went on, "Sometime during the fall, we found out that your mom was pregnant. She wanted to get married right away, but I didn't want to rush it, so I talked her into waiting until after you were born."

Pops interjected, "Don't lie to him."

"I'm not lying."

"You're leaving out an important part of the story."

"What are you talking about?"

With a look of disgust, Pops turned to Luke and said, "He wanted your mother to have an abortion."

Brad slammed his fist into the table, causing Luke to flinch. "Why did you tell him that?"

"Because it's the truth and he has a right to know."

"If Stephanie had gone through with the abortion, she'd be alive today. Don't you wish that she was still here?"

The passion in their voices escalated as the discussion heated up.

Pops continued, "I miss my daughter more than you'll ever know, but if she would've had the abortion, Luke wouldn't be here. Obviously you don't care about that because you left."

"That's a cheap shot!"

Luke stood up and shouted, "Stop!"

The other customers turned to look, curious about what was going on.

Luke slowly sat back down and calmly said, "If you guys are going to continue arguing, I'm out of here. I mean it. I'll walk home by myself."

Brad said, "Luke, I'm sorry." Looking at Pops, he added, "Let's keep this civil for Luke's sake."

Pops replied, "Tell him what you need to tell him. I'll keep quiet."

The waitress brought the food to the table and dropped it off. Pops said a quick prayer and they began eating.

Between mouthfuls of food, Brad resumed his story. "So, the plan was to wait until after you were born, then have a nice wedding. Unfortunately, things didn't work out that way. As you already know, your mother died while giving birth to you."

Brad paused while his eyes filled with tears. "I didn't know what to do. I felt like the whole world was crashing down on me. Your mom meant so much to me and I couldn't imagine life without her. I knew that I couldn't raise you by myself. I'm an only child and my parents were already dead, so I had nobody to turn to."

Luke felt a little compassion for him, but still wanted answers. He gave him a cold look and asked, "Do you think that excuses you for abandoning me?"

With a shake of his head, Brad answered back, "Not at all. I hope you understand that I thought about you every day since I left."

"But you still left. Now you come back and expect everything to be alright. Well, it's not alright. All these years I've been wondering where you are, what you were doing. I didn't know if you were dead or alive. Worst of all, I had no idea why you left. Why didn't you want to be a part of my life?"

Brad put his hands over his face, then slowly lowered them. "I wish I had an easy answer."

Luke frowned as he asked, "Where have you been all these years?"

"After the funeral, I took you to your grandparents house. I asked them to watch you for a few days while I figured out what I was going to do."

"A few days? It's been fourteen years!"

"I know and I'm so sorry. After I dropped you off, I went out and got drunk. The next morning, I started thinking about how I was going to raise you by myself. I never felt so overwhelmed in my life."

"So you left."

Nodding, Brad said, "Yes. I intended to come back, but one thing led to another and it didn't work out that way."

"What was so important that it kept you away for fourteen years?"

"It wasn't any one thing. I decided that a road trip might help me clear my mind. I had a couple thousand dollars left from my mother's life insurance, so I closed out my bank account and started driving west. I didn't have a particular destination in mind. I was just driving. I got as far as Kansas City the first day, Denver the second, and Las Vegas the third. I'd never been to Vegas before, so I got off the freeway and stopped at the first casino I saw."

Brad hesitated for a second, looking up to the ceiling before going on. "As I walked through the casino, I couldn't help thinking about your mother. I had promised to take her to Vegas when she turned twenty-one. Now, there I was, in Vegas without her."

Luke had been listening patiently, wanting to know the whole story, but was starting to get annoyed. "Don't you think that the life insurance money would have been better spent on your baby?"

"In retrospect, I agree, but I wasn't thinking clearly at the time."

"It took you fourteen years to figure that out?"

Brad sighed deeply. "I know that I made a lot of mistakes. You asked me to tell you everything, so I am."

Irritated, Luke nodded and said, "Go on."

"Okay, where was I? Oh yes, the casino. I walked around for a few minutes taking it in. I eventually made my way to one of the casino bars. I struck up a conversation with the bartender. It turned out that he was from Pennsylvania, too. He kept telling me how great of a town Vegas was. Warm winters, good paying jobs, a great night life. Everything he told me made me want to live there. I turned around in my barstool and looked over to the blackjack tables. I watched some of the dealers and thought to myself, 'I can do that.' I enrolled in a dealing school and two weeks later I was dealing blackjack in a casino. I did that for about five years before being promoted to pit boss."

Pops broke his silence. "You've been in Vegas this whole time?"

"Yeah."

Luke asked, "Why didn't you at least tell me where you were?"

"I wanted to. It was hard for me. I've kept in close contact with a friend here in Benworth. He assured me that you were doing well with your grandparents, so I thought it would be best for you if I stayed away.

As much as I hate to admit it, I knew that your grandparents would raise you much better than I could have."

"It still would have been nice to hear from you once in a while. A phone call. A Christmas card. Something. Anything."

"I know. I should have. I lost fourteen years of time that I should have been spending with you. I'd like for you to give me the chance to make up for it. I have four weeks of vacation time from my job, all of which I'm taking now. I'm staying with my buddy that I told you about, so I'll be around. Let's spend some time together."

Luke gave him a condescending look. "Do you really think that you can make up for fourteen years in four weeks?"

"No. That's just the beginning. What I'd really like to do is take you back to Vegas to live with me."

Pops stood up and said, "Over my dead body!"

Luke added, "No way! I'm not living there. Benworth is my home. I like living with Pops. All of my friends are here. I'm playing football and I'll be wrestling after that. Forget about it."

"They have football and wrestling in Vegas, too. As far as friends go, I'm sure you'll adjust."

"Not a chance. I'm staying here."

Pops said, "You have a lot of nerve coming back here after all this time. Do you think I'll just sit here and let you take him away?"

Brad answered, "I'm ready to take this to court if necessary."

"I had a feeling that you might try this someday, so I did some research. The courts will most likely leave the decision up to Luke, and he's already told you how he feels about it."

"I can take better care of him and I think the courts will agree with me."

Pops face turned red with anger. "What are you talking about? You just said that you thought that he'd be better off here and that's why you never came back for him!"

"That was when your wife was alive. Now that it's just you, I have doubts that you can raise him adequately."

"You arrogant piece of trash! I spent the last fourteen years raising a respectable young man while you were living the high life in Vegas. Don't tell me that I can't raise him properly!"

"We'll let the courts decide that."

The table fell silent as Pops looked like he was ready to explode. Luke slouched in his chair and wished that he could crawl under the table. What had started out as a great weekend, watching his friend Matthew lead the football team to a great victory, had turned into a nightmare. Receiving a beating from Jude and now his father returning unexpectedly left him dazed and stunned.

The rest of the meal was eaten in silence. When they finished, Pops and Luke got up to leave. Brad gave Luke a yearning look as he said, "Please give me a chance. Spend some time with me while I'm here."

"I'll think about it."

"Okay. I'll be in touch."

Pops shook his head as he walked to the exit with Luke close behind. They walked outside as the sun was setting. Darkness settled over the town as they drove home, but it was nothing compared to the darkness Luke was feeling in his heart.

CHAPTER 4

The ride home seemed like it took forever to Luke. When they finally got there, he quickly went to his room and changed into some comfortable clothes. A part of him wanted to climb into bed and fall into a deep sleep and another wanted to run outside and scream at the top of his lungs.

From the living room he could hear Pops turn on the TV. For a second he thought about joining him but discarded the idea. Thoughts of reading and listening to music crossed his mind, but none of it appealed to him.

What he really wanted to do was vent to someone. He knew that John usually turned his phone off at night and Mark wasn't much of a listener, so that left Matthew. He was someone Luke could always count on in the past, so he grabbed his cell phone off of the dresser next to his bed, leaned back against the pillows, and called him.

It rang a number of times, and just when Luke thought it was going to go to voicemail, Matthew answered.

"Hello."

"Hey. It's Luke."

"What's up?"

"I could really use someone to talk to."

"Let me call you back. I'm on the other line with Kylie."

"Oh. Alright."

"As soon as I hang up with her, I'll get back to you."

"Okay. Talk to you soon."

Luke closed his phone and sat up in his bed. He was itching for someone to talk to, but didn't know who else to call. He wished Emmanuel was here to give him some advice.

He left the bedroom and joined Pops in the living room. Luke tried to get interested in the reality show that Pops was watching but was too distracted to get into it.

After a few minutes, he gave up and set off for the kitchen, where he took a can of soda out of the fridge. He popped it open and took a long swig from it. He went over to the sliding glass doors that led to the back patio and looked out.

He couldn't believe his eyes. Emmanuel was sitting out there!

Looking very relaxed in one of the chairs surrounding a circular table with an umbrella coming up through the center, Emmanuel calmly motioned for Luke to join him. A chuckle escaped his throat as he noticed Emmanuel wearing his gray hoodie while holding up an identical one for Luke to wear.

Luke looked back toward the living room, saw that Pops was completely absorbed in his show, and knew that it was safe to go outside undetected. As quiet as possible, he slid the glass door open. He slipped outside and eased the door shut. Peering through, he could see that Pops hadn't heard a thing.

He turned around as Emmanuel rose from his seat to give him a hug. Tears filled Luke's eyes as they embraced. He felt the warmth course through him as he realized that no matter what, Emmanuel would always love him. He put the hoodie on to prevent the evening chill from getting to him.

They sat down, turning the chairs inward to face each other. Luke ran his fingers through his reddish brown hair and sighed deeply. "My father showed up today."

"I know."

"Everything is changing."

"Change isn't necessarily a bad thing."

Luke looked away and shook his head. "For years, I secretly wished that he'd come back and we could have a typical father-son relationship."

Emmanuel nodded his understanding. Luke continued, "Now, I just want him to leave."

"Why?"

"This wasn't the way I pictured it. I don't like the fact that he and Pops hate each other. I can't believe that he expects me to live in Las Vegas with him. This is my home, here with Pops."

"Very few things in life will happen the way you expect them to."

"I understand that, but he has a lot of nerve showing up out of the blue and wanting me to drop everything and start a new life with him on the other side of the country."

Emmanuel reached over and put his arm on Luke's shoulder. "Don't worry about that. Whatever happens, you're going to land on your feet."

"I'm not moving to Las Vegas. I'll run away before I let that happen."

Emmanuel chuckled. "You and I both know that you would never do that."

Frustrated, Luke responded, "I know."

He got up and began pacing back and forth across the patio. Emmanuel stayed seated and calmly watched him. Luke stopped, put his hands on top of his head and looked to the sky. A full moon looked back at him. He let out a deep breath and said, "I've heard it said that crazy people come out during a full moon. Is that why my father chose today to come back?"

Emmanuel laughed out loud and said, "Your father isn't crazy."

"He's crazy if he expects me to willingly go to Vegas with him. He said that he'll take it to court if he has to. What will I do if the courts order me to go with him?"

"Then you'll be obedient to the ruling and go with him."

Shocked, Luke replied, "That's not the answer I was looking for."

"I know, but sometimes life happens. When it does, you have to make the best of it."

"I don't want to start over in a new city and a new school. What if they don't like me there? What if I can't make friends?"

"Matthew's friend Kylie is going through that right now. She's doing fine."

"Yeah, but she's a pretty girl with an outgoing personality. It's easy for her."

"What makes you think that it won't be easy for you?"
"Because I'm homely with red hair."

Emmanuel smiled and said, "You're not homely. Do you have any idea how many girls admire you?"

Luke felt a rush of excitement. "Who?"

"Just some girls from your school. Open your eyes and maybe you'll be able to figure it out."

"You're not going to tell me?"

"It's not important right now. I just want to assure you that if you do have to move, you'll be fine."

Luke sat back down and said, "I don't care. I like it here in Benworth and I don't want to move."

"I know you don't. Nobody in your situation would, but I'm here to tell you that it won't be the end of the world."

"I can't believe this is happening."

"You seem a little ungrateful."

"What do you mean?"

With a serious look on his face, Emmanuel looked him in the eyes and asked, "Do you think I didn't hear what you were praying for all these years?"

Confusion engulfed Luke. "I don't understand."

"Since you've been old enough to talk, you've been praying that your father would come back. Today, that prayer was answered."

"Yeah, but I wanted him to live here."

"Well, start praying for that."

"I don't think it'll do any good. From what he told me today, he really loves it in Vegas."

"Do you doubt the power of prayer?"

Luke lowered his head and answered, "No. I'm just confused and angry."

"People's hearts can be changed. It happens every day."

"If my father really loved and cared about me, he wouldn't want to take me away from my home."

"But aren't you expecting the same thing from him?"

"Huh?"

Emmanuel sighed. "Your father has a job, a home, friends, and a life in Las Vegas. Is expecting him to give all that up to come live here any different from what he's asking you to do?"

Luke felt a little embarrassed as he said, "I see your point. But still, he's the one who ran out in the first place. Shouldn't he be the one to make the adjustment?"

"I agree. I would like to see that."

"Is he a Christian?"

"Unfortunately, he's not, but I haven't given up hope for him."

"He said that he wants to spend time with me over the next few weeks. Maybe I could use that time to tell him about you."

A huge smile crossed Emmanuel's face. "I think that's a great idea. Share the gospel with him."

"Should I tell him about our meetings?"

"No."

"Why not?"

"Has anyone else believed you?"

"Good point."

"He's been living in the world for a long time, and he likes it there, so don't get discouraged if he doesn't respond favorably right away."

"What should I say?"

"I think the right words will come to you."

"You can't help me out here?"

"This will be a good experience for you. There are people out there who don't know about me and it's up to believers like yourself to tell them. Your father will be a good place to start, but don't stop there."

Luke suddenly felt overwhelmed. "Wow. Nothing like putting a little pressure on me."

Emmanuel laughed as he replied, "I'm not asking you to save the world. I just want you to tell people about me."

"That makes me nervous."

"Sometimes a person's biggest spiritual growth comes when they step out of their comfort zone."

"What if I say the wrong thing? I don't want to push someone farther away."

"Every time you tell someone about me, you'll be planting a seed. It might stop there with you, but somebody else could come along and water that seed. Do you understand?"

Luke nodded. "I think so."

"It's rare that someone becomes a Christian overnight. It's usually a gradual process where a person slowly comes along. If everyone does their part, eventually that seed will blossom."

"I'd like to see that happen with my father."

"Me too."

Luke leaned back in his seat and looked to the sky. "I'm scared."

Emmanuel stood up and softly took Luke's wrist, easing him up out of his chair. He hugged him gently. "You have nothing to be scared about. I will never leave you nor will I forsake you."

"That's good to know."

"Give your father a chance. Get to know him. He's made a lot of mistakes, but I'm willing to forgive him. I'm asking you to do the same."

"I'll try."

With a smile, Emmanuel said, "You should probably go back inside before your grandfather comes into the kitchen and sees us out here."

"Can't we just hang out and talk some more? I don't want you to go."

"I would love to, but you have some homework that you've been putting off. Go back in and take care of that."

Luke cringed and said, "I almost forgot about that."

"There's one more thing that I want you to do before you go to sleep tonight."

"What?"

"I want you to pray for Jude and his friends."

A feeling of disgust filled Luke from head to toe. "I don't want to pray for them."

"I know you don't, but I'm asking you to anyway. Will you do that for me?" Reluctantly, he said, "Yes."

Emmanuel smiled his approval. Luke took off the hoodie that Emmanuel had given him and handed it back. "Here. I better not keep this. I'd have a hard time explaining to Pops where it came from."

Emmanuel accepted it back and hugged him one more time. He quietly walked down the four steps that led from the patio deck down into the back yard. In a matter of seconds, he disappeared from Luke's view.

He stared out into the darkness for a minute or two until the chill of the night air started to get to him. He went back through the sliding glass doors and locked it behind him.

Pops heard him come in and shouted out from the living room, "What were you doing outside?"

He lied, "I just went out to think for a while."

Returning to his TV show, he said, "You should've put on a jacket. It's cold out there."

For the first time all day, Luke smiled, but it quickly vanished as he retreated to his bedroom. He checked his cell phone to see if Matthew had called back while he was outside, but he hadn't.

He grabbed his school bag and took his textbooks out, setting them on his desk. For the next hour or so, he got lost in his homework assignments. When he finished, he looked at the clock and saw that it had been almost two hours since Matthew said that he would call him back. He wondered what was taking him so long.

To kill time, he surfed the net on his computer for a while, but quickly lost interest. Weariness was setting in, so he got into bed. As he was starting to dose off, he was suddenly jolted awake. He had promised Emmanuel that he would pray for Jude and his friends.

He got up and dropped to his knees at the side of his bed. He obediently prayed for them, although it wasn't very enthusiastic. He took one last look at his phone and felt disappointed that Matthew hadn't returned his call. This certainly wasn't like him.

Once back in bed, he fell asleep fast, but the sleep was restless due to repeated dreams of enrolling in a new school in Las Vegas.

CHAPTER 5

Luke woke up Monday morning feeling as though he hadn't slept at all. He sluggishly got ready for school, all the while wishing that he could stay home.

Pops seemed distracted as he sat in his recliner, reading the newspaper. He would occasionally look up to glance at the morning talk show coming from the TV, but he was clearly fidgety, often shifting in his seat in an attempt to get comfortable.

Luke noticed that Pops wasn't himself but chose not to say anything. He had enough going on without getting involved with what was bothering Pops. Plopping down on the sofa, Luke tried to watch what was on the TV while he waited for his friends to show up to walk to school together.

Pops looked over the top of his newspaper at Luke and asked, "Aren't you eating breakfast this morning?"

"I'm not hungry."

His eyes narrowed as he replied, "You're not going to school without something in your stomach. There's plenty of food in the kitchen. Find something to eat."

Luke didn't want an argument, so he dragged himself into the kitchen and poured himself a bowl of cereal. While robotically shoving spoonfuls into his mouth, he thought about why Matthew didn't call him back the previous night. It certainly wasn't like him.

He convinced himself that it was no big deal and finished eating. As he rinsed his bowl out in the sink, Pops entered the kitchen, got a jelly donut from the cupboard, poured himself another cup of coffee, and returned with them to his recliner.

Following him back into the living room, Luke thought about saying something to Pops about his eating habits, but before he could, Pops asked him, "Are you ready for Bible study tonight?"

A week earlier, Matthew and Kylie, at the suggestion of Zeke, organized a youth Bible study to be held on Monday nights. Pops had agreed to lead it. The first one was scheduled for that night.

Caught off guard, he retorted, "I guess."

"You don't sound too enthused."

He answered with a shrug.

"You're going to be studying God's Word with your friends. You should be excited about that."

Not wanting to talk about it, Luke was grateful when the doorbell rang, indicating that his friends had arrived to walk to school with him. With haste, he slipped his jacket on and headed for the door.

With his school bag slung over his shoulder, he stepped outside where John and Mark were waiting for him. He quickly zipped his jacket when the chilly air of the morning greeted him rudely.

He heard Pops call out behind him, "I'll see you at the JV game this afternoon. Don't forget about the Bible study tonight!"

John answered back, "We won't. Looking forward to it."

When the door was closed, Mark turned to Luke and asked, "What happened with your dad yesterday?"

They began their walk toward school. Luke looked to the ground as he said, "We went to Mario's for dinner."

Mark tilted his head and asked, "And?"

Luke had conflicting emotions. On one hand, he desperately wanted to talk about it, and on the other, the whole thing left him with a sick feeling which made him want to forget it. He raised his head to meet Mark's gaze and said, "Well---"

Before he could finish the sentence, Matthew came rushing out of his house as they made their way to it. He quickly called out, "Hey guys, what's up?"

The other three all turned their heads to see him trotting through the front lawn to meet them on the sidewalk. He joined them and they continued their walk to school.

Luke nudged Matthew with his elbow and asked, "Why didn't you call me back last night?"

As though he didn't hear him, Matthew said, "The JV game should be interesting. This will be Caleb's first time starting at quarterback."

Matthew was referring to Caleb Young. Caleb had been Matthew's backup quarterback throughout middle school and the first few JV games. Now that Matthew had been promoted to the strater on the varsity team, he would no longer play in the JV games. This vacancy allowed Caleb to step up and quarterback the JV squad.

John shrugged his shoulders and said, "I'm sure he'll do fine."

Matthew shook his head. "I don't know. He's looked kind of shaky in practice."

John answered, "I'm not worried about it." Turning to Luke, he asked, "So, tell us what happened with your father yesterday?"

Luke opened his mouth to answer, but before he could, Matthew jumped in. "I talked to Kylie about it last night and she agrees with me. She thinks Caleb isn't ready. I wish I could still play in the JV games, but the coach would never go for it."

Luke looked to John and said, "My dad wants me to move---"

Matthew interrupted, "I wonder why Coach King won't let Cody drop down to quarterback the JV team. I know he's done a lousy job with the varsity, but he'd still be a better choice than Caleb."

Luke stopped in his tracks and scowled at Matthew, who kept walking, seemingly unaware that anything was wrong. John turned and saw the look on Luke's face. He motioned for him to keep going. As Luke caught up, John asked him, "What does your dad want you to do?"

"He said he wants---"

Again, Matthew interjected, "How about that Steelers game yesterday? Best game I've seen in a while. It shouldn't have been so close though. They made a lot of stupid mistakes."

Luke tried again, "He wants me to---"

"Kylie said the Patriots game was good too. Too bad I can't convert her to a Steelers fan. Then we could watch the games together. At least they play each other in a few weeks. We'll watch that one together for sure, even though we'll be rooting for different sides."

Luke's jaw dropped in frustration. He shouted out, "How many times are you going to interrupt me?"

With a stunned look, Matthew asked, "What are you talking about?"

Dumbfounded, Luke just stared back.

John stepped between them and said, "We've been trying to find out what happened yesterday with him and his dad."

Matthew's eyebrows went up. "Oh yeah! What happened with that?"

With aggravation in his voice, Luke said, "We could have talked about this last night, but you never called me back."

A puzzled look came across Matthew's face. "Huh?"

"I called you last night. You said you were on the other line with Kylie and you would call me back after you hung up with her."

"Oh, yes. Sorry about that. We talked pretty late into the night. It must have slipped my mind. Besides, right after my call with her, I got another call from Alyssa Wright."

Mark asked, "Alyssa Wright? Isn't she a senior?"

"Yeah. So?"

"Why is a senior girl calling a freshman guy?"

Matthew nonchalantly asked, "Why wouldn't she?"

John chimed in, "How did she get your number?"

"Jocelyn gave it to her. They're pretty good friends."

"What did she want?"

"She just wanted to talk. She did say something about a party this weekend. She wanted to know if I was going."

Mark asked, "Are you?"

"I don't know. My folks won't be too keen on it, so I may have to come up with a cover story."

As Matthew, Mark and John continued talking, Luke got lost in his own thoughts. He remained quiet the rest of the way to school, and the others stopped asking about his father.

When they got there, Luke, John and Mark went to their usual table in the cafeteria, but Matthew immediately went over to a table with upperclassmen, most of whom were starters on the football team. He laughed and joked with them for a couple minutes before inviting Kylie over. She joined them, but looked uncomfortable and out of place. She quickly excused herself and went back over to her girlfriends.

Luke watched this and tried not to get mad. Matthew was acting different, and he didn't like what he was seeing.

Leaning back in his chair, he suddenly dreaded the thought of going through the school day. He thought about going to the office and saying he was sick, but he knew that if he did, he wouldn't be allowed to play football that afternoon. He also knew that Pops would see right through his charade, and he didn't want to have to deal with that. He slouched down and accepted the fact that he would have to make it through the day.

Mark turned to Luke and asked, "Are you okay?"

"I guess."

John asked, "Do you want to tell us what happened with your dad?"

Luke stared a hole through him as he answered, "Matthew might have something more interesting to say."

Taken aback, John responded, "Whoa! He was the one who kept interrupting you, not me!"

"You certainly didn't seem to mind. Both of you were in awe of Matthew's new found popularity. As soon as you heard that a senior girl had called him, you were all in his business, wanting details!"

Mark jumped in, "What's your problem?"

"No problem! No problem at all!" Luke bolted out of his chair and hurriedly exited the cafeteria, bumping into a few of his classmates along the way. John and Mark watched him go with their mouths hanging open.

Luke went down the hallway toward the classrooms and quickly ducked into the restroom. Two students were inside, one standing at the urinal and the other washing his hands at the sink. He brushed past them both and slipped inside an empty stall, closing the door behind him.

He suddenly felt embarrassed for lashing out as his friends. Leaning back against the door, he caught his breath. After a couple minutes, he felt that he had calmed down enough to return to the table. There was still a few minutes left before the bell would ring to start the school day.

As he made his way through the throng of students, he caught sight of Matthew, still laughing and joking with the upperclassmen. A closer look revealed that Alyssa Wright was standing by his side. She would toss her long auburn hair back as she laughed at what he was saying, and lightly touch his shoulder when she said something to him. It was clear that she was showing an interest in him, and he gave the impression that he didn't mind. In fact, he was obviously enjoying the attention.

Luke wondered why Matthew would flirt with her, knowing that he was crazy about Kylie. He shifted his gaze to Kylie, seated a few tables away, and saw that she had her back to him. Was she even aware of what was going on?

He kept moving until he got back to his table. He slowly sat down and said, "Sorry guys."

John answered, "We're sorry, too."

"I feel like I'm in a bad dream that I can't wake up from."

Mark said, "I take it that things didn't go well with your dad."

"He and Pops argued most of the time."

"Did he at least tell you where he's been all these years?"

"Las Vegas. He wants me to move there with him."

John asked, "How do you feel about that?"

"What do you think? I'm not leaving Benworth, and I told him that. He said that he wants custody of me because he doesn't think that Pops can take good care of me on his own. He's willing to take it to court if necessary."

Mark chuckled as he asked, "How did Pops react to that?"

"He just about went through the roof!"

"I'll bet."

John added, "I'm sure he wasn't the only one who was irate."

"An understatement. I don't want to move and I'll know that Pops will fight it every step of the way."

Mark asked, "What happens now?"

"He said he'll be in town for a few weeks. The last thing he said was that he wants to spend some time with me while he's here. I told him I'd think about it, and really had no intention of doing so, but Emmanuel came to visit me last night and told me to give him a chance."

Mark asked, "You saw Emmanuel last night?"

"Yeah. We talked for a bit on my back patio. He said he's willing to forgive my dad so I should too."

John said, "Forgiveness is one thing, but picking up and starting over in a new city is another."

"Well, Pops and I will do everything we can to prevent that from happening."

The school bell rang, bringing an end to the conversation. As the day went on, Luke found it hard to concentrate in class. He looked around to all the familiar faces seated around him and wondered what it would be like to enter a classroom filled with strangers. How long would it take him to make new friends? Would he be accepted quickly or be considered an outcast? He knew that he was as guilty as anyone in the past of not making new students feel welcome and suddenly felt bad about that. Not that he treated them poorly, but he made no attempt to even talk to them.

This wasn't any different to how the majority of students acted toward the new kids, but Luke now had a new found compassion for them, knowing that it was possible that he would soon be a new student himself.

The day dragged on, and Luke did no more than go through the motions. He barely spoke during lunch and didn't voluntarily contribute to any of the class discussions.

When the final period of the day ended, he was eager to get across the street to the football locker room, and then to play in the JV game. He changed into his uniform, a red jersey with a white number eighty-three, and gray pants. As he ran onto the field for warm ups, he saw one of the assistant coaches talking with the new quarterback, Caleb Young.

Caleb was shorter and stockier than Matthew, not to mention much slower. Luke hoped that Caleb could get the job done, but had serious doubts. The JV team was undefeated to this point, but that was with Matthew playing quarterback. This game was Caleb's first career start, and he looked tense as the coach talked to him.

John came running out of the locker room and went straight up to Caleb. "Good luck. You have the support of the whole team. Just relax and have fun."

Caleb nodded and gave a nervous laugh. Luke immediately thought that the team could be in trouble. Caleb showed no signs of confidence.

Shortly before the game started, Luke scanned the bleachers and found Pops sitting about halfway up, stuffing his face with popcorn and a soda. He smiled to himself, but the smile quickly faded when he saw his father leaning against the fence that kept the spectators off the field. He was abruptly overcome by a sick feeling. He didn't want to play in front of his father.

Once the game was underway, Luke tried to forget that his father was watching, but couldn't shake it. The early part of the game was uneventful for Luke, as Benworth called mostly running plays. Mark did a good job picking up good chunks of yardage, and even scored a touchdown on a long run late in the first quarter.

The defense, on the other hand, struggled. At halftime, they trailed 14-7. Caleb had only thrown three passes and completed two of them. None of them had been thrown in Luke's direction.

In the second half, things fell apart for Benworth as they gave up another touchdown and Caleb threw an interception. At the end of the third quarter, they found themselves in a 21-7 hole.

The first play of the fourth quarter was a pass play to Luke. He ran a slant pattern, and as the ball got to him, he was jarred by a bone crushing hit from an opposing linebacker. He hit the ground hard as the ball slipped out of his hands for an incomplete pass. He felt woozy as he got up slowly. He staggered a little as he made his way back to the huddle, prompting the coach to substitute for him.

Luke felt a little relief as he went to the sideline. He dropped to one knee next to the bench, trying to get his bearings. For a second, he thought that he might vomit, but the feeling quickly passed.

Just as he felt like he was ready to return to the game, he heard his father's voice behind him. "You need to hang on to the ball!"

He pretended to not hear him as he went back to the coach, informing him that he was ready to go back in. It was third and long and another pass play was called. Luke ran his pattern, but dropped the ball when it was thrown to him. He returned to the bench, disgusted with himself. Seeing his father shaking his head with his hands on his hips made him feel even worse. He refused to make eye contact and turned his back to him.

When they finally got the ball back, there wasn't much time left and they were still behind by fourteen points. Caleb threw two more passes to Luke, but he dropped them both. They turned the ball over on downs, and the game ended a short time later, giving the Benworth JV team their first loss of the season.

Luke was repulsed by his performance. He'd been playing football since he was eight years old and had never had a game this bad. He fought back tears as he changed back into his street clothes.

John joined him as they went outside, with Mark a step behind. Luke shook his head as he said, "I can't believe how bad I played."

John responded, "We all have off days. Don't let it get you down. We'll do better next week."

"I hate losing!"

Mark added, "Me too."

Trying to stay positive, John said, "It was Caleb's first start. Things will improve once he gets some experience."

With his head down, Luke replied, "He threw good passes. I just didn't catch them."

"Like I said, we all have off days. You'll work on it in practice and next week will be a different story."

They made their way through the parking lot where Pops was waiting by his minivan, talking to some of the other parents. As they approached, Luke's father appeared from the opposite direction. Luke cringed as he saw him.

"What happened out there? You should've caught those balls."

Luke shrugged but didn't answer.

Pops ended his conversation and turned toward the sound of Brad's voice. He looked like he was about to say something, but glared at him instead.

Brad said, "I'm going to buy you dinner tonight."

Pops stepped in, "No you're not. We're hosting a Bible study tonight. He needs to go home and get ready for that."

Luke felt a rush of relief at Pops statement.

Brad asked, "A Bible study? They're kids. Are you forcing your beliefs on them?"

"Actually, it was their idea. I just agreed to host and lead it for them."

"That's crazy!" Turning to Luke, he asked, "Is that something you really want to do?"

Meekly, he said, "Yeah."

"You don't sound too sure."

Pops said, "Maybe tomorrow. We have to go now."

The kids filed into the minivan one at a time. Pops got into the driver's seat, started it up, and pulled out of the parking lot. Luke looked out the window as they drove away, seeing his father standing alone, watching them as they left. For a split second, Luke felt a little bad for his dad as he watched. He remembered that Emmanuel had instructed him to give him a chance.

As they went down the street, Luke shifted his body so he could see out the back window. He continued watching him until he was out of sight. He turned back around and slouched in his seat, remaining silent the entire ride home.

CHAPTER 6

The doorbell rang, signaling that the first guest for Bible study was at the door. Pops called out from the kitchen for Luke to answer the door. Luke sighed from his spot on the sofa, not wanting to get up. He was enjoying an episode of *Who wants to be a Millionaire,* and wasn't in the mood for company.

He picked himself up and walked slowly to the front door. Trepidation came over him as he was about to turn the knob. What if Jude is on the other side of the door? As silly as it sounded to him, he still found himself thinking that it was possible. He peeked through the peep hole and saw a mane of blond hair staring back at him. He exhaled deeply as he opened the door.

Kylie's bright smile greeted him as she stepped forward to give him a hug, which he lightly returned.

"Hi Luke! It's great to see you. Is Matthew here yet?"

Stepping back to allow her room to enter, he quietly replied, "No. You're the first one here."

Seeing Pops enter the living room, Kylie rushed over to hug him as well. "I'm so excited for tonight. I can't wait to get started."

With a big smile, Pops said, "I wish Luke shared your passion."

Turning to Luke, she asked, "What's wrong? Don't you want to do this?"

"I've just had a bad day. We lost our football game today and I didn't play well."

Pops added, "The last couple days have been rough on both of us."

"What happened?"

Pops ran his fingers through his thick gray hair, hesitated for a second, and said, "I'm not sure how much of Luke's past you're aware of, but his father abandoned him when he was a baby. Yesterday, he showed up out of nowhere and says he wants to take Luke away from here and live with him in Las Vegas."

"I'm sorry. Is there anything I can do?"

Pops chuckled as he patted her on the back. "Being here is enough. We're going to hand this situation over to God and let Him take care of it according to His will."

"I'll be praying."

"We appreciate that."

Pops left the room, then returned a minute or so later carrying two wooden, folding chairs. He set them up in front of the TV, then turned the set off. He took a seat in one of the two recliners across the room facing the TV. Luke sat at the end of the sofa on one side of the room, while Kylie parked herself on the love seat on the opposite side.

Little by little, the others started showing up. Mark came with his sister, Madison. Mark took the other recliner while Madison sat in the middle of the sofa, next to Luke.

John came next and immediately sat next to Madison. Mark didn't look happy as he gave them a nasty stare. It was becoming more apparent that John and Madison were warming up to each other. Luke thought to himself that it was only a matter of time before it turned romantic.

A few minutes later, Kylie squealed with glee as another cute girl with long blond hair came in with a tall, thin, male companion with straight brown hair that covered his ears, and bangs that fell just below his eyebrows. Kylie ran up to hug the girl and said, "I'm so glad you're able to make it."

Luke smiled as he watched. The girl could easily pass for Kylie's sister, but he knew they weren't because he recognized her from school, although they had never been introduced.

Kylie turned to the rest and said, "Everybody, I want you to meet my friend Carli, and her boyfriend, Josiah."

John and Madison rose quickly and welcomed them. Mark stood up and shook hands with Josiah and nodded politely to Carli. Luke stayed seated and watched, which drew an angry look from Pops. Upon seeing the look from his grandfather, he groaned inwardly and got up to join the others.

The room split into two groups, the girls in one and the guys in the other. Luke merged with the guys just as John asked Josiah, "Don't you play basketball?"

"Yeah. I used to play soccer, too, but they cancelled the program."

Mark asked, "Why didn't you come out for football? Some of the other soccer players made the switch."

"I thought about it. Maybe next year."

John asked, "You're a sophomore, right?"

"Yeah. Me and Carli both are."

"I've seen Carli in church before, but not you. Do you attend somewhere else?"

"Actually, I've never been to church. I only came tonight because Carli said it would mean a lot to her."

"What about your family? Do any of them go to church?"

Josiah looked a little uncomfortable as he replied, "No. My parents got divorced when I was five. My mom got married a second time, but that didn't last long. He took off after a year, which was fine with me. I never liked the guy."

Mark asked, "What about your dad?"

"I see him one weekend a month. We're not close. I have a half-sister that he fathered through an old girlfriend. I think she's six years old, but I haven't seen her since she was a baby."

Luke thought about sharing his own experience of growing up without his father, but didn't feel like unloading his problems on someone he just met.

They continued with some light conversation until Pops announced, "I think it's time to get started."

Kylie exclaimed, "Wait! Matthew isn't here yet. We can't start without him."

Pops said, "Luke, give him a call and see what's keeping him."

Luke started toward his bedroom to retrieve his cell phone when the front door opened and Matthew came strolling through.

Kylie sarcastically asked, "Don't you bother knocking?"

Matthew ignored the jab and gave her a big hug, lifting her off the ground a few inches. They all went back to their seats, with Matthew sitting next to Kylie on the love seat, and Josiah and Carli taking the two folding chairs.

Pops opened the study with a prayer, then looked across the room to Josiah and said, "I overheard what you were telling the guys about never having been to church."

"Yeah. Carli has been trying to get me to go to church for a while, but it just doesn't interest me."

"Why are you here tonight?"

"For Carli's sake. She said it would mean a lot to her. I told her that I would come once, but no promises about the future."

Pops smiled as he said, "Well, we're glad you're here. I'm going to put you on the spot. Tell us what you know about Jesus."

Josiah looked a little embarrassed as he replied, "Not much. Just a little of what Carli told me. To be honest, when I was a little kid, I thought his name was just a cuss word."

Laughter filled the room. When it died out, Pops switched his attention to Carli. "What have you told him?"

She smiled deeply as she reached over to hold Josiah's hand. "I explained to him that Jesus is the Son of God and that he died for the redemption of all our sins."

Pops asked, "Anything else?"

"That Jesus is the only way to heaven."

Josiah chimed in, "I have a problem with that. I believe that God exists and I believe in heaven and hell, but I don't understand why I have to accept Jesus into my life in order to get to heaven. I'm a good guy and I lead a good life. Why isn't that enough?"

A serious look came across Pops' face. "When you say that, you're demeaning everything that Jesus did for you. Romans 3:23 says, 'For all have sinned and fall short of the glory of God.' You see, Josiah, none of us can get to heaven on our own. That's why God sent his Son to die on the cross. If being good was enough, then Jesus wouldn't have had to do what he did. Jesus chose to die for you because he loves you and wants you to be with him for eternity."

Josiah scratched his head and said, "I never thought of it like that."

Pops smiled and said, "Just think about it." He started thumbing through his Bible and continued, "Okay, lets all open our Bibles to Luke's Gospel, chapter eight and we'll begin in verse twenty-two."

The sound of ruffling paper filled the room as the kids hurried to find the page. When Luke found it, he scanned the room at the others. Mark was still searching, seeming to be having a hard time. Matthew looked uninterested as he was whispering something in Kylie's ear. Josiah didn't have a Bible, so he scooted his chair a little closer to Carli's so he could look at hers. John and Madison sat and waited patiently for Pops to go on.

Once everyone had found their place, Pops said, "I thought that we would take a look at a very interesting passage of scripture. How many of you have heard the story of Jesus calming the storm?"

All the hands went up except for Josiah's. He looked ill at ease as his eyes went around the room. "Maybe I'm in the wrong place."

Pops answered, "No. Trust me. You're in the right place."

Josiah sat silent and nodded his head.

Pops asked, "Could I get a volunteer to read out loud?"

Kylie wasted no time raising her hand enthusiastically. Pops chuckled and said, "Thank you, Kylie. Start in verse twenty-two and read through verse twenty-five. Loud and clear."

Kylie cleared her throat and began reading, *"One day Jesus said to his disciples, 'Let's go over to the other side of the lake.' So they got into a boat and set out. As they sailed, he fell asleep. A squall came down on the lake, so that the boat was being swamped, and they were in great danger.*

"The disciples went and woke him, saying, 'Master, Master, we're going to drown!'

"He got up and rebuked the wind and the raging waters; the storm subsided and all was calm. 'Where is your faith?' he asked his disciples.

"In fear and amazement they asked one another, 'Who is this? He commands even the winds and the water, and they obey him.'"

Pops asked the group, "Does anyone have anything they'd like to say about that?"

Josiah slowly raised his hand and said, "I have a hard time believing that this really happened."

Pops asked, "What don't you believe about it?"

"It just doesn't sound very realistic. It sounds great, but I think it's probably intended to be used as a metaphor. You know, trust God and the storms in your life will vanish."

"It very well can be used in that way. Storms are going to come. Life is going to happen. The question is, how are you going to handle it? Are you going to rely on yourself, others, or God?"

Josiah leaned forward and said, "It could be any or all three, depending on the situation. I've had problems that others have helped me with, and I've solved some on my own. I'll be honest, I haven't used the God option before."

"That's a good point. It can be any or all. Have you ever considered that when other people have helped you, that it was God who put them there? Or when you solved them on your own, that the wisdom to do so came from God?"

"I guess it could've been, but how do you know if it is or not?"

Kylie jumped in, "That's where faith comes in. Whether you realize it or not, God is active in every aspect of your life. It's no coincidence that Carli asked you to be here tonight. God is reaching out to you. Embrace it."

Matthew whispered something to Kylie and she gave him a nasty look. She was clearly offended by what he said. She shifted her body to the end of the love seat, putting a couple feet of space between them. Matthew just sat there with a cocky smile on his face.

Josiah nodded slowly as he let her comment sink in. "What I'm still not sure of is the historical accuracy of these Bible stories. Did they really happen, or are they just fables to teach us things?"

Pops said, "I have chosen to accept the Bible as fact. There are some crazy things in there, but I've learned over the years that nothing is impossible with God. As far as this story is concerned, yes, I believe it wholeheartedly. What we just read came from Luke, but Matthew and Mark also included almost identical versions of this story in their Gospels. Three different men writing about the same event at different times, each completely unaware of the others accounts."

"Well, I guess there's some credibility there."

Carli leaned over and kissed his cheek. "God loves you and wants you to accept Him. Open your heart."

Josiah blushed a little as he leaned back in his chair.

Pops continued with the study by saying, "Let's take turns talking about a storm that you've gone through and you know that God came through for you."

One at a time, they each told a story of something from their past. As they were speaking, Luke watched Matthew keep trying to say things to Kylie, but she was getting more and more upset with him.

After a time, Matthew and Luke were the only ones left who hadn't spoken. Pops asked them if they wanted to share, but they both declined. Pops didn't look happy with Luke, and it made him feel ashamed.

The truth of it was is that Luke couldn't think of anything to talk about. He was going through a storm right now, and was waiting for it to pass. Maybe when it was all said and done, he would have a great story to tell, but for now, he just wanted to be left alone.

Pops closed out the study with a prayer, and they all got up, putting their jackets on and saying their goodbyes. Pops made a point to invite Josiah back for the following week, and he agreed to come back.

Kylie looked outside and saw her father pulling up to drive her home. "There's my dad. Goodbye everybody." She brushed right past Matthew without acknowledging him and went out the door.

Matthew stood there with a shocked look on his face. Luke walked over to him and asked, "What did you say to her that made her so mad?"

"It was nothing. I was just joking around. I don't know why she reacted that way."

Luke felt uncomfortable as he asked, "If you have some time now, could we talk about some stuff? I've got a lot on my mind right now." Matthew said, "I should get home. I still have some homework and I need to call Kylie later to smooth things out. I'll call you after that."

"Are you sure? You said you'd call last night, but you didn't."

"Yeah. Sorry about that. I'll definitely call you tonight." He gave Luke a fist bump and walked out the door.

Within the next few minutes, everyone had left, leaving Luke alone with Pops. Pops asked him, "Why didn't you want to talk in front of the group tonight?"

"I couldn't think of anything to say. I'm going through a storm of my own right now and God hasn't responded."

"You should have said that. Maybe they would have had some good advice for you. Remember what we talked about tonight? Sometimes God puts people in your life to help you."

"I don't feel good about dumping my problems on everyone."

"You really should talk to someone. I'm here if you need me."

"Matthew said he would call be tonight. I'll talk to him then."

Pops looked deep in thought as he asked, "Speaking of Matthew, what was with him tonight? He didn't seem himself."

"I don't know. He was acting odd on the way to school this morning, too."

"Well, I'm sure it's nothing. Just one of those days, I'll bet." The conversation ended and Luke went to his room. He tackled his homework assignments, trying to get his mind off of how bad he felt. When he finished, he looked at the clock and saw that it was time for bed.

He suddenly remembered that Matthew hadn't called as promised, so he checked to make sure that his phone was turned on. It was, and he saw that he had no missed calls. He decided to take the initiative and call him, but it went straight to voice mail. Frustrated, he flipped his phone closed and set it on the dresser.

Two nights in a row, Matthew broke his promise to call. What had gotten into him? He shook his head and tried not to let it bother him, but deep down, he felt like Matthew didn't care and it hurt. If necessary, he would take a bullet for Matthew and couldn't understand why Matthew was acting this way. Knowing that he couldn't do anything about it at this time, he turned out the light, slipped into bed and fell into a dreamless sleep.

CHAPTER 7

Tuesday seemed like it took forever to Luke. He barely spoke a word on the way to school and wasn't really listening to what his friends were saying. A couple times he almost asked Matthew why he didn't call for the second night in a row, but chose to remain quiet.

He remained uninterested in his classes, occasionally wondering if he would even be in this school for much longer.

Looking out the windows brought his mood even lower as he watched a downpour of rain drench the grass outside. He had been eagerly anticipating football practice, but was now thinking that it might be cancelled due to the weather. Fortunately, the rain let up by the end of the school day, so Luke was raring to go as he ran out onto the practice field.

That eagerness quickly turned sour when practice began, as the coaches rode him hard for his dropped passes in the previous day's game. He worked with Caleb for most of the time, running pattern after pattern, catching pass after pass. Caleb seemed upset that he had to do these drills, and his body language suggested that he blamed Luke.

The day's rain had spotted the field with puddles and the worn out grass had given way to patches of mud. It didn't take long for everyone on the team to be soaked from head to toe, and the uniforms were caked with sludge.

When practice ended, Luke was cold, wet, exhausted, and feeling down right miserable. He wanted nothing more than to get back into his regular clothes and get home, where he could enjoy a long, hot bath. While he changed in the locker room, he watched on as Matthew clowned around with some of the varsity starters. Luke grimaced as he saw him snap his towel at the buttocks of another freshman player, which drew cheers from the upperclassmen. It was evident that Matthew was loving his new found popularity.

Luke changed clothes as fast as possible and waited outside for his friends. Mark and John came out shortly after, and they hung out by leaning against the fence that ran along the sidewalk, waiting patiently for Matthew to emerge. That patience turned to irritation when it took a long while for him to come out. Ten minutes later, he finally appeared, walking briskly past them, then turning around and looking at them expectantly, as though he were the one annoyed by the delay.

"Let's go. It's getting late." Peering to the sky, he add, "Looks like it might rain again. We better hurry."

Luke tried not to get upset. He walked without talking, listening to Matthew talk critically about the JV team's poor performance, and how they would've won if he'd played quarterback instead of Caleb. Just like the walk to school that morning, the other three talked while Luke sulked along side of them.

Matthew went on talking about how excited he was to be making his first varsity start, a home game against Grove Mills, this coming Friday. From there, he bragged about how Alyssa, the pretty senior who had called him a couple nights ago, had called again after bible study last night. This explained to Luke why he hadn't called, but he was still bitter that when he tried calling Matthew, it went straight to voicemail.

Luke thought about asking Matthew why he was so happy that Alyssa was calling when he was obviously interested in Kylie, but decided that it would be best if he let it go. He knew that if older girls were calling him, he'd be loving it too. As he thought about it a little longer, he'd be happy if any girls were calling him.

Thinking of girls was making Luke feel even worse. It looked as if Matthew had his choice between Kylie and Alyssa. It only seemed like a matter of time before John and Madison became an item, and Mark had confidence with the opposite sex like no one else he knew. There were a number of girls throughout the school who would date Mark in a heartbeat. Luke, on the other hand, rarely talked to girls unless they spoke to him first, which in itself was rare.

He remembered what Emmanuel had told him on his patio about girls at his school who admired him, but no matter how much he racked his brain, he still had no idea who they might be. The only time recently that he had any one on one interaction with a girl was a few weeks earlier at Mario's Pizza, when he and Mark flirted with a couple sophomores names Sarah and Rachel. He recalled having a good time talking to Rachel before Sarah got angry with Mark and left in a hurry, taking Rachel with her. Luke had hoped that when he saw her in school the following week, that maybe they could talk some more, but up until now, he still hadn't worked up the courage to approach her. He'd seen her a few times in the hallways and in the cafeteria, but he always looked away when they made eye contact. He would always beat himself up mentally afterward, wishing he could have Mark's self esteem.

Just as he thought that things couldn't get any worse, they made the turn onto Main Street and saw Jude, Scott and Ethan walking toward them. Upon seeing them, Luke stopped abruptly and contemplated running in the opposite direction, but fear kept him rooted.

When Jude saw them, he mockingly said, "Well, well. Look what we have here!" Scott and Ethan smiled at their friend's remark.

John moved ahead of the rest and said, "Look, we're not looking for trouble."

Jude advanced toward him but John stood his ground. Jude stopped just in front of him, looking down at the shorter John. "You've got guts. I'll give you that." Motioning toward Luke and Mark, he added, "Not like those wimps. They tried running away the last time I saw them. It didn't work out too well for them."

Luke glanced over at Mark, who looked just as scared as Luke felt. Matthew stood with his hands on his hips, looking more curious than worried.

John said, "I think it's time that we made a truce. This whole thing is ridiculous."

With a look of contempt, Jude replied, "It doesn't work that way. I'm not the forgiving type. Do you think that I've forgotten that you called me a 'pot smoking loser?'"

Ethan and Scott started moving to each side, flanking the group. Ethan was swinging his arms around and swiveling his body back and forth, stretching and getting ready for action. Scott had a menacing look in his eye and he looked poised to strike at any second.

Matthew stepped up and got in Jude's face, nudging John out of the way. "What are you going to do, steal our shoes like you did with Luke the other day?"

"I'll do whatever I want and you can't stop me!"

"You don't want to do this. We've got a lot more friends than you do, and you're not hard to find."

Enraged, Jude reached up with an open hand and shoved Matthew in the face, forcing him backward. Matthew staggered a few steps, but managed to stay on his feet. He didn't appear to be hurt, but had a stunned look. Jude's strength surprised him and he looked as if he wasn't sure what to do next.

John turned to look at Matthew, and Jude seized the opportunity by grabbing John from behind, wrapping his right arm around his neck in a choke hold.

Ethan ran over and squared off with Matthew, who was backing away and looking for an exit. Scott circled around and confronted Mark, who got into a fight stance, but didn't look like he really wanted to fight.

Luke, being the only one without an attacker, started to run to the nearest house, hoping to get help. After only a few steps, he lost his footing and fell into the wet grass, soaking his clothes. He dragged himself to his feet just as he heard screeching tires on the road.

He turned to look and saw his father jump out of his car. Brad yelled, "What's going on here?"

Luke felt a bit of relief as Brad walked toward the altercation. Ethan and Scott immediately left Matthew and Mark alone and turned to face Brad.

Jude, still holding on to John, called out, "Get out of here, old man. This doesn't concern you."

Brad looked fierce as he answered, "It concerns me now. Let these kids go and walk away."

Ethan and Scott both laughed as they pressed forward. Ethan faced him while Scott circled around, trying to get behind him. Brad moved around, not allowing Scott to get out of his sight. Ethan got close enough to throw a haymaker, but Brad easily blocked it, while at the same time delivering an open hand strike just under Ethan's chin, snapping his head back. Brad followed it up with a kick to the groin, doubling Ethan over, which allowed Brad to drop an elbow to the back of his neck. Ethan fell to the ground and laid there, perfectly still.

As Ethan went down, Scott was running toward him. With his back to him, Brad threw his elbow backward, connecting with his face, dazing him. Turning to face him, he kneed him in the gut, then round kicked him to the side of the head, knocking him to the ground with blood gushing from his nose.

When he was sure that Ethan and Scott were staying down, Brad focused his attention on Jude, who had a shocked look on his face, but still held his choke hold on John.

Seeing that John was turning blue and about to go unconscious, Brad said, "Let him go."

Using John as a shield, Jude said, "I don't know who you are, but you're in a lot of trouble. Those guys are only seventeen. They're minors. You're going to jail for this."

"That was self defense. They attacked me first." Motioning to the kids, he added, "I've got four witnesses who'll testify to that."

"You're crazy." Jude shoved John forward and ran in the opposite direction.

Brad shouted out, "You better run, you coward!"

John wobbled a few steps before dropping to his knees. His face regained its natural color as he breathed deeply, giving his lungs the air it desperately needed.

Brad ran over to him, asking, "Are you alright?"

Between breaths, he managed, "I'm okay . . . I just need a minute."

Luke, who had been watching the whole thing from where he had fallen, walked cautiously back to the others. He was grateful that his father was there to save them, but wished that it could've been somebody else.

Brad turned to the rest and asked, "Is everyone else okay?"

Mark nodded and Matthew said, "Yeah. I'm fine."

Brad gave Luke a puzzled look and asked, "Where were you running to?"

"I … I was … I was going to find help."

"Going for help? These guys needed you. By the time anyone could've gotten here, it would've been too late."

Feeling embarrassed, Luke said, "I didn't know what else to do."

Shaking his head, Brad said, "You're lucky I happened to be driving by, or this would've turned out bad."

Brad went back over to Ethan and Scott, who had both regained their senses enough to raise themselves to a sitting position. "Are you guys okay?"

Ethan glared at him as he said, "I'm fine." Scott just nodded.

When Brad was satisfied that they weren't hurt badly, he went back to the kids and said, "Get in the car. I'll drive you home."

Matthew shouted out, "Shotgun!" He wasted no time getting into the passenger's seat. John and Mark climbed into the back while Luke stayed put.

As Brad was getting into the driver's seat, he looked at Luke and said, "Don't let the grass grow under your feet. Let's go."

Luke snapped out of it and got into the back with John and Mark. His wet clothes were clinging to his body, making him cold and despondent.

As the car pulled out and they made their way down Main Street, Matthew said, "That was awesome. Where did you learn to fight like that?"

Brad answered, "For the last few years, I've been learning a self defense system called Krav Maga."

"Krav Maga? I've never heard of it."

"It's a system developed in Israel. It's taught to both their police and military. It uses techniques from a variety of martial arts and is a great way to learn to defend yourself. As you just saw, it works."

"I would love to learn how to fight like that."

"You should check to see if there are any Krav Maga schools in this area."

Matthew nodded and said, "That's not a bad idea."

Brad looked over and asked, "You're Matthew Peters, the new quarterback of the high school team, aren't you?"

"Yeah."

"My buddy was telling me about you. He said that you played an amazing game last Friday."

Matthew smiled deeply and said, "Thanks."

Luke watched from the back seat as his dad and Matthew continued talking like old friends. He tuned them out and looked out the side window, watching trees and houses whiz by. He started to feel like he might throw up and wondered if he might be coming down with something.

They pulled into Luke's driveway and Brad said, "I'll take the rest of you home in a few minutes, but first, I'd like for you guys to come inside with me while I talk to Luke's grandfather."

Matthew answered for them all as he said, "That's cool."

They exited the car and headed to the front door, which opened before they got there. Pops came storming out, pointing his finger at Brad. "What are you doing here?"

"I gave the kids a ride home."

"If you want to spend time with Luke, that's fine, but call first. I'm willing to work with you on this, but you need to stop showing up out of the blue."

Matthew ran up and said, "Whoa! Pops, he just saved our skin."

"What are you talking about?"

"We had another run in with Jude and his friends. If he hadn't shown up when he did, we would've gotten our butts' kicked. You should be thanking him!"

Scowling at Brad, Pops asked, "Luke, is that true?"

Reluctantly, Luke answered, "Yeah."

Matthew added, "You should've seen it, Pops. He fought off Scott and Ethan at the same time, knocking them both out, then scared Jude off. He ran away like a frightened little girl!" He went over and gave Brad a high five.

Pops said, "Those guys may be bullies, but they're still kids. You can't be hitting them."

Brad raised his hands as if he were surrendering. "Hey, they attacked me first. I was defending myself."

"Well, I guess they deserved it. They've had it coming for a long time."

Matthew said, "I just wish you could've gotten your hands on Jude before he ran away. That would've been great."

Pops said, "The important thing is that you kids are safe." A light rain started to trickle down. Pops held his hands out to feel it, then said, "Let's get inside."

They all followed him in. Luke took the opportunity to slip into his bedroom to change out of his wet clothes. As he changed, he wondered what his father wanted to talk to Pops about.

—

Luke's bedroom door closed, and Brad turned to Pops and said, "We need to talk about Luke."

"What about him?"

"I hate to say this about my own son, but he's turning out to be a real wimp."

Pops was furious as he asked, "What are you talking about?"

"When I jumped out of my car to help them out, he was running away! The other three were about to get pummeled, and he wasn't even helping out. He said he was going for help, but I don't see how running away was helping."

John tried defending him. "He was trying to find someone to come help us. We were overmatched and he knew it."

"Like I said earlier. By the time anyone could've gotten there, it would've been too late. He was scared and was running like a coward."

Pops was getting more angry with every word. "You may not be aware of this, but Luke just got beaten up by those guys a few days ago. It was pretty bad. I don't know anyone who wouldn't be scared in a situation like that."

John said, "He's not a coward. We were all scared."

Brad ran his fingers through his hair. Looking Pops in the eye, he said, "These kids need to learn how to defend themselves. What's this bully's name? Jude? I've seen his type before. He's dangerous and won't stop until you stop him."

Mark asked, "What are we supposed to do? He's older and a lot bigger than us."

Pops added, "Violence isn't the answer."

"Try telling that to Jude. He'll be back, mad as can be. I might not be there the next time. Then what?"

Pops said, "I see your point. What do you have in mind?"

"Well, Matthew was asking how I learned to fight. When I got to Vegas, I heard about a school that teaches Krav Maga. Are you familiar with it?"

"I've heard of it. It's that Israeli fighting system, right?"

"Yes. I've been learning this system from some great instructors. It's a great way to learn how to defend yourself. Unlike traditional martial arts, everything in Krav Maga is applicable to real life situations."

"And you think the kids should learn it as well."

"Let's go on your computer and see if there are any schools in the area."

They all shadowed Pops as he made his way to his den, where the computer was located. He turned it on and they all waited patiently while Pops got online. Pops sat in the chair while the rest looked over his shoulders.

Luke reappeared in a t-shirt a sweat pants. He asked, "What's going on?"

Matthew answered, "We're checking for self defense schools."

"Why?"

Brad said, "Because you guys need to learn how to defend yourselves. I won't always be there to bail you out."

Pops said, "I think I've found one." He clicked on the link and a few seconds later, they were on the schools website. Turning around to Brad, he asked, "This place is only about ten minutes away. What do you think?"

Brad took control of the mouse and started scrolling up and down, reading about it. "This looks promising. Look, they have a class for teens on Saturday mornings at 10:00."

Pops said, "That would fit into their schedules nicely."

Matthew sounded excited as he said, "Let's do this. It sounds awesome!"

Mark nodded while John said, "I'll give it a try."

Brad asked, "What about you, Luke?"

He shrugged his shoulders and said, "I guess."

Pops said, "I'll email the link to everyone. Show it to your parents and have them check it out. This costs money, so make sure they're okay with it."

Brad said, "This was my idea, so I'll pay for Luke's training."

Pops raised his eyebrows as he replied, "We'll each pay half."

"Okay. It's a deal."

Matthew said, "I can't wait. This is going to be so cool!"

John responded, "Too bad Tim didn't know about this stuff. His dad would've thought twice about messing with him."

Brad looked confused as he asked, "What are you talking about?"

Pops answered, "They had a friend who was being abused by his father. It's over now. The boy is living in Philadelphia now, with his grandparents."

Brad's confusion turned to anger as he asked, "Does this guy live in Benworth? I'd like to have a few minutes alone with him. I can't stand guys who hit their kids!"

Pops retorted, "At least he didn't abandon him."

For a few seconds, it looked like Brad might strike Pops, but then he breathed out and said, "I'm done explaining myself to you."

"Don't worry about Tim's father. Tim is safe and his dad is getting the help he needs. I saw him at church Sunday. He's on the right track to getting his life in order. It's none of your concern."

An awkward silence followed, which was finally broken by John. "Could you take us home now? I'm sure that my dinner is probably waiting for me."

—

A couple minutes later, Brad had left with the rest, leaving Luke alone with Pops. They had a quiet dinner of spaghetti and meatballs, with no conversation.

When he finished eating, Luke drew himself a hot bath. He sat in the tub for a long while, wondering if things could get any worse. The hot water felt good on his body, but he still felt worse than he could ever remember. He felt like he was in a nightmare that he couldn't wake up from. While still in the bathtub, he prayed. He cried out for God to help him through this, but still felt like it would end badly.

CHAPTER 8

The next couple days went by quietly. Luke didn't see his father on Wednesday or Thursday, but received a phone call from him both nights. Both calls lasted about ten minutes, and were equally uncomfortable for Luke. His dad asked a lot of questions about his life and tried to pump him up for the upcoming Krav Maga class.

Truthfully, Luke wasn't excited at all about the self defense class. He liked having his Saturdays free to relax in the mornings and to do things with his friends in the afternoon. He only agreed to do it because his friends seemed eager to.

Now, Luke sat in the locker room, listening to Coach King give a pep talk for tonight's game against the Grove Mills Wolf Pack. Both teams came into the game with identical 2-2 records. The coach was stressing how important this game was if they wanted to make the state playoffs.

Knowing that he most likely wouldn't play unless the game was a blowout, Luke found it hard to get motivated. He only played in one varsity game so far, the first game of the season against Valley Prep. The other three games were close and went down to the wire, so Luke spent the duration of those games on the bench. While the other players were getting fired up, Luke sat fidgety, distracted by what was happening in his life.

Coach King called for the team to get ready to take the field. Luke stayed behind with several players for the pre-game prayer. They weren't suppose to be doing this because Benworth was a public school, but the coaching staff pretended to not know about it and allowed the players who wanted to pray, to have their prayer time.

As they circled around to pray, Luke scanned the room and noticed that Matthew wasn't there. This surprised Luke a bit. Matthew had never skipped the prayer before.

When they finished praying, they rejoined the rest of the team by the locker room exit, waiting for the PA announcer to introduce them. Luke noticed Matthew standing near the front of the team, leading them in some cheers, inciting the players and creating a rowdy atmosphere.

They heard the team be announced, and they all ran out, storming the field. Luke found it hard not to get caught up in the excitement as he looked into the bleachers. A huge crowd had shown up to support the home team. It appeared that after last weeks come from behind win, the town once again had hope that the team could live up to its preseason expectations, which was to contend for the state championship.

Once he got to the sideline, Luke scanned the crowd for his father, but couldn't find him in the multitude of people crammed into the bleachers. He picked a spot on the sideline where he could watch, knowing full well that he wouldn't play unless the game was out of reach in the fourth quarter. He stood there with his helmet cradled in his arm, watching Matthew throw some warm-up passes to Dylan Judge, the team's best wide receiver.

The cheering subsided a little when the captains went to midfield for the coin toss. Grove Mills won the toss and elected to receive, but that didn't dampen the spirits of the Benworth Eagles faithful. The energy coming from the fans was electric!

The defensive players gathered together and got ready to take the field. They psyched themselves up with shouts and slapping each others shoulder pads.

Across the field, dressed in yellow jerseys with blue numbers and pants, the Grove Mills Wolf Pack was doing the same. A look into their stands showed a smaller crowd, but just as passionate.

Luke glanced over to Matthew, who was engaged in a discussion with the offensive coordinator and the linemen. It was clear that he was chomping at the bit to get on the field.

As much as he wanted to share his team's fervor, Luke found himself feeling indifferent to what was going on around him. Even as the Eagles took a 7-0 lead when Matthew threw a thirty yard touchdown pass, Luke just watched as the rest of the team celebrated. He even started feeling envious of Matthew when his teammates praised him for his excellent play.

As the game went on, it was obvious that Grove Mills was overmatched. Benworth dominated the game and when the final gun sounded, the Eagles had completed a convincing 27-6 victory, improving their record to 3-2, but more importantly, elevating the team's confidence level.

Matthew's stats were impressive as well. He completed twenty-one of twenty-five pass attempts, with three touchdowns and no interceptions. Luke overheard players and coaches saying that he was just as good as his older brother, if not better.

Despite the lopsided score, Luke never got into the game. He wasn't upset about it, mainly because he knew that his father was somewhere in the crowd, and he didn't want another disappointing performance in front of him. The memory of his dropped passes in the last JV game was fresh in his mind and he was terrified of repeating it.

While many players were mingling on the field, celebrating the win with high fives and back slaps, Luke made his way to the locker room. Just before he got there, he looked over his shoulder and saw Matthew in the middle of a group of players and cheerleaders, smiling ear to ear, enjoying the adulation of his peers.

Luke shook his head and slipped inside. He took his time changing back into his street clothes, trying to decide if he would go to Mario's, which was becoming somewhat of a Friday night tradition with his friends. A part of him wanted to go because it was always a good time, but the thought of going home and playing video games also appealed to him.

By the time he finished changing, most of the team had returned from the field. Amidst the shouting and yelling from happy players that filled the room, Luke made his way to John and asked, "Are you going to Mario's?"

"Yeah. I told Madison that I'd meet her there."

Luke glanced over to Mark, sitting a few feet away, to see his reaction. If Mark heard him over all the noise, he gave no indication as he changed out of his uniform. Luke shouted to him, "Mark! Do you want to go to Mario's?"

Without looking up, he answered, "Sure. Sounds good."

With his voice loud enough for both to hear, Luke said, "I'll find Matthew and let him know we're going."

He scanned the locker room in search of his friend and found him just as he finished talking with an assistant coach. Luke rushed up to him and said, "We'll wait for you outside to go to Mario's."

Matthew replied, "Actually, I'm catching a ride with some of the guys. I'll see you over there."

"Oh … okay."

Matthew walked away to his locker, leaving Luke there by himself. After a couple seconds of indecision, Luke went outside to wait for John and Mark. They emerged together shortly after, talking about the game. If Mark was still upset about how close John and Madison were getting, he wasn't showing it.

Luke said, "Let's get going before all the tables are taken."

John answered, "Let's wait for Matthew."

"He told me that he's getting a ride from someone."

"From who?"

"He didn't say."

John shrugged and said, "Okay. I guess we should go then."

While they walked, John and Mark continued talking about the game. They appeared happy that the team was back on track, winning two in a row after a couple of disappointing losses. Luke didn't say much during the walk, but was pleased that the animosity between John and Mark had seemed to subside.

When they got to Mario's, they went inside, found a table and ordered pizza and sodas. The overall mood of the place was ecstatic. Talk about making the state playoffs, which seemed unlikely two weeks before, was back on everyone's tongues.

While waiting for the food to arrive, Luke visited the restroom, where he heard other students talking very highly of Matthew. They talked about how amazing it was that a freshman could play so well at the varsity level, and what an incredible future he had. Luke wanted to be happy for his friend, but was feeling more jealous than anything else.

He returned to the table just as Matthew walked in, accompanied by two seniors that Luke recognized as Chad and Brock. Although he didn't know them personally, he knew they were both on the wrestling team. Chad wrestled at heavyweight and Brock at one-hundred-eighty-five pounds. It appeared that Brock would have to lose some weight before the season started, as he looked as big as Chad.

Mark saw them come in as well. He asked no one in particular, "What is he doing with them?"

John asked, "What do you mean?"

Before he could respond, shocked looks came across all of their faces as Ethan and Scott walked in. Anger filled Luke as he watched for Jude, who surely must be close by. He'd never seen Ethan or Scott without Jude. He felt a little nervous, but not too bad because he knew that they wouldn't start anything in a place like this. There were too many people around who would come to his aid.

A couple minutes went by and Jude never appeared. Luke relaxed a bit and went back to talking to his friends.

—

David Peters sat in a corner booth with his two best friends. Dylan Judge and Hunter Daniels sat across from him as they discussed the football team's winning effort. Although it pained him to not be playing football anymore, he was happy for his friends. They both played well in the Eagles win and he was proud of them. He was even more proud of Matthew. His little brother filled in at his former quarterback position when he went down with an ACL tear, and he was pleasantly surprised by his play. He was finally coming to terms with his injury and was truly glad to see the team back on the winning track.

He tensed up when he saw Ethan and Scott approaching their booth. He hadn't seen them since an altercation in front of his house a month or so earlier.

After an uncomfortable stare down, Scott asked, "Can we talk?"

Dylan responded, "Sure. What's up?"

Ethan grabbed two empty chairs from a nearby table and pulled them up to the booth. They sat down and remained silent for a few seconds. They looked at each other and then back to David.

Scott finally said, "We'd like to apologize for what happened the last time we saw each other." Fixing his gaze on Hunter, he added, "We especially want to apologize to you for Jude dropping the N bomb that day. I want you to know that Ethan and I have no problem with black people and don't share Jude's view."

Hunter replied, "Don't worry about it. I'm not upset."

David eyed them suspiciously and asked, "Speaking of Jude, where is he?"

Ethan shrugged. "We're not sure. We haven't seen him since Tuesday. To be honest, we really don't care where he is. We're pretty much sick of him and the influence he has over us."

Dylan asked, "What brought this on?"

Looking at David, Scott asked, "Did your little brother tell you what happened Tuesday afternoon?"

Confused, David said, "No."

Scott continued, "We had another run in with Matthew and his friends. We were getting ready to rough them up when some guy we never saw before pulled up in his car. To make a long story short, Ethan and I got our butts' kicked by this guy while Jude ran away."

Hunter asked, "He just left you there?"

Ethan said, "Yeah. For the two of us, it was the last straw. We were already tired of his bullying ways, but we feel like he showed his true colors that day. We've been following him around for years, allowing him to control us like puppets."

Scott added, "Don't get us wrong. We're not trying to come off as saints. We willingly went along with him even though we knew we shouldn't. I think it's time to turn over a new leaf."

David asked, "How so?"

"First of all, we want to return to school. We talked to the principal today and explained to him that we only dropped out because of Jude's nagging. He failed most of his classes last year and was going to have to repeat his junior year, so he took the easy way out by quitting. He said that if we were really his friends, then we would drop out with him. I know it sounds stupid, but he was very convincing when he told us that we don't need a diploma."

"We're already a month into the school year. How are you going to make up all that work?"

"That's what we talked to the principal about. He said that we could do the make up work, but it would take a lot of effort on our part. We're really going to have to hit the books hard, but I think we're up to the challenge."

Dylan asked, "Why are you telling us this?"

Ethan said, "We'd like your help. We did a lot of stupid things over the years and most of the school hates us. You guys are popular and have a lot of influence. If you could say a few good words about us, it would go a long way in helping us to be accepted."

David said, "We can do that, but you should take the first step by apologizing to the people you've hurt."

Ethan and Scott both nodded slowly. After an uncomfortable silence, Scott said, "Thanks for your time. I guess we'll see you around."

"Hold up a minute. There's a party tomorrow night at Brandon Hall's house. A lot of people from school will be there. Maybe you guys should go. It would be a good opportunity to tell people what's going on. That way they won't be so shocked when they see you Monday morning."

Scott answered, "That's a good idea. We'll see you there."

Ethan added, "We can even start doing that tonight."

After returning the chairs to the table they belonged to, Scott and Ethan went to the video game area and disappeared into the crowd. David smiled as he watched them go, then returned to his conversation with his friends.

Matthew was enjoying the praise he was receiving from the upperclassmen. Not a minute went by without someone saying to him, "Great game," or, "You looked good tonight." He didn't even know some of their names, but recognized them from seeing them at school. He thanked each for the compliments as he mingled through the packed house at Mario's.

Chad and Brock stayed by his side as they socialized with the most popular kids from school. He was having a great time being the center of attention.

After spotting Kylie a ways off, he quietly dismissed himself from Chad and Brock by saying, "I'll be right back."

He made his way through the crowd toward her, and when she saw him coming, she smiled and stood up, anticipating his arrival. Just before he got to her, Alyssa suddenly stepped between them and wrapped her arms around his neck, smothering him with a huge hug.

"Congratulations on the game. You were amazing to watch out there."

Once the shock of her abrupt appearance wore off, he lightly returned the hug while looking at Kylie with eyes open wide. "Thank you."

"Have you heard about Brandon's party tomorrow night?"

"Yeah. Everyone's talking about it."

"You should come. I'd love to see you there." Turning to see Kylie standing there, Alyssa asked, "Do you want something?"

With Kylie looking dumbfounded, Matthew said, "This is my friend, Kylie. I was just coming over to talk to her."

Alyssa looked at her with contempt in her eyes. Kylie looked intimidated as she dropped her stare to the ground. With a smirk, Alyssa returned her attention to Matthew, putting her hand on his shoulder. "I guess I'll see you tomorrow night."

After she walked away, Kylie asked, "Who is she?"

"That was Alyssa. She's friends with my brother's girlfriend."

"Jocelyn? I've never seen them together."

Wanting to change the subject, he asked, "What do you think about that party? Do you want to go with me?"

"Why? So you can see Alyssa?"

"Of course not. I don't care if she's there or not."

Sarcastically, she said, "Yeah. Sure."

"Come on, Kylie. If I wanted to see her, would I be asking you to go with me?"

After a few seconds of consideration, she answered, "I guess not."

"So, what do you say? Let's go. It sounds fun."

"I don't know. From what I've heard, it's going to be mostly juniors and seniors there. We'll probably be the only freshmen. Won't that make you uncomfortable?"

"Not really. I think it's kind of cool."

She stared back at him, then said, "I'll go, but only if Carli and Josiah come with us."

"Sure." He put his arm around her shoulder and said, "Come on. I'll introduce you to some of the people who will be there."

"Hold on. Let me go talk to Carli and make sure it's okay with her. Josiah just got his driver's license, so he can drive us."

"That sounds great. I'll be over there."

Kylie went back to her table and started talking to Carli, who started nodding enthusiastically. Matthew smiled to himself and started walking back toward Chad and Brock.

Mark got up from the table and made a bee line for Matthew, who looked as though he was heading back to where Chad and Brock were standing. Luke and John quickly bolted from their seats and followed him.

Mark got to him first and cut him from his path. He asked, "Did you come here with those idiots, Chad and Brock?"

Matthew looked shocked as he replied, "They're not idiots, but yeah, they gave me a ride."

"Why are you hanging out with them? Those are the guys who threw you into a trash can on the first day of school."

Matthew rolled his eyes. "They were just having some fun. A little innocent freshman hazing."

John asked, "Have they apologized for it?"

"No. Why would they? Like I said, they were just having a little fun."

Luke shook his head, then said, "We have a table over there. You're welcome to join us."

"Maybe I'll stop by later. I have some people I want to see first." They watched Matthew hurriedly walk away and rejoin Chad and Brock, where he wasted no time laughing and joking around with them.

Luke looked back at Mark and John and wondered if they were as worried about Matthew as he was.

They returned to the table and sat down. No one said anything until Madison came over and sat next to John. They immediately started talking amongst themselves, leaving Luke and Mark sitting there silently.

Mark just stared at his sister as she talked to his friend. After a few minutes, he got up without saying a word and went to the video game area. The question in Luke's mind about whether or not Mark was upset was answered with a resounding yes.

Luke remained where he was, not sure what to do. He looked around and noticed Rachel a few tables away. He thought about going over to talk to her, but got nervous thinking about it. He kept looking in her direction, and even made eye contact with her a few times, but he always looked away.

Before long, it was time to go home. He never worked up the courage to talk to Rachel, and Matthew never joined them at the table.

Pops seemed surprised to find out that Matthew wouldn't be riding home with them, but didn't say anything about it.

Mark was just as surprised when Madison got into the minivan with them, sitting extra close to John. Mark asked, "Why aren't you going home with your friends?"

She shrugged and said, "I want to go home with you guys."

The only conversation on the ride home was between John and Madison, and that was done with whispers. It was clear that Mark was seething.

With everything that was going on, Luke felt exhausted. All he wanted was to get into bed and sleep in, but knew that he had to get up the next morning for his first Krav Maga class. He groaned inwardly at the thought. He desperately wanted for things to go back to normal, but knew that it wasn't going to happen any time soon.

CHAPTER 9

Luke followed Pops and his dad through the front door of the Krav Maga school. John and Matthew were already there with their fathers, talking with a large, muscular black man at a counter just inside the entrance.

Identifying him as the instructor, Brad interjected himself into their conversation by introducing himself. "Brad James. I'd like to enroll my son into this school."

Shaking his hand firmly, he replied, "Derrick Cavanaugh. Chief instructor. I'll be teaching today's class." Shifting his gaze to Luke, he asked, "Is this your boy?"

"Yes. This is my son, Luke."

Derrick offered his hand and Luke shook it lightly. "Come on. That's the weakest handshake I've ever felt. Shake my hand like you mean it."

Luke felt embarrassed and squeezed Derrick's hand tighter this time. "Okay. That's more like it."

Mark walked in with his father and Madison in tow. He gave John a sour look, then turned to Derrick and shook his hand. Madison went straight to John and gave him a warm hug, causing Mark to walk past them without even acknowledging that John was there.

Pops stepped up to Derrick and said, "I'm Luke's grandfather." Motioning to the other kids, he added, "These boys have been good friends for a long time. Lately, they've been having trouble with some bullies in the area."

Derrick folded his arms across his chest and nodded. "There's been a lot of that going around." Gesturing to some of the students already on the mat, stretching and warming up, he continued, "Probably half of these kids here today had the same story when they first came in."

Pops said, "Luke got beat up pretty bad last week. They even stole his shoes."

"They stole his shoes?" Shaking his head, Derrick added, "Cowards."

Brad said, "Exactly. I saw these kids getting roughed up a few days ago. Luckily, I happened to come along and was able to help them."

"How so?"

"I've been training at the Las Vegas Krav Maga school for a few years now. When I saw what was happening, I jumped out of my car and fought a couple of them off. The third ran away like the coward he is. These were some big, intimidating kids. It's no wonder our boys were scared. My first impression was that they need to stand up to them, but they lack the confidence. I know how much Krav Maga has helped my self esteem, so I recommended that they come here."

Derrick looked him up and down before saying, "Good for you. I'm familiar with the Las Vegas school. I've heard nothing but good things about it."

"It's pretty intense, but I love it."

"We train just as hard here, I can assure you. Let's get them signed up."

While the parents looked over the paper work, Luke went on the mat and looked around. The room was rectangular in shape, with a row of punching bags hanging from the ceiling along the length of the right side. The left side had a full length mirror from floor to ceiling. The mats were a mixture of black and red, creating stripes up and down the room. In the back were three doors, two were entrances to the restrooms and the third led to an office.

A few of the other students came over to introduce themselves, welcoming them. He noticed that they were all wearing an assortment of different Krav Maga t-shirts and shorts. A quick look to the front of the room showed that the apparel was available to buy. He liked the clothing and hoped that Pops and his dad would buy him some before they left.

Luke felt small in comparison to the others in the class. As he looked around, he saw that he was the smallest, with the exception of two girls who were talking amongst themselves toward the back. He assumed that the rest of them were older because they were so much bigger.

John joined them when Madison went to talk with the girls. Mark did a good job of ignoring him.

After about five minutes, Brad called for Luke to come over. He walked slowly back to the front of the room and looked back and forth between his dad and Derrick.

Derrick took a step toward Luke and bent down a little to look him in the eye. Luke felt a little unsettled as he looked back. Derrick asked him, "How did it make you feel when those cowards beat you up and took your shoes?"

Feeling about as uncomfortable as he could imagine, he looked down and said, "I don't know."

"Luke, look at me."

He picked his head back up and looked him in the eye. Derrick went on, "You don't ever have to feel that way again. I can help you, but you have to want it. Do you want it?"

Very meekly, he replied, "I guess."

Sighing deeply, Derrick said, "You can get back what they took from you, and I'm not talking about your shoes."

Luke nodded and looked back down. He was never crazy about taking this class to begin with, and now wanted to leave. One look at his father changed his mind.

Brad gave him an intense look and said, "You're going to love this."

Luke quietly walked back onto the mat and found a spot by himself to stretch and loosen up.

A minute or two later, Derrick called out in a booming voice, "Everybody circle around!"

The group of about twenty students, all but three being boys, gathered around the instructor and dropped to one knee. The parents that had come watched from the front of the room, some in the chairs provided and the rest standing behind them.

Derrick said, "We've got five new members of the tribe." He introduced Luke, his friends, and Madison. The people close by offered handshakes and welcomed them.

The class began with Derrick leading them through about fifteen minutes of exhausting cardio, leaving them all breathing heavy and sweating profusely. Luke thought he was in pretty good shape after two months of football practice, but this class was already pushing him to his limits.

After a minute long break for a drink of water and to towel off, they returned to the mat. Derrick had them spread out across the mat, facing the mirror. He went over some of the basics, which included proper fight stance, body movement when throwing a one-two combination, and defending different attacks.

He called for them to pair up with a partner for the next segment of the class. The kids who had been there for a while and knew each other quickly got together. Matthew and Mark nodded to each other and made a pair. John and Madison did the same which drew another nasty look from Mark.

Luke stood there alone, looking around for someone who didn't have a partner. He finally found the only other one at the other side of the room, an overweight kid who looked to be about seventeen. He looked like he was already going to keel over from the workout and Luke wondered if this kid could last the whole two hours.

At the urging of Derrick, Luke crossed the room and joined his new partner. After a fast handshake and introduction, he learned that his name was Jeremy and he was a senior at Benworth's arch rival school, Northway.

They began a drill where one partner would wear a set of focus mitts while the other would hit them with different combinations. Randomly throughout the drill, the one wearing the mitts would simulate an attack that the other would have to defend. Every two minutes, they switched roles. Derrick spent this time walking around the mat shouting encouragement and correcting the students form and technique when necessary.

It didn't take long for Luke to get sloppy from fatigue. Derrick seemed to take a special interest in him as he spent a lot of time watching him, riding him hard when he made mistakes. He would shout things out, such as, "Don't drop your hands!", and, "Your opponent doesn't care if you're tired. He still wants to steal your shoes! You need to dig deep!"

As much as Luke wanted to keep going, he felt like he didn't have anything left and dropped to his knees, breathing hard and feeling like he might pass out. Derrick got in his face and screamed, "Don't give up!"

Luke shook his head and said, "I can't."

Brad called out from across the room, "Come on, Luke! You can do this."

"I need a break."

Jeremy looked on with sympathy and softly said, "I know it's tough, but it gets easier the more you do it."

Luke felt embarrassed that this fat kid could outlast him in this class. He stood back up and looked around to the other students, who were all still going strong through the drill. The timer sounded and it was time to switch roles. Luke took the focus mitts and held them up for Jeremy to start hitting. He used the next two minutes to get his wind back while Jeremy worked hard. Luke could hear Derrick giving support to the others around the room, and even felt a tinge of anger when he heard him give Matthew praise for how well he was doing, calling him a fast learner.

After switching back and forth a few times, they began working on kicks. Front kicks, side kicks, round kicks, and even groin kicks. One partner would hold a large pad while the other would practice their kicks on it. Just like with the punches, they switched roles every two minutes. They worked at a frantic pace and were all showing signs of weariness.

Just when Luke thought that he couldn't go on, Derrick called for a five minute break. Luke grabbed his bottle of water and found a spot against the wall, sitting between two punching bags. Brad came over and crouched in front of him.

"So, what do you think?"

"It's a lot harder than I thought. Way harder than football practice."

"That's good. We have a saying at the Vegas school. 'The more you sweat in here, the less you bleed out there.' Hang in there. It'll get easier the more you do it."

"I'm so tired. I can't believe we're only half way done. I don't think this is for me. I'm ready to go home now."

Brad looked at him with scorn. "Don't wimp out! You need this training to protect yourself. I won't always be there to bail you out when those guys attack you."

"I don't care. This is too hard."

Pops came over and said, "Brad, don't force this on him. If he wants to leave, then we're leaving."

Brad turned to face Pops. "If he's not prepared to defend himself, then he's nothing more than his attacker's accomplice. Do you think that those bullies are just going to go away?"

"No, they won't, but there must be other ways."

Waving his arm across the room, Brad said, "Take a look around. None of the other kids are complaining. Luke needs to suck it up and stop being a wimp, and you need to stop telling him it's okay to be one."

Pops face burned red with anger. He glared at Brad for a few seconds before turning to Luke, asking, "Do you want to stay or go?"

Luke looked back and forth between Pops and his dad, then quietly said, "I'll stick it out. I'm not a wimp!"

Pops nodded slowly and said, "Okay. I'll be over here if you change your mind."

Brad watched as Pops returned to the chair he was sitting in. He returned his attention to Luke and said, "Good choice. You won't regret this." He continued talking with him, giving advice on things he could do to improve until Derrick called out that it was time to start the second half of the class.

Luke pulled himself up and lazily walked to the center of the mat. He saw Matthew approach him and gave him a tired nod.

Matthew said, "This is so cool. I'm glad your dad recommended this."

Luke wished he could share his friend's enthusiasm, but was already sorry that he decided to stay. He glanced over to his dad, who looked back at him and pumped his fist. The only reason he was staying was because he didn't want to look like a wimp in front of his dad.

The class resumed with Derrick teaching them how to defend different types of chokes. He emphasized to the class that when they practiced on each other, to really choke them. This way they would get a sense for what it really felt like, and give them confidence that the defense will really work in a real life situation.

Luke once again worked with Jeremy, applying chokes to each other and working the defense. Jeremy had no problem escaping Luke's chokeholds, but when they reversed roles, Luke struggled with it. Sometimes he could get out but other times he needed to tap out to get Jeremy to release the hold.

Brad wasn't happy about it and voiced his displeasure, which drew several looks from Pops. Brad's comments were making Luke angry, but rather than use that anger to be more explosive on the mat, he bottled it up inside and continued to struggle through the class.

His frustration was prolonged when he saw that Matthew and Mark were having no problem getting out of each others chokes. John and Madison seemed to be having a great class as well. He was beating himself up inside, wondering why he couldn't get this.

Brad called him over to the side of the mat, where he was watching from. "You're not being aggressive enough. You can get out of these chokes if you try harder." He clapped his hands together a few times and added, "You can do this!"

Luke wearily walked back onto the mat and went on with the class, but his father's words of encouragement didn't help as he toiled away through the rest of the class, but not really getting any better.

When Derrick finally announced that class was over, Luke breathed a sigh of relief. He went over to Pops and asked, "Can we get out of here now? I just want to go home and watch college football."

"Sure. Why don't you ask your friends if they want to come over and watch with us?"

Luke went over to where Matthew was talking with Mark and John. Luke invited them over and Mark and John quickly agreed. Matthew said, "I can't. I think I'm going to stay here for the fight class that starts in a few minutes."

John asked, "What fight class?"

"I heard some of the other kids talking about it. It's basically just sparing. They wear sixteen ounce boxing gloves, shin guards, and head gear. They take turns fighting two minute rounds. I think I'm going to try it. It sounds pretty cool. Do you guys want to try it?"

John replied, "Maybe next week. I'd like to get a little more experience with this before mixing it up."

Luke added, "Come join us at my house after the class."

Matthew said, "I've already made other plans."

"What are you doing?"

"Chad and Brock are picking me up. Chad's father is going to show me how to shoot guns. We're going target shooting. Doesn't that sound awesome?"

Mark asked, "You're hanging out with those guys again?"

"Yeah. They're pretty cool once you get to know them."

Mark shook his head and walked away, joining his dad and Madison. He called over his shoulder, "I'll see you guys later," then disappeared out the door.

John looked at Luke, then back at Matthew. "Well, if you change your mind, you know where we'll be."

Matthew nodded and went to get the gear for fight class. Luke and John went over to where Brad and Pops were waiting. John said, "I wish I'd known those choke escapes earlier this week. It would've come in handy with our altercation with Jude."

Brad responded, "That's exactly what I was talking about. You can never be too prepared."

Luke stood there silently, not sure what to say. Finally, Pops said, "Come on, the Pitt game starts soon. Let's get home before the kickoff."

Luke was happy to walk outside into the autumn chill. He climbed inside the backseat of the minivan and remained silent the whole way home. He kept wanting to tell Pops and his dad that he didn't want to go back the next week, but knew that his dad wouldn't relent and would just talk him into going anyway, so he kept it to himself.

He could hear Pops and Brad bickering back and forth, but wasn't paying any attention to what they were talking about. He just blocked it out and wished that he could wake up from this nightmare.

CHAPTER 10

Matthew waited impatiently for his ride to the party. Kylie told him over an hour ago that she was leaving with Josiah and Carli to come pick him up. What was taking them so long? Three times in the last ten minutes, he'd gotten up to look out the front window, and each time got more frustrated because they weren't there yet.

He was excited about the party. He expected it to be the perfect end to a really fun day. After Krav Maga class, he stuck around and participated in fight class. He fought three different kids and held his own against them all despite having much less experience. He loved it and looked forward to doing it again next week.

When he got home, Chad and Brock were close behind in picking him up for target shooting. He had a blast firing different types of guns owned by Chad's father. He thought that it was a hobby that he could really get into.

Now he was ready to go to his first high school party, if his ride would ever show up. David had already left with his friends over thirty minutes ago. With his arms folded, he stared out the window.

"A watched pot never boils." He turned to the sound of his mother's voice, who was sitting with his father in the living room, enjoying a night of movies that they'd rented from the *Red Box* at the local grocery store.

He dug his cell phone from his pocket and was getting ready to call Kylie, when he saw the headlights approaching from down the street. He watched as the car slowed down and pulled into the driveway.

He muttered under his breath, "It's about time." He grabbed his jacket from the closet and headed to the door.

"Have a good time."

He barely acknowledged his father's comment as he burst through the front door. Ignoring the cold wind hitting his face, he walked swiftly to the car. He jumped into the back seat and was greeted by Kylie's smiling face.

Instead of returning the smile, he blurted out, "What took you so long? I've been waiting for an hour!"

Josiah replied, "Sorry. That was my fault. I got a call from my folks right after we picked up Kylie and I had to run home for a few minutes."

Matthew grumbled, "Who knows how much of the party we've already missed?"

Kylie said, "Relax. It's still early. Besides, it's cool to be fashionably late."

He stared back at her with a look of contempt, then turned to look out the opposite side window. She gave him a lighthearted shove and said, "You'll be the life of the party with that attitude."

He disregarded her remark and stayed silent while the other three talked about what they might expect from the night's social gathering.

They found the house without any difficulty, but finding a place to park was another story. Cars lined both sides of the street, leaving no place for them to park. They circled the block to no avail and finally settled on a spot two blocks away, giving Matthew another excuse to grumble.

"I can't believe how far we have to walk."

Kylie responded, "I think it's a good thing. With this many cars, that means the party is a big hit. It should be fun."

Matthew stuck his hands into his jacket pockets and used his long legs to walk speedily toward Brandon's house, forcing the others to pick up the pace to keep up. When they got a few houses away, they could start to hear the bass from the music being played. The closer they got, the louder the music became.

When the house came into view, they saw about fifteen people mingling on the front porch and yard. As they walked up the sidewalk, the comments toward Matthew started coming.

"Great game last night!"

"Yeah! Good job!"

Matthew gave a nod in their direction as he went to the front door. He pulled open the screen door to allow the other three to enter ahead of him. The hip hop music was being played at a very loud volume, and the lyrics contained a lot of violent and sexual references, in addition to a variety of cuss words.

Matthew saw Kylie and Carli give each other a look that showed they didn't like the music. He quickly went over to them and said, "I know the music is lousy. Just try to ignore it and have fun."

They both smiled and nodded.

Matthew smiled back and started looking around. His smile got broader as he saw how many people were there. The place was packed with people, most of whom he recognized as upperclassmen from school. A few more congratulatory remarks came his way as he led the four of them through the throng. He felt excitement rush through him as he took in the scene.

The living room was full of people. Some sitting on the furniture and others on the floor, all of them talking loudly to be heard above the music, and laughing just as loud. In the adjoining dining room, a group of kids sat around the table, playing a drinking game. There were several pitchers and plastic cups of beer filling the table top.

Upon seeing this, Kylie said to Matthew, "You didn't tell me there would be alcohol."

"It's a party. What did you expect?"

"I don't like this."

He turned to her and said, "Nobody is going to force you to drink. You don't have to if you don't want to."

The look she gave him showed that she didn't want to be there, but he chose to ignore it and walked toward the kitchen. He immediately saw Chad and Brock, both with a beer in their hand.

"Matthew! It's about time you got here." Nudging his buddy, Chad continued, "Go get him a beer."

Brock went over to the keg that was sitting next to the refrigerator, and drew a beer from the tap. He brought it back and handed it to Matthew, who accepted it with a smile.

Kylie wasted no time in stepping in front of him and asked, "What are you doing?"

"I'm having a beer with my friends."

Clearly irritated, she asked, "Why?"

"Why are you acting like this? Take a look around. Everyone is doing it."

"I'm not. Carli's not. Josiah's not."

"Well, you're the only ones. I came here to have fun."

"You can have fun without drinking." She snatched the beer from his hand, walked to the sink and proceeded to dump it down the drain.

Others in the kitchen who witnessed this began making comments. "What a waste!"

"What's wrong with that girl?"

Alyssa, who had been standing in the corner, stormed over and jumped in Kylie's face. "Who do you think you are? I helped pay for that beer, and you think you can just throw it away?"

"Shut up! This has nothing to do with you!"

"Oh! You think you're tough, little freshman?"

Matthew quickly jumped between them and said, "Alyssa! I'll handle this."

Backing off reluctantly, she said, "You better."

Directing his attention back to Kylie, Matthew angrily asked, "What is your problem?"

"I hate alcohol and I don't want anything to do with you if you're drinking!"

Matthew stared at her for a few seconds, feeling rage building up inside. Before he could say anything else, he felt the vibration of his cell phone from his pocket. He took a step back and pulled it out, looking at the caller ID, and saw that the call was coming from Luke. He allowed the call to go to voice mail and shoved the phone back into his pocket.

Kylie asked, "Who was that?"

"Luke."

"Why didn't you answer it?"

"It's too loud in here. I wouldn't be able to hear him."

"Then step outside for a minute. That was rude."

"I'm being rude? He knows I'm at this party. Why does he have to call me now?"

"It might be important."

Matthew's irritation was getting to the boiling point. "He has Pops and his dad to go to if he needs something. Besides, I'll see him tomorrow at church."

Kylie stared at him with a look of shock in her eyes. "I can't believe you. I don't want to stay here."

Josiah came over and said, "Carli and I don't want to stay, either."

"Leave if you want to, but I'm staying. I'll find a ride with someone else." With a wave of his hand, he walked out of the kitchen and back into the dining room, where the drinking games were being played.

He stood behind the table for a few seconds, watching the others play a game where they tried bouncing a quarter into a cup of beer. He probably would've been amused by it if he wasn't so livid with Kylie. He took a glance toward the front door and saw Kylie leaving with Josiah and Carli. She paused for a second to give him a cold look, then disappeared out the door.

A part of him wanted to run out after her, but he refused to give in to that urge. He stood rooted to the floor while staring at the door, hoping she would return, but knowing that it was highly unlikely. He turned his head back to look at the game, but instead, saw Alyssa standing in front of him.

She asked, "Why do you hang out with her? She's a dweeb!"

Not sure how to respond, he answered, "I don't know."

"Are you two dating?"

"Just friends."

"Good, because you could do so much better."

Matthew wanted to defend Kylie and say that she was the most beautiful girl he knows, but chose to keep silent. He came to the party to have fun, and he was going to do his best to accomplish that.

Alyssa suddenly squealed with delight as David and Jocelyn walked into the room, with Hunter and Dylan not far behind. Alyssa and Jocelyn hugged as David limped over to greet them.

Alyssa said, "David, it's so great to see you without the crutches."

"Thanks. It feels good to be walking on my own again. The doctor says that my recovery is going great. I won't be ready in time for basketball, but he sees no reason why I won't be able to play baseball in the spring."

"That's great. Your knee will be as good as new in no time."

Jocelyn said, "The doctor is amazed at how fast his rehab is coming along, but I'm not. He gives a hundred percent in everything he does. I joke with him sometimes that he should get a tattoo on his neck that says 100%."

David blushed a little, then asked Matthew, "Where are your friends?"

"They left. They weren't too happy about people drinking."

David nodded and replied, "Yeah. I know what they mean. We're thinking about leaving too. This isn't my scene."

Jocelyn looked at him and said, "It's not too late to catch a movie."

"Good idea." David leaned in and gave her a quick kiss on the lips, then turned to Matthew. "Would you like to join us?"

The invitation surprised Matthew. He stammered, "Uh … No thanks. I'll stay here a while."

Jocelyn looked at Alyssa and said, "Keep your eye on him." With a wink, she added, "Don't let him get into any trouble."

Alyssa raised her eyebrows up and down a couple times and said with a smile, "Of course."

After David and Jocelyn walked away, Alyssa took Matthew by the hand and led him back to the kitchen. "You need a beer."

They went back to the keg and she drew another cup of beer for him. She handed it to him and he took his first drink. He thought that it tasted awful, but didn't say so out loud. Instead, he brought it back to his mouth and guzzled it all. He was disgusted by it, but hid his true feelings and pretended to love it.

A huge smile came across Alyssa's face. "Whoo! That's what I'm talking about!" She got him another and he did the same with it.

Chad came over and said, "Check you out! I think some of these upperclassmen can learn a thing or two about partying from you."

Matthew smiled heartily, enjoying the attention. Before long, he completely forgot about Kylie and was having a great time with his newfound friends. The more he drank, the looser he felt. Alyssa stayed by his side the whole time, never letting him out of her sight.

A few times, Matthew noticed Hunter and Dylan giving him disapproving looks, but he was having too much fun to care.

After his fourth beer, he found himself really loosening up. Any thoughts of Kylie faded away as he shared laughs with Chad and Brock. He didn't even mind being the butt of some of their jokes. It was a price he was willing to pay to be the only freshman at the party.

He felt his good mood abruptly turn to anger when he saw Ethan and Scott come in. Why were they here? Was Jude with them? His eyes scanned the immediate area, but he saw no sign of Jude.

He looked to Chad and Brock and asked, "If I get into a confrontation here, do you guys have my back?"

Brock answered, "Yeah. Of course."

Chad added, "What's up?"

Matthew smirked and said, "Follow me."

He made his way through the crowd and stopped in front of Ethan and Scott. Chad and Brock flanked him on each side. Whether it was the effects of the alcohol or the fact that he had two formidable friends by his side, he wasn't sure, but he felt no fear as he stepped up the challenge these two people who had terrorized him for years.

"I'm the only underclassman at this party, so if you're looking for someone to bully, you've come to the wrong place."

Ethan looked at Scott, then back to Matthew. "I'm real sorry about what happened the other day."

Scott added, "Me too."

Matthew was a little surprised, but after letting it settle in, he decided not to let them off so easy. "What? Do you think an apology is going to make up for the way you've treated me and my friends all this time?"

Scott said, "We understand why you feel that way. We've been jerks and want you to know that those days are over."

Looking around, Matthew asked, "Where's Jude? Shouldn't you be licking his boots right now?"

Laughter filled the area as a crowd had gathered around to see what the fuss was about. Brock took a step forward and said, "You guys aren't so tough without your ringleader, are you?"

Ethan said, "We're done hanging out with that guy. We've allowed him to drag us down for long enough. We're coming back to school and are trying to turn our lives around."

Matthew asked, "Why should we believe you?"

"Look, we know that we don't have the best track record, but we're trying to do the right thing. We came here to apologize to the people we've hurt, and we're starting with you."

"I don't care about your apology and neither does anyone else. You're not wanted here, so why don't you leave?"

Just then Hunter stepped up, saying, "Hold on! We invited them."

With fire in his eyes, Matthew turned to Hunter and screamed, "You invited them? What were you thinking?"

Dylan jumped between them and said, "Calm down."

"Don't tell me to calm down! Do you have any idea what I've endured over the years because of these morons?"

"Hey! They have good intentions. We talked to them at Mario's last night and we believe that they really do want to do the right thing. Give them a chance."

"Easy for you to say. You're not the one who's been picked on."

Hunter said, "You might want to try forgiving them. They've already apologized. What more do you want?"

Dylan added, "Even your brother is on board for giving them a second chance."

Matthew turned his gaze back to Ethan and Scott. "Watch yourselves! I've got a lot more friends here than you do."

He turned and walked back toward the kitchen to get another drink. He noticed Alyssa smiling at him. She seemed to be impressed with the way he stood up to the older kids.

As the night wore on, he felt himself not caring about anything. People he'd never met before were coming up to him and congratulating him for his performance on the football field the night before. He was having the best time that he could remember and loving the attention that he was receiving.

He eventually lost count of how many beers he'd drank, but he noticed that the more he had, the less the taste bothered him. He also quickly learned how fast beer goes through the body, as he made frequent trips upstairs to the restroom.

After one of his many visits to the restroom, he came out to see Alyssa waiting for him. He didn't know what time it was, but knew it had to be pretty late. He didn't want to leave, but also didn't want to get in trouble with his parents.

"Do you think you could give me a ride home soon?"

With a mischievous smile, she said, "Sure, but not yet. Come with me."

"Where?"

"You'll see."

She took him by the hand and led him down the hall and into one of the bedrooms. She closed the door behind them, muffling the music and other sounds from the party. The only light in the room came from a streetlight outside that shown through the window.

Matthew remarked, "It's dark in here."

"I know. I like it that way."

She turned to look at him, then wrapped her arms around his neck and pressed her lips to his. Once his initial shock of the kiss passed, he put his arms around her waist and returned the kiss. Although he would never admit it to his friends, this was his first kiss and he felt a rush of nervousness go through him. His fear quickly went away as he got lost in the kiss. She pulled him onto the bed and they continued kissing passionately. He wasn't sure how long they kissed on the bed as time didn't seem to exist. He found himself really liking it and didn't want to stop.

He eventually pulled away when she reached down and started unbuckling his belt.

"What are you doing?"

She put a finger against his lips and said, "Relax. I'm not going to hurt you."

Thoughts of Kylie suddenly rushed through his mind and he started feeling guilty. Although he was attracted to Alyssa, his heart belonged to Kylie.

"I don't think we should be doing this."

"Are you a virgin?"

The answer was yes, but Matthew didn't want to admit it, so he stayed silent.

She went on, "It's okay. I promise that you'll enjoy it."

The fear returned, sobering him up in an instant. "I'm not comfortable with this. I'd like to go home now."

"What are you afraid of? I started having sex when I was your age. There's nothing wrong with it."

More visions of Kylie entered his head and the thought of staying there any longer started to make him feel like he might throw up.

"I'm sorry, but I can't do this." He buckled his belt and stood up. Alyssa sat up on the bed and gave him a nasty look.

"Do you know how many guys at this party wish they could be in here with me? You have no idea what you're passing up!"

Matthew felt vile rising in his throat. Without saying a word, he made a mad dash for the bathroom, dropped to his knees and puked into the toilet. The nausea he felt was overwhelming him to the point that he wasn't sure if he would ever be able to get up again. He knelt there, clinging to the toilet seat, wishing more than anything that he could feel better.

He managed to look to the door and saw Alyssa standing there with her hands on her hips. "You've got a lot of growing up to do, little boy!" She shook her head and walked away, leaving him alone.

He now felt like a fool. He hoped he hadn't blown it with Kylie, but wanted nothing more now than to get into his bed and sleep it off. After a few minutes, he managed to pick himself up and went back downstairs. Most of the people from the party had left. Only a handful of people remained. He looked around for Alyssa, but she was nowhere to be found. He saw Chad sitting on the sofa finishing off a cup of beer. He staggered over and sat next to him.

"Can you give me a ride home? I don't feel too good."

"Yeah. Let me go find Brock and we'll get out of here."

In the back of his mind, he knew that Chad was probably in no condition to drive, but didn't really care at that time. All he wanted was to go home.

A minute later, Chad returned with Brock, who looked as bad as Matthew felt. They said their goodbyes to Brandon and thanked him for hosting the party.

As they went outside, the cold air felt good to Matthew. He stumbled a few times as they walked to the car, drawing laughter from Chad and Brock.

"Come on, lightweight, you can make it." More laughter followed.

Matthew didn't like being the butt of their joke, but had no choice but to endure it. As they got to the car, Hunter came up and said, "I'm taking Matthew home."

Chad looked at him and shrugged his shoulders. "Suit yourself."

Hunter added, "Brandon is letting people sleep on his living room floor. Maybe you guys should do that instead of driving home. I'd hate to read about you in the paper tomorrow."

Brock replied, "We're fine. We've done this a thousand times before."

They got into Chad's car and quickly drove down the street. Matthew watched Hunter's expression, which showed a lot of concern.

Hunter said out loud, "Lord, protect them."

Matthew turned to look in the direction that Chad and Brock had driven, but they were now out of sight. Despite his drunken stupor, he was aware enough to be grateful that Hunter offered to give him a ride home.

Hunter led Matthew away and toward his car which was parked on the other side of the street. Matthew climbed into the passenger seat and said, "Thanks for taking me home."

While starting the ignition, he replied, "No problem. Those guys shouldn't be behind the wheel. I'm sober, so you'll be safer with me." As he put the car into gear and started down the street, he added, "You know, you shouldn't have been drinking like that. Even though you're only a freshman, you're still one of the leaders of the football team. You need to be a good example. If the other players see you doing that, they'll think it's okay to do it themselves. Think about that in the future."

Matthew didn't respond. He just sat there with his head against the side window. A tongue lashing from one of his teammates was not what he wanted right now. The only sounds that filled the car for the remainder of the ride home came from the radio.

When he got home, he saw that the lights in the house had all been turned off. His parents were sleeping, which gave him much relief. As quiet as he could, he unlocked the door and made his way to his bedroom. Without even bothering to undress, he collapsed onto his bed on top of the covers. He felt the room spinning and hoped he wouldn't throw up again. Eventually, he drifted off into unconciousness.

CHAPTER 11

Sunday morning came much too soon for Matthew. When his mother opened his bedroom door and called for him to wake up, her voice sounded like it was coming from a bullhorn. He tried to pick his head up from the pillow, but the constant throbbing from his alcohol induced headache wouldn't allow him to. The slightest movement caused his head to pound and to feel like he was going to throw up.

He laid still and after a couple minutes, he dozed off again. His head screamed again when his dad came in.

"Matthew! Wake up! It's time to get ready for church."

Without opening his eyes, he mumbled, "I don't want to go. I'm sick."

"No you're not. You're hungover."

His eyes shot open as he looked at his dad who was standing at the foot of his bed. How did he know that he was drinking last night? Not knowing how to respond, he kept silent.

"Don't try denying it. Hunter called David last night and informed him of what you did at the party last night. David then told your mother and I. That's why we didn't bother waiting up for you. Hunter promised to make sure you got home safe."

Matthew felt a mixture of anger and fear. Anger at Hunter for ratting him out and toward David for telling his parents. Fear for the repercussions that were sure to come as a result of his parents finding out.

He managed to spit out, "I've never felt this bad."

"That's what happens when you drink heavily. Hopefully you'll remember how you feel right now the next time you're in a situation like that."

"Can I stay home? I really don't think I can get up."

His dad ran his fingers through his hair and appeared deep in thought. "I should make you go. If you ever needed to hear a message from God, now is the time."

"Please. I won't do this anymore. I promise."

"Alright, but don't get used to this. You're going next week."

His dad left the room, leaving him by himself. He knew that it wasn't over. His father was just being merciful to his condition.

With great effort, he propped the pillow up against the headboard and sat up. His head felt like it might explode but he forced himself to stay in that position. Noticing that he was still in the clothes he wore to the party, he thought about changing into something more comfortable, but knew that the effort required would make his head pound even harder.

He sat there wondering what his punishment would be. Would he be grounded? No TV? No computer? No cell phone? The thoughts kept coming, but he knew all of those things were too light. He screwed up big time, and the consequence was sure to be severe!

He cringed at the thought. The not knowing was started to gnaw at him. He heard his father's footsteps coming toward his room and he felt even more sick to his stomach.

His dad returned to his room with a bottle of water in one hand and a pill bottle in the other. "I brought you some ibuprofen. It should help with your headache. Try to drink a lot of water today. That'll help too, but the only real cure for a hangover is time."

Matthew gladly took the medicine, then asked, "How much trouble am I in?"

His dad paused a few seconds before answering, "Consider this your one and only 'get out of jail free' card."

Matthew's eyes widened in surprise. That was it? No real punishment? He didn't know what to say. He was so dumbfounded, but grateful at the same time.

His father continued, "Don't get me wrong. Your mother and I are incredibly angry and disappointed with you. We really thought that you knew better than to do something like this. I know you won't do this again because if you do, you're off the football team."

The shock of that final statement caused Matthew's stomach to churn. Was he serious? Would he really forbid him from playing football? He'd played football every fall since he was eight years old. The thought of not being allowed to play was unfathomable.

"Dad, don't worry. I learned my lesson from this." He desperately hoped that he was buying it. He wanted nothing more than for this discussion to be over so he could rest and feel better.

"Okay. Take it easy today and you'll feel better in time."

His dad walked out and left him alone. He was relieved that there would be no punishment, but still felt worse physically than he could ever remember.

About forty-five minutes went by and he heard the rest of his family leave for church. In spite of the silence in the house, there may as well have been someone yelling directly into his ear. He wished that he could fast forward time so that the pain would go away.

He finally pulled himself up and out of bed. He changed out of the clothes he was wearing and put on a t-shirt and sweats. He slowly made his way to the bathroom and relieved himself. As soon as he finished, he fell to his knees. The gagging and dry heaves started and he felt like it would never stop.

He found himself praying and promising God that he will never do this again if He would just make the pain stop.

With great effort, he got back to his feet and went to the living room. He eased himself onto the sofa with his feet up and his head resting on the cushions. He grabbed the remote from the coffee table and turned the TV to *ESPN*. He could hear the analysts talk about the day's NFL games, but wasn't really listening. Who were the Steelers playing today? He wasn't sure, nor did he care at this point.

He figured that Luke would probably call to invite him over to watch the game, but he would have to decline. He didn't think that his headache could take all the screaming and shouting that was sure to take place over there. In fact, he decided to turn his cell phone off. That way he wouldn't have to explain himself. It would also prevent him from having to talk to Kylie in the unlikely event that she would call. He would rather not have to deal with any of that until he felt better.

Thinking of Kylie made him think about Alyssa's attempted seduction of him the night before. He was quite sure that there were people at the party who knew that they had been in the bedroom together. Would they talk at school about it? He didn't want to face questions about it. If he told the truth, then he'll be known as the guy who chickened out. If he lied and said that he went through with it, then he would be known for having been with a girl of questionable reputation. He could always just say that it was none of their business, but that would leave it open for people to draw their own conclusions, and that could lead to all kinds of rumors. It was making his head spin worse than it already was. There was no easy solution to his predicament.

One thing he knew about Alyssa was that she loved to gossip, and if she had the chance to make someone look bad, she would. Depending upon how the rest of the school talked about it, she may decide to do just that. He thought about calling her to try to smooth things out, but didn't want to do anything to lead her on since he had no intention of having anything to do with her again.

After laying there and contemplating it for a bit, he decided to wait until tomorrow and see if anyone said anything. If so, he would decide what to say at that time.

At his father's advice, he continued sipping water and watching the NFL pre-game on TV. The ibuprofen and water weren't helping much as he still felt terrible. He closed his eyes and started to doze off when he was jolted awake by the ringing of the doorbell.

He asked aloud, "Who could that be?"

He slowly got off the sofa and lazily walked across the living room to the front door. Without bothering to look through the peep hole, he pulled the door open. He stood there frozen with disbelief as he saw Emmanuel standing there.

Looking very relaxed in his gray hoodie and blue jeans, Emmanuel said, "Good morning."

Matthew thought that the morning was anything but good. "After our last conversation, I wasn't sure if I'd ever see you again. Why are you here?"

"We need to talk."

"About what?"

"A few things. Can I come in? It's kind of cold out here."

Matthew opened the screen door and allowed Emmanuel to enter his home. Looking at the clock, Matthew said, "We don't have a lot of time. My parents will be back from church soon."

"I assure you that I'll leave before they get back."

Matthew accepted that with a nod and went back to resume his position on the sofa. Emmanuel sat on the recliner and leaned forward, looking intently at Matthew.

Feeling uncomfortable with the stare, Matthew grabbed the remote and turned the TV off. He looked back at Emmanuel and asked, "What do you want to talk about?"

"First of all, let me congratulate you for your excellent performance in Friday night's game. You're taking the athletic ability that my Father gave you and you're making the best of it."

"Were you there?"

"I saw the whole game."

"Cool. I think that the team is back on track and we have a great chance to get into the playoffs after all."

"Keep working hard." Emmanuel sighed, then added, "Unfortunately, I'm not here to talk to you about football. There are a few other things that I'm not too pleased with."

Matthew felt a tinge of anger run through him as he asked, "Like what?"

"For starters, the way you acted last night."

"What are you talking about? I'm the one who put on the brakes with Alyssa."

"I'm not talking about that, although I am glad that you didn't go through with it. However, you shouldn't have allowed yourself to be put in that situation in the first place."

"She tried to allure me. What could I do?"

"If you hadn't been drinking, you wouldn't have been in a position for her to do so."

Matthew threw his hands in the air and exclaimed, "So that's what this is about. I had a few drinks and now you're here to lecture me."

"I thought that you knew better than to drink like that."

"What did I do that was so wrong?"

"I think you know."

"Wait a minute. Didn't you change water into wine once? If you're against drinking, why did you do that?"

"There's a big difference between having a drink and getting drunk. You were drunk. Very drunk! It is written in Ephesians 5:18, 'Do not get drunk on wine, which leads to debauchery. Instead, be filled with the Spirit.'"

"So I got drunk. So did a bunch of other people. Are you making house calls to all of them too?"

Emmanuel sat there in silence.

Matthew added, "I didn't think so. I may have gotten drunk, but it didn't affect my judgment. You saw that I still made the right decision regarding Alyssa."

"What about Ethan and Scott?"

"What about them?"

"Why did you give them such a hard time?"

"Why wouldn't I? They've been giving me a hard time for years."

"You heard them say that they're trying to turn their lives around."

Matthew's eyes widened as he responded, "Do you expect me to believe that?"

"Why not? I do."

In a mocking tone, he said, "I guess the next thing you're going to tell me is that you forgive them."

"Of course. Just like I've forgiven every sin that you've ever committed."

Matthew sat back and stared at the wall, shaking his head. After an uncomfortable silence, he asked, "What about Jude? Have they really ended their friendship with him?"

"It appears that way. They haven't had any contact with him since your encounter with them last Tuesday. Jude is a different story. He's even angrier than usual due to his former friends not answering his calls. You already know how dangerous he is, and it's going to be worse now that he's alone. Continue to pray for him, but more importantly, be extra cautious if you see him."

Matthew sat back up and looked across the room. "Kylie's pretty mad at me, isn't she?"

"Do you blame her?"

"Yeah! She totally overreacted."

"I don't think so. I think she acted admirably. I'm proud of her for having the courage to stand up for her convictions."

Matthew looked back at him in disbelief. "You're taking her side?"

"I think I made it clear that I'm not happy with how you acted last night, not to mention the last week."

His jaw dropped before he asked, "What are you talking about?"

"You've been arrogant and haven't been a very good friend to Luke."

"What does Luke have to do with it?"

"You've been ignoring him in his time of need."

"How so?"

"He's been trying to talk to you since his dad showed up. Every time he's called you, you've either not answered or rushed him off the phone, and you haven't called him back any of the times that you promised to."

"Why does he want to talk to me? He should talk to Pops, not me."

"Do you remember the conversation we had in your backyard last week?"

"Yeah. Why?"

"I told you that your friends were about to go through some fiery trials and they were going to turn to you for help. You said that you would be there for them."

Matthew dropped his head into his hands. This visit from Emmanuel wasn't helping his headache. In fact, it was making it worse. Lifting his head back up, he asked, "What am I suppose to do?"

"Listen to him. That's all he wants. Let him get things off of his chest and offer advice and encouraging words when necessary."

"I don't have any advice for his situation. If anything, he should be happy. His dad is back after all these years. Now he can have the relationship with him that he's always wanted."

"Unfortunately, it's not that simple. He needs the support of his friends right now, and I expect you to lead the way."

A wave of irritation went over him. "I've got enough problems of my own without having to solve his too. He doesn't need me. He just needs to stop being a baby and man up."

"Do you really think that your problems are that bad?"

"I feel a lot of pressure. Keeping up with my school work after coming home exhausted from football practice takes a lot out of me."

"It's no different than anyone else on the team goes through."

"Yes it is. There's more pressure on me because I'm the starting quarterback. Not everyone can handle that. Cody sure couldn't!"

"I tell you the truth when I say that Luke is going through a much tougher time than you are. If you want to be a true friend, take the time to listen to him. It'll do wonders for him."

"Why can't you do it?"

"I want you to do it."

"I don't want to."

Emmanuel closed his eyes and shook his head. "You're showing very poor leadership skills."

"Maybe I don't want to be a leader."

"Whether or not you want to be isn't the issue. As the starting quarterback, you're a leader on the field, and that's going to carry over to other areas of your life. You asked earlier if I was making house calls to everyone who got drunk last night, and the answer is no. I'm here because as a leader, more is expected of you."

Matthew slammed his fist on the coffee table, causing the remote control to fall onto the floor. He stared a hole through Emmanuel. "I feel bad enough today without you making it worse. If you really want to help me, then lay hands on me and take this headache and nausea away."

Emmanuel looked at him with sadness in his eyes. "I could do that, but I won't. The way you feel is a direct result of bad choices you made, and I'm not going to use my healing powers for that."

Matthew stood to his feet as his face turned red with rage. "You won't help me?"

"Not this time. Not under these circumstances."

"Then I want you to leave!"

Emmanuel rose to his feet. "Is that what you really want?"

"Get out! Now!"

With a nod, Emmanuel slowly walked to the door and slipped outside. Matthew quickly slammed the door shut and locked it. He picked up the remote from the floor and turned the TV back on as he plopped back down on the sofa.

He sat there in disbelief. How could Emmanuel not help him? He felt the bile rising up in his throat again. He made a dash for the bathroom and got there just in time as he threw up once again. He got even angrier at the thought that Emmanuel could have remedied this but chose not to. In bitter defiance, he resolved to ignore all of the advice that Emmanuel had given him.

—

Outside the house, Emmanuel made his way down Forest Street with his head down just as Matthew's parents drove into the driveway. His hands were in his pockets and the hood of his jacket was pulled up. When he got to the first intersection, he stopped and looked into the sky, revealing his face and showing tears as they rolled down both of his cheeks.

CHAPTER 12

Luke finished his homework and exhaled slowly. He leaned back in his chair in front of the desk and closed his eyes for a few seconds. He opened one eye long enough to glance at the digital clock and saw that it was almost time for his friends to show up for the Monday night Bible study.

Just like last week, he wished that he could get out of it. He was tired and wanted to be left alone. Curling up with a good book until *Monday Night Football* started sounded like a much better option, but he knew that he had to be a good host, so he went to the living room and watched *Sportscenter* while he patiently waited for the guests to arrive.

Reflecting on the last few days, he felt worried about Matthew. He could understand why he didn't want to watch college football with the guys on Saturday, but when he tried calling him on Sunday to find out why he wasn't at Sunday school, it went straight to voicemail, indicating that his phone was turned off. Even some calls in the early evening went unanswered.

That morning, Luke walked to school with Mark and John, but Matthew opted to take a ride from Chad and Brock. This was the first time that he could remember the four of them not being together on the walk to school, with the exception of when one of them stayed home due to illness.

Matthew didn't sit with them in the cafeteria before class or at lunch either, choosing instead to sit with Chad and Brock. Surprising to Luke, neither Mark nor John talked about him much.

The rest of the school, however, spent a lot of time talking about Matthew. Luke overheard a number of students whispering and gossiping about how Matthew and Alyssa had spent a considerable amount of time together in a bedroom at Brandon Hall's party Saturday night. Speculation was widespread as people guessed and gave their opinions about what may or may not have happened behind those closed doors.

When class ended, they hopped on the bus to the JV game. Luke considered asking Mark and John what they thought about the rumors that swirled around the school about Matthew, but they seemed more intent on talking about the upcoming game. He wasn't sure what to think about it. He wanted to believe that Matthew had better sense than to be with Alyssa. Her reputation throughout the school was less than commendable. Luke knew that if he were in the same situation, he would run away as fast as possible. He wanted to ask Matthew about it, but since being promoted to starting quarterback, he was no longer on the JV team, so he wasn't on the bus with them.

Luke was nervous for the game. He didn't want to repeat last week's poor outing. He didn't think he could handle dealing with more dropped passes, especially if his dad was in attendance.

Sure enough, when the time came for them to take the field, he looked into the bleachers and the first person he saw was his dad. He groaned inwardly and secretly wished that they wouldn't throw the ball his way.

He got his wish. Mark had a fantastic game and the Eagles running attack dominated. They found themselves in very few passing situations, and when they did, no balls were thrown to Luke. The defense also had a big day as they shut their opponents down and kept them off the scoreboard. In the end, the Benworth JV team completed a 28-0 shutout victory.

His phone rang and he grimaced when he saw his father's number on the caller ID. Reluctantly, he answered and tried to sound cheerful.

"Hello."

"Hey buddy, how are you tonight?"

"I'm pretty good. Just waiting for my friends to show up for Bible study."

"I'm glad to see your team get back on the winning track today. It would've been nice to see you more involved, but it was still a good win for your team."

"Well, I can't control how many passes get thrown my way."

"No. I guess not."

After a few seconds of silence, Luke asked, "So what are you up to?"

"Getting ready to go to Floyd's Pub to watch the football game. I just thought I'd give you a call before I went out."

Looking for a reason to end the call. Luke said, "I don't want to hold you up. I'll talk to you later."

"Hold on! Have you given any thought about moving to Vegas with me?"

"I already told you that I like it here in Benworth. I don't want to move."

"I'm telling you, you'll love it there. The winters are mild. The women are beautiful. It's only a four hour drive from the beach. I could go on and on."

"I don't mind winters and the girls here in Pennsylvania are beautiful too. I could care less about the beach. This is my home and I want to stay here with Pops."

His father stayed silent on the other end. The ringing of the doorbell gave him his second chance to end the call and he seized it. "Look, my friends are here, so I have to go. I'll talk to you soon."

They hung up and Luke started feeling guilty. He was sure that his dad's feeling were hurt, but he also knew that he had to be honest if he was going to get his point across.

Little by little, the study group started showing up. Before long, everyone who had been there the previous week were there again, with the exception of Matthew. Luke didn't think much about it because Matthew had been the last one to arrive last week too.

They could hear Pops talking on the phone in the kitchen. While they waited for him to come in and start the study, they were gathered in two groups. Kylie, Carli, Josiah and Madison made up one group while Luke, Mark and John sat on the other side of the room, killing time with small talk.

Kylie left her group and walked across the room to where the others were sitting. They all looked at her curiously.

She took a deep breath and asked, "Is Matthew coming tonight?"

Luke answered, "I assume that he is. He didn't tell me otherwise."

"Well, we had an argument at the party Saturday night and haven't spoken since."

John asked, "What did you argue about?"

"Drinking. He wanted to and I didn't. As soon as I saw that there was alcohol at the party, I told him that I wanted to leave, but he insisted on staying. I left with Carli and Josiah and he stayed behind."

Mark said, "I heard that he got drunk. I even heard that he tried to start a fight. I'm not sure what to believe. You know how rumors get started."

Kylie looked to the front door, as if she expected Matthew to walk through at any second, then turned back to the guys. "I heard those things too, in addition to another rumor that makes me sick to my stomach."

The other three nodded, knowing exactly what she was referring to, but not wanting to speak it out loud.

She went on, "I seriously considered not coming tonight because I don't want to see him, but I knew that Carli and Josiah wouldn't come if I didn't. I had to come for their sake." Shifting her gaze on Mark, she asked, "Will you sit next to me? I don't want to sit with Matthew."

A puzzled look came across Mark's face. "I don't want to get in the middle of this."

"Please? It would mean a lot to me."

"Alright, but if he shows up and looks mad in any way, I'm getting up and sitting somewhere else."

"Thank you. Don't worry. I really don't think he'll get mad."

She got up and rejoined her friends on the other side of the room.

Luke turned to his friends and asked, "What do you guys think? Do you think Matthew really slept with her?"

Mark answered, "It makes sense. Why else would they have gone to the bedroom?"

John said, "Don't jump to conclusions. We weren't in there with them, so we have no idea what really happened."

Luke's phone rang again and he quickly answered when he saw that the call was coming from Matthew.

"Hello."

"Hey. Is Kylie over there?"

"Yeah. Why?"

"Well, we had a falling out and I'm not sure if it's a good idea if she and I are in the same room together."

Not wanting anyone else to hear, he slipped into his bedroom and closed the door. "Are you aware that the whole school is talking about you?"

"Yeah. I figured they would."

"Did you do it?"

"No. She wanted to but I couldn't bring myself to. We kissed for a bit, but that's all."

"Well, that's good to know. You should probably come over. Don't worry about Kylie. I'm sure you two will work it out."

"Not tonight. I think it's best if I give it some time to blow over. Just tell everyone that I'm not feeling well."

"Okay. I'll tell them, but I don't think they'll buy it. You looked fine at school today and when they see you there tomorrow, they'll know something is up."

"Sorry bro, but I just can't do it tonight."

"Are you going to walk to school with us tomorrow?"

"Yeah. Chad said that he doesn't have enough gas to drive tomorrow."

"Alright. I'll see you then."

When he returned to the living room, Pops was in his chair and everyone else was in their spots, waiting for Luke so they could get started. He noticed that Mark was sitting next to Kylie, just like she had asked him to.

With all eyes on him, Luke realized that they were waiting for him to say something about his phone call. He took his seat and said, "Matthew's not coming. He's sick."

Josiah said, "It's more likely that he's still hungover."

Pops looked across the room and asked, "What do you mean by that?"

Kylie jumped in, "He got real drunk at a party Saturday night."

Carli added, "Not to mention trying to start a fight, and who knows what he did in the bedroom with that slut?"

"Let's watch the kind of names you're using."

Looking embarrassed, Carli said, "I'm sorry. We're all a little angry with him. He acted like a real jerk that night, and from what we've heard, he got even worse after we left."

With a look of concern on his face, Pops asked, "Luke, is this true?"

"That's what everyone at school was saying."

"Have you asked him about it?"

"He didn't say anything about the drinking, but he denied doing anything with Alyssa."

Kylie leaned back with her arms folded. "Do you really believe that?"

Luke shrugged and said, "I don't know what I believe."

John added, "I see no reason not to give him the benefit of the doubt."

Shaking her head, Carli said, "People who were at the party said that they were in there for a long time. What do you think they were doing in there? Playing checkers?"

John looked irritated as he defended his friend. "All we know for sure is that they were in a room together. No one else was in there with them, so we don't know what went on. Everything is speculation at this point. I've known Matthew a long time and one thing I know for sure is that he's not a liar. If he says that nothing happened, I believe him."

Pops said, "Well said, John." Shifting his gaze to Kylie, he added, "I know that this is probably tough on you. I see the way you two are together and it's obvious that the two of you have feelings for one another."

Kylie dropped her head and looked into her lap. Pops went on, "Your anger is understandable. I've seen a change in Matthew over the last week or so. It seems that that his popularity from his football success has been going to his head. You say that he's acting like a jerk, and I agree, but that doesn't mean that we should jump to conclusions. We have no proof that anything inappropriate went on in that bedroom."

Kylie nodded her head but remained silent. When nobody else spoke up, Pops said, "In light of this, I think that I know a fitting passage of scripture to discuss tonight." He flipped through his Bible until he found what he was looking for. "Let's turn to the Gospel of John, chapter eight."

When everyone had found it, Pops said, "Madison, would you read out loud? Start with the beginning of chapter eight and read through verse eleven."

Madison leaned forward with her Bible in her lap and began reading. *"But Jesus went to the Mount of Olives. At dawn he appeared again in the temple courts, where all the people gathered around him, and he sat down to teach them. The teachers of the law and the Pharisees brought in a woman caught in adultery. They made her stand before the group and said to Jesus, 'Teacher, this woman was caught in the act of adultery. In the Law Moses commanded us to stone such women. Now what do you say?' They were using this question as a trap, in order to have a basis for accusing him.*

"But Jesus bent down and started to write on the ground with his finger. When they kept on questioning him, he straightened up and said to them, 'If any one of you is without sin, let him be the first to throw a stone at her.' Again he stooped down and wrote on the ground.

"At this, those who heard began to go away one at a time, the older ones first, until only Jesus was left, with the woman standing there. Jesus straightened up and asked her, 'Woman, where are they? Has no one condemned you?'

"'No one, sir,' she said.

"'Then neither do I condemn you,' Jesus declared. 'Go now and leave your life of sin.'"

Pops said, "Thank you, Madison."

You could hear a pin drop in the room as everyone understood why Pops chose that story. Luke looked around and saw that no one was making eye contact with anyone else.

Pops said, "I think it's time to cut Matthew a break."

Everyone nodded in unison around the room. Kylie said, "I'm still mad at him but I think the best thing I can do for him now is pray for him."

Pops replied, "Excellent. I propose that we all pray for him on a daily basis. If we all do this, I'm sure we'll see God move in a mighty way."

Madison said, "Not to change the subject, but something about this story really bothers me."

"What's that?"

"Well, they said that she was caught in the act of adultery. If that's true, then why did they only want to stone her? What about the guy? Why isn't he brought out to be questioned? Sounds like a double standard to me."

Pops smiled for a moment, then answered, "That's a really good question. I wondered that myself in the past, so I looked into it. Most Bible scholars believe that the event was staged to trap Jesus. She probably was a harlot. We can see this by Jesus telling her to leave her life of sin. So if the event really did happen, then they probably did in fact have the man in custody, but they chose to bring the woman out alone to try to snare Jesus. Of course, there's a lot more to the story than just adultery."

John asked, "What did Jesus mean by 'without sin?' Was he pointing out their hypocrisy?"

"Not only that, but he knew exactly what they were trying to do. You see, at that time, Jerusalem was under Roman rule, and the Romans didn't allow the Jews to carry out death sentences, so if Jesus had said to stone her, he could have been in conflict with the Romans. If he had said not to stone her, he could have been accused of not supporting the law."

Kylie said, "So he was caught between a rock and a hard place."

"Exactly, but he knew just how to handle it. When they first accused her, Jesus bent down and wrote in the sand with his finger. What do you think he was writing?"

Blank stares greeted him. Luke reread what was written and spoke up, "It doesn't say."

"No it doesn't, but do any of you have any guesses to what it may have been?'

Madison asked, "The Ten Commandments?"

"Possible."

Kylie said, "Maybe he was writing the sins of her accusers. Letting them know that they were no better than her."

"Another good idea. The truth is, we have no way of knowing if she really was caught in adultery or what Jesus was writing. The same is true with what Matthew did in the bedroom with that older girl. Rather than talk badly about him, we should be more concerned with getting the sin out of our own lives."

The discussion went on, but Luke felt his mind start to wander. The next thing he knew, Pops was praying and ending the study. When he concluded, Luke stood up to say goodbye to everyone.

John was the last to leave, and just before he did, he pulled Luke to the side and asked, "Is Pops okay? He doesn't look too good."

Luke felt a tinge of pain in his gut. "I've noticed it too. He doesn't eat healthy and is gaining a lot of weight."

"It's not just the weight. He looks pale."

"Yeah. I've tried making comments about his eating habits, but it falls on deaf ears. I'm really worried about him."

"Is he under any stress?"

"Yeah. My dad wants to get custody of me and take me to Las Vegas. Although he hasn't talked about it much, it's got to be eating him up inside."

"Sure. Let's be sure to keep him in prayer."

Luke agreed and John left to go home. He watched as John made his way into the darkness and then went to his bedroom. He thought about calling Matthew, but decided against it. He would have time to talk to him in the morning when they walked to school.

He had a little time before he went to sleep, so he got on the computer and started looking at sights about Las Vegas. He was trying to convince himself that life wouldn't be too bad there, but everything inside of him screamed against the idea. Benworth was his home and it was where he wanted to stay.

Feeling frustrated, he shut the computer off and got into bed. Despite his mind spinning, he quickly fell into a dreamless sleep.

CHAPTER 13

It's going to be one of those days. Luke couldn't stop thinking this while he laid in bed. It was almost time to get up for school, but all he wanted to do was stay home. Bad things won't happen to him here. He could hear music coming from the stereo, indicating that Pops was up and about.

He sat up and looked around his room. He smiled a little while he admired the posters on the wall. One wall was dedicated to his favorite bands, *Skillet, Disciple, Thousand Foot Krutch, and Red*. The opposite wall was decorated with posters of his favorite players from the Pirates, Penguins and Steelers. He took a minute to stare at the bookshelf that contained some of his favorite books that he'd read over the years.

He really loved this room. This had been his bedroom for all of his fourteen years. It was his hideaway when he wanted to be alone. The comfort he felt when he was here couldn't be matched anywhere else.

His mind drifted to the game room that Pops had built in the basement. Another smile crossed his face as he reminisced about some of the good times he had with his friends in that room, playing video games and air hockey.

How much longer would he be able to enjoy these things? After his conversation with his dad last night, it was clear that he still wanted Luke to move to Las Vegas with him. How could he convince his dad to forget the idea? Even with Pops' assurance that the courts would never side with his dad, he couldn't help from feeling anxiety over the situation.

Another look around the room made him want to stay even more. He took a deep breath, ran his fingers through his hair, and got out of bed. He made his way to the kitchen, where Pops was shoveling a glazed donut into his mouth.

Between mouthfuls, Pops pointed to a box of assorted donuts on the table, and said, "Help yourself."

Luke stared at Pops for a few seconds, remembering what John had said the previous night about how Pops wasn't looking too good. He looked happy at the moment, with a donut in one hand and a cup of coffee in the other. The morning newspaper was spread out on the table in front of him.

"I think I'll have some cereal instead."

Pops shrugged and said, "More for me."

While pouring some *Cheerios* into a bowl, he said, "Maybe you should try something healthier for breakfast."

Without looking up from the paper, he answered, "My health is fine."

Luke knew from his tone that it was best to drop the subject. He poured the milk into the bowl and sat on the opposite side of the table from Pops, where he ate his breakfast in silence, listening to the music coming from the stereo, tuned in to the local Christian station.

He took his time getting ready for school. He wished that he could stay home and relax. With everything that was going on, he felt weary. The thought of laying on the sofa and watching a funny movie really appealed to him. Knowing that there was a field trip the next day that he didn't want to miss, he knew that this wasn't the time to fake being sick.

He finished getting ready and went outside just in time to see John and Mark coming down the street. Matthew came out and they all started down Forest Street together.

John immediately asked Matthew, "Why weren't you at Bible study last night?"

"I didn't want to see Kylie. We haven't talked since the party. She acted so prissy that night."

"From what we heard, she didn't want anything to do with the drinking that was going on. I can't say that I blame her. It doesn't make her prissy, if you ask me."

Matthew gave him a nasty look and said, "I didn't ask you."

John stopped walking and raised his voice. "What's with you lately? Why are you acting like such a jerk?"

With a surprised look, he responded, "What are you talking about?"

"Let's see. You're arrogant. You're hanging out with losers---"

"What losers?"

"Chad and Brock."

"They're cool."

"You're the only one who thinks so. Nobody else can stand them."

Matthew waved his hand and started walking again. "You're just jealous."

"Jealous of what? You're getting drunk, trying to start fights, ignoring your friends, blowing a chance with a great girl, and fooling around with a girl who has the worst reputation in school! You've changed, and not for the better."

"I haven't blown it with Kylie. I just need to give her time to cool off."

Mark said, "I hope you plan on waiting a long time, because she's pretty ticked off."

Matthew shot him a look. "What did she say?"

"She didn't want to go either, but knew that Josiah and Carli wouldn't go unless she did, so she went for them. She was nervous about what would happen if you were there. She even asked me to sit with her so that you wouldn't be able to."

Matthew chuckled. "What did she say when you told her that you wouldn't sit with her?"

"I did sit with her."

Matthew stopped again and got in Mark's face. "What are you talking about?"

Mark was taken aback as he answered, "At first, I told her I didn't want to. I didn't want to get caught in the middle of your fight, but she pleaded with me. I agreed, but told her that if you showed up and had a problem with it, I'd give the seat up for you."

"You shouldn't have sat with her in the first place! What are you trying to prove?"

"Nothing. I was doing a favor for her."

Matthew shoved him in the chest as he said, "Stay away from her!"

Mark shoved him back. "She's my friend too! Stop acting like she's your girlfriend!"

"She's not yet, but she will be. Everyone knows that!"

"You don't care about her! If you did, you'd never have been in the bedroom with Alyssa!"

"Nothing happened in there! It was just a little kissing!"

"That's not what the rest of the school is saying!"

John jumped between them to prevent a fight. "Calm down! Both of you! If Matthew says that they were just kissing, then I believe him."

Mark asked, "Why are you taking his side?"

"I'm not taking anyone's side. I just don't want you two to fight!"

"Do you really believe that he didn't go all the way with Alyssa? Half the school has, so he probably did too!"

Matthew shouted out, "I didn't! I already told you what happened!"

John added, "Let it go!"

Mark gave John a shove and said, "Don't tell me what to do! You have no room to talk. Who knows what's gone on between you and my sister?"

"Nothing has happened with me and Madison. We're just friends."

"Do you expect me to believe that you two don't like each other? I see the way you look at her!"

"Yes, I like her, but we've decided to keep it as friends until we know each other better. I haven't even kissed her yet."

Mark gave him another shove and said, "You better not!"

John sighed and calmly said, "Don't push me again or you'll regret it. As far as Madison goes, anything that happens between her and I is none of your business. If I want to kiss her and she feels the same way, then there's nothing you can do to stop us."

Luke had watched this whole altercation without saying a word. He was too stunned to say anything. The four of them had been friends for years and never had more than a minor argument. He didn't like what he was seeing.

Out of nowhere, a rage built up inside of Luke and he shouted, "STOP IT!"

The other three looked at him with shock on their faces. "This is so stupid. None of this is that big of a deal. Let's just walk to school and talk about something else."

Mark's anger wouldn't be deterred as he turned to Luke. "It's not a big deal? This is my sister we're talking about! You don't have a sister, so you wouldn't understand."

"If I did have a sister, I'd be thrilled if she wanted to date someone like John. Would you rather have her date Chad or Brock? Or worse yet, Jude? At least you know and like John."

Directing his attention back to John, Mark said, "There's a lot of pretty girls in our school. Why do you have to like my sister?"

"It's not like I planned it this way. If someone had told me a couple years ago that I would like her someday, I never would've believed it." Trying to lighten the mood, he laughed a little as he asked, "Do you remember how we used to mess with her during sleepovers at your house?"

Mark shook his head and started walking swiftly toward school, clearly still angry and not wanting to joke about how they used to harass his sister.

Luke had to practically run to catch up. "Come on. What are you so upset about?"

"Leave me alone!"

"You have to admit, those were some fun times."

"I don't want to talk about it."

Luke fell back and allowed Mark to walk ahead of them. Matthew and John caught up with him and they walked several paces behind Mark.

Speaking quietly so Mark couldn't hear, John said, "Maybe I should keep it as friends with Madison. I had no idea it would bother Mark so much."

Matthew replied, "Don't do that. If you two like each other, then you should be together."

"Not at the cost of losing a friend."

"He'll get over it. You two will be great together, just like me and Kylie."

John smiled and said, "You have some work to do with that one. She is really mad at you."

"I don't see why. All I did was have a few beers. Everyone was doing it."

"It's not just the drinking. She's heard the same rumors that the rest of the school has heard. How would you feel if there was a rumor that she had sex with some random guy?"

"But I didn't do it!"

"She doesn't know that. You'd better let her know the truth, and you'd better be convincing."

"If she would've stayed at the party, none of this would've happened."

John looked astounded. "You're putting the blame on her?"

"Of course! You should've seen the way she was acting. I never realized how immature she is until I started hanging out with some of the upperclassmen. She has a lot of growing up to do."

"Are you serious? From where I'm standing, it looks like just the opposite. She did the mature thing by walking away."

Matthew scowled at him. "You weren't even there. Everyone was drinking and having a great time. You'd have done the same thing if you were there."

"No, I wouldn't have. I might've stayed, but I wouldn't have been drinking. You say that everyone was drinking, but I know that's a lie."

"How could you know that? You weren't there!"

"I talked with Hunter the next morning, before Sunday school. He told me everything. He was embarrassed by how juvenile you were acting!"

"He didn't say that. He gave me a ride home. Why would he do that if he had a problem with me?"

"He gave you a ride because you were about to get into a car with Chad and Brock, who were just as drunk as you were."

Matthew's eyes widened with surprise as he suddenly grasped the fact that John really did know the truth. "Hunter was drinking too."

"That's not what he said. He told me that neither he nor Dylan had anything to drink all night, so your story that everyone was doing it is also a lie. He also said that there were plenty of people there who didn't drink, including most of the football players that were there."

In a mocking tone, Matthew asked, "What else did he tell you?"

"He said that David and Jocelyn left at the same time that Kylie did, and for the same reason."

In the same condescending manner, he said, "Well, if my big brother didn't drink, then nobody should."

"Maybe you could learn a thing or two from him."

"Listen to you, Mister goody-two-shoes!"

Luke couldn't take it anymore. "Shut up! Both of you!"

They turned to look at him. John with a calm look, but Matthew had rage in his eyes. Mark, who had created quite a bit of distance between them, also turned from half a block away to see why Luke had shouted.

Matthew took a step toward Luke and said, "Don't tell me to shut up!"

John stepped between them and said, "He's right! We're arguing over stupid things."

Turning back to John, Matthew said, "Then stop being stupid!"

"I'm going to pretend I didn't hear that." John turned around and continued walking toward the school.

Matthew whispered, "Wimp."

If John heard him, he gave no indication as he briskly walked away. Luke shook his head and said, "Let's just get to school."

There was no more talking as they went the rest of the way to school. To anyone watching, it looked odd as they walked single file, with several feet between each of them. Luke, already upset about what was happening in his life, felt even worse. Everything was changing, and he didn't like it.

CHAPTER 14

The weather warmed up considerably on Wednesday, which was good for the first field trip of the year. History was John's favorite subject, so he looked forward to the trip to downtown Pittsburgh's *Point State Park,* where the class would visit the *Fort Pitt Museum* and *Block House.*

John felt the hot, stuffy air as he boarded the bus. He spotted Luke a few rows back staring absently out the window. John sat next to him and immediately took his jacket off.

"It's burning up in here. Could you open the window?"

Without answering, Luke reached up, opened the window and continued to look outside. John considered him for a moment and wondered why he seemed so distant. He knew that Luke was under a lot of stress lately due to his father's unexpected return, but he couldn't help thinking that there was more to it.

Not much was said between the four friends after the previous day's arguments. Matthew had gotten a ride home from football practice and again to school that morning, leaving the other three to walk without him. The tension between John and Mark was thick, so they barely spoke to each other. Luke seemed to be in his own world, so the walks were done in almost complete silence.

John watched Matthew blow right past him without even acknowledging that he was there. John looked over his shoulder and saw him take a seat in the back of the bus. He looked smug as he leaned back in his seat with his arms folded.

Mark came on a minute later, exchanged an uncomfortable look with John, then found a seat of his own about halfway back.

John had made a point not to call Madison the night before. He wanted to, but didn't want to rock the boat with Mark any more than he already did. How was he to choose between the girl he likes and one of his closest friends? Sure, he thought that Mark was being unreasonable, but he had to respect his feelings all the same.

When the bus started moving, the breeze coming through the open windows made it nice and cool inside. A few times, John glanced over to Luke, and every time he had the same disinterested look on his face. He finally nudged him with his elbow and said, "Lighten up. We're going on a field trip. Enjoy it."

Luke looked tired as he answered, "I'm just thinking about some stuff."

"Do you want to talk about it?"

"I keep thinking that this could be my last field trip at Benworth. If my dad gets his way, I'll be living in Las Vegas soon."

"Pops will never let that happen."

"He might not get a say in it. My dad is ready to take this to court. What if they side with him?"

"From what I understand, they'll ask you who you want to live with. Unless they deem that Pops is unfit to take care of you, they'll let you stay with him."

Shaking his head, Luke said, "I don't want to move. I like it here."

John put his arm around Luke's shoulder and said, "You're not going anywhere. It would be too much of a commute for Emmanuel to keep going back and forth between Pennsylvania and Nevada."

Luke laughed a little and asked, "Have you seen Emmanuel lately?"

"It's been a couple weeks, but I'm sure he'll be around."

"I saw him two Sundays ago. I talked to him on my back patio. He said that if the courts rule in my father's favor, then I need to be obedient to that."

John nodded. "Sounds like something he would say."

They both laughed again and the mood was light for the remainder of the bus ride.

When they exited the bus, they had a short walk to the park, which the locals have always referred to as *The Point*. One of the more scenic spots in the city, it's located at the tip of Pittsburgh's *Golden Triangle*.

Enjoying the unseasonably warm weather, John looked around before they went into the museum. On his left, the Monongahela River came down to meet the Allegheny River on his right. They met and merged into the beginning of the Ohio River, forming a Y shape.

Gazing up to his left, he could see Mt. Washington looking over the city. Behind him, skyscrapers towered above, creating a breathtaking skyline.

A crowd was forming around him as the rest of the students arrived, waiting to go inside the museum.

Matthew was among them. He pointed across the river and asked out loud, "Do you guys see that?"

Everyone looked to where he indicated and saw *Heinz Field,* the stadium where the Pittsburgh Steelers and Pitt Panthers football teams play their home games. The open end of the facility faced them, revealing a mixture of black and yellow seats.

When Matthew was sure that he had the attention of the onlookers, he went on, "I'll be playing on that field someday."

Some people smiled and patted him on the back, giving him words of encouragement, while others looked disgusted by his arrogant comment. John was with the latter. Spotting Mark and Luke, it was apparent that they didn't like the remark either.

John turned to go inside when one of the teachers chaperoning the trip announced that it was time to go in. They formed a line and went into the *Fort Pitt Museum.*

Once the tour began, John listened intently to the tour guide as she explained how Pittsburgh played a pivotal role in the French and Indian War, and the American Revolution.

Being a history buff, he was in his element and took in everything he saw. They went into rooms that recreated life inside the fort that existed two and a half centuries ago, that included a fur trader's cabin, a casement storage room for munitions, and a British soldiers' barrack.

Some of the artifacts they saw were an American Indian powder horn, item's from General Braddock's expedition such as musket balls and rifle locks, General Lafayette's cannon, and a writing desk that once belonged to Josiah Davenport, who happened to be Ben Franklin's nephew and a local fur trader.

John was fascinated by what he was seeing and felt like he could spend all day here. He got a great understanding of how important Pittsburgh was to the early history of the United States. The only down side to it was hearing Matthew make snide comments about the exhibits. A few people laughed at what he said, but John only felt irritation from it.

The tour ended much too soon for John, but he took solace knowing that they still had a visit to the *Block House* before going back to school.

The *Block House* is the only surviving structure left from the original Fort Pitt. It's not only the oldest building in Pittsburgh, it's also the oldest building west of the Allegheny Mountains. It was mostly known for providing quick cover to soldiers caught outside the fort when it came under attack.

It's a very small, black brick, square structure that almost seemed to get lost in the park. John pondered how many soldiers could actually fit inside, and how much protection did it provide? He tried to picture how it looked back when it was used during wars based on the paintings he saw in the museum, but with all the changes the city had gone through over the years, it was hard to imagine.

Due to the small size of the building, they would have to go inside to hear the presentation in groups, as the class was too large for all of them to enter together. John went in with the first group. He shook his head as he heard Matthew say that the building resembled an outhouse. Why couldn't he keep his comments to himself? Did he really think that he was that funny?

When his group was finished they waited outside for the other groups to take their turn. With a little time to kill, the students were given permission to walk around and enjoy the beautiful day, as long as they didn't wander too far.

John walked slowly with his hands in his pockets, looking around at the sights around him. Living in a suburb, he didn't get many opportunities to see this gorgeous town. Aside from an occasional ball game, his family didn't make it to the city very often.

He looked across the river to *Heinz Field* once again and thought about what Matthew had said. John couldn't help but wonder the same thing about himself. He wasn't the star quarterback like Matthew was, but he was a pretty good linebacker in his own right. Did he have the talent to someday make it to the NFL? Or at least college? If he chose to attend Pitt, then it was likely that he would one day play in that stadium too.

He smiled at the thought. His smile got even brighter when he looked in the direction of something that caught his eye. Leaning against a nearby tree was Emmanuel, dressed in his usual gray hoodie and jeans.

Emmanuel motioned for him to come over. John looked around and when he saw that no one was looking his way, he ran the short distance to Emmanuel and gave him a huge hug.

With a big smile, Emmanuel said, "You were right when you told Luke that I'd be around."

"You heard that?"

"Of course."

"I should've known."

John sat down in the grass and Emmanuel sat a few feet away, facing him. Once again, John scanned the area around him and saw that none of his classmates were watching, which relieved him. It wasn't that he was embarrassed to be with Emmanuel, but rather he didn't want to have to explain who he was and why he was talking with him. He'd had enough of that with Pastor Alex and his parents a few weeks ago.

With a smile, John asked, "What brings you here? This is the first time I've seen you outside of Benworth."

"I thought it would be a good time to talk to you."

"Should I get the other guys and bring them here?"

"No. I want to talk to you, alone."

"About what?"

"A few things. First of all, how do you feel about Matthew right now?"

John lowered his head and said, "He's acting like a jerk."

"Is there anything that you could do to help him?"

"I've tried talking to him, but he gets so defensive. I was hoping that Kylie being upset with him would knock some sense into him, but it seems to have had the opposite effect. What's gotten into him?"

"This is common when someone becomes popular. When you have so many people telling you that you're great, it's hard to not let it go to your head."

"It's done more than just go to his head, it's changed him. I used to love hanging out with him, but now I can't stand to be near him."

"He thinks you're jealous of him. What do you think about that?"

"I don't know. Maybe I am a little. When I see him on the football field during the varsity games, I find myself wishing that I could be out there too. I'm happy for him. I think it's great that he won the starting job, but I don't like what it's done to him."

Emmanuel looked at him closely. "You mentioned Kylie a little bit ago. How do you think she could help him?"

"Well, he's crazy about her. I figured that he would do anything to win her affection. If she can't get to him, I don't know who can."

"His pride won't allow that."

"How so?"

"Let me use your wrestling experience as an example. When you wrestled in middle school, how did you feel when you lost a match?"

"Terrible. I would beat myself up inside, constantly going over the match in my head and thinking about what I could have done differently."

"Okay. What about when you won?"

"I felt like I was on top of the world. Like I could accomplish anything."

"Do you see? That's how Matthew feels when he quarterbacks his team to victory. That success has led to pride. He's starting to think that he's invincible. His pride won't allow him to admit to Kylie that he was wrong. He actually believes that he did nothing wrong and he's waiting for her to apologize."

"I don't see that happening. She's way too angry with him."

"Not to mention the fact that she has nothing to apologize for."

"Now that I've heard this, I find myself hoping that he falls on his face Friday night. That would bring him down to earth, but I don't want it to be at the expense of the team. The seniors who have their last shot at a state title don't deserve that."

"Okay. That's enough about Matthew. What about Mark?"

John stretched his legs out in front of him and looked to the sky. "That's a tough one. I really like Madison and I think we would be great together, but I can't let her come between my friendship with Mark. I wish there was a way to make him understand."

Emmanuel leaned over on his side, resting on his elbow. "This is difficult for him. His parents aren't getting along and he's scared. He feels like his family is falling apart. He knows that his parents are close to divorce so he's starting to cling to his sister for support. He views you as a threat to that."

"I would never do anything to hurt him. He must know that."

"He knows that you would never do anything purposely, just like his parents wouldn't hurt him purposely, but every time they argue, he is hurt by it. He's lashing out at you because if you and Madison become an item, he'll have no one to turn to. His sister has always been there for him when his parents weren't."

"I never thought of it that way. What should I do?"

"Talk to Madison about it. She has no idea that Mark is so upset. When you're not around, they get along really well. If she talks to him and explains that a relationship between the two of you won't come between them, it could go a long way."

"Okay. I'll do that, but what about in the meantime? We've barely talked to each other since yesterday morning. I can't believe he pushed me. He's never done that before. Things are so awkward and I don't like it. I wish things were easier."

Emmanuel lifted his hand in front of his face, revealing a caterpillar crawling across the back of his hand. He smiled as he watched it slowly moved up to his wrist. Looking back to John, he asked, "Where do you think this caterpillar was going before he found my hand?"

Confused, John answered, "I don't know. He was probably going somewhere to build a cocoon so he can change into a butterfly."

"How does the butterfly get out of the cocoon?"

Trying to remember what he learned in science class, he thought for a few seconds, then replied, "They have to fight their way out, breaking the cocoon apart from the inside."

"What would you do if you saw a butterfly struggling to break out of it's cocoon?"

John scratched his head in thought. "I guess I would have compassion on it and rip the cocoon open so he could get out sooner."

Emmanuel nodded his head and smiled. "I like that answer, but it's not the right one."

"What do you mean?"

"If you did that, the butterfly would die within hours."

"How?"

"The process of breaking out of the cocoon gives strength to the butterfly. Without the struggle, it's wings will never get strong enough to fly, thus making it an easy target for predators."

"I never knew that."

"Does that explain to you why life can never be easy? It's through our struggles that we learn and grow stronger."

"That makes sense. That's something that Luke needs to hear. He's going through a rough time."

Emmanuel put his hand back to the ground, allowing the caterpillar to crawl back onto the grass and back on it's way. "I want you to start calling Luke more often."

"Sure. I can do that. Is there any particular reason?"

"He's desperate for someone to talk to. He's tried talking to Matthew, but he's not getting any response from him. Just lend an ear to him and give advice when he asks for it."

"Is there anything specific that you want me to tell him?"

"Tell him the butterfly analogy that I just told you. I think he'll receive it well."

"Okay. What about the others?"

"Nothing for Mark because he won't listen to you right now anyway, but let Matthew know that I forgive him."

"For what?"

"He'll know. That's between he and I."

"Alright. I'll pass the message."

"Pray for all three of your friends. They need it."

"I will."

They hugged once again and Emmanuel walked away. John watched him as he made his way toward the buildings that made up downtown. When he was out of sight, John went back to where the rest of the students were gathering to go back to the bus.

He spotted Matthew staring straight ahead. He checked to see what he was looking at and saw Kylie standing a ways off with her friends. If she knew that Matthew was ogling at her, she gave no sign of it.

John cautiously walked up to him and said, "If you apologize to her, I'm sure that everything will be cool again."

Matthew looked at him as though he were crazy. "Are you kidding me? She should be the one apologizing to me."

Not wanting to push the issue, he said, "Guess who I just saw."

Shrugging his shoulders, Matthew said, "I really don't care."

"Emmanuel. He wants me to tell you that he forgives you."

"Whatever."

"What happened? He wouldn't tell me."

"Nothing happened. I don't know what you're talking about."

John stood there dumbfounded while Matthew walked away, joining some other classmates that John didn't know well. He felt like he was in a daze as he followed the other students back to the parking lot.

Getting back on the bus, he saw Luke sitting in the same seat that he was in on the way there. John sat next to him again, and proceeded to tell Luke about his talk with Emmanuel. Luke remained silent as John told him about the butterfly.

John took the silence as understanding. When they got back to the school, he hesitated before getting up and said, "I'm here for you if you need to talk."

Luke softly said, "Thanks."

While John mentally prepared himself for football practice, he couldn't help but feel for Luke, and he hoped the storm he was in would pass soon.

CHAPTER 15

Thursday night youth group was always one of the highlights of the week for John. He watched for Matthew, but wasn't surprised when David showed up without him. He figured that Matthew wouldn't be there.

John purposely sat away from Madison, instead choosing to sit with Luke and Mark. She looked a little hurt as she eyed him from across the room. He would wait until the lesson was over, then talk to her and explain the situation.

As Zeke started the worship music, he noticed that Kylie kept looking to the door, almost as if she expected Matthew to walk in at any time. She seemed distracted and John wondered how much Matthew's behavior change was affecting her. He even found himself looking to the door, not really wanting to see him come in either.

When the worship ended, John sat down and listened to Zeke lead a forum about forgiveness. He didn't participate in the talk, as most of it was done by the upperclassmen. David, Hunter and Dylan dominated most of the discussion, giving their views on the subject.

Madison spoke up a few times, looking over to John each time. He tried to keep from looking at her too much, because when he did, it made him want to be with her even more.

He watched Luke and Mark at times and saw that they both appeared to be preoccupied. Luke looked straight ahead and didn't give the impression that he was listening at all. Mark looked down and fiddled with the zipper on his jacket. While he sat there wishing that things could go back to the way they were before, his thoughts kept going back to the butterfly, breaking out of it's cocoon. It was a good reminder that he and his friends were going to learn and be strengthened through this.

The lesson ended and they were free to socialize and play games. John stood up to stretch and saw Madison walking straight toward him.

"Why did you sit over here? I was saving a place for you."

John sighed and said, "We need to talk."

A worried look came over her face. "What's wrong?"

A glance around revealed that there were a lot of people close enough to hear them, so he gently led her by the arm to the other side of the room. When he was certain that no one was within earshot, he asked, "Are you aware that Mark doesn't approve of you and I being so close?"

"What? Did he say something?"

"Plenty. He's made it clear that he wants me to stay away from you."

"Is that why you haven't called all week?"

"Pretty much."

John's heart was being torn up as he watched her face show signs of pain and betrayal. About thirty seconds of very uncomfortable silence ensued before Madison finally asked, "Does this mean you don't want to see me anymore?"

"Not at all. Trust me, that's the last thing I want."

"But you can't let me come between your friendship with my brother."

"Exactly."

"There's got to be some way to make him understand that I would never try to come between you two."

"I think it's the other way around."

"What do you mean?"

"I think he's afraid that I'll come between the two of you."

As she stood there with a perplexed look, John continued, "With the problems your mom and dad are going through, I think he's clinging to you for support. He's scared that if you and I get together, then he'll have no one to turn to."

"What makes you think that?"

Treading carefully, he paused to think of the right words to say. He couldn't let her know that Emmanuel gave him this information. With her staring into his eyes, waiting for an answer, he said, "It's what my gut feeling is telling me."

"How do you know that my parents are going through a rough patch? Did he say something?"

"He mentioned it a few weeks ago on the way to school. He's pretty sure that they'll get divorced."

Looking a little angry, she said, "I told him not to tell anyone."

117

"Don't hold it against him. We kind of dragged it out of him. We could tell something was bothering him, so we hounded him until he told us."

It wasn't the complete truth, but it seemed to satisfy her. She looked at him with sadness in her eyes and asked, "Where does this leave us?"

"It doesn't change the way I feel about you."

"I know, but that's not what I asked. Does this mean that we can't be together?"

Looking at the tears forming in her eyes, he felt an urge to forget all about Mark and take her into his arms, but he knew that wasn't a realistic solution. "Will you talk to him? Assure him that you'll always be there for him. Tell him that he'll always come before me in your heart."

She nodded as the first of the tears ran down her face. "I'll do that. I just pray that he'll understand."

He smiled and said, "I want this as much as you do."

"I don't know about that." A smile lit her face up as she added, "My friends have been ribbing me pretty hard about you."

"What are they saying?"

"They're only joking, but they give me a hard time about liking someone two years younger than me."

He laughed as he asked, "So you've been telling your friends about me?"

"Of course. Haven't you told your friends about me?"

He shrugged. "They know we've been talking, but I don't think they know how close we've become."

"Well, Mark is about to find out. I really hope I can make him understand because all my friends think we're going to become a couple. It would be real embarrassing to tell them that I got turned down by a freshman."

"You'll just have to think of a lie to tell them."

"I guess I will."

They both laughed and embraced in a hug. When they pulled away, John said, "Maybe you should go hang out with your friends before Mark see us together and gets even more angry."

She looked at him longingly as she took the first few steps, then turned and joined her friends on the other side of the room.

John watched her go, then looked to see where Mark and Luke were. He didn't see them and figured they were in the other room playing one of the games.

He started to head that way when he saw Kylie walking toward him. Motioning to Madison, she asked, "Is there something going on between you two that I should know about?"

John chuckled and answered, "We're just friends."

With a sarcastic tone, she said, "I don't know. You looked awfully cozy there."

Thinking fast on his feet, he quickly retorted, "No more cozy than you and Matthew have looked recently."

The smile that had been on her face suddenly vanished. "That's the reason I came over to talk to you. Do you have a minute?"

"Sure."

She looked over her shoulder to see if anyone was listening, then guided him against the wall to ensure that they had privacy. "I really thought that he was a great guy. The first few weeks I knew him, I had such a great time getting to know him. Now I'm beginning to wonder if I ever knew him at all. You've known him a lot longer than I have. Is the way he's acting lately the real him?"

"No. Not at all."

"Then what's gotten into him?"

Leaning against the wall, he sighed and responded, "You're not the only one who's noticed it."

"But why? How can someone go from being sweet and funny to being a complete jerk?"

"If you ask me, I think it has to do with how popular he's become since he took over the starting quarterback position."

"I was thinking that too. That's when I saw the change in him."

John nodded. "I'm getting to the point where I'd like to see him have a terrible game tomorrow night, but not at the expense of the team."

"I don't think that'll happen tomorrow night. I've heard that the team you're playing hasn't won a game all year."

"That's true."

"Do you think you could talk to him for me?"

"If I get the chance. I don't see much of him anymore."

Puzzled, she asked, "Why not?"

"He seems to like his new friends a lot better. He's getting rides to school in the morning and after practice. I tried talking to him during the field trip, but he just walked away."

"This is so disappointing. I was really starting to like him."

"If he apologized to you, would you forgive him?"

"I've already forgiven him. If there's anything I learned from tonight's lesson, it's that forgiveness is my choice and it has nothing to do with anything that he does or says. An apology would be nice. It would show maturity on his part, but what I really want to see is the old Matthew. That's what I miss."

"Me too. I'd love to talk to him for you, but I don't think it'll do any good. His arrogance and pride are so high right now that it's going to take a lot more than words to bring him down."

She looked sad as she nodded. "It's crazy how fast someone can change."

"Everything seems to be changing lately."

"What else is going on?"

Shaking his head, he replied, "It's nothing."

She looked into his eyes and said, "Talk to me. I might be able to help." When he didn't say anything, she asked, "Is it because Mark doesn't want you dating his sister?"

A wave of shock ran through him. "How did you know about that?"

She shrugged and said, "I'm not blind."

"Great. How much more of my personal life does everyone know about?"

"I don't think anyone else picked up on it. It was obvious to me from the body language at Bible study the last two Mondays."

"It's a tough situation. I like her, but I can't let a girl come between me and one of my best friends."

She snickered and said, "And I was worried that I would be the one coming between Mark and Matthew."

"Maybe you could talk to Mark for me and I'll talk to Matthew for you. Then maybe we can both be with the one we like and not hurt any friendships in the process."

"I think that's a good idea."

John wanted to feel good, but instead felt a little nervous about agreeing to talk to Matthew, knowing that he probably wouldn't be receptive to anything he had to say. Kylie must have seen the worry on his face because she added, "Everything will turn out fine. You'll see. I'm going to go find Mark and talk to him now."

"Okay. I'll call Matthew."

He smiled as she walked away despite the uneasy feeling he had. He took his cell phone out of his pocket and called Matthew. While it was ringing, he tried planning what he would say, but nothing was coming to mind. He thought about hanging up and trying again later after he was better prepared for what he wanted to tell him, but decided to go through with it. It was better to get this over with.

After the fifth ring, it went to voicemail. John breathed a sigh of relief. Was he really not available to talk, or was he choosing not to answer? It didn't matter. He would rather have some time to think about what he would say to him.

He waited for the tone, then said into the phone, "Matthew, this is John. Call me when you get this. I have something to discuss with you. Talk to you soon."

He closed his phone and put it back in his pocket. He hoped that Matthew would call him back that night, but doubted that it would happen. Checking the clock, he saw that he still had about thirty minutes before Pops would be coming to pick them up. There was still time to get a game or two of ping pong or air hockey before he went home.

He walked into the adjoining room and almost bumped into Kylie. "Whoa!"

"Sorry. I was going to talk to Mark, but he's in the middle of a game of air hockey. I'll wait until I have a chance to talk with him one on one, if you don't mind."

"No problem. Matthew isn't answering his phone, so I'll have to do it later, too."

As she started walking away, she said, "Okay. Good luck."

"You too."

He went over to the ping pong table, where Hunter and Dylan were engaged in a fierce back and forth volley. He waited until Hunter scored the point, then asked, "Can I play the winner?"

Dylan responded, "Find one of your friends. We'll play doubles."

"Sure." John searched the room for Luke, but couldn't locate him right away. A closer look found him in the corner, talking frantically into his cell phone. John's stomach started churning as he quickly realized that something was wrong.

He ran over just as Luke hung up. His face was absent of color and he looked like he was on the verge of a panic attack.

"What's wrong?"

With tear filled eyes, Luke said, "That was Matthew's mother. Pops has just been rushed to the hospital. They think he's had a heart attack!"

CHAPTER 16

Luke was numb. The downward spiral he'd been on the last couple weeks kept spinning out of control. What else could go wrong?

John stood in front of him, staring in disbelief. There was indecision on the part of both of them. Neither seemed to know what to do or say. Finally, John said, "Let's tell Zeke."

He whirled around and soared into the other room. Luke followed at a slow pace, feeling like it was a great effort just to get his legs to move. By the time he got to the next room, John was already talking to Zeke.

With a wave of his arm, Zeke motioned for Luke to come over, which Luke did unhurriedly.

Zeke asked, "What other family do you have in town?"

Luke scratched his head. "It's just me and Pops."

John interjected, "No. Your dad is still here."

Luke gave him a bemused look. Why did John mention his dad? He might be Luke's biological father, but Luke hardly considered him family.

Zeke asked, "Where is your dad?"

Luke gave a vague shrug as he responded, "Who knows? Probably at the bar."

"Call him. Have him come get you and take you to the hospital." Switching his attention to John, he added, "Get everyone together. Tell them we're having an emergency prayer session."

John immediately darted to the other room to tell the others. Luke watched him go then looked back to Zeke. "I don't really want to involve my father in this. He and Pops don't get along."

"Call him anyway. He needs to know and you need to be with him now."

He shook his head and lazily took his phone out. Before he had the chance to make the call, Kylie came storming into the room with worry on her face and tears in her eyes.

"Oh my gosh! I can't believe this." She ran over and hugged Luke tightly. "I'm so sorry."

Luke politely hugged her back and said, "I need to call my father."

"Okay. We'll be praying."

She released him and joined the other students who were gathering around. There was a lot of commotion as everyone came together. Nobody seemed to know why their game time had been interrupted.

"What's going on?"

"Who's grandfather?"

"Is he alive?"

The questions and confusion were too much for Luke. He slipped outside into the brisk evening air. He breathed deeply and made the call to his father. After a few rings, he finally got an answer.

"I need your help!"

"With what?"

"It's Pops! He's in the hospital! They think he's had a heart attack!"

The silence that ensued made Luke wonder if they'd lost the connection. Eventually, he heard his father's voice say, "I'm sorry to hear that."

"Can you come get me? I need someone to take me to the hospital."

"Okay. Are you at home?"

"No. I'm at the church."

"Alright. I'll be there in a few."

Luke leaned against the wall while he absently watched car headlights zip up and down the street. He suddenly felt the need to be at the hospital as soon as possible, even though there was nothing he could do for Pops. He felt very helpless standing in front of the youth center.

Feeling restless, he paced back and forth in front of the door. His attention was diverted by someone walking on the sidewalk on the other side of the street. The darkness prevented him from being able to see who it was. All he could see was a silhouette, but it seemed familiar. He felt a longing to see Emmanuel, but the physique was wrong. Nonetheless, he was pretty sure that he knew who it was. He resisted an impulse to call out to whoever it was, as he saw that he was about to pass under a street light.

Luke's eyes widened as the man's face was uncovered. It was Jude! Luke stood there frozen with his heart pounding inside his chest. He prayed that Jude wouldn't see him. He felt a little reassured that he was so close to the youth group, and the fact that Jude was alone, but the memory of the beating he recently took was still very fresh in his mind.

At one point, Jude looked in his direction, but if he saw Luke, he gave no indication as he kept walking at the same pace with no hesitation. Luke's eyes never left him until Jude was far enough down the street that he lost sight of him. He breathed a little easier once he knew that the danger was over for the time being, but just as quickly, the worry over Pops returned.

He glanced through the glass door and saw everyone with their heads bowed. Zeke stood at the front of the room with his hand extended, talking a mile a minute. Luke couldn't hear him through the closed door, but knew that prayers for Pops were being lifted up. He contemplated whether or not he should go inside and be a part of the prayer, but felt like he should stay outside so he'd be ready to jump into his dad's car when he pulled up.

He dropped to the ground and sat, leaning back on the wall. His stomach was turning. It all seemed surreal. How could this be happening to Pops?

While he waited for his dad, he thought back to his grandmother's death. He couldn't believe that it had been four years since she died. A victim of brain cancer, she held on for a year after being diagnosed. He watched her health deteriorate as she underwent chemotherapy and radiation treatments. She appeared to wither away right before his eyes.

When she finally breathed her last, he felt relief that her pain was over, despite the incredible sadness that went along with losing a loved one. He took solace in knowing that she was in heaven now, and would never feel pain again.

He remembered praying at her funeral that when it came time for Pops to go, that it would be quick, so he wouldn't suffer the way she did. He now regretted that prayer.

He stood up and looked around the parking lot, hoping to see Emmanuel, but he wasn't there. Sadness overtook him as he fell to his knees. He cried out, "Lord! Please don't take Pops away from me now! I need him!"

The tears started flowing as he wept. He wasn't sure how long he knelt there, but he kept his eyes closed until he felt a hand on his shoulder. He immediately jumped to his feet and raised his hands to defend himself. For a second, he thought he saw Jude standing in front of him, sending a jolt of fear through him. When he realized that it was John, he relaxed a bit but his heart still pounded.

"Calm down. It's only me. Are you okay?"

Luke dropped his hands and said, "Not really. Please don't sneak up on me like that."

John nodded in understanding. "Sorry. I didn't mean to scare you. Is there anything I can do?"

"I don't know. I can't believe this is happening." Glancing at his watch, he asked, "What's taking my father so long?"

"I'm sure he'll be here soon." John put his hands on Luke's shoulders. "There's a whole room full of people in there praying. Pops is in a hospital with great doctors working on him."

"I know, but it doesn't make me feel any better."

Headlights illuminated the area as Luke's father pulled into the parking lot and eased to a stop next to them.

"It's about time."

John said, "I'll see you soon. My parents are on their way. We're going to the hospital too."

Luke nodded as he ducked inside the car. He closed the door and was greeted by loud music coming from the radio, tuned in to the local classic rock station. Luke reached over and turned the volume down as his father put the car into gear and made his way through the parking lot and onto the main drag.

Neither of them said anything for the first minute or so, then his dad asked, "How bad is it?"

"I'm not sure. Mrs. Peters just said that he was complaining about chest pains and numbness in his arm. She called 911, and by the time the paramedics arrived, he was unconscious."

"That doesn't sound good."

They both remained silent again. Luke watched his dad as he drove and saw no concern on his face whatsoever. He showed no urgency at getting to the hospital and looked as if he were taking a leisurely Sunday drive.

Luke knew that his dad didn't like Pops, but he still felt resentment toward him for not showing any distress at all.

As they got close to the hospital, his dad casually said, "You know, even if he does pull through, you probably won't be able to stay with him anymore. The courts will definitely rule in my favor when they learn that he's not in good health."

Luke was flabbergasted. How could he be so insensitive? They weren't even sure if Pops would live or die, and all he could talk about was where Luke was going to live? He wanted to shout at him, but was too appalled to say anything.

Where he was going to live was not what he wanted to think about. He lowered his head and once again prayed for Pops to live.

The hospital parking lot was packed. It took them some time to find a parking spot, and once they did, they had to walk a distance to get inside. Luke and his dad went through the emergency room entrance where they saw two middle age ladies sitting behind a counter. One was talking on the phone while the other gave them a cold greeting.

Luke's father looked at him and said, "Have a seat and I'll find out what I can."

A look around revealed a large waiting room filled with hard plastic chairs and coffee tables with magazines spread over the tops of them. A flat screen TV hung on the far wall that was tuned in to *CNN*. Most of the seats were taken, some by people who were waiting for medical attention, and others by people who were with them.

Luke found a couple seats next to each other that were unoccupied and took one, saving the other for his dad when he finished talking to the receptionist. He did his best to ignore the sounds coming from the TV and closed his eyes, trying to clear his mind. While he wanted to convince himself that Pops would be fine, the nagging feeling in his gut told him otherwise.

Thinking back to his grandmother and how sick she was in the months leading up to her death, at least it gave him time to prepare for it. When he got the news that she had died, he wasn't surprised. He thought that if Pops were to die now, it would be too soon and shocking. The silent prayers continued as Luke asked God to give Pops more time.

From where he was sitting, he could see his dad talking to the hospital employees. A part of him wished that he could hear what they were saying, and another part was grateful that he couldn't because he didn't want to hear any bad news.

Closing his eyes once again, he started reminiscing about good times that he and Pops shared over the years. One of his earliest and fondest memories being pulled around in a red wagon at the county fair when he was no older than three or four. Pops would take him out to go on some of the childrens rides or to ride the ponies. It was the first of many times he could remember eating cotton candy, which would become one of his favorite treats at these types of events. He even smiled for a second when he reflected on the stuffed dog that Pops had won for him at that fair. He had watched in awe as Pops, looking like a major league pitcher, threw a ball and knocked over a stack of tin cans, thus winning the prize for Luke. That stuffed dog, which he had given the name 'Lassie', became Luke's sleeping companion for the next few years.

Learning how to swim at the public pool at Acorn Park was another recollection that he loved. Pops would hold him up while Luke would kick his legs and flutter his arms in the simulation of him swimming by himself. Pops would let him go and then grab him again if he started to sink until he finally stayed afloat on his own.

Pops also taught him to dive from the diving boards at the same pool. Luke, in turn, was able to teach Matthew, Mark and John how to dive, while Pops watched from a distance with a smile on his face.

The patience that Pops showed when Luke was trying to ride his bike without training wheels for the first time was more than most could endure. Holding on to the back of Luke's seat while they went up and down the driveway, Pops would periodically let go and Luke would lose balance. They would do it over and over again until Luke eventually got the hang of it. When he got enough confidence to take the bike out to the sidewalk in front of the house, Pops would sit for hours and watch him ride back and forth.

Riding his first roller coaster with Pops by his side was a huge thrill. He loved visiting *Kennywood Park* and riding *The Racer* and *The Jackrabbit*, and when he got a little older and braver, he dared to face the adventure of riding *The Thunderbolt* and *The Phantom's Revenge*. Amusement parks and roller coasters in particular became one of the highlights to every summer in recent memory.

Then there was always the little things, such as teaching him to hit a baseball and catch a football, preparing him for little league baseball and pee wee league football. He always appreciated the time that Pops was willing to spend with him in those areas, as it gave him a head start over his teammates and helped him to earn starting positions on those teams.

He wasn't ready to let Pops go. There were more memories to be created in the future, and he wanted Pops by his side for as many as possible.

Still with his eyes closed, he could feel a presence near him. His eyes snapped open and he jumped to his feet, putting his hands up to guard himself from the attack that he was sure was coming. For a split second, he thought he saw Jude standing in front of him, then became conscious of the fact that it was just his father.

"Relax."

"Sorry. I thought you were someone else." Luke sat back down.

Taking the seat next to him, Brad asked, "Are you still jumpy from getting beat up a couple weeks ago?"

"I guess. I saw him earlier tonight."

"Where?"

"Outside the church while I was waiting for you to pick me up."

"What was he doing?"

"Nothing. Just walking down the street."

"Did he say anything to you?"

"I don't think he saw me. He was on the other side of the street."

Brad turned to face him and asked, "What would you have done if he confronted you?"

"I don't know. I probably would've gone back inside to get help."

Brad shook his head and said, "You need to stand up for yourself. What if you weren't at the church? What if there was no help to turn to?"

"I'm pretty sure I could out run him if I had to."

"That didn't work out too well for you the day you got your butt kicked."

Luke shot him a nasty look. He was starting to sound like Matthew. "What do you suggest?"

"Fight back! The best way to beat a bully is to beat him at his own game. Show him you're not scared and give him a taste of his own medicine. You do that, and he'll never bother you again."

"I'm afraid that if I do that, the beating I receive will be worse than the last time."

"That's why I want you to learn Krav Maga. You're going back Saturday, aren't you?"

"That depends on what happens with Pops. Did you find anything out?"

Brad nodded. "He had a massive heart attack. They almost lost him. He's stable now, but in critical condition. He's in for a lengthy hospital stay."

"Can I see him?"

"Not now. They said to come back tomorrow and they'll be able to tell us more. Why don't you stay with me tonight at my buddy's house?"

Before he could answer, he heard John call out, "Luke!"

He turned to see John walking toward him, with his parents close behind. Jim, John's father, quickly made his way over to them and asked, "How is he?"

Brad answered, "Critical, but stable."

Maggie, John's mother, asked Luke, "How are you doing?"

"I've been better. I want to see Pops, but they won't let us until tomorrow."

Maggie replied, "Keep praying. God can bring him through this."

John said, "Come home with us. Spend the night and we'll go to school together in the morning."

Brad interposed, "He's going to stay with me tonight."

Luke said, "I'd rather stay with my friend if you don't mind."

Brad looked hurt, but said, "Okay. If you'd be more comfortable there, I understand."

The five of them slowly made their way out to the parking lot, where Brad asked John, "How did you like the Krav Maga class?'

"I thought it was really cool."

"Are you going back?"

"Yeah. I want to be able to handle myself with the likes of Jude."

"That's what I'm trying to get Luke to recognize. You have to stand up to this guy, because deep down, he's a coward. You saw the way he ran off when I challenged him. That's his true colors."

John nodded. "It doesn't change the fact that he's a lot bigger and stronger than us."

"Very true. That's why you need to learn how to fight."

"Speaking of fighting, I'm thinking about staying for the fight class on Saturday."

"Great idea." Switching his attention to Luke, he added, "You should do that too. It would be a good experience for you."

Luke shrugged and said, "I'm more concerned with Pops right now. I'll worry about fighting when I know that my grandfather is going to be alright."

This marked the end of the conversation as they reached Brad's rental car. They shook hands and Brad drove off.

Luke said nothing on the ride to John's house. He spent the time thinking and praying for Pops. They made a quick pit stop at Luke's place, where he got a change of clothes and his school books, then went to John's.

Jim set up an air mattress and a sleeping bag next to John's bed. Luke laid there for a long time, weeping at times, and just thinking at others, but not sleeping at all. John was quiet in the bed next to him, and Luke wondered whether or not he was asleep. He wanted to talk, but didn't want to disturb him if he really was sleeping, so he kept to himself.

He wasn't sure how long it took, but eventually he drifted off to sleep. Dreams of hospitals and funeral homes plagued him throughout the night, causing him to wake up in a cold sweat more than once. One thing after another kept making this storm that he was in feel like it was turning into a hurricane!

CHAPTER 17

In the visiting locker room of Washington Heights High School, Coach King was giving his pre-game pep talk, but Luke wasn't listening. It had been a long day already. After the previous night's events and a restless night of broken sleep, he felt emotionally drained.

The day began with him sluggishly getting ready for school while John's mother called the hospital to see if there was any change in Pops' condition. Luke thought about not going to school so he could be at the hospital with Pops, but was talked out of it by John's father. Pops was still unconscious and there was nothing that he could do for him, so Luke reluctantly agreed to attend classes.

He spent most of the school day in a daze. Fortunately, there weren't any tests given, so his lack of attention to his studies didn't hurt him.

During lunch, he checked his cell phone and saw that he had a text message from his dad telling him that he would pick him up after school to take him to the hospital. He was grateful that his father was willing to do this because he had only a two hour window between the end of class and the bus leaving for the football game, and he wanted to make the most of the time available.

At the hospital, they learned that Pops was coming in and out of consciousness. The doctor told them that he kept calling out the names Debbie and Stephanie. Luke informed him that those were the names of his wife and daughter, both of whom had passed away years ago.

While visiting in his room, Pops woke up twice. The first time he muttered something unintelligible before falling asleep again, and the second time, he stared at them as though he recognized them, but couldn't quite place it. It broke Luke's heart to see Pops this way.

When the time came to leave for the game, Luke mentioned to his dad that he didn't want to go. Being the third string tight end, he wasn't likely to see any playing time, and they were playing a team that was still looking for their first win of the season. He wanted to stay with Pops, but Brad talked him out of it, saying that the fact that they were playing a second-rate team that would probably result in an easy win meant that he had a good chance to get some playing time. Once again, he went against his heart and left for the game.

Now, the warm-ups and pep talk were over, and it was time to take the field. The Benworth Eagles charged the field, showing intensity and excitement as they fired themselves up for the game. Luke was in the midst of it, but failed to share their enthusiasm. All he could think about was being by Pops' side.

Luke felt bad looking into the crowd, knowing that Pops wasn't there. This was the first Benworth Eagles game that Luke could remember in which Pops wasn't in attendance. Going back to when Luke was a small child, Pops took him to every game, whether it was at home or away, sometimes driving halfway across the state for playoff games, Pops was a fixture in the bleachers, and was known for being one of their staunchest supporters. He knew that his dad was watching, but he didn't feel like looking for him, instead choosing to try to focus on the game and get his mind off of Pops.

As hard as he tried, he couldn't stay interested in the game, despite the fact that the Eagles were putting on a dominating performance. Washington Heights was winless on the season and it quickly became apparent why. They turned the ball over often on offense and were very poor tacklers on defense.

Benworth, on the other hand, played flawlessly. Matthew's passes were right on target, the offensive line was opening huge holes for the running game, and the defense was hitting hard, intimidating their opponents and forcing a lot of Washington Heights mistakes.

The game was a complete mismatch. At halftime, the Eagles led 28-0. Matthew had thrown three touchdown passes and Hunter added the other score on a long run, breaking a number of tackles along the way.

The atmosphere in the locker room was enjoyable and relaxed. A lot of joking and laughs filled the room as everyone had some lighthearted fun. Except for Luke. He sat in front of his locker with a heavy heart. He was feeling agitated and was resentful of the other players for having such a good time while he was miserable.

John came over and sat next to him. "Lighten up, buddy."

Luke gave him a sad stare. "I don't want to be here. I should be at the hospital."

"I can understand you feeling that way, but there's nothing you can do for him."

"I know, and it makes me feel helpless. Being here is doing nothing more than frustrating me. It's not like that team can beat us. If this was a home game, I'd just slip out the door and go be with Pops. The coach probably wouldn't even know I was gone."

"If I know Pops, he'd want you to stay. He loves this team."

Luke gave him a discouraged look. "It's not like the team needs me. The game's a blowout."

John scolded him, "Don't say that this team doesn't need you! Everyone on this team plays an important role!"

"Come on! I'm the third string tight end. If I quit, the team wouldn't be affected in any way."

"That's not true. Take Matthew, for instance. He started the season as a third stringer. All it took was one injury and the backup getting benched for him to get thrust into the starting lineup."

"That's different."

"How so?"

"He's a much better athlete than I am."

"You're a lot better than you give yourself credit for."

Luke dismissed his comment with a wave of his hand, then said, "You saw how many passes I dropped in the JV game a couple weeks ago."

"That was just one game. We all have bad games from time to time."

"Then why didn't they throw any passes my way in the last game?"

"Because we didn't need to. We were preserving a big lead and kept the ball on the ground."

Luke let loose an unenthusiastic chuckle. "That just proves my point. I'm not needed."

"Please. There's a lot more to your position than catching passes. You're an excellent blocker for the running game."

Luke responded sarcastically. "Yeah, right."

"You are. Mark told me after the last game that some of his long runs wouldn't have been possible if it wasn't for some key blocks that you made."

"He said that?"

"Yes! You helped spring some big plays!"

"Okay, maybe I did, but that was the JV team. This is varsity. It's a whole other world."

"That's true, but that doesn't change the fact that you're important to this team. Crazy things could happen to put you on the field, and you need to be confident that you'll be ready if that comes to pass."

Luke lowered his head. "Confidence is something that I don't have much of right now. I feel like the world is falling in on me."

John put his arm around Luke's shoulder and said, "I know that you're going through a tough time, but I want you to know that I'm here for you in any way you need. When I saw Emmanuel the other day, he told me to be there for you. I felt good after my talk with him. It helped me to remember that God is always in control."

"That's easy to say when you're looking from the outside in."

John sighed. "Do you remember what Romans 8:28 says?"

Having learned it a few years earlier from Pops, Luke recited it from memory, "And we know that in all things God works for the good of those who love him, who have been called according to his purpose."

"Exactly. I know that what you're going through isn't easy, but I also know that you'll come out of this stronger. Think about what I told you on the bus ride home from the field trip."

Luke was confused as he wasn't sure what he was referring to. Seeing the blank look on his face, John added, "About the butterfly."

Recalling the conversation now, he nodded. Waiting a few seconds, he said, "I appreciate you trying to cheer me up, but what I really want right now is to be with Pops. I know I'm supposed to try to be positive, but I can't help think that this could be the end. If it is, I want to spend as much time with him as possible."

John rubbed the top of Luke's head, messing his hair a little. "I know. I'm worried about him too. I love him as if he were my own grandfather."

"I know you do, and he loves you, Matthew and Mark as if you were his own grandchildren."

John smiled and got a little teary eyed. "Alright. Let's change the subject before I start crying."

Luke laughed and suddenly felt a little better. "Why don't you come with me to visit Pops after the game?"

"You mean tonight?"

"Yeah. I figure that by the time we get back to Benworth, we'll have about an hour before visiting hours are over."

"Of course I'll go with you. In fact, I'll do you one better. I'll round up the guys and get them to go too."

Luke's smile broadened. "I'm sure Pops will love that."

"I think he will too. Now, let's get our heads right. If this game keeps going the way it has, we both should see some action. That will give you something cool to tell Pops. News like that will be good for him."

For the first time since his terrible performance in the JV game, Luke was excited about playing football. When Coach King called the team to return to the field for the second half, Luke felt like he was the most eager player on the team.

Standing on the sideline, he watched and anxiously awaited to be called. John stood next to him and said, "Another touchdown or two, and we'll definitely get in."

Luke nodded and looked on attentively.

The second half began much like the first, with the defense coming up big and forcing a punt. Matthew wasted no time in adding to the lead, as it took him only two plays to throw his fourth touchdown pass of the night, tying a school record for touchdown passes in a single game, a record he now shared with his brother and another player from a few years earlier.

Talk on the sideline was all about whether or not Matthew would break the record. He had plenty of time to do it, as it was still early in the third quarter.

It didn't take long for him to get his chance. On the next play from scrimmage, the Washington Heights quarterback threw an interception that was returned all the way to the eight yard line. Luke watched with keen interest as Matthew led the offense back onto the field.

The sideline was buzzing with anticipation. They all knew that it would be a pass play and every eye was glued to that end of the field. Luke found himself shifting his weight from one leg to the other in expectation. Despite the way Matthew had been acting lately, he still wanted to see his friend do well. He also wanted another touchdown for the team, knowing that it would increase his chances of getting into the game.

Matthew lined up in the shotgun formation, with Hunter as the lone setback to his right. There were four receivers lined up, two on each side of the offensive line. The snap was a little high, but Matthew snagged it effortlessly and calmly stood in the pocket while his receivers ran their routes. The line gave him excellent protection as he looked for an open man to throw to. The Washington Heights defense looked confused as their coverage broke down, leaving Dylan wide open in front of the goal post. Matthew saw this and fired a bullet right on the numbers, which was easily caught for the touchdown.

A roar erupted from the Eagles' sideline. Matthew raised both fists into the air as he jogged back to the bench. David, dressed in his jersey and blue jeans, was the first to give him a congratulatory hug. It warmed Luke's heart to see David legitimately happy for his younger brother, who had just broken his record.

With the score 42-0, Coach King started substituting players, and it wasn't long before Luke, Mark and John all got their chance to play. Due to the huge lead, they didn't call any more pass plays, but that was just fine for Luke. He remembered what John had told him about his blocking skills and used his time on the field to hone them.

Mark got a few carries at running back and picked up some nice gains. Even without throwing the ball, they still had no trouble moving the ball at will.

While on defense, Luke concentrated his attention on John. He played his linebacker position as though it were a tie game. He looked intense out there, making tackle after tackle, and not allowing them a first down.

By the time the game finally ended, they had added two more scores, completing a 56-0 rout of the hapless Washington Heights squad. The jovial mood in the locker room continued onto the bus the entire ride back.

When they got back to the school, Luke was quick to put his equipment back in his locker. He couldn't wait to get to the hospital and see Pops. He found John and Mark and asked them if they were ready to go.

John said, "I haven't had the chance to let Matthew know where we're going." Spotting him entering the room with his equipment bag slung over his shoulder, John ran over to him with Luke and Mark on his heels. "Hey. We're heading over to the hospital to see Pops. Are you coming with us?"

Matthew looked a bit surprised as he answered, "Oh. I already promised some people that I would be at Mario's."

"That's okay. Visiting hours will be over soon. You can go to Mario's after that."

"I can't. My ride is already outside, waiting for me." As he walked away, he yelled back, "Say hi to Pops for me."

Luke felt a hint of anger, but did his best not to let it show. John and Mark didn't say anything either, but it was clear that they were bothered by it too. Without saying a word, Luke walked outside and headed straight to his dad's rental car, which was parked by the curb. He got into the passenger seat while John and marked climbed into the backseat.

As Brad started the drive to the hospital, he said, "Your team is looking good."

John answered, "It's easy to look good when you're playing one of the worst teams in the area. Next week will be the real test."

"What's next week?"

"We're playing Allbridge. They're undefeated and ranked number one in the state!"

"Sounds like it should be a great game."

Luke sat there while the conversation continued between his dad and John, but he was no longer listening. He was feeling antsy and was growing impatient with how slow his dad was driving. The time was short that he had to see Pops tonight, and he didn't want to waste a second of it. With every red light they stopped at, he would check the clock on the dashboard and his annoyance would escalate.

Once they got to the parking lot and found a spot, Luke had unbuckled his seatbelt and was out the door before his dad had even turned off the ignition. He swiftly walked through the lot toward the entrance, creating distance between himself and the others.

Just in front of the doors, he turned to see how far back they were and called out, "Hurry up!"

His father yelled back, "What's the rush? He's not going anywhere!"

Luke's face turned red with anger. He felt as though that comment was completely inappropriate and wanted to call his dad an insensitive jerk, but bit his tongue. Instead, he waited for them to catch up, then darted to the elevator and hit the up button. They rode it to the fourth floor and found Pops' room.

Luke was taken aback when he entered and saw Pops laying in the bed. Pops looked as if he'd aged twenty years overnight. His eyes were open but had a vacant look to them. The room was silent with the exception of the beeps and tones of the machines he was hooked up to.

Mark and John followed him in and went to Pops' left side while Luke stood to his right. Brad stayed back and leaned against the door frame.

Once the initial shock of his grandfather's appearance wore off, Luke smiled and greeted him. "It's good to see you, Pops."

Pops answered with a very weak voice that was almost inaudible. "Sorry I missed your game."

"Me too. You would've loved it. We won 56-0 and Matthew broke the school record with five touchdown passes!"

A slight smile formed on Pops' lips. He struggled to look around with glassy eyes, then asked, "Is Matthew here?"

"No, but he wanted us to tell you that he said 'hi.'"

Luke grabbed one of the nearby chairs and pulled it over to the bedside. He positioned himself so that he was close to Pops' face because he was having a hard time hearing what he said.

Pops looked back to Luke and asked, "Did you play?"

With a giddy smile, he replied, "Yes. I played most of the fourth quarter. We weren't passing the ball at that point because we had such a big lead, so I just concentrated on making good blocks. Mark had some nice runs, and John made a lot of tackles. It was a good night for all of us."

With another feeble smile, he said, "That's great." With great effort, Pops raised his head enough to look at Brad, who was still standing by the door with his arms folded. Pops laid his head back down on the pillow and said to Luke, "Tell your father to come over here. I need to ask him something."

Confused, Luke turned to Brad and said, "He wants to ask you something."

Brad took the few steps to stand behind his son with a bewildered look on his face. He leaned down close to Pops and asked, "You wanted to see me?"

Pops seemed a little short of breath for a few seconds before he managed to say in a hoarse voice, "I want you to look after Luke while I'm here."

The surprise was equal for both Luke and Brad. Pops added, "Stay in my house. Luke will be more comfortable there."

Brad said, "Of course."

After a few seconds of raspy breathing, Pops looked up to Brad, "I'm sorry I was so hard on you when you returned. I want you to know that I forgive you."

A tear slid out of the corner of Pops' eye and rolled down to his ear. Luke reached over and wiped it for his grandfather as he fought back tears of his own. Luke looked over his shoulder to see his dad, who just stood there with a stunned look.

Finally, Brad managed to say, "Thank you. I'll take good care of him."

Luke looked back to Pops, whose eyes were now closed. When it became clear to them all that Pops had fallen asleep, they quietly left the room and made their way back to the car. There was very little talking during the ride home.

Luke was pretty sure that everyone was in shock over what Pops had said. He was still trying to make sense of it himself. Why had Pops suddenly changed his tune? It made him think that if Pops was willing to forgive his dad, then maybe he should too.

After dropping Mark and John off at their homes, they went to where his dad had been staying. They went inside and Luke sat on the sofa while Brad collected his belongings, then they went back to Luke's house.

There was an awkward aura throughout the house as Luke showed him where the guest bedroom was. Not much was said between them before Luke went to his room for the night.

Laying in bed, his mind raced as he thought back on what had been a crazy day. His emotions had gone through a rollercoaster of highs and lows. Exhaustion eventually won out and Luke fell asleep, but not before he prayed a silent prayer that Emmanuel would show up and perform one more miracle of healing!

CHAPTER 18

Saturday morning began with Luke wanting to sleep the day away. The last couple days had taken its toll on him and he had never felt so weary. The only reason he got out of bed was his desire to see Pops.

Walking through the living room on the way to the kitchen, he saw his dad sitting on Pops' favorite recliner, drinking a bottle of beer. Luke stopped in his tracks. After a quick check of the clock, he said, "It's only 8:30. You're drinking already?"

Looking very relaxed, Brad answered, "I like to start the day with a beer. It gets me going. Some people start their day with coffee. I start mine with beer."

Luke was horrified as he said, "You're supposed to drive me to Krav Maga class and then to the hospital."

"Yeah… And?"

"And you're drinking! You can't get behind the wheel now!"

Brad sighed, "Of course I can. I do it all the time."

"I don't like this!"

"It'll be fine. A couple beers is not enough to get me drunk."

Knowing that he wouldn't convince his dad to stop, he chose to drop the subject and went to the kitchen and poured himself a bowl of cereal. He ate it silently at the kitchen table while the sounds of his father channel surfing in the next room filled the house.

Upon finishing his breakfast, he joined his father in the living room and watched *ESPN* and their pre-game coverage of the day's college football games. They talked a little about who they thought would win some of the marquee match-ups of the day.

Before long, it was time to leave for Krav Maga class. Luke was not enthused about going and even mentioned briefly to his dad that he would like to skip it in favor of visiting Pops, but Brad swayed him into believing that Pops would want him to go to class.

They talked a little more on the drive and even shared a few lighthearted laughs. Aside from a couple awkward silences, the ride was enjoyable for Luke, and it did a good job of getting his mind off of Pops.

As they parked the car in front of the school, Brad said, "You should stay for fight class."

Luke didn't like the idea of mixing it up with the other students, in fact, it down right scared him. Looking for an excuse to get out of it, he said, "I want to visit Pops, so I don't want to spend all day here."

"It won't be all day. We'll have plenty of time for a visit."

Luke lethargically got out of the car and slowly walked to the entrance. They were a little early, so there weren't very many people inside. Derrick greeted them with a wave from the other side of the mats, where he was showing one of the other kids a technique for defending a choke from behind. Brad urged Luke to pay attention in case he needed to use it in a future encounter with Jude. Luke remembered being taught it at his first lesson. He watched closely and made a few mental notes.

When Derrick was done showing the defense, Luke found a spot on the mat and began stretching. While he got loose, Luke saw from the corner of his eye, Derrick and his dad talking quietly by the front door. He noticed them look his way a few times, so he knew that they were talking about him. An uneasy feeling overtook him.

Dread overtook him as Derrick walked slowly toward him with Brad on his heels. Luke continued his stretching and pretended to not notice them. While sitting on the mat with his legs extended, Luke reached down and grabbed his toes, letting his muscles get warm. He could feel Derrick's huge frame looming over him, but he said nothing.

"Your father tells me that you're reluctant to participate in fight class. Why is that?"

Raising his eyes to look up, he saw Derrick looking down at him with his hands on his hips. Not wanting to admit his fear, he said, "I don't want to spend too much time here because I want to see my grandfather in the hospital."

Lifting his hand to rub his chin, Derrick replied, "Yes. I'm real sorry to hear about him."

"Yeah. So I hope you understand why I want to get out of here as soon as the regular class is over."

"Have you seen that bully since the last time I talked to you? What's his name?"

"It's Jude, and yes, I saw him two nights ago."

"Did he say anything to you?"

"No. I don't think he saw me." Luke continued to tell him about seeing Jude outside the church, but left out the part about how scared he was.

When he finished, Derrick asked the question he was hoping to avoid. "How did you feel when you saw him?"

Luke shrugged. "I didn't feel anything at all. I had just gotten the news about Pops and was more concerned about that."

"What would you have done if he'd confronted you?"

"I had a room full of friends that I easily could have ducked into."

Derrick nodded slowly. "What would you have done if your friends weren't there?"

"I don't know. I guess I'll deal with that at the time, if it ever happens."

"That's why you need to be at fight class. This guy lives in your neighborhood, so it's not a case of if, but when. There is no maybe about it. You will see him again and have to deal with it. The experience you get from fight class will equip you with the skills and confidence you'll need to handle it."

Luke still didn't like the idea of having to fight the other students who were more experienced and trained than he was, but the thought of facing Jude alone scared him even more. Against his better judgment, he said, "Alright. I'll stay for fight class."

"Good choice. Don't worry. We've been doing this for years and nobody has ever gotten hurt. Just like I said last week, You can get back what that coward took from you. You can get your pride back. You can walk tall again. You can live a victimless existence, but you have to want it."

Luke gave a sheepish smile and continued his stretching. The butterflies started forming in his stomach, but he tried not to think about it. In the back of his mind, he wondered what he'd gotten himself into.

As the time for class to begin drew nearer, the rest of the students started trickling in. Mark and Madison arrived together, followed shortly by John. Luke watched as John and Madison exchanged an uncomfortable look, then went to opposite ends of the room without saying a word to each other. Luke briefly wondered what was going on, then slipped back into his own world.

Matthew's entrance was a loud one. It seemed like everyone wanted to congratulate him for his record breaking performance, including Luke's father and Derrick. While Luke looked on from a distance, he did his best to keep the disgust from showing on his face while Matthew soaked in the praise from his peers. Was it possible for Matthew's head to get any bigger?

A glance at the clock showed that it was time for class to start, but Derrick was busy talking with some of the parents. Luke was getting restless. He wanted to get this class over with so he could go see Pops. He paced around with an anxious feeling in his gut. His impatience showed as he drew looks from some of the other students.

Five minutes behind schedule, class started. It began the same way it did the prior Saturday. Another tiring round of cardio followed by some of the basics. When it came time to pair up with a partner, Luke once again found himself searching the room and having to team up with Jeremy again. He didn't have a problem with Jeremy. He was a nice enough guy, but he wished that he could train with someone closer to his own size.

Luke made it through the class a lot easier this time. He was tired, but when the two hour class ended, he was still on his feet and feeling like he could keep going if necessary.

Brad came over and said, "Much better this week. Are you ready for fight class?"

The feeling of dread returned. "Can't we go see Pops? I'll fight next week."

"Don't chicken out on me now. It's only an hour. We'll have all afternoon to see your grandfather."

Luke resigned himself to the fact that he would be fighting, whether he wanted to or not. He sighed and sat against the wall. He saw the other kids putting on shin guards and boxing gloves, so he followed their lead. When he finished putting on his gear, he looked over and saw his dad saying something to Derrick, who nodded slowly. Once again, he knew they were talking about him, but he had no idea what it could be.

Roughly half the students had left and the ones who remained were shadow boxing in front of the mirror or practicing their strikes on one of the heavy punching bags. Not wanting to look like he didn't know what he was doing, Luke mimicked the others by the mirror.

Derrick called for the class to circle around and take a knee while he explained the rules. Everyone would fight a two minute round against three different opponents. No head butts and no kicks, knees or elbows to the head. Other than that, they were free to fight as they wished. If the fight happened to go to the ground, they would continue until a stalemate ensued or until one fighter achieved a dominant position, at which time they would resume the fight on their feet. No winners or losers would be declared. This was just to give the kids some fighting experience.

Luke listened while the churning in his stomach got worse. He checked out who was still left in the class and thought about who he would like to fight. Jeremy was too big. Matthew, Mark and John were too good of friends. Madison and another girl whom he didn't know would probably be easy fights, but he didn't want to fight a girl. The other five students were kids from other schools, so he knew nothing about them, but they all looked athletic and had been doing this much longer than he had. None of the prospects appealed to him. He sighed and hoped for the best.

He hated how nervous he was and didn't want to be there, but at the same time, since there was no escaping it, he wanted to be called first so he could get his first fight behind him. The tug-of-war inside his head was going nowhere, so when Derrick called the first two fighters and he wasn't one of them, he exhaled slowly but got more edgy at the same time.

Two of the more experienced students went to the center of the mat, touched gloves and waited for the timer to sound. The rest sat down at the edge of the mat to watch. Luke's tenseness level went through the roof as he watched the first fight and saw that they were hitting hard.

The second fight saw Matthew take on a much larger opponent, but he did quite well, matching him punch for punch and stopping two take down attempts.

Madison and the other female student went at it with a ferocious array of strikes and kicks. Luke had second thoughts about them being easy fights.

Another fight between two kids that he didn't know sent shivers down his spine as they went at it with a fury that he'd never seen before. Had he bitten off more than he could chew?

As that fight came to a close, he looked around and saw that the only ones left who hadn't fought yet were himself, John, Mark and Jeremy. He didn't like how this was shaping up. When Derrick called John and Mark to the mat, Luke felt a bit of terror run through him as he realized that he would be fighting Jeremy next. Not only did Jeremy outweigh him by at least sixty pounds, but he was considerably stronger than Luke.

Luke closed his eyes and swallowed. When the timer sounded to start the fight between John and Mark, Luke looked on and quietly wished that it wouldn't end.

He suddenly forgot about his fear as he watched Mark come at John with an irate look in his eyes. He threw furious combinations and kicks while John struggled to defend. This surprised Luke. He had always considered John the strongest and most athletic of his group of friends. He'd often joked with his buddies, saying that if the chips were down, he wanted John on his side. Now he stared with wide eyes as Mark was taking the fight to John.

John managed to withstand the barrage, and about a minute into the fight, he grabbed hold of Mark and proceeded to take him to the mat. From there, John's wrestling background took over and he controlled Mark, preventing him from getting back to his feet. Mark's frustration was evident as he repeatedly tried to escape from John's grip, but without the wrestling skills that John possessed, he was unsuccessful.

The timer chimed, signifying the end of the fight. John stood up and held his glove out for Mark to tap, but instead, Mark rose to his feet and shoved him. Derrick immediately rushed between them and quickly reprimanded Mark for his lack of sportsmanship.

Mark and John continued to stare each other down. John had a look of disbelief on his face while Mark's showed nothing but disdain. Luke knew that Mark wasn't happy with how close John and Madison had been getting, but he had no idea that it was this bad.

They went to opposite sides of the mat and Derrick called Luke and Jeremy to fight next. Luke put his mouth guard in and tried not to look as scared as he was. He looked at Jeremy on the other side of the mat and saw how imposing he looked. His breathing became labored and panic was starting to set in. Did Derrick really expect him to fight someone so much bigger?

Luke barely heard the timer but swiftly put his hands up when he saw Jeremy advancing toward him. They lightly touched gloves and started circling the mat.

Luke didn't have a clue as to how to approach this fight. He thought twice every time he wanted to throw a punch, fearing that it wouldn't do any damage and not wanting to be counter punched. Brad was shouting instructions, but he wasn't really listening. He felt very stiff as he apprehensively waited to see what Jeremy would do.

He wasn't sure how long they went around, but it seemed like a very long time. Just when Luke started to relax a little, Jeremy threw a round kick to Luke's left leg, a few inches above the knee. Luke winced as the sharp pain shot through him. He tried to counter with an identical kick, but before it landed, Jeremy hit him with a stiff left jab that was followed by another. His knees buckled a little but he stayed on his feet.

Again, his dad was yelling things out for him to do, but he was too afraid to try them. He started back pedaling, but Jeremy was faster than he looked and stayed on top of him. A right cross connected on his chin, bringing back the bad memory of having his jaw broken by Jude. Jeremy followed up with a one-two combination that sent Luke staggering backward a few steps and then down on his butt.

In his disoriented state, he could hear his father yell out, "Come on, Luke! Get up!"

He looked up and saw Jeremy standing a few paces away, waiting patiently for Luke to get back to his feet, but he had no desire to resume the fight. Feeling dazed, he sat there for a few more seconds, drawing Derrick to the mat.

"Luke! You have to get up and fight back!" When Luke didn't respond, he added, "I know you're scared, but you have to fight through it!"

Slowly, Luke dragged himself to his feet. A few seconds later, he was flat on his back looking up at the lights. As he laid there, he wasn't sure how he got there. Did Jeremy knock him down again? He pulled himself up to a sitting position and looked up at his opponent, but he no longer saw Jeremy standing there. Where Jeremy had been standing, he now saw Jude glaring down at him with a cold look in his eyes.

Quickly regaining his senses, he searched the room for Derrick, finding him off to the side. Trying to appeal to him with his eyes, he desperately wanted Derrick to put an end to the fight, but it was not to be.

"You have to fight back! No one is coming to help you!"

With his spirit crushed, Luke once again rose to his feet. How much longer would this go on? This was the longest two minutes of his life. He just wanted the fight to be over. Demons of fear and doubt were standing in front of him in the form of his opponent!

Getting back to his fight stance, he squared off with Jeremy. Still seeing Jude's face, he hoped the timer would sound so he could escape the onslaught. Just survive, he thought to himself.

From all sides of the room, he could hear the other kids shouting encouragement to him, but it all sounded like a jumbled mess.

Derrick bellowed from the side of the mat, "You have to fight! No one is coming to help you! Fight him! Fight him! Fight him! Go forward! Do not back up! Don't give in to your fears! FIGHT!"

Something caught his eye from the corner of the room. He risked a glance to see what it was and saw Emmanuel standing there. Everything seemed to be going in slow motion as he looked at his Lord and Savior.

Emmanuel didn't say a word, but simply nodded to him, which spoke volumes to Luke.

A rage began boiling inside. He was tired of being timid. He was sick of allowing people to walk over him. While time stood still, he set aside every fear that he'd ever had and made a promise to himself. *No more fear! I am a warrior! I am not a victim! I will fight! I will never break! I will never bow! Fear does not consume me! Fear can't kill me! Fear can't defeat me and I know it now!*

With a resolve that he'd never felt before, he walked forward to face his opponent. Jeremy threw a right, but instinctively, Luke ducked out of the way and circled to his left. Jeremy hurriedly closed the gap and threw a left, which Luke again avoided with a duck and circled around. Bit by bit, confidence arose in him. It didn't take him long to see that he had a significant speed advantage.

He heard Derrick call out, "Nice! Now hit him back! You haven't thrown a punch the whole fight!"

When Jeremy closed in on him again, Luke threw a flurry of punches. Most of them were blocked, but it sent Jeremy backward and Luke felt no fear. Jeremy countered with a round kick that was intended for Luke's ribs, but Luke's wrestling experience suddenly kicked in. He caught the kick and advanced toward him, taking him down to the mat. In no time, he had mounted his opponent and landed two punches to his face as the timer sounded.

As bad as Luke wanted the fight to end just seconds before, he was now a little disappointed that it was over. Now that he had gained the advantage, he wanted to fight some more.

Derrick came out on the mat and said, "Nice finish! That's the kind of aggression I've been looking for since you got here."

Luke tried to suppress a smile but was unsuccessful. It felt great to finally hear some praise from his instructor. Hoping to hear the same from his dad, he was a little saddened when he remained silent.

Walking to the side of the mat, he became aware of how winded he was. He grabbed his water and took a long swallow, then sat with his back to the wall so he could watch the next fight. He peered over to the corner where Emmanuel had been standing just seconds before, but wasn't surprised when he wasn't there anymore.

Before the class concluded, he fought two more times. Once against Mark and the other against John. He was proud of himself for holding his own in both of the bouts.

Despite his exhaustion, and a lingering headache from some of the shots that Jeremy hit him with, Luke felt amazing at the end of class. For the first time in his life, he felt self-assured that if he got into a confrontation, he would be able to handle himself. He still wasn't crazy about the idea of running into Jude in the streets again, but he now had an small arsenal of weapons that he could fight back with. He wasn't scared anymore.

—

The hospital trip was uneventful. Pops was sleeping and showed no signs of waking up, so they cut the stay short with the agreement that they would return later.

Brad offered to buy Luke lunch, which he readily accepted. He was famished after the lengthy Krav Maga class and was eager to eat. Luke offered a few suggestions of places in Benworth, but his dad rejected them all.

"Let's head down to Pittsburgh. I haven't been to Station Square in years and I know they have plenty of good restaurants there."

Luke asked, "Why do you want to go all the way into the city?"

"It's been a while since I've been there and I miss it. Every time I watch the Steelers on TV, I see the aerial shots of downtown and I get a little homesick. I'd really like to go down and see the sights. Besides, I have a little surprise for you."

"What surprise?"

With a mischievous smile, he said, "I'll let you know when we get there."

They hopped in the car and started driving through Benworth and into the neighboring town of Northway, the arch rival of Benworth High School. While they drove, Brad told stories of things he and his friends did when he was Luke's age. With every store, park and restaurant they passed, Brad had a tale to tell about it.

As they went past Northway High School, Brad motioned to the football field behind it and told Luke about the games he played in on that field. Luke enjoyed hearing the stories his dad told and even smiled and laughed a few times.

Once they got through Northway, they got on the freeway and made their way to Pittsburgh. Luke loved coming into the city from this way. As they got close, they rounded a bend in the interstate and the skyline of downtown opened up in front of them. No matter how many times he'd seen it, it always took Luke's breath away.

The talking ceased while they both admired the view as they approached their destination. They were forced to slow down a little as the traffic got heavier. On their left, Luke saw *PNC Park,* the home of the Pirates, and a minute or so later, they eased past *Heinz Field* on their right. Looking into the stadium parking lot, he saw lots of fans tailgating as they awaited the start of the Pitt Panthers football game that was scheduled to be played in a couple hours.

They crossed the Fort Duquesne Bridge and a few seconds later, the Fort Pitt Bridge, just a short distance from the confluence of the Allegheny, Monongahela and Ohio Rivers. They exited the highway and pulled into the parking lot of Station Square, a collection of stores, restaurants and entertainment venues on the south side of the Monongahela.

They parked the car and started walking around. The place was packed. The beautiful autumn day brought a lot of people out to enjoy an afternoon of shopping and dining. After a quick look around, they found a quaint little sports pub to have lunch in.

A circular bar encompassed the center of the room and was surrounded by tables and booths. Big screen TV's were placed sporadically throughout, each showing a different college football game. There was a buzz of activity going on with waitresses rushing to serve the patrons and people cheering for the games. Luke smiled to himself as they found an empty table with a good view of the TVs. He looked from TV to TV, getting updated on all the scores. The atmosphere was fun and he was relishing the experience.

A cute waitress in her mid-twenties came and took their drink order, a coke for Luke and a draft beer for Brad. Luke felt a little giddy as the waitress flirted with him and gave him a wink as she walked off to get their drinks. Although a tad bit embarrassed, he loved the attention.

While looking over the menu, Luke casually asked, "Why do you drink so much?"

Looking surprised, his dad answered, "I don't. At least not any more than the average guy."

Closing the menu and leaning back in his seat, he said, "You just told me this morning that you like to start your day with a beer instead of coffee. I may be young, but I know that isn't normal."

"Maybe not, but I can assure you that I don't have a drinking problem."

"Just remember, I don't have a drivers license, so you have to do all the driving today."

"I know how many I can have and still be safe behind the wheel."

Luke decided to drop the subject as the waitress returned with their drinks. She set them down in front of them and asked, "Are you ready to order?"

Luke said, "I'd like a dozen hot wings with a side of ranch."

His dad responded, "Fish and chips with a bowl of clam chowder."

"Excellent. I'll put your order in right away." As she left, she put her hand on Luke's shoulder and stroked it across his back as she walked away.

Brad smiled and said, "I think she likes you."

As his face turned as red as his hair, he jokingly asked, "Well, who can blame her?"

"I haven't had the chance to ask you since I got here. Do you have a girlfriend?"

"No."

"Anyone you're interested in?"

With a sly grin, he said, "There's a girl from school who has caught my eye."

"What's her name?"

"Rachel. I'm not sure if she likes me or not. She's a sophomore and probably wouldn't want to date a freshman."

"Don't be so sure. Does she know that you like her?"

"I don't know. We talked for a bit a few weeks ago at Mario's after a football game, but she left in a hurry when Mark made her friend angry."

"Tough break. Why haven't you talked to her since?"

"I don't know. I guess I haven't had the chance."

"Haven't had the chance or haven't had the courage?"

Laughing nervously, he asked, "What do you mean?"

"You know exactly what I mean. You attend the same school. You know where she hangs out on Friday nights. If you wanted to let her know how you feel, you've had plenty of opportunities to do so."

Nodding, he replied, "Yeah. I just get a little scared when it comes to approaching girls."

"That's normal. All guys are like that, but just like you faced your fears at class today, you'll have to do the same with girls. Otherwise, you'll spend your whole life lonely."

"Okay. You have my word that the next time I see her, I'll start a conversation with her."

"Cool."

They continued talking about a variety of topics while they waited for the food. For the first time since they met, Luke was actually enjoying his father's company. It was good for him in many ways, but particularly in helping him temporarily forget about Pops condition. It was a nice escape.

The food arrived, along with another round of flirtation from the waitress, causing more embarrassment for Luke. While they ate, they watched and talked about the football games being shown on the screens around them. Luke was having a great time talking to his dad about football. He was impressed by his knowledge of the game.

When the meal was finished, Brad asked him, "You really love football, don't you?"

"It's my favorite sport."

"I already know that the Steelers are your favorite pro team, but who do you root for in college?"

"Pops is a huge Pitt fan, so I've been watching them with him for years."

Reaching into his inside jacket pocket, Brad pulled out a plain, white envelope and set it on the table in front of Luke. "Go ahead and look inside."

Looking skeptical, he asked, "What's this?"

"Just open it."

"Is this the surprise you were talking about?"

"Just open it already."

Luke grabbed the envelope and pulled its contents out. His eyes lit up as he saw what it was. "These are tickets to the Pitt game!"

"That's right. Fifty yard line."

"How did you get these?"

"The guy I was staying with has a few connections."

"This is so cool. I've been to lots of Pirates and Penguins games, and even saw the Steelers play a couple times, but I've never seen Pitt play in person before."

"We better get moving if we're going to make it before kickoff. There's a shuttle that will take us to the stadium. Let's go catch it."

Smiling ear to ear, Luke was filled with excitement as he followed his dad out of the pub. They rode the shuttle bus to the other side of the river and hurriedly found their seats just in time to watch the start of the game.

He enjoyed the full game experience, having nachos and soda while cheering his favorite college team. The only downside was watching his dad order a beer every time the vendor came to their section. At halftime, Luke urged his him to stop drinking so he'd be sober enough to drive home. Brad compromised with him by telling him he'd only have one more, which Luke reluctantly agreed to.

When the final gun sounded, Luke was emotional and physically drained. It had been quite a day. They capped it off by visiting Pops in the hospital and telling him everything that had happened. Pops gave a few faint smiles as he listened, but still looked very feeble in his bed.

Just before they left, Pops called Brad over to his bedside and whispered, "Thanks."

"You're welcome. Thank you for giving me a chance."

"Do me a favor. Make sure Luke gets to Sunday School tomorrow morning."

"Sure."

Luke felt himself get a little teary eyed as he heard this. They said their goodbyes and left to go home. The ride was a quiet one as they were both pretty tired from the long day. Upon getting home, Luke really felt the fatigue hit him as they went inside. He set his alarm clock and was about to get into bed when he saw his dad standing at his bedroom door.

"I really had a great time with you today."

"So did I."

CHAPTER 19

Brad drove into the church parking lot, pulled up to the curb in front of the youth center, and said, "I'll pick you up when it's over."

Luke responded, "Aren't you going in for the church service?"

"No. Church isn't for me."

"You should give it a chance. You might like it. Besides, what else are you going to do on a Sunday morning?"

"I'm going to see my friend. I need to thank him for the Pitt tickets."

"You can do that anytime."

"I know, but I'd feel better if I did it now."

Knowing that he was fighting a losing battle, Luke got out of the car. As his dad's car disappeared from the parking lot, he looked through the hustle and bustle of kids entering the youth center and adults heading to the main sanctuary. He was hoping to find his friends, but they either hadn't arrived yet or were already inside. Eager to tell his buddies about his experience at the Pitt game, he went inside to his classroom.

Zeke was there to greet him. "How's your grandfather doing?"

"He's weak, but I'm hopeful that he'll pull through."

"He's in my prayers."

"Thank you."

Luke found his usual seat next to Mark, who looked uncomfortable as he stared into space. He seemed uninterested as Luke told him about going to the Pitt game. Just when he was about to get frustrated with Mark's lack of attention, Kylie walked in and took the seat to his other side. After a quick hug and greeting, Luke switched gears and told Kylie all about the good time he had with his dad. She listened with a smile and looked as if she were genuinely happy for him.

When the class began, Luke noticed that Matthew wasn't there for the second week in a row. He'd shown up late before, so maybe he would wander in later. Luke leaned back in his chair and listened as Zeke started talking.

It didn't take long before his mind started drifting. Thinking back to the fun he had the day before, and looking forward to visiting Pops in the hospital kept him from paying attention to the lesson. The next thing he knew, Zeke was praying for Pops while the class bowed their heads. Snapping out of his daydream, Luke quickly lowered his head as well.

When the class was dismissed, a few students came to him and assured him that Pops was in their prayers. He did his best to thank them and be polite, but he was anxious to get outside so he and his dad could go visit Pops.

Walking outside, he immediately saw his dad's car parked along the curb. He was surprised to see his dad standing next to the car, talking to Matthew, both of them laughing and joking as though they were long time friends.

Approaching Matthew, he asked, "Why weren't you in class?"

With a lazy shrug, he answered, "I didn't feel like it."

"Where were you?"

"I went over to Chad's and played video games."

Shaking his head, Luke looked to his father and asked, "When are we going to visit Pops?"

"I just invited Matthew over to watch the Steelers. We'll go to the hospital after the game."

Feeling disappointed, Luke suggested, "We could record the game on the DVR and watch it tonight. That way we could spend more time with Pops."

Matthew interjected, "I think Pops would want us to watch the game together, like we always do. Besides, you'll have plenty of time to see him tonight."

His dad added, "Tell your other friends to come over too. It'll be just like every other week."

Not liking what he was hearing, Luke said, "It won't be the same as every other week because Pops won't be there."

Looking irritated, Matthew asked, "What difference does it make if you visit Pops now or tonight?"

"The difference is that my grandfather means a lot more to me than a football game."

His dad came over and put his arm around Luke's shoulder and said, "I understand how you feel, but the chances are that he won't even be conscious when we get there. Let's just go home and watch the game with your friends, then I promise you that we'll go see him as soon as the game is over."

Knowing that he wasn't going to change his dad's mind, he reluctantly agreed and got into the car. They drove home with little conversation.

Once home, Luke sat on the sofa and watched the pre-game show. Mark and John showed up a few minutes apart, but didn't have much to say to each other. Just before kickoff, Matthew walked in and sat in Pops favorite chair.

Throughout the game, Matthew and Brad talked back and forth, both nitpicking and disapproving of every decision the Steelers made, despite the fact that they were building a huge lead.

At halftime, the Steelers held a three touchdown lead, so Luke asked if they could leave for the hospital since the game was a blowout, but his idea was quickly shot down. Luke did his best to stay patient, but it wasn't easy as the second half was the same as the first. Finally the game ended, but instead of being happy that his favorite team won, he was incredibly agitated. All he wanted to do was visit Pops, and no one else seemed to care.

Luke invited his friends to come along and visit Pops at the hospital. John and Mark readily accepted but Matthew declined, saying he had things to do and hastily dismissed himself. Luke was ready to go and waited by the front door, but his dad was taking his time, putting things away in the kitchen.

The sound of the telephone ringing startled Luke. Walking slowly toward it, he said, "We hardly ever get calls on our land line anymore."

Before he got to the phone, Brad beat him to it and answered it. Luke stood and watched for a second, then turned around and plopped back onto the sofa, annoyed by yet another delay. He could hear his father giving a lot of one word answers to whoever he was talking to.

Just when he thought that his patience was coming to an end and he might lose it, he heard the sound of the phone hanging up. Bolting to his feet, he started toward the door.

"Luke, I need you to sit down."

Stopping in his tracks, he turned around and saw a solemn look on his dad's face. Right away, he knew that the phone call contained bad news. A look at his friends showed that they too had concern regarding what Brad was about to say. His legs felt weak as he made his way back to the sofa, where he sat leaning forward with his elbows resting on his knees.

His dad sighed as he sat on Pops' easy chair. "That was the hospital on the phone. Your grandfather has had another heart attack."

"What?"

"I'm sorry."

"Is he still alive?"

"Right now, yes, but they don't expect him to survive the night."

"NO!"

John quickly went across the room to comfort his friend, but Luke brushed him off. With his face turning red and tears filling his eyes, Luke said, "We have to get to the hospital. I have to see him."

Brad got up and said, "Okay. Let's go." Turning to John and Mark, he added, "Their only allowing immediate family to visit him, so maybe you guys should go home."

John, with his cell phone already in his hand, said, "I'm calling my parents so they can get a prayer chain started."

Mark dug into his pocket to get his own phone. "Good idea. I'll do the same."

With tears rolling down his face, Luke responded, "Thanks guys. I'll call you later when we know more."

After a quick hug from his friends, Brad and Luke made a dash for the car and got inside. Ignoring speed limits and barely slowing down at stop signs, they made it to the hospital faster than Luke thought possible. As soon as a parking spot was found, Luke was opening the door before his dad even put the car in park.

Luke was practically running to the entrance, leaving Brad behind, struggling to keep up. Luke darted inside and went straight to the elevator, hitting the up button over and over again in an attempt to make the elevator doors open faster. With his stomach in knots, he did his best to control his emotions while he waited for what was surely the slowest elevator in the world.

In his frustration, he turned around to see if his father had caught up yet, but was instead surprised to see Pastor Alex walking up to him.

"What are you doing here?"

"John's parents called me and told me the news. I came over as soon as I heard."

The elevator door finally opened and they slipped inside. Luke held the door open while Brad jogged up and joined them inside. The number four lit up when Luke punched the button and they felt themselves being lifted up as the elevator took them to their desired floor.

When the doors slid open, Luke exited first and bee lined for Pops' room, with Brad and Pastor Alex close behind. Luke stopped short when he walked inside the room. At first, he thought he had walked into the wrong room, as he didn't recognize the man laying in the bed, but he suddenly realized that it was indeed Pops, but he looked considerably worse than he had the day before. Luke gasped at the realization of how bad it was.

Tubes and wires connected his body to machines that made noises and showed numbers on the screens that Luke didn't understand. Pops was unconscious and if it wasn't for the beeps corresponding to his heartbeat coming from one of the machines, Luke would have been sure that he was dead. Trying to get his mind around what he was seeing, Luke felt his body go numb. This couldn't be happening.

Brad and Pastor Alex followed him in. Luke went to the left side of the bed while Brad and Alex took spots on the opposite side. Pops had the room to himself as the other bed was empty. There were no nurses or doctors around, But Luke was sure they would make an appearance soon.

Once the initial shock of how bad Pops looked wore off, Pastor Alex quietly said, "Let's pray."

Brad and Luke both bowed their heads and closed their eyes as the pastor began praying. Luke could hear his voice but wasn't comprehending what was being said. He felt like he was falling into a dreamlike state. More memories of his childhood filled his mind and it felt like he was reliving them. He even felt himself start to smile a few times as he recalled some of the fun times he shared with his grandfather.

He no longer felt like he was in a hospital room, but rather was in ball fields, parks, and even his own home as he remembered all the great times they had over the years. He simply wouldn't accept that it was ending. Pops wasn't going to die. Not today. Not tomorrow. Not anytime soon. Somehow, someway, Pops was going to pull through and defy the odds.

Luke snapped back to attention as Pastor Alex finished his prayer. "I'm going to give you guys some privacy and get back to my family."

Brad shook his hand and said, "Thanks for coming out. That was very nice of you."

"My pleasure. He's been a very important member of our church for years. This is the least I can do. Call me if you need anything."

Upon Pastor Alex's departure, Brad and Luke stared at each other for a few seconds, neither one knowing what to say. Finally, Luke ended the stare down by grabbing a chair and pulling it next to the bed. He sat down and took Pops' hand in his. He looked down at his grandfather and began speaking out loud, his voice cracking as the tears started to flow.

"Pops, I don't know if you can hear me or not, but you have to listen to me. You have to wake up and get better. I know you still have a lot of years left in you. You can't leave me now."

He paused while his dad handed him some tissues, then stood behind him with his hand on Luke's shoulder.

Luke continued, "Football season isn't over yet, and you have to watch me play. In the winter, you're going to watch me wrestle and in the spring, watch me play baseball. You have to join me at Bible camp next summer. All the kids love it when you're a counselor there."

He stopped talking while the weeping overtook him. He sobbed uncontrollably as his dad rubbed his shoulders, doing his best to comfort his son. After a deep breath, Luke managed to go on, "I know it's still a few years away, but you have to be there when I graduate from high school. You have to be there to see me off to college. You have to be there when I get married. I know you want to be there for these things and it won't be the same if you're not there. This can't be the end!"

His crying prevented him from talking anymore. A minute or two went by, then Luke stood up and hugged his father, burying his face into his chest. Brad wrapped his arms around his son and kissed the top of his head. "I'm so sorry you have to go through this. I wish there was something I could do."

Luke broke the hug and stepped back, looking up into his dad's eyes. "Just being here is enough." They smiled at each other and hugged again, holding it for a couple minutes.

Luke suddenly felt the need to pray by himself, so he said, "I'm going to the restroom."

Brad nodded and said, "Okay. I'll be here."

Luke slipped inside the bathroom, located next to the entrance to the room. He closed the door behind him, lowered the toilet seat and sat down. He closed his eyes and began praying out loud.

"Father God, please let my grandfather live. I don't know what I'll do without him. I'm not scared for him, because I know where he's going after he dies, but I'm not ready to give him up yet. I need him! Matthew, Mark and John need him too. He's too important to us for You to take him away now! I'm begging you to let him live longer!"

More tears stared falling as he fell to his knees. He cried out, "Emmanuel! Where are you? Please come and heal him!"

He wasn't sure how long he stayed on his knees crying, as he lost all sense of time, but it must have been a while because he heard his dad knock on the door, asking, "Are you okay in there?"

"Yeah. I'll be out in a second."

Luke stood up and washed his face in the sink. He took a deep breath and regained his composure. As he came out of the bathroom, he saw his dad standing against the wall with his arms folded. Luke wondered if his father heard him praying, but if he did, he gave no sign of it.

"We should get going. It's getting late. I just talked to the doctor and he promised to call us if there's any change to his condition."

Luke nodded and went back to Pops' side. "Good night Pops. You hang in there and we'll be back tomorrow." He leaned down and kissed Pops on the forehead, then slowly turned around and walked out of the room, glancing back for one last look. He couldn't help but think that this might be the last time he would see him alive. He shuddered at the thought.

They walked side by side down the corridor to the elevator. Once again, they stood there waiting. Luke looked to his dad, who was staring at his shoes while they waited. He looked back down the hallway toward Pops' room and his heart stopped.

Emmanuel was standing outside the room!

Luke's heart stared beating faster than he'd ever felt before. Excitement filled him as he knew exactly why Emmanuel was there. Luke smiled as he and Emmanuel stared at each other from the length of the hallway. The smile was returned as Emmanuel nodded to him, then disappeared inside the room.

The elevator door opened and Brad stepped inside while Luke stood still, gazing toward Pops' room.

"Luke. Come on."

Still grinning ear to ear, Luke casually joined his dad inside the elevator. As they descended to the ground floor, Luke looked to his dad and said, "Pops is going to live."

"I like your enthusiasm, but please don't get your hopes up. You know what the doctor said."

"I don't care what the doctor said. God is going to heal him. I know it!"

With a skeptical look, Brad replied, "I hope you're right. I really do."

The elevator door opened and they walked back to the car and went home in silence, but Luke smiled the whole way.

Once they got home, Luke called his friends one at a time and assured them that Pops would be okay, telling them about seeing Emmanuel and knowing that the healing was already done. They all sounded thrilled to hear the news, even Matthew.

Luke felt relaxed as he went to bed. His sleep was filled with dreams of he and Pops doing all sorts of different things together. The smile remained on his face throughout the night.

CHAPTER 20

Monday morning arrived and Luke laid in bed, feeling more peaceful than he could ever remember. The restful night of sleep had done a world of good and he felt energetic. He was especially looking forward to the JV game that afternoon and was excited to play again.

The house was silent and he wondered if his dad was awake yet. As he got out of bed, the telephone rang. Luke assumed it would be the hospital again, since no one else ever called the house phone.

He started toward the kitchen to answer it but his dad was already there. Luke stood in the center of the living room and watched as his father talked with the phone receiver in one hand and a can of beer in the other. Luke shook his head with disappointment as he saw his dad drinking early in the morning again.

He listened in on his dad's side of the conversation.

"You're kidding!"

"How can that be?"

"That's crazy!"

"That's fantastic news!"

After hanging up, Brad stood there with a disbelieving look on his face. He looked at Luke, who stood there calmly. "Your grandfather is conscious. He's talking, breathing, and eating on his own."

"I know."

"How did you know that?"

"I told you last night that God was going to heal him and He did."

"You know it doesn't work that way."

"Of course it does. How else can you explain this?"

Brad shook his head, went to the kitchen table and sat down. Luke followed him and sat on the opposite side. After a few seconds of silence,

Brad said, "I don't know how it happened. Maybe it was God. I don't really believe in that kind of thing, but something unexplainable happened. I'm just happy that he's going to be alright."

"Me too. When does he get to come home?"

"The doctor isn't sure yet. He's totally stumped. He said he's never seen anything like this before. They want to run some more tests to be safe, but there's a chance that he'll come home tomorrow."

With a huge smile, Luke pumped his fist and said, "Yes! Are you still going to stay here after he comes home?"

"I'd like to, but that will be up to him."

"I'm sure he'll agree to it. I'll be sure to let him know that I want you to stay."

Brad and Luke shared a few laughs together and then it was time for Luke to get ready for school. He was full of joy as he brushed his teeth and got into the shower. He even caught himself singing *How Great is our God,* while washing himself.

He got dressed and ate a bowl of cereal, then watched from the window to see when John and Mark would be coming down the street so he could join them.

When Brad saw him looking out the window, he offered, "I'll drive you to school if you want."

"No. You're drinking."

"I'm okay to drive."

"I'm sure you are, but I'd rather walk with my friends. We do this every day and I like it. Besides, I'm anxious to tell them about Pops. I know they're going to be as excited as I am."

"Alright. If that's what you want. Let me know if you change your mind." He returned to the kitchen, opened the fridge and popped open another can of beer.

Luke thought about saying something about it, but just then, he saw John and Mark as they walked in front of the house. "They're here. You're coming to the JV game this afternoon, aren't you?"

"I'll be there. Have a good day in school."

"I will." Luke dashed out the door, eager to tell his friends about Pops' recovery. Just like he thought, they were thrilled to hear the good news.

When they got to Matthew's house, Luke was a little let down to hear that he was getting a ride from Chad and wouldn't be joining them on their walk to school. Luke, John and Mark enjoyed the walk despite not having their other friend with them. All of them were excited about playing football that afternoon. Luke wasn't sure what he was more enthusiastic about, playing in the game or seeing Pops afterward.

As the school day progressed, Luke caught himself smiling repeatedly. Knowing that Pops was going to be okay made him want to shout out how awesome God is.

When it came time for the JV game, Luke couldn't wait to hit the field. His demeanor had changed so much in the last couple days. His improving relationship with his father, Pops' recovery, and his increasing confidence on the Krav Maga mat had him feel like nothing could stop him.

His play on the field that day couldn't have been better. He caught every pass thrown in his direction and even scored two touchdowns. His blocking on running plays was superb. Benworth won in convincing fashion, and as the game concluded, Luke received a lot of accolades from the coaching staff and teammates alike.

He kept reminding himself that he needed to stay humble. The last thing he wanted was to allow a good football performance to go to his head. He smiled to himself as he thought that Benworth wasn't big enough for two Matthews. Every time he received a compliment, he answered it with, "To God be the glory."

He quickly changed out of his uniform and met his dad out front. He was eager to go see Pops and see for himself how fast his recovery was going. When he greeted his father by the car, Brad was on his cell phone. Upon seeing Luke approaching, he said into the phone, "Do what you can and I'll talk to you later. I have to go."

Closing his phone and shoving it into his front pocket, he turned to Luke and said, "That was some game. Why didn't you play like that a couple weeks ago?"

Luke shrugged and said, "Even the best players in the NFL have their good and bad games."

They got into the car and started driving to the hospital. Curiosity got the best of Luke as he asked, "Who were you talking to on the phone?"

"A friend."

"You hung up pretty quick when you saw me coming. Are you keeping something from me?"

"Not exactly. Let's just say that I might have another surprise for you lined up this weekend."

"What is it?"

"If I told you, it wouldn't be a surprise."

"Come on! Give me a hint at least."

Brad laughed as he replied, "Just be patient. My friend is working on something for me, but there's nothing guaranteed."

Luke let it go and tried to keep his excitement level in check as they got close to the hospital. Rather than show his haste when they parked the car, he calmly walked by his dad's side as they went inside and rode the elevator to the fourth floor. Another casual stroll down the hallway led them to Pops' room.

As they walked in, they were greeted by a huge smile from Pops, who was sitting up in bed, munching on some grapes while watching highlights from yesterday's football games.

"Looks like I missed some good games. Oh well, I'll make up for it next week."

Luke was taken aback when he saw how Pops' appearance. He looked as good as he had before his first heart attack, if not better. Was he actually looking younger? Luke chalked it up to how bad he looked the day before. Once his initial shock wore off, he ran to the bed and hugged his grandfather tighter than he ever had before.

"I'm so glad you're alright!"

"Me too!"

Fighting back tears, Luke said, "I was so scared that I was going to lose you."

"Nope! You're stuck with me for a little longer. God isn't done with me yet."

Luke laughed as the first tear rolled down his cheek. "I knew that God would answer my prayers."

Pops reached over and wiped the tear off Luke's face. "The time for crying is over." Switching his gaze to Brad, he added, "Thank you for watching over him while I was here."

Brad smiled and replied, "Thanks for trusting me."

Luke said, "We went to the Pitt game on Saturday."

"I know. I may have been weak when you told me, but I heard it all. So, tell me about your game this afternoon."

"We won and I scored two touchdowns!"

Pops playfully slammed his fist into the mattress beside him, feigning anger. "Dang it! I missed it! I told these doctors that I'm fine, but they still won't release me."

Brad chuckled and said, "Cut them some slack. They're just being cautious. Just yesterday, they thought you weren't going to make it. To be honest, I'm shocked that you're doing this well."

"God can heal a whole lot faster than these doctors or any medicine."

Luke motioned to his dad, "I told him this morning that God was responsible for your recovery, but he's skeptical."

Pops nodded. "You've never given your life to Christ, have you?"

Brad ran his fingers through his hair, obviously uncomfortable with where the conversation was going. "I've never had any use for religion."

"It's not about religion. It's about a relationship with God. Do you realize that God loves you so much that He sent His only Son to die in your place?"

"Please don't take offense to this, because I know you mean well, but I'm not interested in talking about this. If you want to believe that God healed you, that's fine, but I think there's a more logical explanation that doesn't have anything to do with the supernatural."

"No offense taken, but I can assure you that God is real. Call me crazy if you want, but I know for a fact that God is responsible for bringing me back to health."

"How can you know that?"

Pops' smile widened. "Once again, you're going to think I'm nuts, but Jesus Christ appeared to me in a dream last night."

Luke's ears perked up but he remained silent.

Brad looked at him doubtfully. "A dream doesn't mean anything. You were near death and heavily medicated. You were probably hallucinating."

"Oh, it was no hallucination. It was as real as can be. He stood right here by my bedside."

Luke asked, "Did He say anything to you?"

"He said plenty, but most of it was between Him and myself. What I can tell you is that He told me to eat healthier. He told me to be there to cheer you on as you compete in different sports. He wants me to be a counselor at Bible camp next year. He doesn't want me to miss your graduation. He wants me to see you off to college, and He wants me to be in attendance at your wedding."

Brad shook his head. "Those are all things that Luke said to you last night. It wasn't Jesus. The medication made you think what Luke was saying came from God."

Luke jumped in, "I didn't say anything about his eating."

Pops added, "He also said that Matthew, Mark and John will need me too. Those kids are like family to me."

Turning to his dad, Luke said, "That's something I prayed about by myself, so he couldn't have heard that from me."

Brad didn't respond, but still had a suspicious look on his face.

Luke looked back to Pops and said, "I believe you."

"I know you do." Pops looked back and forth between Brad and Luke. "You never know when God is going to show up, and in what form, so you need to always be ready."

Luke responded, "I know exactly what you mean."

Brad shook his head. "I think it's great that you're better, but I don't think it's a good idea to fill Luke up with false hope."

"False hope? Listen, Brad, you can believe what you want, but God is real and He healed me. The fact that I'm sitting here telling you about Him is all the proof you should need. Keep your eyes open, because He may show up in your life at an unexpected time."

After a few uncomfortable seconds, Luke looked into his grandfather's eyes. "I have something I need to ask you."

"Sure. What is it?"

"Well, I know you'll be coming home soon, and it would mean a lot to me if my father can stay with us until it's time for him to go back to Vegas."

"That will be fine."

Luke looked back to his dad and they smiled at each other.

Pops cleared his throat, getting their attention back to him, then said, "There's no good time or easy way to bring this up, so I'll just ask you. Are you still planning to fight for custody of Luke?"

Looking ill at ease, Brad hesitated before answering, "I want my son to be in my life, especially now that I've gotten to know him over the past couple weeks. I know it won't be easy for you, but I'm sure we could arrange something so the two of you could still see each other."

Luke interjected, "Look, it's been great getting to know you too, but I really want to stay in Benworth. This is my home."

"I really think you'd love Vegas if you gave it a chance."

"But what if I don't? I already love it here. Besides, I already promised you that I'd talk to Rachel the next chance I got. You wouldn't want me to leave after I've started a relationship, would you?"

Brad and Luke both smiled as Pops asked, "Who's Rachel?'

Their smiles escalated into laughter as Luke answered, "She's a girl from school that I like."

Pops sighed. "I was wondering how long it would take before you showed an interest in girls. It's about time."

"Hey! I've liked girls for a long time. I just haven't told you about it!"

Pops joined in the laughter. The mood was suddenly lighter and talk of the custody battle was dropped. After a time of small talk between the three, in which they all shared numerous laughs, Pops finally said, "I don't want you and your friends to miss out on your Bible study. I called Zeke this afternoon, and he agreed to lead the study in my absence. You guys need to get home to let them in."

A surprised Luke replied, "Wow. With everything that's been going on, I'd forgotten all about the Bible study."

Luke hugged his grandfather and they said a quick goodbye. He and his dad left and started on their way back to the house. Luke was amazed at how God was working in his life and couldn't wait to see what He would do next.

—

Luke looked out the window for the third time in about five minutes, prompting his dad to say, "They'll get here soon."

Checking the clock, Luke replied, "They're usually here by now."

He was anxious to tell his friends about how great Pops looked and about the dream, which Luke understood not to be a dream at all, but an actual encounter with Emmanuel.

The Bible study itself was something Luke was excited about too. He smiled to himself as he thought about how much things had changed in such a short amount of time. Just last week, he didn't even want his friends to come over.

He took his spot on the sofa and flipped through a magazine that was sitting on the coffee table. The TV was on, but he wasn't paying it any attention.

Zeke got there first, and after a quick introduction, Brad stated, "I'm curious about what's going on here. If you don't mind, I'd like to sit in and listen."

Zeke replied, "No problem."

Kylie was next to show up. She was her usual bubbly self and seemed extra excited that Pops was going to be coming home soon.

Matthew's appearance surprised Luke. He didn't expect to see him after he'd skipped last week's study and the last two Sunday school classes, but sure enough, he was there acting as if nothing was out of the ordinary.

When Matthew tried to make eye contact with Kylie, she immediately started playing with her cell phone, doing her best to ignore him. Luke didn't like the obvious tension between them and was relieved when the rest of the group started arriving in rapid succession.

Before long, everyone was there and they were ready to begin. Kylie was the last one to take her seat, and as she scanned the room, there were two spots left. One on the sofa next to Matthew, and the other on the love seat next to Mark. She looked back and forth between the two, then plopped down next to Mark.

It was clear to Luke that Matthew wasn't happy with her for choosing to sit with Mark, but he was trying hard to not let it show. Luke couldn't help but think that if Matthew would just stop acting so cocky, everything would be fine between him and Kylie again. He even thought about praying for a humbling experience to bring Matthew's inflated ego back in check.

Zeke opened the study with a prayer, then asked if anyone had any prayer requests.

Luke spoke up first, saying, "Mine has already been answered!"

A round of applause filled the room, with everyone smiling over the good news. When the clapping died down, Zeke said, "What an amazing testimony about the power of prayer. God really did perform a miracle through your grandfather. We're all so happy that he's recovering so well." Looking around the room, he asked, "Anything else?"

Matthew raised his hand, and after a nod from Zeke, said, "The football team has a big game Friday night. We're playing the number one ranked team in the state."

Zeke responded, "Yes. I'm looking forward to watching you guys play. I think it'll be a great game, but don't be too upset if you lose. There's no shame in losing to an undefeated team."

With a look of disgust, Matthew replied, "We need this win. We can kiss the playoffs goodbye if we lose another game. We should be undefeated ourselves. In fact, we would be if Coach King didn't have his head up his butt earlier this season."

"Hey! That'll be enough of that. You don't talk about your coach that way."

"Why not? It's true! Everyone here knows that if I'd played quarterback in the two games we lost, we would've won."

There wasn't a person in the room who wasn't repulsed by what he said. Matthew's arrogance had been taken to a new level. Luke glanced over to Kylie and saw that she wasn't even looking at Matthew. The ghastly look on her face showed true disdain for him.

Even Zeke seemed appalled. Once his initial shock wore of, he suggested, "I think the game is worth praying over, but not the result. We'll pray for the safety of the players."

Matthew retorted, "Yeah. That did a lot of good for my brother."

Ignoring the last remark, Zeke asked, "Any other prayer requests?"

Luke, not wanting to hide his loathing of Matthew's behavior anymore, blurted out, "I think we should pray for everyone in this room to be humble."

Mark jumped in, "I second that!"

While glaring at Matthew, Kylie added, "Me too!"

If Matthew was upset about the comments directed toward him, he didn't show it. He just leaned back in his seat, chewing his gum, and smiling out the side of his face.

In an effort to regain control, Zeke said, "Okay. This isn't getting us anywhere." He reached down into his bag and pulled out a CD. "Maybe we should all keep quiet for a little bit and worship the Lord."

He continued talking as he walked over to the stereo. "I have a CD here from a new artist named Beth Williams. Her CD is entitled, *You can be Loved.* Let's listen to a few songs and invite the Holy Spirit to be here with us."

The music started and Luke closed his eyes, listening to the lyrics and enjoying the angelic voice coming from the speakers.

After the third song, Zeke ejected the CD and returned to his seat. "What did you think of the music?"

Kylie answered, "I loved it. What is her name again?"

"Beth Williams. I was introduced to her music by a friend of mine in Bakersfield, California. He sent me a copy of her CD and I haven't been able to stop listening to it."

Writing the name on a notepad, she said, "I'm going online as soon a I get home and ordering one for myself."

Luke thought to himself that he might do the same. He wondered if the rest of the group enjoyed it as much as he did. A gander around the room showed smiles from everyone, except Matthew, who sat there looking stoic while he chomped on his gum. Luke tried to keep his contempt for him under wrap.

Zeke went back into his bag and retrieved his Bible. "Let's all open to Luke, chapter nine." He gave the kids a few seconds to find the page, then asked, "Will someone start reading aloud, starting with verse eighteen?"

Kylie, always eager to get involved, swiftly raised her hand. Zeke motioned to her with his arm, and she began. *"Once when Jesus was praying in private and his disciples were with him, he asked them, 'Who do the crowds say I am?'*

"They replied, 'Some say John the Baptist; others say Elijah; and still others, that one of the prophets of long ago has come back to life.'

"'But what about you?' he asked. 'Who do you say I am?'

"Peter answered, 'The Christ of God.'

"Jesus strictly warned them not to tell this to anyone."

Zeke interrupted, "Let's stop there for a minute. Why do you think Jesus didn't want his disciples to tell anyone that He is the Messiah?"

Silence engulfed the room as everyone looked around, waiting to see if someone would answer Zeke's question. Luke felt awkward and hoped that he wouldn't get called on.

When no one volunteered to speak up, Zeke went on, "I know it doesn't seem to make sense. The Jewish people had been waiting for centuries for the promised Messiah, and when He finally arrived, He didn't want the public to know who He really was. Now, think about it. Why would He give these instructions to His followers?"

Luke thought about his own experiences with Emmanuel, then sheepishly raised his hand.

"Luke. What do you think?"

"Maybe Jesus thought that no one would believe them."

Zeke gave a slow nod. "That's a possibility, but why wouldn't they believe? He'd been performing miracles all over. He healed the sick, gave sight to the blind, demons were cast out, lepers were cured, the dead were raised, the paralyzed were made to walk again. What more proof did they need?"

John spoke up, "I think the people had preconceived notions about who the Messiah would be, and Jesus didn't fit them."

"Very good deduction. He still had a lot more to teach the people before He could reveal who He really was."

Josiah, who had been silent up until now, asked, "What did He have to lose? Not too many believed Him when He finally did make known who he was, so why wait?"

Madison answered, "Because He still had a lot of time left in His earthly ministry. If the people got wind of it too soon, then they might have had Him killed before His work was finished."

Zeke's eyes widened. "Another great insight. Let's get back to what John touched on. The Jewish people of that time had preconceived notions of what Messiah would do, most of which were false. What were some of them?"

Carli was quick to offer her thoughts. "They expected Him to be a political leader who would usher in a revolution against Rome."

"Exactly! The Jews desperately wanted to be out from under Roman tyranny. One of the names that they had for the promised Messiah was 'Deliverer.' They believed that Messiah would be a political, or possibly military leader, that would deliver them from Rome and bring Israel back to prominence."

Mark asked, "So they had the wrong idea of what 'Deliverer' meant?"

"Yes. They didn't realize that He was going to deliver them from their sins. They had it all wrong and Jesus knew it, so He had to keep His identity from the general public to prevent them from demanding that He lead a coup."

Zeke paused to look around, and when he was sure that they understood, he said, "I think it's time to move on. Carli, would you pick up where we left off? Start with verse twenty-two and read through verse twenty-seven."

Carli looked down to her Bible, resting in her lap. *"And he said, 'The Son of Man must suffer many things and be rejected by the elders, chief priests and teachers of the law, and he must be killed and on the third day be raised to life.'*

"Then he said to them all: 'If anyone would come after me, he must deny himself and take up his cross daily and follow me. For whoever wants to save his life will lose it, but whoever loses his life for me will save it. What good is it for a man to gain the whole world, and yet lose or forfeit his very self? If anyone is ashamed of me and my words, the Son of Man will be ashamed of him when he comes in his glory and in the glory of the Father and of the holy angels. I tell you the truth, some who are standing here will not taste death before they see the kingdom of God.'"

Zeke observed the kids' reactions to the passage, then asked, "Does anyone have any comments about what we just read?"

After a few seconds of an uncomfortable hush, where they all looked around at each other, waiting to see if someone else wanted to speak, Mark at long last said, "Not only did Jesus know that He would die, but He talks about taking up your cross, so He also knew how He would die."

In a confused manner, Josiah asked, "What does taking up your cross mean? Jesus isn't asking everyone to die in the same way that He did, is He?"

Zeke answered, "No. He used it as an analogy. Like I mentioned earlier, Israel was under Roman rule at this time, and their preferred method of execution was crucifixion, so they were all familiar with it. Not only was Jesus predicting how He would be killed, but was also teaching His disciples in a way that they would comprehend."

Still unsure, Josiah inquired, "Then what did He mean by it?"

Zeke responded, "That's a good question. What do you guys think?"

John was quick to answer, "Before He says anything about the cross, He says that we must deny ourselves. It sounds to me like He's telling us to put Him first in our lives, no matter how much the world is telling us not to."

Madison added, "A few verses later, He talks about gaining the whole world, but forfeiting your very self. I think what Jesus is trying to tell us is that there will be a lot of tempting and alluring things out there, but they'll just take us away from God. We're better off ignoring those things and focusing on God."

Zeke smiled. "Very good. What are some of those tempting and alluring things?"

The kids began throwing out answers.

"Money."

"Fame."

"Drugs and alcohol."

"Sex."

Then Zeke asked, "Why are these things so tempting?"

Kylie replied, "One of the biggest reasons is because TV and movies glorify them so much."

"Very true. Anything else?"

John said, "Peer pressure."

"A big one. Now, how do we keep ourselves from falling victim to these things?"

Once again, the responses came quick.

"Pray more."

"Read our Bibles."

"Talk to our parents about it."

"Call a friend for advice."

Zeke closed his Bible and said, "I think you guys got it. You have the tools to avoid these temptations, now it's up to you to use them. Also, if any of you need to talk about anything, I'm here for you. You all know how to get a hold of me."

Zeke said a prayer over the kids and closed out the study. Shortly thereafter, the parents started showing up to pick the kids up, and before long, it was just Luke and Brad left in the house.

Luke asked his father, "What did you think about the study?"

Brad nodded and said, "I think it's great that you and your friends do this. I'm still not into all this religious mumbo jumbo, but I guess it beats going out and getting into trouble like I did at your age." After a brief pause, he asked, "What's with Matthew? Has he always been that arrogant?"

"No. He was one of the nicest, most down to earth guys I've ever met until he won the starting quarterback position. That was when all the upperclassmen started showing him a lot of attention and it went straight to his head."

"Do me a favor. Don't ever act like that."

Luke chuckled and said, "I thought you liked him."

"At first, I did. I was even secretly wishing that you could be more like him. Now, I couldn't be happier that you're not."

With a smile, he dismissed himself and went to his room to do some school work. When he finished, he dropped to his knees and thanked God, not only for healing Pops, but for bringing his father back into his life. Even with the possibility of having to move to Las Vegas looming over his head, he felt an inner peace like he'd never felt before. Somehow, he knew that it would all turn out okay. He was willing to take up his cross and take it wherever God led him.

CHAPTER 21

Football practice ended on Tuesday and Luke was anxious to get home. During the brief time between the end of school and the start of practice, Luke had checked his phone and read a text message from his dad, telling him that Pops had been released from the hospital and was home.

His first inclination was to skip practice and go home to see his grandfather, but he knew that Pops would want him to practice, so he stayed.

Hurriedly changing back into his street clothes, he started to get irritated with John and Mark for not changing fast enough.

"Hurry up, guys! I want to get home and see Pops."

John cracked a smile and said, "Relax. Do you think it would be okay if Mark and I came over for a little bit. We'd love to see Pops."

"I'm sure he'd love that."

"Cool. Let me call my folks and let them know I'll be a little late."

Matthew came over and asked, "Did I hear you right? Pops is home?"

"Yeah. He went home earlier today. I'm in a hurry to get home, but these guys are taking their sweet time."

"You guys should come with me. I'm getting a ride home from Chad and Brock. Chad's got a pretty big car, so I'm sure we could all fit."

Turning to the others, Luke called out, "Get a move on. We're getting a ride with Chad."

Five minutes later, they were all in the parking lot, piling into Chad's car. It was a tight fit, but they all managed to squeeze in.

As they drove off, Luke ignored the small talk that was going on as he let his mind wander. He was desperately hoping that the animosity that Pops and his dad had for each other a week or two ago would come to an end. With the exception of their differences about faith, they seemed to be getting along pretty well at the hospital.

His biggest desire was for the two of them to become friends so they could all do things together. Even though his dad was planning to go back to Las Vegas in a week, he knew there would be a lot of opportunities for the three of them to bond and have fun together in the upcoming years. Even if Luke would have to relocate to Vegas, he still wanted his dad and grandfather to have a good relationship.

Closing his eyes, Luke silently prayed for hearts to be changed and for all the bad blood to be forgiven and forgotten.

His eyes opened quick when he heard Matthew exclaim, "There's Jude, and he's by himself! Pull over!"

Sure enough, there was Jude on the right side, walking toward them with a cigarette protruding from his lips and his hands stuffed into the pockets of his blue jean jacket.

With screeching tires, Chad suddenly stopped the car by the curb. In no time, Matthew, Chad and Brock were out of the car and confronting Jude on the sidewalk.

Luke, along with John and Mark, stayed inside, watching out the window. Luke wasn't sure how he felt about this situation. He wasn't scared because he knew that his friends had his back, but he didn't really like what he was seeing either.

John nudged Luke and said, "Let's go out."

Luke didn't want to get out of the car. He couldn't see anything good coming from this. Slowly, he followed John and Mark out of the car and watched what was going on.

Jude stood still, looking like a deer caught in the headlights. Chad and Brock flanked him while Matthew boldly walked right up to him.

"Where are your friends, Jude? Huh? Where are Ethan and Scott?"

When Jude didn't answer, Matthew continued taunting him. "Oh yeah! They don't hang out with you anymore, do they? They finally wised up and saw what a loser you are."

For the first time ever, Luke actually saw fear in Jude's eyes. The bully was becoming the victim and he had nowhere to run. It was hard to feel sorry for him, knowing all the things he'd done in the past, but Luke still had a check in his spirit about this. Even if Jude deserved what was coming, Luke didn't want to be a part of it.

Matthew gestured toward Luke and Mark, then continued, "You see my friends over there? The ones you jumped and beat a few weeks ago? Well, what goes around comes around! Revenge is going to be sweet!"

Chad and Brock grabbed hold of Jude, pinning his arms behind his back in a painful manner. As Jude struggled against them he grunted, "You'll never get away with this!"

Matthew got right in his face and shouted, "What are you going to do about it?" He followed that with an open hand slap across his face, creating a loud cracking noise that echoed down the street.

Chad howled with laughter as Brock yelled, "Nice shot!"

Jude glared back at him, but he knew he was helpless. He continued to try to wriggle free, but after Brock lifted a knee into his ribs, he reluctantly accepted his circumstance and fell to his knees.

As much as he didn't want to, Luke started to feel some compassion as he watched Jude's predicament. Jude looked pathetic and weak as he kneeled before them with his head hanging down, allowing his stringy hair to fall over his eyes. Chad and Brock still had a tight grip on his arms, not giving him an opportunity to escape.

All Luke could think was how wrong this was. Despite the fact that Jude had mistreated them for years, he didn't feel right about this. A glance to John and Mark indicated that they felt the same way.

Not wanting to see anymore, Luke stepped forward and said, "Alright. That's enough. Let's get going."

Matthew spun around to face Luke. "Are you crazy? This is our chance to get even with this jerk!"

Luke shook his head. "I don't like this."

"What are you afraid of?"

"I'm not afraid of anything, but this isn't right!"

Matthew waved him away and turned back to Jude. "Pick him up!"

Chad and Brock complied and lifted Jude back to his feet. Matthew ran up to him to get some momentum and delivered a powerful kick to Jude's groin, doubling him over and forcing a moan. While he was still hunched over, Matthew grabbed the back of his neck and brought his knee up, connecting solidly with his nose, just like he'd been taught in Krav Maga class.

Jude fell back to his knees, and probably would have collapsed forward if Chad and Brock hadn't still been holding on to him. Matthew grabbed a fistful of hair, jerking his head up and revealing a trickle of blood coming from his nostril. Jude kept spitting in an effort to keep the blood out of his mouth.

The cigarette that Jude had been smoking had fallen on the sidewalk in front of him, still smoldering. Matthew picked it up and held the lit end about a half inch from Jude's eye, causing him to blink and squirm. In a mocking voice, he said, "Don't you know that smoking is bad for you? Let me put it out for you!"

Still having a firm grip on his hair, he put the cigarette as close as he could to Jude's eye without actually touching it. Jude pleaded, "Don't do it!"

"Why not? If anyone deserves this, it's you!"

"Come on, man! This isn't funny!"

"I'm not trying to be funny. Just like you weren't being funny all the times you picked on me and my friends. Now, if you apologize, I won't blind you." Looking back to his friends, he asked, "Doesn't that sound fair?"

Luke shook his head and said, "Let him go. You've done enough."

Matthew fixed his gaze back on Jude. "Oh no! I'm just getting started! I'll give you five seconds to say you're sorry. If you don't, you'll be in a world of pain! Five, four---"

"Screw you!"

Luke yelled, "Don't do it, Matthew!"

Chad followed it with, "Yes! Do it!"

"Three, two---"

"You're crazy, man!"

"One!"

Jude's voice cracked as he cried out, "I'm sorry! I'm sorry!"

Matthew flicked the cigarette off to the side, into the grass next to the sidewalk. He lowered his head to put his face just above Jude's. "I could kill you if I wanted, but you're not worth it!" He shoved his head backward as he walked away. He went back to Luke, looked him in the eye, then pointed back to Jude and said, "Go get your revenge!"

Luke just stood there, not sure what to do. He looked to John for help, but he had a blank look on his face.

Chad and Brock started shouting out encouragement to him, urging him to follow Matthew's lead. Matthew shouted out, "What are you waiting for? Don't you remember when he kicked your butt? This is the chance we've all been waiting for! Don't waste it!"

Brock added, "You may never have an opportunity like this again. Take advantage of it!"

Luke felt his blood start to boil. All the years of abuse rushed through his mind. His hands involuntarily balled up into fists. With Matthew, Chad and Brock egging him on, he began walking toward his helpless foe. Rage welled up within him as he walked up to Jude, who by now had recovered enough to rise back to his feet.

Matthew was now beside himself with anticipation, bellowing, "Hit him! Hit him now!"

Just like in fight class, he could feel something changing inside of him. He could hear his inner voice rise up, shouting in his head. *I will not be bullied anymore! This guy has scared me for the last time! This guy has hurt me for the last time! Never again will I fear this pitiful excuse for a man! I refuse to live in fear anymore!*

The time for feeling sorry for him had passed. He was almost enjoying the look of terror in Jude's eyes. Despite the chaos that was going on with the others yelling and screaming for him to take his years of frustration out on the bully, everything seemed to get quiet. All of his emotions were calling for him to absolutely thrash his adversary, but yet he stood there doing nothing. There was fire in his eyes and his hatred of Jude consumed him.

Without even realizing that he was doing it, he positioned his body into the fight stance that Derrick had taught him. He cocked his right hand back, getting ready to unload. Jude cringed, awaiting the impact.

Something caught Luke's eye to his right. He looked over to a nearby house and saw Emmanuel standing on the porch. With a very concerned look on his face, Emmanuel passionately shook his head, doing his best to let Luke know that he didn't approve of what he was about to do.

Luke froze. All of the anger suddenly left him. He dropped his hands to his side and exhaled slowly.

Matthew shouted out again, "Hit him! What are you waiting for?"

He could hear what Matthew was saying, but it was drowned out by his inner voice, except this time, it wasn't shouting. Instead it was very calm and controlled. *I don't have to do this! I'm not going to stoop to his level! Emmanuel loves him as much as he loves me!*

Luke casually closed the distance between himself and Jude, put his face inches away, and softly said, "I forgive you."

He turned on his heels and went back to the car. John walked over and put his hand on his shoulder, letting him know that he'd done the right thing in his eyes.

Matthew, on the other hand, was furious. "Don't let him off the hook! Get back over here and kick his butt!"

Luke looked back at him. "It's just like you said. He's not worth it."

"You're just going to let him get away with what he did to you?"

"Not like this."

Luke looked back to the porch, but just as he expected, Emmanuel was no longer there. He stood next to Chad's car and waited for the others.

He could hear Matthew trying to get Mark and John to do something, but they too, declined. He watched as Chad and Brock released Jude, who took the opportunity to get away in a hurry. Luke watched him rush off, lighting another cigarette as he did.

Brock walked up to Luke and asked, "Why are you such a wimp?"

Luke felt shocked and embarrassed. "I'm not a wimp!"

"Only a wimp would do what you just did."

"Only a coward would do what you just did!"

Brock shoved Luke backward. "Who are you calling a coward?"

John quickly jumped between them. "Cool it! Both of you!"

They continued staring at each other until Chad said, "It's getting late. Let's get going."

Chad and Brock got back in the car, but Luke started walking down the street. Matthew called out, "Where are you going?"

"I'm walking the rest of the way."

"Why?"

Luke turned back around and faced Matthew. Pointing to Chad and Brock, he said, "I don't like those guys. If you want to be friends with them, that's your decision, but I don't want anything to do with them. I'm walking home. You guys are welcome to join me."

John and Mark wasted no time in standing next to Luke. Matthew stood there with a confused look. He looked back to the car, then said, "Don't you want to see Pops? We can get there a lot faster if we take the ride."

Luke stuck to his guns. "I don't care."

Matthew's indecision lasted a few more seconds before he slowly walked back to the car and climbed inside. Luke refused to look as they drove past.

Luke shuddered at the thought of what he may have done if he hadn't spotted Emmanuel when he did. As much as he disapproved of the way Matthew had been acting lately, he came within a whisker of doing something similar. Yes, he'd made the right decision in the end, but he still felt shame for even thinking about retaliating. It was one thing to defend yourself from danger, but another entirely to tee off on someone who was helpless.

The walk home started off in silence, which was fine with Luke. He didn't feel like discussing what just happened, but he was grateful that Mark and John stuck by him. They didn't get far before Luke heard footsteps behind him. Spinning around with his hands up to protect himself, he expected to see Jude coming for him, but was relieved when he saw that it was Emmanuel.

"Relax. It's just me."

Luke let out a small laugh. "I should've known."

The three took turns giving Emmanuel a warm hug, each pleased to see him. They began walking together, each wondering what Emmanuel had to say. They didn't have to wait long.

"That was quite an altercation you had there."

Mark asked, "Did you see it?"

"I sure did."

John said, "You know, as much as I wanted to see Jude get what's coming to him, I found myself feeling sorry for him."

"That's because you have a compassionate heart. The way you helped your friend Tim a few weeks ago showed that."

"Yeah, but Tim is a great guy. Jude's been giving us a hard time for as long as I can remember."

"It doesn't have anything to do with them, but rather what's in your heart. Do you understand?"

John nodded. "I think so."

Luke asked, "Jude isn't going to let this go, is he?"

"Only time will tell, but I think you guys will be able to handle yourselves from now on. I'm proud of you three for not taking advantage of the situation."

John said, "I just couldn't bring myself to hurt him. He looked so helpless and pitiful."

Luke added, "A part of me wanted to, but I felt like I wouldn't be any better than him if I did."

Emmanuel smiled. "It's good to see that you have that kind of conviction about it. It shows me that the Holy Spirit is working inside of you." Turning to Mark, he asked, "How are your parents getting along?"

"Terrible. They argue every night."

"Are you doing okay with it?"

"I guess."

"How about your brother and sister?"

"I talk to Madison now and then. She seems like she's got it under control."

"What about Jacob?"

"He's having a tough time. He hides out in his bedroom whenever they fight. I go in sometimes to see if he wants to talk, but he shuts down. I'm worried about him."

"Is it just how he responds to your parents' fighting that has you worried?"

"No. He's been complaining about being sick a lot. My mom thinks he's just acting out to get attention."

Luke said, "I remember when we are watching football at your house. He said his stomach was hurting."

Mark replied. "Yeah. He says that a lot."

Emmanuel nodded slowly. "You might want to tell your folks to take him to the doctor."

"Why? Is it something serious?"

"I can assure you that he's not just acting out, like your mother seems to think."

Mark looked concerned as he said, "I'll mention it to my parents."

"Good. I've got one more thing to say before I go. Be there for Matthew. You guys are his true friends and he's going to realize that soon."

John shook his head and asked, "What's gotten into him?"

They waited for an answer but were greeted with silence. When they looked to see what was taking Emmanuel so long to answer, he was gone.

—

When they got to Luke's house, Matthew was waiting for them on the porch steps. He asked, "Is it still okay for me to see Pops?"

"Of course."

Luke burst through the front door. His dad and Pops were seated in the living room. Pops bounced out of his chair and gave his grandson a huge hug. John, Mark and Matthew followed and each took their turns embracing Pops. Luke found himself wanting to cry again and he saw that John and Mark were teary eyed as well. Although Matthew smiled at the sight of Pops, his eyes remained dry.

His cheer was taken down a notch when he saw the bottle of beer in front of his dad. He couldn't help but wonder what Pops was thinking about it. Over the years, Pops was adamant that he didn't want alcohol in his home.

The smile on Pops' face showed that he was overjoyed that Luke's friends took time out of their busy day to see him. He asked around to find out what everyone wanted to drink, then retreated to the kitchen to accommodate them.

While they waited, Brad asked, "How was practice?"

Luke shrugged. "Typical practice. Coach worked us hard as usual."

Matthew chimed in, "We had an interesting encounter on the way home."

"Yeah, what happened?"

As Pops returned with the drinks, Matthew recounted the events that took place with Jude, but conveniently left out the part where he threatened to extinguish the cigarette in Jude's eye, but was quick to inform them that Luke walked away from the situation. He looked smug as he finished the story.

Brad asked his son, "Why didn't you hit him? If anyone has it coming, it's that guy."

"I didn't feel right about it."

"He would've done it to you. In fact, he has."

"I didn't like the fact that he was being held down. It would've been different if he was a threat, then I would've defended myself, but I'm not going to hurt somebody who can't defend himself. It's just not right."

Brad looked confused, but didn't say anything else.

Pops said, "I wasn't there to see it, but from what I can gather, you made the right choice. I'm proud of you."

Luke smiled while Brad just shook his head.

After a few minutes, Matthew excused himself and went home. John and Mark stayed a little while longer, but then they left as well.

Once he said goodbye to his friends, Luke said, "I'm hungry. What's for dinner?"

Another smile crept across Pops' face. "Remember a couple weeks ago, you suggested that we have a big salad for dinner? Well, Jesus told me to start eating healthier, so I made the salad this afternoon."

Pops ran to the kitchen and a few seconds later he reappeared with a large bowl with all the fixings.

Luke couldn't help but laugh. The three of them gathered around the table and each had two platefuls of the most delicious salad Luke ever tasted. They talked about the one thing they all had in common; their love of football.

They talked about Benworth's big game against Allbridge on Friday night, Pitt's game against Notre Dame on Saturday, and the Steelers game against the Patriots on Sunday. Luke thought about how great it was going to be to have such an awesome weekend to spend with his dad and grandfather.

He felt like he had weathered the storm, but couldn't stop thinking about Matthew. He wanted his friend back. It seemed to Luke as if Matthew was going through a storm of his own, but wasn't even aware of it. Before going to sleep that night, Luke prayed, asking God to do whatever it takes to bring Matthew back to his old self.

CHAPTER 22

The town of Benworth was full of life with anticipation. The showdown with number one ranked Allbridge was only a day away. Schools, grocery stores, bars, barber shops, and gas stations were buzzing with talk about the big game. Most were in agreement that the Eagles had an excellent chance to pull off the upset.

Matthew loved the encouragement he received from students and adults alike wherever he went, but didn't like that they were considered the underdogs in the game, despite the fact that Allbridge was unbeaten. Benworth would have the home field advantage, and Matthew believed that they would be undefeated as well if he'd been playing quarterback all along. He truly believed in his heart that the Eagles were the better team, and he couldn't wait to get on the field to prove it.

After a relatively easy football practice, Matthew completed his homework quickly. He was feeling anxious and didn't feel like staying home. He remembered that the church youth group was tonight, and even though he skipped it the past two weeks, he felt the urge to go.

A look at the clock showed that his friends would have already left, so he asked David for a ride with him and his friends. A few minutes later, Hunter pulled up with Dylan. David and Matthew got in the backseat and they headed to the church.

They talked excitedly about the game, all of them pumped up about such a big match-up. Matthew couldn't help but feel bad for his brother, knowing that it was probably driving him crazy that he couldn't play.

Dylan kept emphasizing how important the game was and how difficult it would be to make the playoffs if they lost. To Matthew, losing was unthinkable. He couldn't remember the last time he'd lost as a starting quarterback. Of course they would win and make the playoffs. He knew that with this win, all the talk about the state championship that was going around at the beginning of the season would return. He was feeling invincible and believed that he was the man to get the job done.

Hunter found a parking spot and they shared some laughs as they walked to the building. As they went through the door, Matthew was in the rear. Just as he was about to follow the others inside, he saw someone approaching from the corner of his eye.

It was Emmanuel!

Matthew allowed the door to close before him as he stood there watching Emmanuel walk toward him. He wasn't sure how he felt about it. The last time they talked, it hadn't gone well. Not sure what to say he asked, "What are you doing here?"

"I came to see you. Can I have a few minutes of your time?"

He glanced inside the window to make sure no one was looking, then answered, "I guess, but not here. Let's walk down the street."

Emmanuel agreed and they walked slowly, side by side. After an awkward silence, Emmanuel asked, "Are you still angry with me for not taking your hangover away?"

"Not really."

"Tell me what's on your mind."

"Is this really why you're here? You just want to shoot the breeze?"

Emmanuel frowned. "What's happened to you?"

"Nothing. I've never been better."

"You realize that Luke, Mark and John are disgusted with you, right?"

"It's not my fault that they're jealous."

"I don't think they're jealous at all. In fact, I know that they're happy for your accomplishments on the football field. What they don't like is how arrogant you've become."

Matthew wheeled around to face him. "I'm not arrogant!"

"No? When is the last time you had a conversation that didn't revolve around yourself?"

Matthew's face reddened with anger as he glared back at him.

Emmanuel continued, "Luke needed you these past couple weeks and you were so selfish that you ignored him completely, even after I specifically told you to help him."

"I'm not his babysitter!"

"No, but you are his friend. Don't you remember our talk about the book of Daniel? I told you that your friends were about to go through fiery trials and I wanted you to be the one to help them cope. I'm very disappointed in the way that you handled this."

Matthew felt incredible frustration. "Why do you have to bother me with this now? I'm twenty-four hours away from the biggest game of my life. I don't need this distraction right now."

"This is just one of many football games you will play in your life, and it's not more important than your best friends."

"Best friends? You just told me that they're disgusted with me. I have plenty of other friends. I don't need them."

"Luke, Mark and John may not be happy with you now, but they're the ones who will be with you through thick and thin. This new group that you've been socializing with aren't nearly as loyal."

"Of course they are. What are you talking about?"

"They're just clinging to your coattails because of your popularity. Luke, Mark and John truly care about you. I would recommend that you do what you have to in order to save your friendship with them."

"I haven't done anything wrong!"

"Do you really believe that?"

"Yes! Do you have anything helpful to say to me or are you here just to berate me?"

"Do you want advice about Kylie?"

Matthew stopped short. "What about her?"

"Your attitude is the reason why she doesn't want to see you anymore. It's not too late to change that."

"I don't need her. Do you know how many girls there are in this school that like me?"

"Like Alyssa? Kylie is someone who will love you for the right reasons. The rest of them will like you only because you're the starting quarterback. It won't mean anything. You can say what you want, but I know your heart, and I know that Kylie still has a firm grip on it."

Matthew felt his heart break a little. He knew that what Emmanuel said was true, but he didn't want to admit it. His pride got the best of him as he blurted, "It's her loss. If she thinks she could do better, she can go ahead and try."

Emmanuel sighed. "I know that's not how you really feel."

"Why are you giving me such a hard time?"

"I'm not here to give you a hard time. I see you going down the wrong path and I love you too much to just sit back and watch it happen."

"What am I doing that is so wrong?"

"You're turning your back on your friends when they need you the most. You're arrogant. You've developed a mean streak. Should I go on?"

"A mean streak? What are you talking about?"

"You were a second away from putting a lit cigarette in Jude's eye!"

Matthew's jaw dropped before answering, "I wasn't really going to do it. I was just trying to scare him. Anyway, he would've deserved it. He would've done it to me if the situation was reversed."

"My Father still has hope for him. Jude knows that you're a Christian and you were not a good witness at that time. He already believes that Christians are hypocrites and you helped reinforce that notion. Thankfully, Luke did the right thing."

"What? Luke wimped out! How is that doing the right thing?"

"He showed compassion and forgiveness."

"He showed weakness! Jude will never mess with me again because I fought back. Luke will still be a target!"

"Don't be so sure."

"I'm very sure. You'll see! Why do you care about a jerk like Jude, anyway?"

"I love him as much as I love you."

"Do you really think he'll ever accept you?"

"It's happened to worse men than him."

"Like who?"

"The apostle Paul, for one."

"What?"

"Haven't you read the book of Acts? Paul, or Saul, as he was called at the time, was killing Christians before I appeared to him. He repented and went on to be the most effective witness of his time. He even wrote two thirds of the New Testament."

"Yeah, but you don't know Jude the way I do. He'll never change."

"Actually, I know him much better than you do. Just like you're changing for the worse, he can change for the better."

Matthew glared at him. "How can you say that? I see nothing wrong with who I am!"

"I warned you a few weeks ago not to let your football success go to your head, and that's exactly what you let happen. Everything you have can be taken from you in an instant."

"Nothing will be taken from me because I won't let it happen. Now, if you'll excuse me, I have a youth group to attend." He turned and went back in the direction of the church, leaving Emmanuel standing there. He called back over his shoulder with a contemptuous tone, "My fans are expecting me. I don't want to disappoint them!"

He continued walking briskly, refusing to look back. He was furious with Emmanuel and wasn't going to give him the chance to get in the last word.

—

Luke was singing along to the last song of the worship segment of the youth group. As the music died down, the door popped open and Matthew barged in, making sure that everyone saw him.

Zeke was getting his notes ready to begin his teaching while Matthew drifted across the front of the room, looking intently at Kylie, who was sitting in the front row. She stared straight ahead, refusing to make eye contact with him. He eventually came to rest at the back of the room, next to Hunter, Dylan and David. He had a smirk on his face as he leaned back in his seat and put his foot on the empty chair in front of him.

Luke listened to the murmurs around the room as people talked among themselves while they waited for the lesson to begin. Sitting between Mark and John, he kept to himself and silently prayed that Zeke's teaching would be directed at Matthew.

The room fell silent as Zeke started speaking. "Tonight, we're going to talk about the sin of pride."

Luke had to stifle a laugh. He glanced behind him to see Matthew's reaction, but was disappointed to see that he still had that same smug look on his face.

Zeke went on, "I looked up the word pride in the dictionary, and here is what it said. 'A high or inordinate opinion of one's own dignity, importance, merit, or superiority, whether as cherished in the mind or as displayed in bearing, conduct, etcetera.'"

He paused for a second to let it sink in, then said, "I'm proud to be an American." He waited a few more seconds, then asked, "Have I just sinned by saying that?"

Blank stares greeted him, then he asked, "What about if your parents say they're proud of you for getting good grades? Have they sinned?"

More silence came from the students. Zeke chuckled, then said, "How about a Bible verse to help us out. 2 Corinthians 7:4 says, 'I have great confidence in you; I take great pride in you. I am greatly encouraged; in all our troubles my joy knows no bounds.' Did Paul sin by writing that?"

David raised his hand, then spoke up, "I don't think so. He wasn't being prideful about something he had done. He was simply happy that the people of Corinth were doing the right thing. The same applies to your previous question. If my parents say they're proud because I get good grades, they're just saying that they're happy about it. As for being proud to be American, once again, that's not something that any of us have accomplished. We're Americans by birth, so there's nothing wrong with saying that."

Zeke smiled and nodded. "It's a tricky word. One that can easily be misused. Let's see what else the Bible says about pride. We're going to look at a few verses in the book of Proverbs. We'll start with Proverbs 8:13."

Those who had their Bibles with them began flipping through the pages to find the passage. Zeke gave them a minute or so to locate it, then read aloud, "'To fear the Lord is to hate evil; I hate pride and arrogance, evil behavior and perverse speech.' 11:2 says, 'When pride comes, then comes disgrace, but with humility comes wisdom.' 13:10 says, 'Pride only breeds quarrels, but wisdom is found in those who take advice.' One of the more popular scriptures is found in 16:18, 'Pride goes before destruction, a haughty spirit before a fall.' And finally, 29:23 says, 'A man's pride brings him low, but a man of lowly spirit gains honor.'"

Zeke set his Bible down on the podium, then paced back and forth in front of the class. "Anyone have any comments?"

Kylie's hand went up quickly. "The first verse you read mentioned arrogance. That's what I think of when I hear the word pride."

John added, "I agree. I think that instead of calling it the sin of pride, it should be called the sin of arrogance."

Zeke answered, "Pretty good deductions. You're definitely on the right track. When you start taking credit for your accomplishments, instead of giving God the credit, then you're guilty of pride."

Luke resisted the urge to turn around again and see how Matthew was reacting to this, but didn't want to be obvious about it. Instead, he silently prayed that the message would get through to him.

The lesson went on with Zeke driving home the point that you have to be careful not to let pride creep in and to always give God His due.

When the kids started to get restless, he dismissed the class and they broke into groups. Some went into the other room to play pool, ping pong, and air hockey, while others congregated in the class room and talked in clusters.

Luke watched Mark and John play air hockey against one another and listened to them trash talk back and forth. He wondered how serious they were with the insults, knowing that there was still some bad blood between the two.

He looked around and saw Madison talking with some friends on the other side of the room. She kept looking at John, but would look away when he looked her way. Luke tried to see Mark's side, but couldn't understand why he had a problem with her and John liking each other. It was something else he would have to add to his prayer list.

A few minutes later, Matthew came in and looked around the room. Luke noticed that he was staring at Kylie, who was against the wall, talking with Carli and Josiah. It looked like Matthew wanted to go talk to her, but he just stood there watching her. If she knew he was there, she gave no indication.

Eventually, he gave up and came over to the air hockey table. "Can I play the winner?"

Neither Mark nor John answered. They were playing the game at a frantic pace and continued to hurl offensive remarks. Matthew thought it was funny and laughed out loud, doing his best to act as if everything was okay.

For the first time, it was clear to Luke that things were not okay. Mark and John, despite their animosity for each other, were making an effort to show that they were ignoring him. Every comment that Matthew made was either returned with silence or they would go back to knocking each other.

It made Luke uncomfortable. He wanted things to go back to normal. He missed the camaraderie that they had together for years. It got worse when the game ended. Rather than allow Matthew to play the winner as requested, they both walked away and watched the ping pong game between David and Dylan. Matthew stood there gaping.

Luke couldn't help but feel a little bad for him. He walked to the end of the table and asked, "Do you want to play?"

Matthew shrugged and said, "Sure."

They began hitting the puck back and forth, but neither showed much enthusiasm for the game. To break the awkwardness, Luke asked, "Are you ready for the game tomorrow night?"

A cocky smile came across Matthew's face. "I can't wait."

"It won't be easy. This is the toughest team we've played all year."

"I'm not worried. I think they're overrated. They haven't played anyone as good as us yet."

"I don't know about that. Their defense has only allowed two touchdowns all season. They lead the conference in interceptions and forced fumbles."

"I haven't thrown an interception all year, and I'm not going to start now."

"I hope not."

They went on talking, but no matter what subject Luke tried to bring up, Matthew's arrogance always rose to the surface. When the night ended, Luke went home and prayed fervently for his friend. He kept remembering Proverbs 16:18. 'Pride goes before destruction, a haughty spirit before a fall.'

He couldn't shake the feeling that Matthew was headed for a fall if he didn't change his attitude in a hurry. He hoped that when the fall came, it wouldn't have an adverse effect on those around him.

—

Emmanuel stood outside on Forest Street, halfway between the homes of Luke and Matthew. He looked at one house and then the other. As pleased as he was with how well Luke handled his hardship, he was equally displeased with Matthew's behavior.

He thought back to when he asked Matthew to be there for his friends and felt great sadness that Matthew had failed in such a big way. Now he knew that it would be Luke who would have to be there to help Matthew.

He thought about appearing to Luke the next morning to give him some instructions, but decided not to. He knew that Luke was in a place where he didn't need direct guidance. He was going to watch from a distance and see how it all unfolded.

He had confidence that Luke wouldn't let him down.

CHAPTER 23

The Benworth Eagles charged the field to a thunderous ovation from the largest crowd they'd seen all year. Dressed in their home uniforms of red jerseys with white numbers, and gray pants, they were in sharp contrast to the Allbridge Phantoms in their white jerseys with black helmets, numbers and pants.

Bleachers on both sides of the field were packed to capacity with the overflow lined up along the fence that surrounded the field. There were so many people in attendance that the running joke going around was that the game should be played at *Heinz Field* to accommodate the incredible turnout.

Matthew tried to stay focused on the task at hand, but couldn't help but be awestruck by how many people were there. While he stood on the sideline, throwing a ball back and forth with Dylan, he thought that there must be more than just Benworth and Allbridge fans there. It appeared that everybody from the region had shown up to see western Pennsylvania's biggest match-up of the night.

With every toss to Dylan, Matthew's left foot would sink into the soft earth, soggy from a rainfall earlier in the day. The rain had stopped for the time being, but the forecast called for more later in the night. Matthew hoped that the rain would hold off until the end of the game, but many of the fans were prepared, already wearing ponchos or with umbrellas by their side.

The rain had also succeeded in cooling the air as well. With every breath he took, Matthew could see it in front of his face, appearing like wisps of smoke that would disappear into the night. He didn't know how cold it was, but he kept himself moving around to stay warm, blowing on his fingers between throws. His usual pre-game jitters were a little worse tonight.

Matthew was pleased when Benworth won the coin toss and elected to receive. He wanted to get on the field as soon as possible so he could be the one to set the tone for the game. As the receiving team took the field for the opening kickoff, Coach King pulled Matthew aside.

"How do you feel?"

"Good, Coach!"

"Nervous?"

"A little," he lied, "But no worse than usual."

"This isn't just another game. We're playing the number one team in the state."

"I know, Coach. I'm ready."

"You've been playing great the last couple weeks and you had a great week of practice, but this team is something else. You saw the game films. These guys are big, strong, and fast. Bigger, stronger, and faster then you've seen all year."

"I'm up to the challenge, Coach!"

Coach King grabbed him by the shoulder pads. "Be very careful when passing. Their defensive backs have deceptive speed. If the receivers aren't wide open, I want you to either throw the ball away, or tuck it and run! This team averages three interceptions per game and we can't afford to turn the ball over."

"I haven't thrown an interception all year!"

"And I want to keep it that way. The only way to insure that is for you to be extra careful out there. No mistakes! We can't beat this team if we make mistakes, and that starts with you. Make smart decisions and the rest of the team will follow you."

"I will."

"Good. Now, what I want to do is try to establish the running game first. We're only going to pass when necessary."

Matthew felt his heart sink a little. He wanted to get the game started by airing it out. "Isn't this team good against the run?"

"They're good all around! That's why I want to keep it simple early on. If things don't go well, then we'll go to plan B, which will be to rely on your arm."

"Sounds good, Coach! I won't let you down!"

Matthew watched Coach King go back to his spot on the sideline as the teams lined up to start the game. He put his helmet on and began chewing on his mouth guard. He was doing his best to stay calm, but his insides felt like someone was pounding on his stomach with a hammer!

The Phantoms kicked off and the ball sailed high toward the far sideline. Hunter raced to that side, but it soon became clear that he wouldn't get to it before it landed. Matthew was convinced that the ball would go out of bounds and give them good field position, but it came down at the five yard line, just a few feet from the sideline. The spongy field conditions caused the ball to stay put without bouncing or rolling. It just died there at the five yard line.

Hunter got to the ball first and bent over to pick it up. As he did, the Phantom players closed in on him. He had nowhere to go and was quickly driven out of bounds. The Allbridge side of the field was alive with cheers while Benworth's side groaned. The Eagles would begin their first drive at their own five yard line.

Matthew sighed. This was not how he wanted the game to start. Coach King gave him the first play and he ran out on the field, doing his best to keep his head high. They huddled up and Matthew called the play, an off tackle run to the right.

The walk to the line of scrimmage felt like a death walk for Matthew as he saw the size of the defense up close. He couldn't believe how big the lineman and linebackers were. They reminded him of bulls getting ready to charge. Some of them were even snarling and spitting as he called out the signals. For the first time in a football game, Matthew felt intimidated! Maybe even outright scared!

He wanted to believe that the reason his hands were shaking as he held them under the center was because of the cold air, but couldn't deny that his nerves were what was really to blame.

He took the snap and gave the ball to Hunter, who was rudely met at the line of scrimmage for no gain. On the second play, they called an identical run to the left side that resulted in another stop for no yardage.

Facing a third and ten, they called a pass play. Matthew was learning quickly that this defense was the real deal. He lined up in shotgun formation with the heels of his shoes touching the goal line. The linebackers were creeping toward the line, indicating that a blitz could be coming. Matthew called out an audible, warning his receivers that the pass could be coming faster than anticipated.

He received the snap from center and dropped back a couple yards into the end zone. Sure enough, the blitz was coming! The offensive line gave way in a hurry and the defenders were closing in on him. He managed to avoid the first Phantom player with a nifty side step, but two more were right behind him. He saw Dylan make his cut across the middle and let the pass go in his direction just as another Allbridge player reached him, plowing into his chest, shoulder first, driving Matthew into the ground with force enough to knock his wind away.

He never got to see what happened to the ball after it left his hand. While he looked into the face of the opposing player on top of him, he heard cheers, but they were coming from the wrong side of the field. He winced, both from the pain and from knowing the result without even seeing it.

He got up, feeling woozy from the hit, and saw the Phantoms celebrating the interception. Thankfully, Dylan had been able to make the tackle as soon as the defender caught the ball in front of him. He saved what would have been an easy touchdown, but Allbridge would start their first drive only fifteen yards from pay dirt.

Matthew felt a sick feeling rising in his chest. It was the hardest he'd ever been hit, and combined with the outcome of the play, he thought that he might throw up. He tried his best to hide the pain as he returned to the sideline. He found a spot on the bench and drank some water.

Coach King came over and asked, "Are you okay? That was some hit you took!"

Matthew muttered, "I'm fine."

"Okay. Shake it off. Our defense is just as good as theirs. Hopefully we can keep them out of the end zone and regroup."

Matthew nodded and tried to catch his breath. He watched from the bench as the Eagles defense rose to the occasion, stuffing the Phantoms on three consecutive plays, forcing them to settle for a field goal. Despite the 3-0 deficit, it seemed like a moral victory for the Eagles that they didn't give up a touchdown.

They started their second drive with better field position, as Hunter made a decent return to the thirty-one yard line. Unfortunately, they fared no better this time. They had to punt after three plays without gaining a yard.

As the game progressed, both defenses shined. Neither team could get their offenses moving. Every time the Eagles tried to run the ball, it resulted in little or no gain. Matthew became more and more frustrated with each pass attempt. Everywhere he looked, he saw white jerseys. It seemed like they had twenty players on the field instead of eleven. His receivers were always well covered and the pass rush was always in his face. The few times he did manage to complete his passes, it was always for a short gain.

The Eagles defense kept them in the game by playing just as impressively as their counter parts, but as the first half was winding down, the Phantoms put together a drive that put them deep in Eagles territory. Allbridge added another field goal as the second quarter expired, increasing their lead to 6-0.

Matthew walked dejectedly to the locker room. He embraced the warmth that touched him as he went inside. It felt good to get out of the cold, but as he sat on the bench in front of his locker, he could sense the tension of every other player who knew that the tongue lashing was coming from the coach.

As the rest of the team made their way in, Matthew tried to figure out what he was doing wrong. He couldn't understand why the Allbridge defense had an answer for everything the Eagles tried. Going into the game, he really believed that he could lead this team to a win. In fact, he was positive that they would win. He hated the doubt that had crept in as the first half progressed. What did he need to do different?

Coach King entered the room and the team braced themselves, but the tirade never came. Instead, he commended the defense for how well they played and encouraged the offense to get it together. He seemed to be using positive reinforcement to get the offense going.

When the coach finished speaking, Dylan, along with Coach Campbell, the offensive coordinator, came over to Matthew.

Dylan said, "Don't get discouraged. You're doing fine."

"No I'm not! I've sucked out there tonight!"

Coach Campbell chimed, "Don't worry about the first half. That's over now. I've got some ideas about how we can get the ball moving."

Open to any suggestions, Matthew asked, "What do you have in mind?"

"I think timing patterns are the answer. We worked on this a few days ago in practice. This will be a good way to negate their speed advantage."

Dylan added, "Also, I'm taller than them and I know I can out jump them, too. Put the ball up high and I'll go up and get it."

Matthew felt a little life shoot through him. He liked the ideas and even had one of his own. "What about screen passes? With the rush coming as fast as it is, I think I can hit Hunter in the flats, and with his speed in the open field, he can make things happen."

Hearing his name brought Hunter into the conversation. "What do you think about going without a huddle? Matthew could call the plays from the line of scrimmage. I think it would confuse them and keep them on their heels."

Coach Campbell and Dylan's eyes both lit up. They gathered the rest of the offense together and discussed the second half strategy. Matthew started feeling confident that they could put some points on the board, and if the defense could do their part, they might pull this off after all.

—

Emmanuel sat in the bleachers on the Benworth side of the field. Directly in front of him were Brad and Pops. He smiled to himself as he listened to them talk about the game, each offering insight as to what the Eagles needed to do in the second half if they wanted to win. Seeing them get along pleased him.

He pulled the hood of his hoodie over his head as the rain started to fall again. Groans and mumbling could be heard throughout the stands as umbrellas popped open and people adjusted their ponchos and parkas in attempts to stay dry.

In a matter of seconds, the light rainfall progressed into a torrential downpour! High winds accompanied it, making the already chilly night even more uncomfortable.

Emmanuel listened in as Brad complained about the Pennsylvania weather, stating that he was sure that it was warmer in Las Vegas tonight. Pops balked at the comment, saying that this was the kind of weather that football was meant to be played in.

It continued, and Emmanuel had to make a conscious effort not to laugh out loud. Even through the bickering, Emmanuel was satisfied that the hatchet had been buried between the two. He knew that he had Luke to thank for that. He was so proud of how well Luke handled the storm that he had gone through. Although it wasn't completely over, the worst of it had passed, and he had an idea of what he might do to help put an end to it once and for all.

Now, he was going to have to sit back and watch as Matthew went through a storm of his own.

—

Matthew felt his spirit drop a little as he ran back on the field to start the second half. His wish that the rain would hold off until after the game wasn't granted. Now that he'd had a taste of how good the Phantoms defense was, he didn't want the extra disadvantage of a wet ball and shoddy field conditions.

The field had already been wet before the game started, and the furious pace of the first half had torn the field up. Now the rain was turning the field into a mud pit. Matthew wondered how anyone was going to be able to keep their footing in such a mess.

The coaching staff was being very vocal about staying positive, but the weather circumstances weren't helping the matter.

The second half got under way with Benworth kicking off. The defense continued playing well, not allowing Allbridge to get any momentum. After three plays, the Phantoms punted and the Eagles offense took the field, starting at their own forty yard line.

Coach Campbell's plan was put into effect. On the first play, Matthew dropped back to pass, and as Dylan made his cut, the pass was already on the way. He was only open for a short time as the defensive back has amazing closing speed, but he wasn't fast enough to prevent Dylan from making the catch for an eight yard gain.

Matthew ran up to the line, shouting instructions as he did. Allbridge scrambled to get ready and Matthew took advantage of the confusion. He tucked the ball and ran a quarterback draw for the first down.

He completed two more quick passes that took them down to the Phantoms thirty yard line. The Allbridge defense started to catch on to the hurry up offense and began getting ready just as fast. Matthew wasn't disheartened by this. He called for the screen pass, and when the pass rush came after him, he steadily back pedaled and allowed them to come after him. Just as they were closing in on him, he lofted a floater to a wide open Hunter on the right side of the field.

Hunter took the pass and turned up field, dodging a few tacklers before being brought down at the eleven yard line.

The adrenaline was pumping as Matthew lined up for the next play, but his excitement caused his undoing as the wet ball slipped out of his hands as it was snapped to him. He lunged forward to try to recover it, but he was too late. The Phantoms nose tackle had already fallen on top of it.

All of the air had come out of the Benworth sideline. A promising drive had come up short due to another turnover. Matthew unbuckled his chin strap with a snapping motion, letting his emotions show.

Coach King met him at the sideline. "That was a great drive, but we can't afford any more mistakes. You need to concentrate better out there!"

Matthew brushed past him and went straight to the bench, bringing about a hard look from the coach. He lowered his head and stared at his hands resting in his lap. He was so irritated with himself. They were so close to taking the lead, and now they were right back where they started.

Some members of the offensive line were trying to keep the team's spirit high, but Matthew was too angry to listen. His body was feeling the effects from the numerous hits he'd taken and he couldn't help but blame the linemen for not blocking better.

He blinked against the rain that was still coming down hard. The wind was blowing in his face and making it feel like the rain was hitting him straight on. The temperature was dropping as the night wore on, causing his fingers to go numb and tingly. He began rubbing his hands together to try to warm them up so he could still grip the ball.

It wasn't long before he had to return to the field, as the defense continued their fine play and forcing the Phantoms to punt. The field position was even better than the last time, starting at midfield.

Once again, they moved the chains as they drove down the field with quick passes. Before they knew it, they had a first and goal at the three yard line. The Benworth side of the field was alive with excitement.

The Allbridge side was just as loud, as they were shouting their support. They were in danger of losing the lead, something they hadn't done all season long.

Not even the monsoon type conditions could dampen the exhilaration that the fans had for their schools.

Matthew was disappointed when the coach called timeout. They had Allbridge on the ropes and he wanted to deliver the knockout punch. He thought that by slowing the pace, they were giving the Phantoms a chance to recover.

Coach King ran onto the field and joined the offense in the huddle, accompanied by two water boys, who passed water bottles around. Matthew waved the water away when it was offered to him, and waited impatiently for the timeout to end.

He couldn't help himself as he asked, "Why are we wasting a timeout now? We've got the momentum!"

Coach King responded, "Because I don't want to mess this up! We need to make sure that we do this right."

Matthew shook his head and looked away.

Obviously feeling disrespected, Coach King shouted, "Matthew Peters! What is your problem?"

Matthew scowled back at him defiantly, but said nothing. His look was shooting daggers through the coach, as though he were challenging his authority.

The coach grabbed him by the facemask and pulled him forward. "I asked you a question! What is your problem?"

Matthew pushed the coach's arm away and shouted back, "My problem is that you called timeout! Why are you giving them time to catch their breath?"

"Don't you ever question my decisions! Do you understand? I'm the coach of this team, not you! If you talk back to me again, your butt will be back on that bench so fast, it'll make your head spin! We're going to run the ball, and Cody Williams can hand off just as well as you do!"

Matthew stared back at him, but knew better than to say anything. He knew that he needed to stay focused on the game. They were on the verge of taking the lead from the number one team in the state, and he couldn't let his anger get the best of him.

He swallowed his pride and said, "You're the boss. What's the next play?"

Coach King turned his attention to the linemen. "I need you to block hard here. We're going to stick it down their throats!" He grabbed Hunter and looked at him. "The ball is going to you. Take it in!"

Hunter nodded and said, "You got it!"

The coach then told them they were running the off tackle to the right, the same play they ran on the first play back in the first quarter, which made Matthew cringe. The play was a bust the first time they ran it, and he saw no reason why they should run it again. He wanted to voice his complaint, but knew that after the altercation he and the coach just shared, that it would be a bad idea.

The referee blew his whistle, indicating to the coaches that the timeout was over. As Coach King backed away toward the sideline, he said once again, "Linemen, you have to drive them back if this play is to work. Give it everything you've got!"

Both teams were pumped up as they lined up for first down. The timeout seemed to give the Phantoms new life, just as Matthew had feared. They were shouting encouragement to each other and were very animated.

Matthew called out the signals, took the ball from the center, and handed it off to Hunter, who was rudely met at the line of scrimmage and driven hard into the ground, creating a splash of water to shoot into the air like a fountain.

Back in the huddle, the signals came in from the sideline calling for another off tackle run, this time to the left. Matthew couldn't believe it. What was the coach trying to do? The offensive line was clearly overmatched and this type of running play was sure to be ineffective. He sighed and called the play, then lined up behind the center, his confidence dwindling.

Just like the previous play, Hunter was stopped short, bringing up and third and goal. He felt a little better when they called a bootleg option to the right. This was the same play that they ran to score the winning touchdown against Penn Park a few weeks ago. The play was designed for Matthew to fake the hand off to Hunter, then roll to his right. From there, he had the option to run or pass, whichever was the better choice.

Matthew walked up to the line, determination showing on his face. He took the snap, faked to Hunter and ran to the right. Two large defenders had broken through the line and were in his face right away, taking the run option away.

Matthew saw Dylan streaking to the back corner of the end zone without a defensive back anywhere near him. Matthew saw an easy touchdown in the making and let the ball go in his direction, but one of the Phantom players chasing him reached up and tipped the ball, changing the course of the ball as it went right into the arms of an Allbridge player.

Dropping to his knees, Matthew screamed in frustration. Is was his second interception of the night, and the team still hadn't put a point on the board. He didn't want to face anyone on the team as he returned to the bench.

He sat by himself and put his head down. Dylan and Hunter both came by to offer some words of reassurance, but he ignored what they said. He'd never experienced a game like this and wasn't sure how to handle it. The third quarter was ticking away in a hurry and time was running out.

—

Emmanuel, now sitting behind Kylie and her friends, watched to see how Matthew responded to his adversity. He felt his heart break a little as he looked on, seeing Matthew sitting on the bench all alone, rejecting all attempts to comfort him and raise his spirit.

He was also curious to see how Kylie reacted. She'd shown little emotion as the game went on. From his position behind her, he couldn't see her facial expressions due to her pulling the hood of her thick blue jacket, with a New England Patriots logo across the back, over her head, obscuring his view. However, he could tell from his vantage point where she was looking, and it wasn't the field, but rather the Benworth bench. More specifically, directly where Matthew was sitting. He was pretty sure that if he could see her eyes, there would be compassion in them.

—

The third quarter ended and the Allbridge Phantoms were on the move. They had picked up a couple first downs and had moved past midfield. The Eagles defense was digging deep, but with the heavy rain, dropping temperature, and overall fatigue setting in, they were starting to fade.

Matthew kept an eye on the game, but was rapidly losing hope. Twice, he had been within striking distance, and both times, he turned the ball over. They should have the lead, and he felt responsible for that not happening.

As the Phantoms offense moved down the field, he kept watching the scoreboard clock, which seemed to be moving in fast-forward. With each first down, he looked up to see the clock ticking away, and with it, his confidence.

When Allbridge completed a pass inside the Benworth ten yard line, the clock showed less than seven minutes left in the game. It looked as if the Phantoms were about to put the final nail in the Eagles coffin, but the defense rose to the occasion, making three consecutive stops for no gain.

When the Phantoms lined up to kick a field goal, Matthew felt no better than he had before. If they made it, they would fall behind 9-0, which meant they would have to score twice, an unlikely scenario against such a strong defense with little time remaining.

It appeared that many in the crowd were ready to leave if they made the kick. They weren't willing to brave the wet and cold conditions anymore if the game was out of reach.

Life was suddenly restored to the Benworth side when Allbridge mishandled the snap. The ball squirted free and a mad scramble ensued, ending with a pile of players on top of the ball. When the referees cleared up the mess, they signaled that the Eagles had recovered, giving them a first and ten on their own twenty-two yard line.

Matthew pumped his fist, put his helmet back on, and ran to Coach King to get any instruction he may have. The score remained 6-0. They could still win this with a touchdown and extra point!

His adrenaline returned and he caught his second wind. The pain that he'd endured throughout the night left him as he ran back onto the field.

This was his chance to redeem himself and he wasn't going to blow it. A look to the clock showed that there was 5:36 left in the game, plenty of time to march down the field and win this game.

As he lined up in the shotgun formation, Matthew knew that a heavy pass rush was likely. The ball was snapped to him and he almost lost his grip on it. It felt slimy and slippery and he barely held on to it. He had to act quick as the blitz he expected was coming strong from the outside. Matthew stepped up in the pocket to avoid the pressure and he couldn't believe what he saw. The defensive back assigned to cover Dylan had lost his footing and fell face first into the wet mud, leaving Dylan wide open twenty yards down field!

Matthew let a wobbly pass go, almost slipping from his hand, and watched it sail through he air. It wasn't his best throw, but it made it to his intended target nonetheless. Dylan caught the pass, tucked the ball and ran full speed toward the end zone. Both of the Phantoms safeties were in pursuit and their speed saved them, catching Dylan at the Allbridge nineteen yard line. A gain of fifty-nine yards!

While the rest of the Eagles offense was hurrying down the field to line up, Matthew ran to the sideline where Coach King and Coach Campbell were standing side by side.

"Coach! The pressure is coming from the outside. I think a draw play will work here!"

The two coaches looked at each other and nodded. Coach King said, "Go ahead! Run it!"

Matthew was beyond excited as he sprinted to the rest of the team. He quickly relayed the message to the rest of the players, then ran up to the line, hoping to catch the Phantoms off guard.

Just as Matthew predicted, the pass rush came from the outside again. He feigned like he was going to pass, then handed the ball to Hunter, who had stayed in the backfield, pretending to be a blocker. Hunter wasted no time bursting through a gaping hole up the middle. Two defensive backs saw what was happening and tried to adjust, but it was too late. Hunter's explosive speed took him into the end zone before Allbridge knew what hit them!

—

The Benworth bleachers broke out with cheers. No one was sitting, not even Emmanuel. He laughed as he looked at the row in front of him where Kylie and her friends were jumping up and down, screaming with elation!

All around, fans were trading high fives, fists were in the air, and the noise was deafening. The bleachers were actually shaking from all the commotion and one couldn't help but worry that they could come crashing down at any second.

Emmanuel watched as Matthew ran to the end zone and embraced Hunter. A few other players joined in the hug while the sideline celebrated with jubilation, which was in sharp contrast to the Allbridge side where they stood in stunned silence.

The cheering died down a little as the Eagles lined up to kick the extra point, which was anything but automatic with the crazy weather conditions, but when the kick snuck through just inside the left upright, the pandemonium continued.

Benworth had a 7-6 lead with 4:48 left in the game and nobody seemed to care about how wet and cold it was anymore.

—

Pops and Brad were on their feet, being as loud as anyone else in the stands. Any bad blood that they once had for each other was certainly forgotten at this moment as the excitement of the game overshadowed anything else.

Brad turned to Pops and had to yell for Pops to be able to hear over all the noise. "I don't miss this weather, but there's something about Pennsylvania high school football."

Pops smiled back at him. "I wouldn't trade this part of the world for any other place!"

Even with the heavy rain pelting against his face, he knew that Pops was right. There was something special about Benworth, and the longer he stayed there, the more he knew he was going to miss it when it came time to go back to Las Vegas.

He shook his head and concentrated his attention back to the game. It had all the makings of a classic, and he didn't want to miss any of it. The only down side was that Luke was spending the whole game on the bench. He wished his son could be a part of it too.

—

While the rest of the team celebrated, Matthew was more concerned with watching the opposing sideline. He wanted to see how they would deal with the situation.

The Allbridge coach had gathered his players around him and was giving instructions. His arms were flailing around and he was pointing to different areas of the field while the players watched him intently.

Matthew wished that he could hear what was being said. If he was sure of one thing, it was that the Phantoms were not going to give up. There was enough time on the clock for them to drive down the field one more time, and he felt helpless standing on the sideline. He hoped that the defense had enough left in them to make one more stop.

David walked over to Matthew, dressed in his jersey, blue jeans, a red ball cap, and a see-through plastic poncho draped over him. "It's been a rough game, huh?"

Matthew nodded. "Those guys hit hard. I'm sore all over."

"You're doing well out there."

Matthew looked at him as if he were crazy. "I've thrown two interceptions and fumbled. How can you say that?"

"You're going to have games like that, especially against good teams. I threw interceptions and fumbled too."

"Not very often."

David shrugged. "Look, you can't change what's already happened. Just be ready. If they score again, you need to be ready to get back out there. This game is far from over."

"I know."

David gave him a pat on the back and walked back where he came from. Matthew watched him go over to Hunter and Dylan.

He looked back to the field as Benworth kicked off and Allbridge returned it to the thirty yard line. Both teams looked intense as they got ready for the home stretch of this game.

If there was any question as to how the Phantoms would respond to finding themselves trailing for the first time all year, it was quickly answered with how well they drove down the field. Matthew felt powerless as he watched them pick up one first down after another. After each play, he would look to the scoreboard clock, and unlike earlier, where it seemed to be moving in fast-forward, it now had switched to slow motion.

He paced up and down the sideline, getting more nervous with each yard the Phantoms gained. He desperately wanted the clock to run out before they could score, but when they got inside the ten yard line with 1:50 remaining, he started to lose hope.

During a timeout called by Allbridge, Coach Campbell gathered the offense together to discuss what their strategy would be if the Phantoms scored. He kept zoning out as he was more interested in what was happening on the field, bringing a blunt reprimand from the coach.

"Matthew! Pay attention!"

The teams were lining up for the next play and Matthew wanted to watch, not listen to what the coach had to say. When he heard another wild cheer come from the fans, he wheeled around to see what had happened.

The Eagles were celebrating a fumble recovery! Matthew raised his fist into the air. They were going to pull it off!

Coach Campbell yelled out, "Okay! Don't lose your focus! They still have two timeouts left, so let's make them use them on defense. We'll run safe running plays up the middle." He turned to Hunter and went on, "Stay in the center of the field. Make them use their timeouts to stop the clock. If we can get one first down, we can run the clock out. Protect the ball, and whatever you do, don't fumble!"

Hunter replied, "I won't!"

Coach Campbell grabbed Matthew by the shoulder pads and looked intently into his eyes. "The ball is wet and slippery. Make sure that you get a good grip and hand the ball off cleanly."

Matthew felt like the coach was talking to him like a little kid, and he wanted to retort with a sarcastic answer, but knew that this wasn't the time for it. Instead, he put his helmet back on and ran onto the field.

The ball rested on the five yard line and there was 1:45 left on the clock. He called the play and lined up. He was hoping that the Phantoms defense would be discouraged after the fumble, but he was disappointed to see that they looked as intense as ever.

He'd never allowed his nerves to rattle him before, and he wasn't about to start now. He took the snap and gave the ball to Hunter, who was hit hard at the line. The Phantoms immediately called timeout and the clock stopped.

Matthew looked to the clock and saw that it read 1:41. He couldn't believe it. The play lasted only four seconds!

The next play had the same result, and when Allbridge called their final timeout, there was 1:35 left in the game. They faced a third and ten on their own five yard line. Coach King and Coach Campbell came out onto the field and talked to the players.

Coach King said, "We need a first down! I don't want to punt out of the end zone in these conditions." He turned to his offensive coordinator and continued, "We're not going to pick up the first down by running the ball."

Coach Campbell shook his head. "I don't like passing in this situation. If we run and don't make it, at least the clock will go under a minute. I'd rather put it into the defense's hands. They've come through all night."

"They're getting tired. I'd rather roll the dice and throw the ball. They won't expect it. We can catch them off guard."

Coach Campbell looked unsure, but said, "Okay. Let's try it, but let's do it from a running formation so we won't tip our hand."

"Good idea!" Coach King spun around to look at Matthew. "Don't force anything. If no one is open, either throw it away, or better yet, try to run for the first down. The last thing we need is an interception here. Can I depend on you?"

Matthew answered, "Of course!"

The coaches left the field and Matthew called the play. While he called the signals, he'd never seen an opposing defense look more imposing. *Don't be scared! Run the play just like you do in practice!*

He took the ball from center, faked a handoff to Hunter, and dropped back to pass. The running formation worked! Nobody was covering Dylan! He was wide open!

Matthew cocked his arm back to throw, but before he let it go, a blitzing linebacker hit him hard from his blind side and at the same time, smacked his arm just below the elbow, causing the ball the slip from his hand while pain shot up his arm. The jarring hit drove him into the ground and put him in a disoriented state, but he was still aware of what had happened.

He could see the ball laying on the ground, a couple yards away and in the end zone. He instinctively tried to crawl over to the ball, but he couldn't move with the linebacker on top of him. He watched with despair as a Phantom player fell on the ball and the referee raised his arms in the air, indicating an Allbridge touchdown!

Matthew was too shocked to move. His right arm was completely numb from the hit. He thought that it might be broken. His teammates came over to check on him and helped him up to his knees. He gripped his right arm with his left hand while it hung limply. He was opening and closing his fist, trying to get some sensation back.

While the Phantoms celebrated in the end zone, Coach King was on the field screaming at the officials. He was arguing that Matthew's arm was moving forward when he was hit, so it should've been ruled an incomplete pass rather than a fumble, but the referee's stuck to their original call.

Allbridge elected to try for a two-point conversion, but their pass attempt fell incomplete. With 1:28 showing on the clock, The Phantoms led 12-7.

Matthew went to the bench wincing. Coach King saw this and shouted, "Cody Williams! Start warming up!"

When Matthew heard this, he yelled, "No! I can play!"

Coach Campbell ran over and said, "Throw a couple passes here on the sideline. Let's see if you can still go."

Matthew reluctantly got up and picked up a ball. Dylan went about fifteen yards away to catch his throw. A little bit of feeling had returned, but the pain was still excruciating. Pain shot up and down his arm as he released it, but he did his best to not let his face show it. A couple more throws hurt just as bad.

Coach Campbell asked, "How does it feel?"

He lied, "I'm fine. I can play."

"Okay! We have two timeouts left, so we'll have to use them wisely. After each play, look to us and we'll let you know if you should call timeout, spike the ball, or just run the basic two minute drill. Don't lose hope! When we scored earlier, we did it in just two plays. You can do this! Keep the pace fast, but controlled. Keep them on their heels. You're the General out there. Lead us to victory!"

Matthew was listening, but couldn't keep his mind off of how much his arm hurt. His head was whirling over what had just transpired and he tried not to panic. *Stay calm. You can do this.* He tried to clear his mind while he watched the kickoff.

Allbridge squib kicked the ball and a Benworth player fell on top of it at the forty yard line. Matthew breathed a little easier as he saw that they would start with good field position.

He shook his arm a little as he ran onto the field, but when that made it feel worse, he stopped and decided to preserve what little use he had left in it. Everyone in the huddle had a determined look on their faces. "We were in the same situation against Penn Park. We did it then and we can do it now."

He called the play and they ran up to the line. Matthew hoped his arm would hold up, but the pain wasn't reassuring to him. He would have to dig deep!

Little by little, they made their way downfield with short passes, but the time was ticking away. They used one timeout with thirty seconds left, and later, spiked the ball to stop the clock with eleven seconds remaining, with the ball on the twenty yard line.

With one timeout left, Matthew figured that they had time for two more plays. He dropped back to pass, but couldn't find an open receiver. He saw a hole up the middle and took off running. He crossed the ten yard line and knew that he wasn't going to score, so he dove head first, trying to pick up as many yards as he could. He landed on top of his injured arm, bringing the numbness back.

His momentum carried him to the six yard line and one of his teammates called for their last timeout. The clock showed two seconds left.

Matthew got up holding his arm again. Coach King ran out and abruptly confronted him. "Are you okay?"

"Yeah, Coach. I'm fine."

"Don't lie to me! If you can't throw, tell me now."

The thought of being pulled from the game horrified Matthew. There was no way he was going to let someone else come into the game and steal his glory!

"I can do this!"

"Alright! We have one last shot. Receivers, get open! Matthew, get it to one of them! It's that simple!"

—

Emmanuel looked on while all the fans around him cheered madly. He knew that Matthew's arm was injured and that he should exit the game. He kept thinking to himself, *You don't have to do this. No one will think any less of you if you come out of the game.*

The talk around the bleachers varied. It was obvious to everyone in the crowd that Matthew was in pain. Some admired his courage for sticking it out, while others thought that it was best for the team if the coach would replace him.

Emmanuel shook his head when Matthew stayed in the game and lined up for the final play of the game.

—

From the shotgun formation, Matthew awaited the snap. The crowd noise was louder than he'd ever heard before. Fans from both sides were cheering their team on. He took a deep breath and tried to calm his nerves.

The snap was a little high, but he snagged it effortlessly. His arm was throbbing, but he refused to think about it. The crowd noise suddenly turned off inside his head and everything seemed to slow down. The line was blocking better than they had all night, and there was no pressure.

He spotted Dylan cutting across the back of the end zone. He was open! He let the ball go, and as he did, the pain in his arm intensified. The ball sailed through the air, but it didn't have as much on it as Matthew intended. Instead of a tight spiral, it wobbled along, and just before it reached Dylan's hands, a Phantom defender jumped in front of it and made the interception, sealing the win for Allbridge!

Matthew fell to his knees, feeling sick to his stomach. While the Allbridge bench cleared and they ran onto the field to celebrate, Matthew did his best not to cry.

After a minute or so, he got to his feet and lined up to shake the hands of his opponents. The Allbridge head coach pulled him aside and told him not to let this game bring him down, that he was a great young quarterback with a very bright future, but Matthew wasn't in the mood to hear it. He walked way without saying a word.

When his teammates offered words of encouragement, he shook it off and quietly made his way to the locker room.

—

As the bleachers emptied, Emmanuel stayed put, never letting his eyes leave Matthew until he disappeared inside the locker room. His heart was breaking for him. As much as he wanted to go talk to him, he knew it was better if he gave him some space. Maybe he would talk to him tomorrow after he had a little time to get over it.

The rain was still coming down and was expected to continue until morning. Emmanuel wanted the rain to stop falling in Matthew's life, but because a lot of this storm was caused by his own choices, it was going to be up to him whether or not he would calm it.

CHAPTER 24

Luke couldn't believe how packed Mario's was. With the lousy weather and the disappointing loss for the Benworth football team, he didn't expect many people to be there, but it was more crowded than he'd ever seen it.

After being dropped off by Pops at the front door, he stood with Mark and John, looking for an empty table or booth, but there was none to be found. In the time it took for them to change out of their wet uniforms, put on dry clothes, and ride over with Pops, the restaurant had filled up quickly.

Not feeling hungry, Luke was okay with not getting a table. He went over to the video game area and started playing one of his favorite games. Mark was by his side watching while John excused himself to go mingle with the crowd.

While he played, Luke couldn't help but overhear the chatter that was going on around him, most of it about Matthew. The comments were not flattering.

"I guess he's not as good as his brother after all."

"I can't believe he threw three interceptions and fumbled twice. We would've won if it wasn't for him."

"Looks like he was just a one hit wonder."

"It's obvious that he can't handle the pressure of a big game."

Luke finished his game and Mark took his turn. Luke took the time to scan the room, curious to see if Matthew had shown up. He saw Chad and Brock sitting at a table with some other upperclassmen, but Matthew wasn't with them.

He doubted that Matthew would come. After seeing him in the locker room after the game, looking dejected and defeated, Luke figured that he would probably go home and call it a night. He had thought about talking to him at that time, but because he looked like he wanted to be left alone, he thought it would be best if he waited a while.

Continuing to look around the restaurant, he was trying to see if Rachel was there, but the place was swarming with so many people, it was impossible to see everyone. He was a little disheartened when he couldn't find her.

While searching for her, he saw John sitting next to Madison, having what appeared to be a pleasant conversation with her. Luke hoped that Mark wouldn't see it. There had been enough bad feelings between the two of them lately. A look back to the video game showed that Mark's complete attention was fixed on the game, so for the time being, he was unaware of what was going on.

Luke breathed a little easier. He didn't want to have to get between his friends. He supposed that if he could keep Mark busy playing video games, then he might never see John talking to his sister. It was worth a try.

Just when he was about to go back to watching Mark play, Luke spotted Rachel at a table on the other side of the room. When he noticed her look across the restaurant right at him, his heart jumped and he looked away quickly. He'd been looking forward to having the chance to talk with her since he'd made the promise to his dad that he would do so, but now that the opportunity was in front of him, he wasn't sure if he could go through with it. Talking to girls was not a strong point for him and he felt the terror seize him.

He went back to watching Mark play, trying to get his heart to stop pounding. He thought that it would be easier to talk to her if she was by herself, but with all of her friends at the table with her, he wasn't comfortable approaching her. Maybe he would get a chance later in the night.

—

Matthew walked into Mario's, having caught a ride with his brother at the last second. He had planned to ride with Chad and Brock, but couldn't find them after the game. Just when he was about the give up and go home, David offered to take him.

Initially, he thought that maybe Chad and Brock decided not to go due to the weather, but when he saw them sitting at a table with some upperclassmen that he hardly knew, he felt a dash of anger creep to the surface.

He did his best to not let it show that he was mad as he went over to the table. He was met with blank stares. "Why didn't you wait for me? I was looking all over for you."

Brock flatly answered, "We didn't think you were coming."

"Why would you think that? You were the one who called me this afternoon and asked me if I wanted to go."

Chad retorted, "We didn't have any more room in the car."

"Then why did you invite me?" Matthew grabbed an empty chair from an adjacent table, careful to use his left arm because his right was still sore. "Can someone scoot over so I can sit down?"

Chad said, "We don't have room at this table either."

Matthew felt stunned as he got the hint. "Oh. So it's going to be like that?"

Chad shrugged without changing the expression on his face. The body language of everyone at the table showed that he wasn't welcome there. Gradually, what Emmanuel told him about who his real friends were came to the front of his mind.

"So, if we win next week, are you going to want to be my friend again? Is that how this works?"

Chad smirked as he said, "If you're looking for a friend, I think Alyssa might be lonely."

The table busted out with laughter as Matthew felt rage simmer inside. "You know that nothing happened between me and her!"

"All I know is that the two of you went into a bedroom and closed the door behind you. Why should we believe that you didn't do anything?"

Brock added, "You were pretty drunk that night. Maybe you're not remembering everything. Alcohol will do that to you."

More laughter ensued while Matthew started to walk away. He called over his shoulder, "You guys are pathetic!"

Over the noise of the packed house, he heard Chad shout out, "No more pathetic than you played tonight!"

Even more laughter followed and continued until he was out of earshot. He headed to the restroom, but stopped short just before reaching the door as Kylie came out of the girls room. They both stopped as they saw each other. She looked just as ill at ease as he felt. Already feeling as bad as he did, he didn't want to add to it, so he broke the eye contact and ducked inside the door.

He found solace in one of the stalls. He wasn't in there to relieve himself, but rather to have a moment alone. He could hear other people coming in and out, but wasn't really paying attention. He was regretting his decision to come. It wasn't making him feel better like he had hoped.

He was thinking about calling his dad and asking him if he'd come pick him up, but before he did, voices outside of the stall caught his ear.

"So, do you think Cody Williams will be the starter next week?"

"After the way Matthew Peters played tonight, I wouldn't blame the coach if he made that call."

The voices sounded familiar, but he couldn't put faces to them. He wanted to poke his head out to see who they were, but at the same time, he would rather not know.

A part of him wanted to stay in that stall all night, but he knew that eventually, he'd have to face everyone, so he took a deep breath and walked back out into the restaurant.

He felt like every eye was on him, giving him scornful looks. These were the same people who had been congratulating him, patting his back, and singing his praises for the last three weeks. All it took was one bad game for everyone to change their tune.

He already felt bad enough. There wasn't a person there who felt worse than he did. Why did they care so much? They weren't even on the team. He showed up to try to get his mind off of the game, but it was backfiring. No matter where he went, he couldn't escape the stares.

He wanted to ask his brother for a ride home, but he saw David and Jocelyn having a good time together along with some other friends, so he didn't want to interrupt. The thought of walking home crossed his mind, but with the rain still coming down in droves, he quickly eliminated that possibility. He could call his dad to come pick him up, but then he would have to explain to him why he was leaving so early, and he didn't want to have to do that.

Finding a spot against the wall near the video games, he leaned back and closed his eyes. He could still feel eyes gazing at him, but he tried to ignore it. Popularity sure had it perks when things were going well, but the other side of it made him question whether or not it was worth it.

—

John was having a great time with Madison. The ease of the conversation and the laughs that they shared made him remember how much he liked her and why he wanted to pursue a relationship with her in the first place.

This was the first time he'd talked with her since the youth group meeting the night that Pops went to the hospital. Although that chat hadn't gone well, it didn't change how they felt about each other. If anything, it may have made the feelings stronger.

He glanced over his shoulder now and then to see if Mark was watching, but so far he hadn't seen them. With what he was feeling in his heart, he knew the time was coming where he and Mark were going to have to deal with this. He was going to have to find a way to make him understand.

John was a little surprised when Kylie joined them at the table. She gave Madison a quick hug, then grabbed John by the bicep and asked, "Do you mind if I borrow him for a minute? I promise to bring him right back."

Madison lightheartedly said, "He's all yours."

Kylie led John toward the back, near the restrooms, so they could talk without prying ears.

"You and Madison look like you're getting along well. Is everything okay with you and Mark?"

"We've been getting along a little better this week, but then again, he hasn't seen me with his sister lately."

"Is he here? I haven't seen him."

"The last I saw him, he was playing video games with Luke. As far as I know, he hasn't seen me with his sister tonight."

She nodded. "I know I promised to talk to him for you, but I just haven't had the chance."

"I understand. I was supposed to talk to Matthew for you, but with everything that happened with Luke's grandfather, I guess I kind of forgot."

"Yeah. It's been a crazy week."

"Well, both Matthew and Mark are here. Maybe we can talk to them now."

"Good idea. I just saw Matthew by the games. He was just standing by the wall, looking really bummed out."

John ran his fingers through his thick dark hair. "I can imagine."

"Have you heard some of the horrible things people are saying about him?"

"I've heard a little."

"You'd think he just murdered someone with the things people are saying. They need to lighten up. It's just a football game."

"I know what you mean. I guess now is as good a time as any. I'll go talk to Matthew. You can probably find Mark playing games with Luke, as long as you don't mind talking to him with Luke there."

"Hmmm. How does Luke feel about you and Madison?"

"He's on my side. He doesn't understand why Mark has a problem with it."

"Good. Maybe that will work to our advantage. Having an ally with me could really help."

"Great! Let's do this."

—

John found Matthew exactly where Kylie told him hew would, looking despondent. He approached him slowly, wanting to be careful not to set him off.

"Hey, buddy."

"Hey."

"Rough night, huh?"

Matthew shrugged. "I've had better."

"Why are you by yourself?"

"I get the impression that no one wants me around. I want to get out of here, but I don't have a ride."

"I've got a table with Madison and some of her friends. I'm sure you'll be welcome there."

Another shrug. "I don't know. I think I made a big mistake coming here. It's making me feel worse."

"Will going home make you feel better?"

"Maybe not, but at least I won't have to face all these people who don't want me around."

John sighed. "You'll have to face them sooner or later. It probably won't be any different Monday at school."

"I know. It's just that I really wanted to win tonight. I really thought that we would. Now we probably won't make the playoffs."

"There's still a chance we can make the playoffs if we win the rest of our games, and the worst of our schedule is over. Don't give up hope there. Just think, if we get into the playoffs, we might get another crack at Allbridge."

A small smile crossed Matthew's face. "I'd like that."

John smiled back. "Why don't you come sit with us? We'll make room for you at the table, and I promise that no one there will be judging you."

"I wouldn't want to impose on your time with Madison."

"You won't be."

"Not to change the subject, but what's the status between you two?"

"Still just friends. I'd like to be more, but we need to make Mark understand first."

"Yeah. That's a tough one. Maybe I could go knock some sense into him."

John laughed. "Kylie's already on that."

"Really? What's up with that?"

"We agreed to do each other a favor. She's talking to Mark for me, and I'm talking to you for her."

Matthew looked puzzled. "That's what this is about?"

"Not exactly. Yes, I promised to talk to you, but that's not the only reason I'm here. I know that you're hurting right now and I want to help."

Matthew looked away, tears forming in his eyes. "It's weird. Everything was going so well. People loved me. I was feeling good about myself. In the course of one football game, all of that's changed."

"Well, I know some people who still love you."

"Yeah? Who?"

"Me, Mark, Luke, and even Kylie."

"I'm afraid I've lost any chance with her. I saw her a few minutes ago and it was really awkward. We didn't even say a word to each other."

"She still wants to be your friend. She told me so. She just wants things to go back to the way they were when you first met."

His head dropped and he looked at the floor. "I've been acting like a jerk, haven't I?"

"Yeah, but it's not too late to change that. Go talk to her and apologize."

"Not now. Maybe I'll call her tomorrow." He paused for a few seconds, then continued, "I had no idea how much pressure there would be in being a varsity quarterback."

John asked, "Remember the lesson at Monday's Bible study? We're all have our crosses to bear, and we have to do it daily. It's not supposed to be easy."

Matthew nodded. "I guess not. Why don't we go join your friends at the table?"

John smiled and led the way. He felt pretty good about their talk and was confident that Matthew had been humbled enough to go back to his old self.

—

While John went to talk with Matthew, Kylie set out to find Mark. She found him quickly, sharing a laugh with Luke as the video game they were playing came to an end. She approached them with a bright smile.

"How's it going, guys?"

Mark answered with a smile of his own. "Much better now that you're here."

Kylie blushed at the compliment. "I was hoping to have a word with you two."

Mark and Luke looked at each other and nodded in agreement. "Sure. What's up?"

She breathed out, unsure of where to start. After a moment of thought, she said, "One thing I've noticed as a new student at Benworth is that there are a lot of guys here that are absolute jerks!"

Luke smiled. "You've got that right."

"And I've also noticed that there are some really good guys."

Mark responded, "You'll find that at any school. Where are you going with this?"

"Well, I've had some guys show some interest in me, and I'm wondering what I should do about it. Should I go out with the really nice guy, or the jerk?"

Confusion was written all over Mark's face. "Is this about Matthew? Has someone else asked you out?"

"This has nothing to do with Matthew. I'm just saying that there are two guys who want to take me out. One is really nice and the other isn't. Which one should I go out with?"

"I'm sorry, Kylie, but that's a really stupid question."

"But you haven't answered it."

"Who are the guys?"

"That's not important."

"Sure it is. It would be easy to say that you should date the nice guy, but if you don't know these guys well, then you might not be a good judge of their character."

"Okay. The guys are John and Chad."

Both Mark and Luke's eyes widened in surprise. Mark exclaimed, "John asked you out? Does Matthew know?"

"Forget about Matthew for now. Which one of those guys should I date?"

"Well, forget about Chad. He's completely wrong for you."

"I agree. I would never date someone like him, but what about John? Should I say yes?"

"This isn't going to fly with Matthew."

"I already talked to Matthew. He said he doesn't care."

"Really?"

"Yeah."

"Then I guess you should go out with him."

217

Kylie smiled, knowing she had baited the hook and got Mark to bite. "What if we hit it off? If he and I were in a relationship, would you be okay with that?"

"Yeah. Why wouldn't I be?"

"So you think that John is a good guy?"

"Of course. We've been friends forever."

She let out a little laugh, then said, "Sorry I had to do this, but I just made that whole thing up."

Luke bellowed, "I knew it!"

Mark asked, "What?"

"I'm so sorry, but I had to make a point. Neither John nor Chad have ever asked me out."

"Why would you do that?"

"Like I said, I had a point to make."

"What point?"

"I wanted you to say that John is a good guy. If you wouldn't have a problem with him dating me, then why do you have a problem with him dating your sister?"

A look of betrayal came over Mark's face. "That's different. You're not my sister."

"But you just said that you've been friends with him forever. You said that he's a good guy."

"He is. I just don't understand why he wants to date my sister. There's lots of girls in our school. Why does he have to mess with Madison?"

"Would you rather she date someone like Chad?"

"That's the second time I've heard that."

"Well, would you?"

"No. Of course not!"

"Your sister is very pretty and is going to get a lot of attention from guys. Sooner or later, she's going to date someone. If it's not John, then who?"

"I don't know. It'll be weird having one of my best friends dating my sister, that's all."

Kylie turned to Luke. "What do you think?"

Luke answered, "I don't have a sister, but if I did, I would be thrilled if she was dating someone like John."

Mark replied, "But you don't have a sister, so you don't have to worry about it."

"Come on, Mark. We've known John a long time. You know he'll treat her right. You can't say that about anyone else in school."

"I know. It'll be a really tough adjustment."

Kylie asked, "If they do cross that line, are you going to be okay with it?"

"Probably. I just feel odd about the whole thing."

"Cool." She smiled at Mark until he smiled back. "Hey. Why don't you two join me and my friends at our table? We have room for a couple more, and we have a lot of pizza on the way. There's no way we can finish it ourselves."

Mark said, "Sounds good to me." He started toward the dining area.

Luke hesitated, then called out, "Hold up a minute."

Mark and Kylie turned around. "What's wrong?"

"I need some advice."

Kylie said, "Shoot."

He looked nervous as he looked back and forth between Kylie and Mark. "There's a girl here tonight that I like. I promised my father that I would talk to her the next chance I got, but now I'm not sure if I can go through with it."

Kylie smiled and asked, "Why not?"

"I'm scared."

Mark asked, "What are you afraid of? Just go up to her and start talking. I do it all the time."

"Yeah, but I don't have your confidence with girls. This is awkward for me."

Kylie chuckled and said, "Don't worry about it. The best way to get over your shyness is to face your fears." She turned to look around the restaurant. "So, is it anyone we know?'

Luke's face reddened. "It's Rachel."

Mark said, "You had no trouble talking to her a few weeks ago. What's the problem?"

"That was easy. You broke the ice for me by talking to her friend."

"Do you want me to go with you?"

Kylie interjected, "No. Don't do that. I think this is something that Luke needs to do himself."

Luke shook his head and said, "Maybe some other time."

"Come on. What's the worst that can happen?"

"I could be humiliated."

"That's always a risk anytime you ask a girl out, but if you don't do anything, someone else might beat you to it."

Luke looked over to where Rachel was sitting. "She's with all of her friends. I'd feel better if she was alone. It will be embarrassing if she turns me down in front of everybody."

Kylie grabbed Luke by the shoulders. "Listen to me. If you want to impress her, talk to her in front of her friends. I know it won't be easy, but it'll go a long way in how she'll respond."

"You think so?"

"Just try it."

"I don't want her to know how nervous I am."

"Let me tell you something. I've had a few guys ask me out before, and every one of them was nervous. I could tell. We expect guys to be nervous. It's actually kind of cute, if you ask me."

Mark added, "I get nervous too."

Luke looked back at him. "Really?"

"Sure, but I do it anyway because I figure it's better to get rejected than to not know at all."

Luke nodded. "I guess so."

Kylie said, "Just try to relax. You're a nice looking, funny, easy going guy. If she doesn't see that, then it's her loss."

"Okay. Wish me luck."

Kylie smiled as she watched Luke walk across the restaurant toward the table where Rachel was sitting.

—

Luke couldn't remember ever feeling this nervous. His palms were sweating and he felt a little queasy. He couldn't believe that he was really going through with this.

He walked past John and Matthew, who were now sitting with Madison and her friends. He heard John call out, "Hey Luke. Where are you going?"

He looked over his shoulder, and without stopping, he said, "I'll talk to you in a little bit."

He vaguely heard him say, "Alright."

Even though the walk only took a few seconds, it felt like it was never-ending. As he got close, Rachel saw him coming and looked directly at him, causing his stomach to jump. *She saw me. There's no turning back now.*

He took a deep breath and took the last few steps. She watched him the rest of the way and looked up at him expectantly.

She was sitting at a rectangular table with four friends. There happened to be an empty chair next to her. Luke motioned toward it and asked, "Can I talk to you for a minute?"

She looked a little taken aback, but said, "Okay."

He felt clumsy as he plopped into the seat. Every girl at the table was staring right at him, making him feel even more scared. He wanted to turn around and run, but knew that he would never forgive himself if he did. Instead, he figured he would just get it over with.

"I just wanted to tell you that I really enjoyed talking to you here a few weeks ago." When she didn't respond, he went on, "I'd like to get to know you better. If it's okay with you, I'd like to take you out sometime."

Every jaw at the table dropped as they turned to Rachel to see how she would react. Luke also looked at her eagerly, awaiting her reply. She didn't say anything right away, making the suspense even worse.

Finally, she said, "I would like that." Then she playfully shoved him, asking, "What took you so long? I've been waiting since that night for you to ask me out!"

The girls at the table started in with oohs and ahhs. Luke thought that being turned down would be embarrassing, but was now thinking that this was worse. He was happy that she said yes, but was blushing at the response of her friends.

Sarah, Rachel's best friend, clasped her shoulder and said, "I think you two will be really cute together."

Now Rachel was embarrassed too. She turned back to Luke and asked, "What do you have in mind?"

He smiled back at her and said, "This is the last weekend that my father will be in town, so how about next Saturday? Lunch and a movie?"

"Sounds good."

They exchanged phone numbers and he promised to call her soon. They said goodbye and he excused himself, heading over to Kylie's table, where she and Mark were already sitting.

He sat down, grabbed a slice of pizza, and leaned back in his chair. He could feel Mark and Kylie's eyes bearing down on him, but he was enjoying the moment and chose to remain silent.

Finally, Kylie asked, "Well? How'd it go?"

He looked back and quietly answered, "She said yes!"

"Whoo! I knew it. Congratulations!" She got up, walked over to him and gave him a tight hug.

Luke smiled at the attention. Things were starting to look up. Now, if he could only get his father to give up the battle with Pops over custody.

—

As the night went on, Mario's started to empty out. After a while, Matthew, John and Madison were able to join the others by pushing their tables together. Everyone seemed to be having a great time, and before long, any thoughts of the football game had gone away.

Matthew and Kylie looked at each other a few times, but neither said anything to one another. It was obvious that they wanted to, but neither was willing to make the first move.

Although no one saw him, Emmanuel sat at a back corner table, watching them interact with each other. He was happy to see them all getting along.

CHAPTER 25

Brad woke up in his rental car with a splitting headache and overwhelming nausea. His neck was sore from the awkward position he'd slept in. It took him a while to get his bearings and figure out where he was.

He remembered saying goodbye to Luke after the football game when Pops took him and his friends to Mario's, then leaving for a bar near downtown Pittsburgh. After that, it was all hazy.

Due to the heavy rain and dropping temperature, the car windows were covered with ice. The rising sun gave enough light in the car for him to see a twelve-pack of beer on the passenger seat, unopened. He must have bought it when he left the bar, but he had no recollection of doing so.

The morning chill was biting through his skin, so he turned on the car's ignition and cranked the heater up all the way. He looked around for an ice scraper but couldn't find one. The rental company must not have supplied one. He would have to wait for the defrosters to do their thing.

While looking around the car, he spotted a plain white envelope on the passenger side floor. He reached over to grab it, causing sharp pain to run through his head. *How much did I drink last night?* He couldn't recall ever having a hangover this bad.

He opened the envelope and pulled the contents out. He held in his hand four tickets to tomorrow's Steelers game against the Patriots.

Now it started to come back to him. His friend had told him earlier in the week that he might be able to get him the tickets, and after last night's high school game, he got a call on his cell phone telling him that the tickets were his, and to pick them up at the bar. That's why he went into the city in the first place.

He couldn't wait to get home and tell Luke the good news. If he was excited about going to the Pitt game last week, he would be ecstatic about seeing the Steelers.

Once the windows cleared up enough for him to see, he put the car into gear and left the bar parking lot. He was kind of embarrassed that he'd fallen asleep in the car, but the more he thought about it, the more he was grateful. If he couldn't remember what had happened, then it was better that he'd slept it off rather than drive home in that condition.

The rain had stopped, but the roads were still wet. He drove down the street a bit until he came to a convenient store. His mouth was dry and his headache was getting worse, so he went inside and bought a bottle of water and some ibuprofen. He knew that he must be looking pretty bad when he got some unusual stares from the other customers inside.

He quickly paid for his items and slipped outside. As he walked up to the car, he saw a man leaning against it. He was dressed in a gray hoodie and blue jeans. He had shaggy brown hair and a scruffy beard. He looked very relaxed as he gave Brad a slight nod.

Brad's first inclination was that the guy was homeless and looking for a handout, but a closer look revealed that he was clean and his clothes looked relatively new, so he discarded that idea. He thought about saying something about him leaning against the car, but with his head hurting as bad as it was, he wasn't in the mood for a fight.

Instead, he looked at the man and asked, "Can I help you?"

In a relaxed tone, the man replied, "I was hoping to catch a ride to Benworth. Are you going that way?"

Brad stopped short for a second. What were the odds that this random guy would be going to Benworth and be leaning on his car? After a brief hesitation, he answered, "Yes. Hop in."

He wasn't really feeling like company, and didn't really want to give him a ride. As soon as he said it, he regretted it. When he got inside the car, he saw the twelve-pack sitting on the passenger seat, so he picked it up and put it in the back seat, just as the man got in the other side.

Upon seeing Brad move the beer, the man asked, "Do you plan on drinking all of that today?"

"Why? Do you want some?"

"No. It just looks like you had enough last night and having more is probably a bad idea."

Brad looked at him for a second, thought about telling the man to get out of the car, but said nothing. He opened the bottle of ibuprofen, popped a few pills into his mouth, and swallowed them down with the water he'd purchased. The cool water soothed his dry mouth so he continued drinking the water until the bottle was almost empty.

The man watched him the whole time. "Wow! You sure were thirsty."

As he started the car and started to pull out of the parking lot, Brad absently said, "Cotton mouth."

"You know, I have a guaranteed way for you to never have another hangover."

"Yeah? What is it?"

"Quit drinking."

Brad was getting annoyed. "Why would I do that?"

"Because your life would get a lot better if you did."

"We just met, so we don't know anything about each other, so don't pretend to know anything about me."

"I know so much more than you will ever understand."

Brad stopped at a red light and turned to look at the man. "Who are you?"

"I'm known by a few names, but my friends around here call me Emmanuel."

"Well, Emmanuel, my drinking and my life are none of your business."

The light turned green and they were back on their way. Emmanuel stayed quiet for a minute, then said, "I'd like to help you with a few things, but I can't unless you are willing to accept it."

"What makes you think you can help me?"
"I help people all the time."

"Yeah? Well, I don't need any help."

The car fell silent again. After a couple minutes, Brad felt uncomfortable without any noise, so he asked, "Why are you going to Benworth? Do you live there?"

"No, I don't live there, but I have a few friends who do. There's one friend in particular that I want to talk to."

"Where do you live?"

"I guess you could say that I'm a drifter of sorts."

"Homeless?"

"Far from it."

Confused, Brad said, "You're very odd, no offense."

"None taken."

Brad laughed to himself. "This trip is anything but what I expected."

Emmanuel smiled and said, "Tell me about it."

"It's a long story."

"I've got time."

Brad spent the next ten minutes spilling his guts to Emmanuel, who listened patiently. He told the story of how he took off when Luke was born, found himself in Las Vegas, and came back fourteen years later to try to get custody of his son.

He finished the story by saying, "I wish I could get Luke to agree to go to Vegas with me. I could give him a good life there."

"It sounds like he already has a good life."

"I guess he does, but now that I've gotten to know him, I don't want to go back to Vegas without him."

"Then don't go."

"What do you mean? That's where I live. I have a good job and a home. My life is there."

"And Luke's life is here. You were the one who ran away, so why should Luke be the one to pay for that?"

"I worked hard to get everything I've got. I don't want to give that up."

"What about what you have with Luke? Isn't that more important?"

"Of course. That's why I want him to come with me." "You're already here. Why don't you just stay?"

Brad felt frustrated. Everything Emmanuel was saying made sense. "How would I support him? All I know how to do is casino work."

"There are casinos here in Pennsylvania."

"I know, but what if they won't hire me?"

"You have fourteen years of Las Vegas experience. That's going to go a long way."

Brad smiled. "Yeah. I guess it will, but that's not the only thing. I've made some good friends and I have my self-defense classes."

"They have a good Krav Maga school right here in town."

"How did you know about Krav Maga? I didn't say anything about it. I simply said self-defense."

Emmanuel smiled deeply. "I was only mentioning that there is a school here."

"Are you familiar with Krav Maga?"

"I have a special interest in things from Israel."

"Yeah? Have you ever been there?"

"I spent quite a few years there."

"Doing what?"

"Ministry work."

Brad nodded enthusiastically. "That explains a lot. You're a Bible thumper."

Emmanuel laughed heartily. "You could say that."

"Did Luke's grandfather put you up to this?"

"Put me up to what?"

"Don't play games with me. Am I supposed to believe that it's just a coincidence that you just happened to be leaning on my car and looking for a ride to where I was going anyway?"

"Trust me. One thing I don't do is play games."

Keeping one eye on the road and the other on Emmanuel, Brad said, "You know too much."

"I told you before, I know more than you will ever understand."

"Yes, but how?"

"It's not important. What is important is what you decide to do about where you're going to live. It's not fair for you to ask Luke to drop everything and go to Las Vegas. It would make a lot more sense for you to move back here."

"I wish it was that easy."

"It is. I think it would show great maturity on your part."

"Where would I live?"

"I'd be willing to bet that Luke's grandfather would let you stay there as long as necessary."

Brad scratched his head. "You're probably right, but I know he doesn't like having alcohol in his house. He hasn't said anything about it yet, but I'm not very comfortable drinking in front of him."

Emmanuel shrugged. "Then don't drink there."

"Here we go again."

"What's that supposed to mean?"

"People are coming at me from all directions about my drinking."

"And that's not telling you something?"

"I know I drink more than I probably should, but I like it."

"How are you feeling now?"

Brad chuckled. "I know. I drank way too much last night, and now I'm paying for it."

"Look, you don't need me or anyone else to tell you about the negative consequences of drinking. You've already lived it. What I can tell you is that you don't need to drink."

"It helps me get going in the morning."

"You will do just fine without it. In fact, you will do better without it. You're not setting a good example for Luke."

"I'll tell you what. I'm not going to promise to stop drinking all together, but I will agree to not drink in front of my son."

"That's a good start." Emmanuel looked into the backseat and asked, "Why don't you let me take that beer off your hands?"

"Why? Do you want it for yourself?"

"No, but I have an idea of what I could do with it."

"Fine. It's yours."

"Thank you."

They were now in Benworth, driving down Main Street. Emmanuel said, "You can drop me off here. I'll walk the rest of the way."

"Are you sure? I can take you to your friend's house."

"No. This is fine. Thanks a lot for the ride. I enjoyed talking to you."

"Strangely, so did I."

Brad stopped the car by the curb. Emmanuel reached into the backseat and grabbed the twelve-pack of beer. As he got out of the car, he said, "You and Luke have a good time at the Steelers game."

Brad did a double take. "How did you know about the game?"

Emmanuel winked back. "Just enjoy the game, and tell Luke to have a good time on his date with his new girlfriend."

"What new girlfriend?"

"Ask him about it. I'm sure he'll be eager to tell you."

Brad sat there stunned as he watched Emmanuel walk down the street with the beer tucked under his arm. His hangover was feeling a little better and he was looking forward to taking Luke to another Krav Maga class, as well as surprising him with the tickets, so he drove on, receiving a wave from Emmanuel as he passed him.

Although he had never considered moving back to Benworth, the thought weighed heavily on his mind. It would make things easier on Luke, and he probably could get hired at one of the local casinos.

He had to admit, being back in Benworth after so many years made him realize how much he missed it. With the exception of the lousy weather, he couldn't think of any other reason not to move back. He would run the idea by Luke and see how he responded. If he really did have a girlfriend now, then there was no way that he could take him to Vegas.

He pulled into the driveway and saw Luke looking out the front window. He was going to have to think up a lie to explain why he was out all night. He couldn't tell him that he slept in the car. He suddenly saw the importance of not drinking in front of him.

He didn't know who that Emmanuel character was, but he sure did make Brad think about things from a different perspective.

CHAPTER 26

The sun was blazing hot. Matthew was standing on the goal line of the high school football field, feeling weak from the heat as sweat dripped from his body. He had no shirt and was starting to feel the effects of sunburn.

He wondered how it got so hot. Just last night, he played on this very field in a cold, wet storm. He'd heard of Indian summer, but this was ridiculous. Despite the heat, the field stayed muddy, slowing down his progress as he tried to get from one end of the field to the other.

What really slowed him down was the huge, rugged, wooden cross that was draped over his shoulder. He wasn't sure why, but he knew that he needed to take the cross to the other side of the field. He looked around to see if anyone was there to help him, but he was alone. Every time he took a step or two, the immense weight of the cross would bear down on him, making him stop to catch his breath.

Splinters were digging into his shoulder and back. His mouth was dry and his throat was parched. He desperately wanted some water, but had none.

Another step, then rest for a second. The muddy field conditions made it even harder to drag the cross, causing the base to continuously get stuck in the muck.

Matthew screamed in frustration. How was he expected to carry this cross the whole length of the field? He'd barely made it a few steps and was already drained of his energy.

He closed his eyes and felt sweat run over his eyelids. He felt dizziness sweep over him and thought that he might pass out.

When he opened his eyes, he saw Emmanuel standing in front of him. Where did he come from? He had just looked around and saw no one.

Emmanuel looked at him with sympathy. Matthew waited to see if Emmanuel would say anything, but he stood there in silence. Why is he here?

If he ever needed help from him, it was now. It appeared that Emmanuel was waiting for Matthew to talk first.

Finally, feeling hopeless, Matthew asked, "Will you help me?"

Emmanuel smiled. "All you had to do was ask."

Matthew waited as Emmanuel walked behind him and picked up the base of the cross, easing some of the pain in his shoulder, but not completely. He managed to take a few steps, but he was still struggling. He stopped just before he was about to fall to his knees.

Anger was starting to overtake him as he realized that completing this journey was going to be more strenuous than he could handle. What was he going to do?

He turned to look back at Emmanuel. "I didn't know that it was going to be so hard."

Emmanuel had a disappointed look on his face as he said, "You don't have to carry it if you don't want to."

Matthew's eyes snapped open. He was back in his bedroom, staring at the ceiling. He breathed a sigh of relief as he grasped the fact that it was just a dream. The sweat, however, was real. He was drenched from head to toe.

Kicking off the covers, he allowed the air to cool him off. The sun was shining through the window at an angle that indicated that it was later in the morning than he was used to waking up. He glanced at the clock and saw that it was too late to make it to Krav Maga class, which was probably a good thing since his arm was still feeling sore.

The house was silent, which was unusual for a Saturday morning. He wondered where his family was. Surely they weren't still sleeping this late.

He slowly stood up, yawning as he did, and walked into the living room. All the lights were off, as well as the TV and stereo. He shrugged and went into the kitchen to pour himself a glass of orange juice.

Upon doing so, he saw a hand written note on the table indicating that his parents had taken David to the doctor for a check-up on his injured knee. He nodded as he remembered them mentioning the appointment earlier in the week.

It wasn't often that he had the house to himself, and he was grateful for it now. The pain of last night's loss still lingered and he thought that some alone time would do him some good. He wanted to feel better, so he turned on the stereo and tuned in to the local Christian rock station. He turned the volume up and listened to the *Skillet* song that blared from the speakers.

He downed his orange juice as he rested his head on the back of the sofa. He relaxed as he thought about what he would do today. He had originally made plans with Chad and Brock, but after the way they treated him last night, he wanted nothing to do with them anymore.

Thinking back to his dream, he speculated what it could mean. Emmanuel had never appeared in one of his dreams before. Maybe it was nothing. He began to doubt if he would ever see Emmanuel again. The last two times they'd spoken hadn't gone well and he wouldn't blame Emmanuel if he chose to never see him again.

Even with the loud music, he found his mind calming down. He kept reminding himself that it was just a football game and he was only a freshman. He would have many more games to redeem himself. He would practice hard all week and get back on the winning track next Friday.

The sound of the doorbell startled him. He wasn't expecting any visitors. The thought of ignoring it passed through his mind, but knew that whoever it was could probably hear the music, so he resigned himself to the fact that he was going to have to answer it.

He groaned as he pulled himself up from the sofa. Lazily, he walked to the front door and opened it. The cold air hit him, making known to him that the heat from his dream was just that, a dream.

A huge smile came across his face as he saw Emmanuel standing there.

"I take it from that smile that you're happy to see me."

Matthew laughed. "I was just thinking about you." He stepped to the side to allow Emmanuel to enter. "My folks should be gone for a while. They took David to the doctor."

Emmanuel held up a twelve-pack of *Gatorade* and showed it to Matthew. "I got this for you."

"You bought that for me?"

"I didn't buy it. I just had an interesting conversation with a very troubled man. I took it off of his hands and I figured since you're an athlete that you would like it."

"Sure. Thanks."

Matthew accepted the gift and retreated to the kitchen to put it in the fridge. He returned to the living room to see Emmanuel turning the stereo down.

"I love music that glorifies my Father, but we need to talk."

Matthew nodded. "I was wondering if you would ever come back after the way I disrespected you the last couple times we talked."

"I was hurt but I never stopped loving you."

With his head down, Matthew asked, "Did you see the game last night?"

"Yes. You almost pulled it off."

"I played the worst game of my life."

"Don't be so hard on yourself. You did your best."

Matthew went back over to the sofa and sat down. Emmanuel sat across the room on the recliner. "You know, I just had a crazy dream."

"I know. I was there."

Chuckling, he responded, "Yeah. I guess you were."

"Do you understand what I was trying to tell you?"

"Sort of. I keep getting reminded of the scripture about taking up my cross."

Emmanuel leaned forward to look at him. "Just like I told you in your dream. You don't have to carry it if you don't want to. It's your choice."

"Yeah, but the scripture says that I have to if I want to follow you."

"Exactly."

Matthew nodded as he understood what Emmanuel was telling him. "I want to follow you. I just wish it wasn't so hard."

"I never said it would be easy. In fact, I said the exact opposite. A life of faith isn't supposed to be easy. It involves a lifetime of hard work, dedicated study, and tough decisions."

"Then why should I do it?"

"Because the rewards for endurance are great!"

Matthew smiled. "Yeah. I guess they are."

"This is nothing new. Going all the way back to my earliest disciples, it was tough. I mentioned the book of Acts the other night when we talked. Did you get a chance to read it?"

"I did, so I'm aware of what they went through. It makes my problems look pretty stupid in comparison."

"I'm glad we see eye to eye on that."

"I know. I just feel bad for the seniors on the team. I feel like I let them down."

"It was just one game."

"Sure, but this is their last chance. Before my brother got hurt, there was talk of winning the state championship. Now those chances have gone out the window."

Emmanuel looked confused. "Why do you say that?"

"Last night was our third loss. We might not even make the playoffs."

"You just gave the number one team in the state everything they could handle. The bounces didn't fall your way. If one or two things went slightly different, you could've won. Don't give up hope."

Matthew chewed on that for a few seconds, then looked back at Emmanuel. "We're a pretty good team, aren't we?"

"You play for a very good team, and you're one of the reasons the team is so good!"

Matthew blushed. "I wish the rest of the school still believed that."

"Don't worry about what everyone else thinks. You continue to go out there and play your best."

"I felt like a fool at Mario's last night."

"It was nice to see you reconnect with your real friends."

"Yeah. It felt good to hang out with them again. I didn't appreciate them the way I should have. It was cool how they acted like nothing was wrong."

"They weren't acting. Even though they haven't been happy with you the last couple weeks, they will always accept you because they are true friends."

"I guess I'm lucky to have them."

Emmanuel had a calm look as he said, "I think you're getting the picture, but there's two more things."

"What are they?"

"First, you spent a lot of time at the same table as Kylie last night, yet you never spoke to her."

Matthew dropped his gaze. "That's a tough one."

"How so?"

"I don't think she wants anything to do with me."

"Don't be so sure."

"What do you mean?"

With a sly grin, Emmanuel answered, "She wants to forgive you, and you're about to be given the perfect opportunity to give her a peace offering."

"What are you talking about?"

"Just be patient. Something is about to fall into your lap. You'll know what it is when it happens."

"Alright. I trust you. What's the other thing?"

"Be there for your friends!"

Matthew felt embarrassed as he said, "I really dropped the ball with Luke."

"Yes you did, but he's coming out of this stronger. You could learn a few things about character by watching him."

"I wouldn't blame him if he walked away from me."

"He won't."

"I wish I could go back and help him the way I should have."

"You can't do that, but you will have another chance to help someone."

"Who?"

"Keep your eye on Mark. Things are happening in his life and are about to get worse. If you think Luke went through a rough time, you haven't seen anything yet."

"Is this about his parents having marriage troubles?"

"That's just the beginning. You'll find out soon enough."

"Okay."

Emmanuel got up and walked across the room. Matthew stood up when he reached him and they embraced in a hug. "Be there for him."

"I will."

"You're going to be alright."

"I hope so."

Emmanuel looked him in the eyes and said, "Stop trying to be popular and just be yourself."

"I will."

"I'm leaving now, but I'll always be near."

"I know."

"Take care of that arm. You're going to need it next Friday."

Matthew watched as Emmanuel went out the front door. A few seconds later, he went to the window and looked out, but not surprisingly, Emmanuel was nowhere to be seen.

—

Returning from another demanding Krav Maga class, Luke sat in the passenger seat while his dad drove. Feeling weary, he looked forward to relaxing the rest of the day while watching Pitt play Notre Dame.

He wanted to ask his dad why he didn't come home last night, but was afraid of what the answer might be, so he kept quiet. His dad was unusually quiet today and he speculated that it was probably because his time in Benworth was coming to an end.

Just before they got home, Brad asked, "Do you have anything you want to tell me?"

Luke suddenly felt nervous. "Am I in trouble?"

Brad laughed a little. "No. I'm referring to the girl that you like."

Luke's face reddened. "You're talking about Rachel. Yeah, I asked her out last night."

"And?"

"And she said yes!"

"Nice!" Brad gave his son a high five as they arrived at the house. "Let's get inside. I have something I need to talk to you and your grandfather about."

Luke burned with curiosity as they went in. Pops greeted them from his easy chair as he chomped on an apple, which was pleasing to Luke. The pre-game show was on the TV as game time was approaching fast.

Luke took his spot on the sofa while Brad plopped down on the love seat. Not sure what his dad was going to tell him, he eagerly awaited, hoping it was something good, but fearing the opposite.

He eased up a little when his dad smiled at him. "Have you told your grandfather the news?"

"No, not yet."

Pops asked, "What news?"

Luke felt a little embarrassed and didn't say anything.

Seeing Luke's discomfort, Brad spoke up. "It appears that Luke has himself a girlfriend."

"Really?"

Luke said, "That's a bit premature. We haven't even had our first date yet."

"What do you have planned?"

"I'm going to take her to lunch and a movie next Saturday."

"How are you going to get there?"

He looked at Pops and said, "I was hoping that you could drop us off and pick us up."

"Sure. I'll do that for you."

Brad smiled. "Well, with that news, I guess there's no way for me to ask you to come back to Vegas with me."

Luke's jaw dropped a little as Pops asked, "Are you saying that you don't want custody?"

"Not exactly. I've decided to move back here."

Luke couldn't contain his excitement. "When?"

"Soon. I spent some time this morning on the computer, applying for jobs at some of the local casinos. I'm hoping that my Vegas experience will help get me a job."

Pops said, "I think that's a great idea."

"What I was hoping for was to stay here until I get the job and get settled, then I'll find a place of my own."

"You're welcome to stay here for as long as you need to."

"Thank you."

Luke asked, "Where will I live once you leave here?"

Pops answered, "I think we'll leave that up to you."

"I don't want to move."

Brad said, "That's fine. As long as we're close and I can still be in your life, that's good enough for me."

Pops gave Brad a nod of approval. Brad then added, "I will have to go back to Vegas for a short time. I need to give my job a proper notice that I'm leaving and put my house up for sale. I'll probably sell most of my furniture and just come back with what I can fit in my car."

Luke felt a huge sense of relief wash over him. He was staying in Benworth and didn't have to move out of Pops' house. He went across the room and hugged his dad. "Thank you."

Once Luke had returned to the sofa, Brad asked, "What do you guys have planned for tomorrow afternoon?"

Luke answered, "We'll be right here in this room, watching the Steelers."

"Are you sure about that?" Brad pulled the envelope from his pocket and took the tickets out. "I have four tickets to the game."

Luke exclaimed, "You're kidding!"

"Not at all. I was thinking that the three of us would go and the extra ticket could go to your new girlfriend."

Pops said, "I appreciate the offer, but after freezing my butt off at the game last night, I think I'll stay here and watch it on TV. The forecast is calling for another chilly day, so I'll stay here and keep warm. Besides, if I stay here, I can eat healthier, instead of stuffing my face with hot dogs and nachos."

Luke added, "I don't think I want to invite Rachel. I'm looking to take things slow with her, so I'd rather not come on too strong."

Brad nodded. "Okay. That leaves us with two extra tickets. How about you ask John and Mark? They're big football fans."

Luke thought for a second, then said, "I have a slightly different idea. Let me make a phone call, then I'll get back to you."

—

Matthew was getting ready to watch the Pitt game when his cell phone rang. It was Luke, inviting him to watch the game at his house with Pops and his father. He readily accepted, not wanting to watch the game alone.

He left a note for his parents, who were still with David at the doctor's office, then took the short walk over to Luke's.

When he got there, Pops welcomed him warmly. "How's the arm?"

"A little sore, but I'll be fine."

"Good. I know you'll bounce back next week."

He sat next to Luke on the sofa just in time to see the opening kickoff. When the game went to it's first commercial break, he asked why Luke was smiling at him.

Luke answered, "We have two extra tickets for tomorrow's game."

"The Steelers?"

"Yep, and since they're playing the Patriots, I was thinking that you and Kylie should come with us."

Matthew stood up. "That's it! That's what he was talking about!"

Brad asked, "What who was talking about?"

"Oh, nobody. Just a friend."

Luke asked, "Is that a yes?"

"Let me call Kylie and make sure it's okay with her."

Pops said, "Don't forget to ask your parents for permission."

"I'm sure they'll say it's fine."

Matthew excused himself and went out to the back patio for some privacy. Butterflies entered his stomach as he took his cell phone from his pocket. He had no idea what he was going to say to her and was hoping that he hadn't burned any bridges with her.

His nervousness increased as he listened to the ring. *Please don't let it go to voicemail! I want to get this over with.*

"Hello."

Matthew's heart jumped. It wasn't the enthusiastic greeting that he had grown accustomed to from the previous times he'd called her, but rather a dull sounding voice, but at least she answered. "Hey. Do you have time to talk?"

"Sure."

"Thank you." His mind was racing as he thought of the right words to say. "First of all, I want to tell you how sorry I am for the way I've been acting. I especially want to apologize for the way I treated you at the party."

"Okay. Since you brought it up, what happened at the party after I left?"

"You mean with Alyssa?"

"Yes. With Alyssa."

"Nothing."

"Really? Nothing?" She did nothing to hide the sarcasm in her voice.

"Well, at least not what people are saying."

"Okay. Explain."

Matthew took a deep breath. He figured that he may as well be completely honest. "It's true that I went into the bedroom with her, but she lured me there. Keep in mind that I was drunk and wasn't in the right state of mind."

"I told you not to drink."

"I know, and I learned my lesson. You won't see me drinking again, that's for sure."

"Okay. Tell me what happened, and please don't lie."

Matthew paced back and forth across the deck. The tone in her voice was harsh, which was making this twice as difficult.

"We kissed. That's all. She wanted to do more, but I stopped her."

"Then why does the whole school believe that you slept with her?"

"I don't know. Probably because they know her reputation."

"That's what confuses me the most. You know her reputation, yet you fooled around with her anyway. I thought you had better taste than that."

Matthew cringed as the sting of her comment hit home. "All I can say is that I had bad judgment that night. I made a lot of mistakes that night, but I learned from them and won't make them again."

Kylie remained silent for a few seconds, but it seemed like a lot longer to Matthew. Finally she said, "I forgive you."

Matthew felt the stress in his body leave as he breathed out. "Does this mean we're still friends?"

He heard a slight chuckle. "Of course."

He laughed and could hear her laughing on the other end. He felt great relief and tried to keep his exhilaration in check. "You know, tomorrow is a big day for our football teams."

"Yeah! The Steelers are going down!"

"We'll see about that!"

"Do you want to watch the game together? It'll be fun to watch you eat crow right in front of me."

"Funny you should ask. It just so happens that I'm going to the game with Luke and his dad."

"Really?"

"Yep, and it just so happens that we have an extra ticket. Do you know anyone who might want it?"

"Me! Me! Me! Me!"

"I don't know. I'm not sure how they would feel about me inviting a Patriots fan."

"Please!"

"Will it be okay with your folks?"

"Let me ask. Hold on."

He could hear her asking for permission, but couldn't hear the response. A minute or so later, she said enthusiastically, "My parents said I can go."

"Great! I guess we'll leave right after Sunday school."

"Okay. Thank you so much for asking me. I'm so excited!"

They hung up and Matthew couldn't stop smiling. He went back inside to watch the rest of the Pitt game, but had a hard time concentrating on it. He wanted to fast-forward to tomorrow so he could get to the game and spend time with Kylie.

—

Luke watched Matthew off and on during the game, happy for his friend. It looked like the old Matthew was back.

While Matthew had been outside talking to Kylie, John and Mark had come over. They arrived together and seemed to be getting along. When they heard about the Steelers game, they sounded happy and showed no sign that they were jealous or bitter about not being asked to go.

At halftime, he called Rachel and had a quick, but pleasant conversation with her, just to let her know he was thinking of her. She sounded genuinely pleased to hear from him.

When he got back to the living room, everyone was having a great time. No one minded that the usual junk food and sodas were replaced with a veggie tray and bottled water. His best friends were all back together, just like old times, but this time it was better because his father was a part of the group.

The best thing that Luke noticed was that Matthew was no longer being critical of the game. He was cheering along with everyone else without a negative comment throughout the game.

When the game ended, Matthew said he needed to get home to take care of some school work, especially if he was going to be spending the next afternoon at the stadium. He said his goodbyes and slipped out the door.

The others all remarked about the change they saw in Matthew, only this time for the better. Luke couldn't help but think to himself that last night's loss was a good thing for him. A humbling experience was all he needed to bring him down to earth.

—

Matthew set off for home, but before he even got off of Luke's property, he was cut off by Jude, who happened to be walking past.

Both of their eyes widened in surprise when they saw each other, but Jude's look quickly changed into an unnerving smile.

Matthew felt fear as the events of a few days ago ran through his head. He stood frozen as Jude looked around.

"Where are your friends, Matthew?" When he said his name, he did so in a scornful tone. He pulled out a pack of cigarettes and continued, "Without your friends here to protect you, I bet I could do something real nasty with these."

Matthew took a step back.

"Not so brave anymore, are you?"

Jude stepped forward and shoved Matthew into the bushes that separated Luke's front yard from the sidewalk out front. Matthew felt the branches dig into his skin and terror filled him as he saw no way out.

—

Luke glanced out the window and saw Jude push Matthew into the bushes. Without hesitation, he darted out the front door.

He heard his father call out, "Where are you going?"

He kept moving without answering. There wasn't time for explaining. He ran through the front yard at full speed, hurdling the waist high bushes at the end.

The look of shock on Jude's face gave Luke confidence. He quickly got between Jude and Matthew, hands up for protection, and ready for a fight!

"Get out of here! Now!"

Jude sneered back. "Get out of my way, little boy, or you're going to get hurt!"

"No way! You don't scare me!"

"You didn't learn from the last time I kicked your butt?"

"I've already taken your best shot, and I'm still standing."

A look of rage came over Jude as he threw a wild, looping right hand. Luke easily blocked it, just like he'd been shown how to do in Krav Maga class, and countered it with a palm-heel strike to Jude's chin, driving him back a few steps.

Jude looked even angrier and came back a second time, but was rudely greeted with a round kick to the side of his knee, buckling it and causing him to fall to his side.

Luke knew that he'd hurt him with the kick, as Jude grasped it while laying on the side walk. He stood there in his fight stance, ready for more, but Jude just sat there.

"Go home now, and this will be over."

Jude responded, "This will never be over!"

"Your choice, but there's nothing you can do to me."

Enraged, Jude got back to his feet and charged, but Luke was ready and delivered a perfect front kick to Jude's groin, doubling him over. He followed it up with an uppercut that sent Jude sprawling. Luke stood there, waiting to see if Jude would get back up, but he seemed to have had enough.

The next thing he knew, John and Mark were standing by his side, and he heard his father say, "Nice job!"

He looked back and smiled while his dad gave him a thumbs up. He turned back to Jude as he pulled himself back to his feet. Without looking back, he started toward his house.

Once Jude was out of sight, he went over to Matthew to make sure he was alright.

"I'm fine. He caught me off guard, that's all."

Luke suppressed a smile. He said his goodbyes to his friends and went back inside. He had school work of his own to do and figured that now was as good a time as any to get it done.

He had weathered the storm and the calmness he felt filled him with peace.

CHAPTER 27

The sun had gone down on another autumn Sunday. The weather was unseasonably cold and the forecast called for a chance of snow flurries later in the night. Luke and his dad had just dropped off Matthew and Kylie, and were just getting home themselves from the Steelers game. The car's heater had finally taken the chill off that had Luke shivering during the course of the game.

The game itself was exciting and breathtaking, and definitely worth sitting through the cold. As they pulled into the driveway, Luke smiled to himself as he thought about how well Matthew and Kylie got along throughout the day, despite the friendly trash talking that went back and forth before and during the game. He had found himself feeling envious at times of the chemistry that they had together, and hoped that once he and Rachel got to know each other better, that they could have something similar.

Any bad blood that existed between Matthew and Kylie was long forgotten. It wouldn't surprise Luke if they were to cross the line from being friends to a couple in the near future. He was happy for them and it made him want to call Rachel, but he didn't want to rush things.

When he got inside, Luke spent a little time talking with Pops, who had been watching on TV, about the game.

Brad had gone to his room to pack for his return trip to Vegas. His flight was scheduled for the next morning. Even though he was only going back for a short time before moving back to Benworth, Luke wished that he had more time with him. As pleased as he was with how everything had turned out, he was going to miss his father while he was gone.

He couldn't believe that only three weeks had gone by since his dad had come back into his life. He thought back to that day, to the feelings of anger and resentment that he had for his father, and was glad that those feelings were gone. They could never get back those fourteen years they had lost, but they could make the best of the future. Luke looked forward to doing just that.

It was getting late and Luke was tired from a long day. He went into his room and changed into some comfortable clothes. He contemplated calling Rachel once again. He didn't want to scare her off, but also wanted to talk to her as often as possible to get to know her. The possibility of an exclusive relationship with her excited him.

He sat on the edge of his bed, staring at his cell phone, wondering whether or not he should call, when it started ringing. He looked at the caller ID, but instead of a number or name, it showed unfamiliar characters. Was that Hebrew letters? He continued to look in disbelief. He'd never seen anything like this on his phone.

Curiosity got the best of him and he answered, "Hello."

"It's nice to hear your voice again, Luke."

Luke smiled as he recognized the unmistakable voice of Emmanuel. "I should've known it was you when I saw the Hebrew letters on my phone. I didn't know you had a cell phone."

"I don't."

Confused, Luke asked, "Are you using somebody else's?"

"What makes you think I'm using a phone at all?"

"But ... How ..."

Emmanuel's hearty laugh came over the phone. "Don't worry about it. We've got a lot to talk about."

Luke scratched his head. "Okay. What's up?"

"First of all, I'm very proud of how well you handled this rough patch that you went through."

"It wasn't easy."

"Do you still wish that your father never came back?"

"Of course not."

Another laugh from Emmanuel. "Remember when I told you to pray that he would move back?"

"Yes, and I prayed for that every day since."

"I know you did. Never doubt the power of prayer."

"I won't ever again."

"Did you share the Gospel with him like I asked you to?"

Luke looked down. "No. It's awkward for me. We're getting along so well, so I don't want to make things uncomfortable between us."

"You may not be aware of it, but you're making a huge impact on him. If there's anyone he'll listen to, it's you."

"I don't know. It all feels so weird to me. I've never told anyone about you before. Maybe I can get Pops to talk to him with me."

"No. Don't do that."

"Why?"

"If Pops talks to him about me, it might not be effective."

Luke was confused. "How so? They're getting along great."

"I know, but there's still some trust issues between them. I want you to tell Pops to not witness to him. Tell him that you want to do it yourself. He'll respect that."

"I don't have much time. He's going back to Vegas tomorrow."

"He'll be back soon enough."

Luke got up and started pacing around the room. "Alright, but I have no idea what I'll say to him when the time comes."

"I'm sure you'll think of something. Pray about it and see what happens."

"Okay."

"Speaking of prayer, have you been praying for Jude?"

"Sometimes. I feel a little bad for him. First, Matthew humiliated him, then there was the encounter yesterday."

"You did well. You showed compassion when he was helpless, and you showed great courage when you helped Matthew out."

Luke blushed a little. "I think I got lucky. What if he comes back? I may not get so lucky next time."

"I don't think you have to worry about that."

"Why not?"

"I don't think you'll be seeing him anymore."

"How do you know?"

"I just do."

Luke smiled, realizing that he shouldn't doubt anything that Emmanuel tells him. "Okay. If you say so."

After a few seconds of silence, Emmanuel said, "You've had a lot of spiritual growth in the last few weeks."

"I don't feel any different."

"You are. You just don't see it yet. Most people would've crumbled in similar circumstances. Now, I want you to help your friend."

"Which one?"

"Mark."

"What do you want me to help him with?"

"He has a trial coming up that's going to make what you just went through seem like a walk in the park."

"Are you talking about his parents? Are they still having problems?"

"That's just the beginning. Right now, as we speak, the wheels are in motion at his house. Things are happening that are going to send him into a tail spin. You, Matthew and John need to be there for him. He's going to need you more than ever. Can you do that for me?"

"I can try, but what's going to happen?"

"You'll find out soon enough."

"How bad can it be?"

"You have no idea."

Luke suddenly didn't like what he was hearing. "Should I call him?"

"Not now. Wait until tomorrow. Talk to him when you're walking to school."

"Sure. You know, right before you called me, I was thinking about calling Rachel."

"I know. Go ahead and call her. She'll be happy to hear from you."

"Okay, I will."

"I'm going to tell you the same thing I told Matthew regarding Kylie."

"What's that?"

"Go slow. Be her friend first. If you push for a romantic relationship too fast, you'll scare her off."

"I'm fine with that. I don't want to move too fast anyway."

"Good. Go ahead and call her now and I'll see you soon."

"Okay."

The phone went dead. Luke sat there for a minute, thinking about what Mark must be about to go through. He knelt down and prayed for him, asking God to give Mark strength to get through whatever it was that he was about to face. He also asked for wisdom to be able to help him the way Emmanuel asked him to.

When he finished praying, he arranged his pillows in a way that would be comfortable to sit up in bed, then sat for a minute reflecting on all that he'd been through the last few weeks. The more he thought about it, the more he knew that Emmanuel was right. He had grown spiritually. He'd faced the toughest storm of his life, and now it was as calm as could be.

He'd kept his faith through it all, and now he was about to reap the reward. His father was back in his life, and with a little help from

Emmanuel, he was sure that before long, he could lead his dad to the Lord. The thought of it warmed his heart.

He got up, went to his dad's room, and gave him a long hug. "I love you Dad."

"I love you too."

It was the first time he'd called his father "Dad," and it felt good. He returned to his room and sat back in his bed. A huge smile came across his face as he dialed Rachel's number.